Thwarting Magic

A Regency fantasy romance
and the sequel to *Round Table Magician*

by Ann Tracy Marr

Copyright © 2008

ISBN: 978-58749-693-6

All rights reserved

Earthling Press ~ United States of America

Thwarting Magic—copyright by Ann Tracy Marr
Copyright 2008

Print edition 2008
ISBN 13: 978-1-58749-693-6

Electronic edition 2008
ISBN 13: 978-1-58749-647-9

All trade paperback and electronic rights reserved
Printed in the United States of America. No part of this book may be used or reproduced without written permission, except in the case of brief quotations embodied in reviews or articles. For more information, please address the publisher:
   www.awe-struck.net
This is work of fiction. People and locations, even those with real names, have been fictionalized for the purpose of this story. Published by Earthling Press, a subsidiary of Awe-Struck E-Books, Inc. To purchase this book, go online to: Amazon.com

Available in most electronic formats and in print

Editors: Kathryn Struck and Dick Claassen

Cover art: Delle Jacobs

~ Dedication ~

The ideal romantic hero: Five days in a car with a cat and he didn't lose his temper once, not even when he had to straddle the litter box.
Thanks for the sanity, Rick.

Chapter One

"She is a pretty bit, but her sister looks more your taste," Adrian Hughes said, warming the tails of his coat at the fireplace.

James Treadway, voice roughened by the rasp of brandy, drawled, "You put your finger on it. But the dear Pater don't care for my taste. He is determined on this match. Has approached Ridgemont already and all but signed the marriage contract." He turned the snifter around and around in his long fingers, peering at it as if the spirits were tainted. "Unless I wish to seriously displease him, I will betroth myself to Miss Ridgemont, though she is a far cry from my ideal." Papers shifted as he leaned against the beveled lip of the walnut desk and blew to warm his fingers. "Can't abide insipid chits. He says she was in town last year; don't remember her at all. But the Pater is determined."

Hughes ran his finger along the frame of an indifferently painted ancestral portrait, dislodging a small clump of beeswax. The drip fell; he stooped and picked it up, depositing it in the pen tray. "Heaven forbid you displease the old martinet."

"And heaven forbid I displease the old martinet. He don't like widows, but Mrs. Whitmill-Ridgemont has a lushness that speaks to me, a flamboyance that urges me to get to know her better, even in crow black. Margaret Ridgemont is much too staid for my taste."

A wisp of sound made Treadway turn toward the library door, at the same time inhaling the heady scent of heliotrope. Framed between the moldings of the double door entry like Guinevere and her handmaiden were the two ladies he referred to. Mrs. Christine Whitmill-Ridgemont, the wearer of the sophisticated perfume, had her arm entwined with that of Miss Margaret Ridgemont, the young lady his father had requested, nay, ordered him to wed.

The first was unmistakably a widow. In a worked muslin gown the color of mourning, Christine Whitmill-Ridgemont was a vision. She wore the dress high around the bust, the tiniest twist of crape confining her bosom, accentuating her finest feature. The hall candles backlit her skirt, lending the black muslin a touch of transparency. His attention seldom slid that high, but her face was acceptable, with arched brows over brown eyes and slightly hooked nose.

To James Treadway, the widow was a picture of perfection with intriguing flashes of passion.

Margaret Ridgemont did not compare in form or style. Dark hair, light dress—what more was there to say? The thick jaconet muslin, plain and tight to the hips with a fall of concealing lace at the bodice, was more than a year behind the fashion. In dull debutante white, Miss Ridgemont was a watercolor wash of dun. She was too petite to suit Treadway, too demure to intrigue, too insipid to inspire. Worse, she epitomized what his father wanted for him. At least she didn't have spots.

No matter his thoughts, Treadway felt the first faint tinkle of his life shattering. The doors to the hall were not far enough from where he stood. The library was too blasted small, the desk too close to the doors. His words could have carried that far. He picked up the scattered papers and tapped them into a tidy pile with numb fingers. They went askew when he set them down.

What he had said was not proper drawing room fare. Gentlemen did not discuss ladies in a derogatory fashion. Especially ladies one contemplated wedding. It just wasn't done. Not publicly, not privately. He glanced from one to the other.

Had the girl heard? Would she complain to her father?

"Ladies," Hughes said. "You are a breath of tropical air in the Arctic. Please, come in."

"I hesitate to interrupt," Miss Ridgemont said. Hughes moved forward.

"No, no interruption. We were about done."

She stood like a block in the doorway, no expression on her face. He'd seen more appealing cows, though to be fair, she wasn't portly. But there was no life to the chit, nothing of passion. No, she must not have heard, else she would be having the vapors and screaming for Papa to call him out. Treadway sighed and turned his attention to the widow. Had *she* heard?

Mrs. Whitmill-Ridgemont propelled her sister into the room. "Our stepmother requests your attendance in the drawing room." Her long lashes fluttered, laying spiky shadows against pearly skin. "We were lonely without your company in any event, were we not, Margaret?"

The cow flushed, nodding agreement with her sister's

pronouncement. Impulsively, Treadway revised his opinion. Margaret Ridgemont wasn't a cow, but a merino. Cows flapped their mouths a lot. Sheep were merely dull.

No, there was no sign the widow had heard.

Crow black glided across the room, swaying to a stop when the widow's feet touched the elaborate medallion curled on the center of the rug. Glancing at the meager fire, she said, "The drawing room is warm with a big blaze in both fireplaces. Not like this chilly old library. Brrr, I need a muff in here."

James smiled. "It is cool, but with the weather, not surprising. Many rooms are hard to heat."

The sheep commented, "Step-Mama thinks too warm a fire encourages must in the books."

"The only thing that could thrive here is icicles." Giggling at her own weak humor, the widow's bodice expanded in an interesting manner. Most affected laughs had Treadway running for the door, but not this one. It sounded like the mating call of the female rake. He responded with the instinct of a full-blooded male. He just couldn't act on it.

"Mold is a concern with books," Hughes said. "It causes the musty smell. Cool temperatures inhibit mold. She is right to be vigilant, especially if Sir Denison has any valuable tomes."

"Papa has an old copy of Sir Thomas Mallory's history of King Arthur." Miss Ridgemont gestured vaguely to the far wall. "I do not know if it is valuable, but he fusses over it. He showed it to me once; it has beautiful illuminations. He keeps it under lock and key."

Hughes raised his eyebrows. "Really. An illuminated *Morte D'Arthur*. That is rare enough to justify all manner of precaution. I would love to see it."

"If you ask Papa, I am sure he would bring it out."

"Do you know who illuminated it?"

"No, only it was done in an abbey. Papa said something about a rose tint to the gold that makes it English. French is darker, I believe."

The widow smiled. "You must come to the drawing room. If you freeze in here, Sir Denison will be irritated. Besides, he specifically desired your presence."

Hughes set his glass on a table and sketched a bow. "We have holed up here too long. My apologies for detaining Treadway, Mrs.

Whitmill-Ridgemont. Wanted to gain his advice about an investment and added too much detail. He's a devil with the funds, y'know." Under his breath, he added, "By Balan, I hope she didn't hear."

Treadway's lips barely moved. "She couldn't have." Before he could extend his arm, the widow tittered and attached herself to Hughes's sleeve. Diaphanous black muslin floated about his legs.

"Investments are boring," she chided. "Better to flirt with me."

"They are my life blood," Hughes protested. "Investments and music. I can't resist violins." The two left the library, the widow's draperies fluttering. Treadway's attention went with them.

Leaving the papers in a smear, he crossed the room and held his arm out to the other lady, the quiet one wearing modest white muslin. The staid one his father had ordered him to wed. "Shall we go to the drawing room? Lady Ridgemont may become impatient and that would not do." Miss Ridgemont dumbly laid a hand on his sleeve. "Hughes and I should not have spent so much time in the library—our poor excuse must be the investment we discussed is involved. He is enthusiastic and I lost track of the minutes.

"My mother raised me well," he continued with a desperate flash of teeth, "though sequestering myself away from the party may not show my manners to best advantage. I shall exert myself to behave better in the future." Ignoring what Treadway trusted may have been taken as a roundabout apology, the chit kept her eyes averted. He paid little attention to her reply.

"I readily forgive your delay, though I had not noticed you gone from the company overly long," she said. "In my experience, gentlemen are forever immersed in their own concerns. During my season at Camelot, ladies complained men hid in libraries discussing the quest for the Ark of the Covenant and other matters rather than dancing. I thought much of the time they merely avoided dancing."

Mismatched in height and step, they walked through the library door and started across the marble-floored hall. Boots tapped an even beat while slippers pattered and skipped. "Step-Mama will not be impatient, I believe, no matter what my sister said. She understands gentlemen must be indulged when they fail to note the passing of time. It is my father who wishes to hasten the business."

"Business," he repeated, bored beyond belief with her colorless conversation. "What business may that be, Miss Ridgemont?"

"The business that brought you to Puckeridge, Mr. Treadway." Skipping a step to match his longer stride, she colored. "The business of betrothal. Unless you have altered your intention. My father wishes the matter done. That is why he sent Mrs. Whitmill-Ridgemont and me to seek you out."

Impertinent chit. He slid his hand to her elbow and stopped them in front of a life-size marble statue of Mercury with wings on his heels, clad in drapery resembling a Scottish kilt. He ignored the vulgar god and glanced at his friend and the widow ahead of them, arm in arm. "Let them go on ahead."

Hughes, the lucky devil, escorted Christine Whitmill-Ridgemont into the drawing room. Schooling his patience, Treadway fastened his eyes on the sheep. "The business of betrothal, hmm. I take it you are aware of why I came to visit."

"Yes sir. My father informed me this afternoon that you intend to wed me. Is that an error?"

"No, but I would prefer to go about this another way. I see no reason to hurry. Would you not like to come to know me better first?" Her eyes flickered to his chin.

"I believe it best we accomplish the matter without delay."

Arthur, she might have been discussing an arrangement to go driving rather than the disposal of her life. Was Margaret Ridgemont made of ice? Was her placidity as bovine as it appeared?

Staid, hah! Dead and laid out inside was more like. Accolon's curse, he was not ready for this. She had little to recommend her at the best of times, but here was the final straw. The sheep could not look him in the eye when she consented to his unstated proposal. She couldn't even wait until he made the proposal to consent. Her clear skin meant nothing if she was as thickheaded as she appeared.

* * *

Running out the door and down the drive was not an option. Margaret had nowhere to go and Papa would only fetch her back. Behind a serene mask, she stamped a mental foot on the marble floor.

Did this man want to marry her? Surely not, not after what she heard. She raised the subject just to get it over and done with.

She said something—she hardly knew what—to let Mr. Treadway know she understood. They were to be betrothed. Papa had decreed.

He stopped her with a hand on her elbow. Panicked though she was, Margaret swallowed a giggle. Step-Mama's pretend Greek statue was taller than Mr. Treadway. More handsome too. To be fair, his was an imposing figure: Mr. Treadway, not Mercury. The broad shoulders of a horseman filled a claret-colored coat cut by a master tailor. With a smooth, neat cravat, he looked like someone consequential. Despite a nose a tad too long and a mouth a smidge too wide, Treadway's features were pleasing. But Mercury was more to Margaret's taste.

"The business of betrothal, hmm," he said. He said more, but she only listened with half an ear. She wanted to smack his cheek. She itched to make a fist and push Mr. Treadway's teeth down his throat. The man sounded bored, for pity's sake. She focused to control her hand.

Papa's bald command echoed in her head. She was to marry this man she had scarce laid eyes on before yesterday, who couldn't adjust his stride to match hers, who gazed at her with hazel green eyes, measured and discounted the total she summed up to. 'A far cry from my ideal' he said. If only Papa had not been obdurate.

If Mr. Treadway went down on bended knee, she would scream.

Oh, to smash Mr. Treadway's nose into Mercury's sporran. She had to say yes, had to tell him she would be his wife. Papa—Step-Mama—would accept nothing less. Composed on the surface, she stared at his chin and said what she really did not want to say.

"I believe it best we accomplish the matter without delay."

* * *

"The drawing room door was open," Lady Ridgemont screeched. "I heard. You cannot rescind your promise."

"I do not deny what I said. Upon reflection, I changed my mind." It was their custom to meet in the drawing room before dinner for a glass of sherry or brandy. Strife was Step-Mama's preference, as the current discussion illustrated.

"Change your mind, why, you ungrateful brat. There is no

changing anything. Your father made the decision. His was the choice. You will do as you are told." Christine graced a chair, nodding her head in time to Step-Mama's noise. Papa distanced himself, hovering over the wine decanters, leaving his wife to chastise his disobedient daughter. Lady Ridgemont was doing so with relish.

"You said 'No delay,' Margaret. The intent was clear. I consider your statement binding." Lady Ridgemont reclined on the sofa, as smug as a knight tapped on the shoulder by the king. "The Lady knows, unlike your mother—may God forgive me for speaking ill of the dead, but she was the most intemperate—I tried to instill obedience and a sense of responsibility in you. Obedience to your elders and responsibility to the family name. Those precepts are the foundation of life. You will wed James Treadway. Without delay, as you promised." Step-Mama was over-doing the dutiful wife role. Papa should fight his own battles. Better, he should pretend this was his battle, not his wife's.

"Not an hour ago, you were agreeable to the scheme," Christine purred. "I like Mr. Treadway quite well. He will make a fine husband."

Margaret turned her eyes from her elder to her younger sister, fading into the wall, pretending deafness. Emma did that much too often. But Margaret must counter Step-Mama's plot, not worry about Emma. "You may like him, Christine, but I fear Mr. Treadway and I will never suit."

Step-Mama ranted. "Your father went to a deal of trouble arranging this. It behooves you to be grateful for his efforts. He had to go to London to chase down Carlton Treadway. You know he dislikes town. He was absent an entire fortnight. It's a wonder he didn't turn bilious. It is not as if you managed to attach a gentleman by your own efforts. Your season was a disgrace. No, you will do as you are told. I will brook no more demurrals."

The older woman listed toward the armrest like a top-heavy sloop at anchor. She must have celebrated the betrothal privately with a bottle of sherry. *You want me gone, you wicked crone, so you don't suffer comparison with my youth. Or comparison with Mama. Drat you for pushing Papa to this.* Thus far, the argument had lasted a quarter hour between her, Step-Mama, and Papa. Papa had said the least.

Aloud Margaret said, "Step-Mama, Mr. Treadway is not to

my taste. How can I wed a man I dislike?" Her own thoughts drowned her protest. *Where is Emma going?* From the corner of her eye, she watched her sister slip out the door to the small salon. She was going to hide, as she did more and more frequently. She wouldn't be at dinner. Lucky Emma.

"Nonsense. I see nothing distasteful. James is a fine young man." Lady Ridgemont's voice rose. "You will have a house in town and an ample allowance; your children will bear a respected name. It's more than you deserve, with this shilly-shallying. Don't think I will put forth the effort to take you to Camelot again, you ungrateful chit. The expense and your father's comfort forbid it."

"The inconvenience," Margaret mumbled.

Christine, dear Christine, heaped coals on the fire. "I wouldn't mind wedding Mr. Treadway. His coats are by Weston. No padding there. And his boots are Hoby. Such a well turned out figure. Margaret is a ninnyhammer. I imagine she has the idea he will mistreat her." She loved to needle her sisters and especially, their brother, Thomas. Margaret likened her elder sister to the knight Blamore, who after siding with Lancelot against the king, died a hermit; Margaret thought his going into seclusion showed a guilty conscience for his perversity, no matter what the history books said. Christine was like that. Someday she would regret her vagary, just like Sir Blamore.

"You may find him a paragon. I do not."

Lady Ridgemont dripped acid. "No man is a paragon. If you look for perfection, you will end your days firmly on the shelf. That will never do. I will not have it said I failed my duty to Sir Denison. He devised a fine match and I will see you obey him."

"The only lack is a title." Christine stretched her hand and admired the massive ruby ring on her finger. "I was not able to gain one; I do not see you doing better." She twisted on the chair. "Papa, Margaret is adamant. You should suggest to Mr. Treadway that I would be amenable to a betrothal with him."

Sir Denison stalked to the comfortable padded chair that was his alone and brandished a wine glass much as the bronze figure on the mantel clock waved her laurel wreath. Sitting, he rested the crystal precariously on his knee and rubbed his hands together. "Nonsense. He's for Margaret, not you, Christine. All settled, not going back on my word. You, Margaret, don't be missish. Nothing objectionable about the Treadway family, nothing wrong with the boy. It's a fine match, a fine match indeed. Settles you most respectably."

"You don't know the meaning of the word unpleasant," Christine interjected.

"I don't see that he is respectable," Margaret said.

Christine tittered. "Respectable. A fine house in town, fashionable carriages. A box at the Opera. What do you find scandalous?"

"Opera dancers."

Sir Denison narrowed his eyes. "Watch your tongue. You should be glad I arranged a match of stunning advantage for you, girl." He swung his arm in an arc, spraying wine. "James Treadway, despite the lack of a handle to his name, stands to inherit some of the neatest acreage in the Isles. The Treadway estate is chock full of sheep and acres of hops. His father had that fellow—what was his name—Benjamin Franklin; that fellow. Had Franklin to stay with him. Carlton Treadway convinced King George it was better to make trade agreements than war. He helped establish the Crown's relations with the new country of America, for Arthur's sake. Prominent family."

"I care not about acreage or politics, Papa."

Christine laughed. "You must have heard something in town about Mr. Treadway. Margaret, all men are rakes, especially the good looking ones."

"He is handsome," Lady Ridgemont said, dabbing at the wine spotting her skirt, "and possesses enough charm to please any woman. A reputation means nothing. The boy has been sowing wild oats, is all. All spirited young men do. Once you are wed, it is up to you to keep him content and at your side."

"Handsome as Adonis," her sister said.

Margaret didn't care for the tone of Christine's remark. She ran a shaking finger over the mantel clock. "Papa, I would like to refuse."

Sir Denison thundered, "NO. That is final, Missie." Face purple, he shook his finger. "No. No. No. The settlements will be signed. The announcement will be in the papers. We will not discuss it again. You are marrying James Treadway and that...is...that."

At the same time, Lady Ridgemont shrilled, "You agreed to this match. I heard you. I will see you wed or you will spend the next ten years in the wine cellar. You will not disgrace us by jilting him." Under cover of the eruption, Christine flounced out.

"I won't sacrifice my wine cellar. Either she does as she's told or she can take up governessing," Sir Denison bellowed. He kicked the footstool, which rolled over and played dead. "The girl is doing better than her sister by a long chalk," he muttered. "I let Christine make her own choice and look what came of it. Looked around before I set my mind on Treadway. Buck of the first water. Many a chit would be delighted to be hooked with him. Fine family—prominent—well heeled. No one can say I didn't do my duty."

"Did you say something, dear?" Lady Ridgemont asked. "I couldn't hear you."

He shook his head. "Females are the very devil."

Margaret, knuckles white as her hands strangled each other, knew defeat. On that cheery note, the door opened and the two guests, James Treadway and his friend Adrian Hughes, entered. Sir Denison bolted for the decanters. Lady Ridgemont fussed with her hair.

Someone should maintain standards. Margaret said, "Mr. Hughes, Mr. Treadway, please come in. Would you care for a glass of sherry before dinner?"

Lady Ridgemont belatedly donned a brilliant smile. "Come sit with me, dear Mr. Treadway," she trilled. "May I call you James?" Sir Denison cleared his throat and glanced at his wife, who straightened on the sofa and nodded vigorously.

The older man thumped a fist against his amply padded thigh. "Treadway, I see no reason to stick my head down the fox hole. You came to Puckeridge for a purpose and I'd like to finalize it now. Do you agree to a betrothal?"

Both guests looked startled. Treadway paused in the middle of the floor and turned a leery eye toward Margaret. "Ah, Miss Ridgemont and I have not—"

Sir Denison interrupted. "Bah. She's female; she'll do as she's told. Do I have your agreement?" The belligerent words hung in the air. Behind Treadway, Hughes stared at a drooping arrangement of hothouse roses.

"Yes, sir," Treadway said, turning dull red.

"Good. When your father arrives, I'll draft a notice to the papers." Ridgemont stomped to the drinks table and hefted a full decanter. "Shall we have a toast to seal the bargain?"

Lady Ridgemont patted the sofa cushion. "What a wonderful surprise. I couldn't be more delighted you young people have found each other. You will be happy together. Come James, tell me your plans. Shall the wedding be soon? I have it planned: Margaret will wear lace and carry her grandmother's prayer book. She was Pitt's mother, you know."

Margaret fought to contain her blazing temper. Turning a stiff back to the company, she noted the time as told by the mantel clock. Almost half past, her moment of doom. She watched the hand on the dial; it seemed as frozen as her soul.

Under her feet, the carpet smoked. Tiny flames flickered in the wool. Not a lot, not enough for a family immersed in strife to notice, but enough to form pinprick holes over the surface. Pile singed and tiny coals dropped through the jute backing before burning out. Unaware of the miniscule bonfires, Margaret shifted her feet. Embers snuffed out. New ones flared.

Chapter Two

Unobtrusively, Hughes moved away from Treadway. His intention was not to shove his nose into this ignoble sealing of a betrothal. It was Tread's business. He had his own to tend. Now it was on the level of a quest, he could do nothing else. Not that he had objected to the task.

Altogether, it was a situation fraught with danger. He'd likely be knighted if he succeeded. He would gain a seat at the Round Table. And England might not crumble into the sea.

Lady Ridgemont held forth at great length on plans for the wedding. He grimaced, noting Tread's gray face. The betrothal was as new as gas lights and the woman had him cribbed and confined. He could guess why his friend didn't want shackles; Tread was a great man for the ladies who couldn't be termed ladies. Keeping to one woman wasn't something he did well.

Hughes glanced across the room. Miss Ridgemont appeared unsteady, as upset as Ophelia before she drowned herself. That must be Sir Denison's maladroit handling. She had achieved that fashionable pinnacle: the Good Match. Nevertheless, forcing Tread's agreement in front of her was bad *nous*. Her father should have dragged Tread into the library alone to finalize things, not blurted it out in front of all and sundry. Tasteless. Shaking himself mentally, he concentrated his senses. They skittered.

A clock on the mantel chimed the half hour. Looked like a Dore piece, with the fine detailing of the draperies on the figure. About twenty inches high, with swags, some sort of scepter, and angels on the Cipollino marble base. Maybe Galle did it. And maybe it was offering a clue. His eyes dropped.

The carpet in front of the fireplace glistened. Miss Ridgemont moved to a seat and Hughes took her place at the hearth. He scuffed his shoe along the rug. He wished he could pick the rug up and examine the pile. Would wager his grandmother's annuity there were holes in it. They'd been made recently; from the sparkling residue, within the last hour. He forgot the clock.

The draperies at the window shimmered. Edging over, he

pulled out his quizzing glass. A thin line of fire crept down the velvet, then sputtered out. A two inch slit smoked and sparkled, an unmistakable sign of deadly magic.

Yes, it was coming from someone in the house. His deductions were correct. Someone connected with Sir Denison was the source of the magic. But he'd lay odds it wasn't Ridgemont himself. Every sign indicated a female.

Lady Ridgemont nattered at Tread. The *torchiere* behind the sofa added depth to her fading blond hair. Dropping lids half over his eyes, Hughes let the forceful lady's figure blur. She looked younger, if one allowed the incipient wrinkles, the light tarnish of her hair, to fade into insignificance. A fine figure of a woman. He could see what had attracted Ridgemont. It was a shame her character wasn't as refined. Well, there was plenty of that sort in society.

What he didn't see was the faint phosphorescence the wielding of magic would give her. The glow it would lend her skin, especially her fingertips. She glowed, but more as if she had been at the sherry bottle. Anyway, it wasn't she. Or was it? He couldn't be sure.

"If we are not to remove to London, the ceremony may be at the chapel in the village," Lady Ridgemont was saying. "It's an adorable place, very Celtic. Enough pews to seat anyone we care to invite, but intimate." Poor Tread looked like porridge warmed in a chafing dish.

Hughes allowed his eyes, still unfocused, to linger on Sir Denison and his daughter. The knight was grumpy, guzzling port and thumping an upended footstool. He hadn't said much once he'd badgered Tread into the betrothal, just sat in his chair and glowered.

The daughter; she's a thoroughbred. How long it would take his friend to realize Margaret Ridgemont was a damn fine woman, as admirable as Lynette, Sir Gareth's love? She had cause to indulge in a full-blown case of the vapors, thanks to Tread and his loose lips. She wasn't even sulking. Miss Ridgemont had graceful fingers wrapped around a thimbleful of sherry. She hadn't done more than sip—kept the conversation light when many a girl would have shrieked. He pinched his leg to distract himself from the ephemeral. Didn't matter, not unless she was the wizard.

No. No sign either father or daughter dabbled.

Balked of his prey, Hughes turned his attention to consideration of personalities. The widow wasn't there yet—dinner was held back for her. Probably primping. The shrew, Lady Ridgemont, simpered when Mrs. Whitmill-Ridgemont sent word she'd be late. Nothing like a little money to grease friendship. Some people don't have the sense to look beyond the bank account and see the mushroom sprouting.

The widow's spouse, gross Martin Whitmill, had keeled over one month after their marriage, cursed by a fish bone in his throat. A man could die of food stuck in his gullet, true, but it was convenient for the widow. Whitmill was a coarse merchant, fattened by a fortune made in coal. Filthy coal, filthy man. His death was too convenient to ignore. Had Mrs. Whitmill-Ridgemont facilitated his death with necromancy? It was a possibility to keep in mind.

The door opened. Mrs. Whitmill-Ridgemont slipped into the room. "I am sorry for the delay," she said. "My hem was coming loose. I miss London *modistes,* don't you, dear Step-Mama? That provincial seamstress didn't knot the thread."

The widow was a feisty armful, willful and passionate. Vulgar. No wonder Tread was interested in her and not the genteel Margaret. He never had much discrimination when it came to females. Hughes unfocused again and eyed the luscious widow.

He rocked on his feet. If he weren't as surprised as Balan. There it was.

He sharpened his gaze and deflated. No, it wasn't. A ray from the candle sconce had fallen on the doorknob. The shimmer of brass was from the light, not the remnants of a spell. Her hands were clean. Could it be the widow? Could she be the bearer of bad magic? He scratched his thumb and pondered his suspects.

He'd narrowed it down to someone in this house. Ridiculous to think a servant could create the havoc. The lower classes hadn't the linguistic training complicated enchantments require; generally, they didn't achieve more than earth wizardry. This rogue was a full wizard. Someone unknown, unacknowledged by the Council of Mages.

It had to be a member of the family. The idea of Sir Denison creating magic was laughable. Better imagine John Bull as an opera dancer. There was a brother at university and a younger sister. The brother was unlikely—the disturbance emanated from this area, not

Oxford. It didn't look masculine. The girl was in the schoolroom, too young to join the company. Emma, that was her name. He'd met her by chance, a fleeting introduction when he and Tread first arrived. She was going out to sketch something or other. Could it be her?

How in the crystal cave was he to find out?

Hughes felt such disappointment at not nailing the rogue wizard, he determined to take the harpy, Lady Ridgemont, in to dinner. Let Tread enjoy his meal in peace; his own was already ruined.

* * *

"Have to head back to town," Hughes mentioned over after-dinner brandy. Sir Denison nodded, lost in the mists of too many tumblers, but Tread flinched.

"I can't leave yet," he mumbled. "Thought you were going to stick with me. The wedding is in six weeks, if they get their way. I'll not stay the whole time. But I can't take a flit till after the Pater comes."

"When will that be?"

"Saturday. Four more days."

"So I'll expect you in London Monday?" Hughes ran a finger around the edge of his glass.

"No later than Tuesday, I swear. I'll leave Monday even if the Pater isn't done. Can't you wait?"

"Wish I could, but I need to meet with Haverhorn. Our enterprise is set to go."

"You and your schemes. Well, if you take the carriage, I'll have to go post. Have you no pity?" Tread whined mockingly.

Hughes laughed, knowing the whine was perilously close to real. He set his empty glass on the table. "I have no pity—not when it is my convenience versus your comfort. You will have to be satisfied that I will return to hold you up at the altar."

Sir Denison hummed a ditty popular with naval gentlemen. Hughes leaned his head on his hand to block at least one ear. Tread's path was nigh intolerable. It was bad enough to have to marry where he felt no urge, but to have given her affront was worse.

Margaret Ridgemont wasn't an antidote. She was adept in conversation—had a pretty figure.

Around his glass, individual threads of the damask tablecloth unraveled with a flash. By the Lady, whoever it was, her magic was gaining potency. Hughes prodded the tablecloth and bits of glitter stuck to his skin. If he could only feel... He closed his eyes, but there was nothing to grab on to.

The prospective father-in-law was slipping down in his chair. "Your civilizing presence is the only thing makes this bearable," Tread moaned. Sir Denison reached for the decanter again and knocked it over. "Maybe."

One servant mopped at the table with a cloth while a footman went for another bottle and Tread propped Ridgemont up. Hughes watched the cloth by his glass as more threads threw out sparks. His gut tightened. No pattern to it, but magic was the logical explanation.

It would be safer to stay and deal with the rogue now, but he needed to bounce his ideas off the duke. Haverhorn would likely know the best way of doing it. A wrong step could be disastrous.

Silent as a ghost, Ridgemont poured brandy from the full bottle into his glass, liberally watering the table in the process. Tread fell into a reverie; not his normal drinking style, but shackles hung heavy on him. The silence left Hughes free to think it out, step by step.

His mind flipped through the calendar. He'd be back in Hertfordshire for the wedding. Not too late, if Merlin's luck prevailed. Not only did Tread deserve his championship at the altar, it would give him an opportunity with the wizard. The sooner the better, if these holes were any indication. He scratched at the tablecloth.

Someone had been fiddling with magic. The Council of Mages knew that much. Not that it was unusual—a lot of people thought they might have ability. With most, a few failed spells made them lose interest. There was nothing better designed to halt foolhardy behavior than failure. A few kept at it, achieving minimal ability to control their environment in one aspect or another. They did no harm; batting away irritants or causing wagers to be successful more than the average didn't make a ripple in the atmosphere.

It was that once-in-a lifetime dabbler who, through talent or determination, managed to corral the essences floating through the air who made trouble. Like the rogue Hughes was in Puckeridge to find.

It had taken five magicians to locate the rogue; the best they had been able to do was narrow her location to Puckeridge. Four magicians had been riding the lanes of the shire for weeks, chasing cloud formations. It was pure chance dropped him here. Or, if not chance, perhaps Merlin was directing events from wherever he was. If he was.

The Council objected to anonymity. Always in the back of their minds was the knowing: witch hunts were set off by a spark. Historically, anonymous spells were a menace. That was the duke's concern.

Hughes had found a further cause for panic. The clouds masked holes in the atmosphere. Holes in hearth rugs and tablecloths were the least of his worries. What if holes riddled the supports of a bridge? Or boat keels? By Merlin, foreheads. He could see people falling like pheasants at a shoot.

Who knew how the atmosphere would react? Was it like punching water? Slap and it slid aside, only to right itself. Or was it like tearing sheets apart? Rip and it fell to rags. A raggedy atmosphere would be worse than random folk with holes in their foreheads. It was imperative: find the magician before serious damage was done. Plotting twists, Hughes let Tread call the footmen when Ridgemont drunkenly slid under the table. He rubbed the charred pattern of holes in the cloth.

Why he was having difficulty pinpointing the culprit, he didn't know. *Wise and discerning, discerning and wise. Work on it, my lad.* Tonight, while everyone slept, he would solve the problem once and for all. Tonight he would know, with Arthur's blessing.

Then he had to see the duke. Countering the damage to the atmosphere was going to be tricky. He needed advice.

Upstairs, almost as far from the dining room as one could get and still be in the house, a puff of smoke leaked under a door and into the hall. Under the disinterested light of a candle flickering in a polished silver wall sconce, it crept away from the door and became bold.

Bunching into a cloud, it emitted tendrils that writhed across the floor. Along its path, the flat weave of the rug shimmered. Reaching the center of the hall, the smoke resolved itself into a rough oval. The color wavered between wispy gray and a lovely shade of violet. Against the dull brown of the rug, it showed like a smear of chalk etched by a drunken hand.

Floating, the smoke ring reached the opposite wall. It turned, sweeping along the wide molding at the bottom of the wall until every puff was off the carpet and sank into the floorboards, leaving a mist of twinkling lights flickering in the grain of the wood.

The door opened. "Oh, Morgan, it went wrong again." Dainty feet obliterated the glittering particles. The only evidence of the smoke's passing was a charged glimmer of sawdust so faint it required the eyes of a magician to see it.

* * *

Late that night, Adrian Hughes bent from the waist and picked up two more twigs. They couldn't be thicker than his thumb or thinner than his tongue. "Gardeners are too efficient," he grumbled to no one. "It's one thing to keep the park tidy, but this is the middle of the home wood, for Merlin's sake. There's supposed to be litter on the ground."

It was dark; he'd had to mark a trail back. Somewhere behind him, straight ahead if he walked between two blackthorns and veered to the left of a honeysuckle, was the house. Keeping his eyes trained on the ground, he moved further into the trees.

"Ah, there's another. Now, how many do I have?" He tramped to the middle of the clearing and counted. "Twenty-seven. That's enough."

A glimmer showed where the moon would soon rise. "Better hurry. Took longer than I thought." Kneeling, he laid the twigs in a spiraling pile. From his pocket, he took a bun and speared it on the topmost twig.

"Now I need an acorn. A nice, firm, ripe one." Hughes had chosen the clearing partly for its showy stand of oaks. He circled under one, scuffing the ground. "Acorns. There should be plenty. The most zealous of gardeners wouldn't waste time gathering all the nuts." He kicked at a clump of grass. A small knob-like shape bounded across the clearing.

"There you are," he boomed and chased the acorn. "Thank Merlin my eyes are sharp."

Scooping up the nut, he looked back to the sticks. A small

squirrel, nose twitching, sniffed at the bun. On its hind quarters, the tower of sticks was just its height. The squirrel waved its plumy tail and leaned forward.

"No!" He threw the acorn at the squirrel. Startled, it snatched the bun in its teeth and bounded across the grass to scale one of the tallest oaks. He watched it scamper up the trunk and jump from branch to branch. Then it was lost in the dark. So was the bun.

"You damned Scotti," he shouted. "What do you mean, taking my bread? I need it for the spell."

Scowling, he kicked the stack of twigs, scattering them. "It's too late now. This spell has to be performed at the rise of the moon. With a bit of bread, by Merlin. There isn't time to get another bun." Squirrels were the most quarrelsome critter. Well, maybe not. Kangaroos kicked. A smile flirted around the corner of his mouth. That roo chasing his brother around the compound was pretty funny. How'd the thing know a well placed kick to the rump would send Christopher flying into the Eucalyptus?

He sobered. Hands thrust in his pockets, the magician contemplated the ground. This spell was a wash. Was there another enchantment that would have the same effect?

No. There was not, not a one he knew. Nothing else would reveal the identity of the rogue wizard at this juncture. He went back over his training; had something been omitted or had he forgotten a detail he could use to his advantage? No.

The old litany, 'What would another do?' failed. Lord Brinston might call the Graces to some effect. That helped not a whit. The Graces ignored Adrian Hughes as an ant in the forest. Hurst, well, to be honest, Hurst should be here. His particular gift was tailored for the situation.

Hurst was in London.

He was so deep in thought, Hughes was not aware a glimmer of magic fell from the sky and caught a patch of grass afire. It smoldered low. After he left the clearing, returned to the house, and fell into bed, the patch of grass sparked, sending a spray of twinkling particles into the air.

Chapter Three

Mrs. Whitmill-Ridgemont waved one last time at the light traveling carriage as it rolled down the drive. "It is unfortunate Mr. Hughes must leave," she murmured in Treadway's ear. "He will have a miserable drive back to town in this weather."

"The condition of the roads won't stop Hughes. He can drive to an inch; was asked to join the Four Horse Club, but the silly chub declined."

"I have seen the club on their monthly excursion." Christine tossed her head and a strand of her hair whipped his cheek. "They wear those ridiculous striped ties; no wonder Mr. Hughes didn't want to be a member. But why must he go?"

"Has business in town. He is a busy man. For being an idler, that is. His latest is an investment with the Marquess of Brinston and the Duke of Haverhorn. They've been arranging it for over a month. Evidently it is now set to go."

"The Marquess of Brinston—that awful man. I thought Mr. Hughes had more refined taste. Brinston's activities have been questionable, you know, consorting with low lifes and smugglers. *On dit* is he sold information to the French."

"I believe that was debunked, my dear. The marquess was working to catch foreign agents."

"Is that so? I hadn't heard." The movement of her body released a cloud of perfume on the wind. Treadway breathed heliotrope, could almost see it whirling about his head, worming its way into his skin. Her scent raised his hunting instincts. It figured the widow would use it. She was made for passion.

He pulled his mind back to the conversation. "Yes, it all came out before his marriage. As to Hughes, I can't find it in me to regret his leaving. I don't like to share treats—and your company, my dear, transcends a banquet."

A warm glance promised much more. From the corner of his eye, he could see his betrothed, standing by the door, reluctant to brave the gusting wind for more than a moment. As soon as Hughes's carriage pulled away, she scurried to the shelter of the portico, where she stood like a sentinel. Graceful, he absently noted, but still a guard.

Sir Denison had already retreated to the hall; Lady Ridgemont had not come downstairs. Poor sendoff for Hughes. As if, achieving their goal, they couldn't be bothered with guests. Which was probably true. Ridgemont wanted to settle his daughter—that was done. What else was there to talk about—crops?

A maid slipped out the half open door and curtsied to Miss Ridgemont. He couldn't hear what the girl said, but with a nod, his betrothed called, "Excuse me. I am needed in the kitchen."

Ahh, time alone with the widow. Bad *ton* to dally under the Ridgemont roof, but she was a good vehicle for thumbing his nose at the elders. Trying not to leer, Treadway said, "Your sister may be occupied for some time. Shall we visit the conservatory?" And visit her heliotrope, her mouth, her breasts. Who wanted plants?

"I can't think of anyone I would rather view it with." There was the giggle again, the one that focused his desire.

* * *

The next afternoon, Treadway's father arrived in Puckeridge. Solicitors showed up next. With great bonhomie, Carlton Treadway and Sir Denison ensconced themselves in the library to thrash out the marriage settlements. It didn't take long. They were in accord before they began.

The younger people congregated in the drawing room. Treadway was desperate for a diversion. It would not do to think about what was happening in the library, how his father was consigning his soul. Might go berserk. Watching Miss Ridgemont's hands as they swooped back and forth, plying a needle, he noted her fingers. Slender, quietly dexterous, but nothing he admired.

Shaking out his cuff, he commented, "The weather looks to be clearing in time for a drive this afternoon. It may be cool, but if you dress warmly, you should enjoy tooling in my phaeton."

Miss Ridgemont looked up from the sheet she was darning, fingering the shears hung by a ribbon around her neck. "The rain has stopped?"

"Oh James, you are so clever." Christine dropped a book of verse to the floor and fluttered to the window. "I am impressed no end! I was dying to escape this gloomy house; how did you guess?"

She perched on the wide windowsill and traced a sensual finger along the glass. "The clouds are clearing."

The muslin of her gown stretched across her derrière and Treadway's fingers itched. He was careful not to look toward his betrothed. Miss Ridgemont looked too much like a wife already. Darning sheets. That was a chore wives did.

"Been cooped up the past days," he demurred. "Stood to reason."

"I adore riding with you. Your horses are strong...muscular..." Christine touched his sleeve. "Dominating."

"If you like, we could head to the next village. The inn there puts out a decent spread." He kept his head turned to Christine. "You said you like sticky buns—theirs are good. They pour a decent mug of ale, too."

"I like sticky buns, but the prospect of a drive with you is better. I don't mind if we have no fixed destination." She fiddled with her hair, throwing her bosom into higher prominence. The one who would be a wife looked like all the wives in the world. He grinned at the widow's bosom.

The lackluster betrothed gazed through another rain-washed window into the garden. *If it rained forever,* Margaret brooded, *I would not have to drive with Mr. Treadway, barbarian that he is. And if dear Christine catches a chill from the bodice she is almost not wearing, it will serve her right.*

Who had his invitation been extended to? A phaeton did not seat three people in comfort and just yesterday morning she had made clear her aversion to the cloying sweetness of sticky buns. Turning away from the pair, her fingers tightened around the sewing shears. In the last novel she read, the heroine stabbed the villain with shears. She saved herself. What a marvelous dream.

* * *

Rubbing his hands together, Sir Denison announced at tea, "It's settled. You can sign the papers tomorrow, after the solicitors finish fair copies."

Carlton Treadway slapped his son on the back. "Ain't that grand, my boy?"

Lady Ridgemont beamed. "So pleasing. Margaret's wedding dress will be done within the week. Isn't it exciting, Emma?"

Emma's presence had been decreed to honor the betrothal. Margaret's sister didn't look honored, but she nodded. A thin girl of sixteen, Emma had spent her adolescence perfecting the art of invisibility. Only her older sister, and occasionally Lady Ridgemont, paid any heed to her. A smaller version of Margaret, but too young to have learned to conceal her thoughts, Emma strangled the glass of lemonade she had carried into the room.

"Emma," Margaret said, stifling a sense of panic, "perhaps you can visit me in London after I marry." The girl looked at her for a moment, then buried her head in her glass. The lack of animation irritated Margaret, but she was distracted by a swerve in the conversation.

"I'll send my man for a special license." Mr. Treadway Senior grinned. "No sense letting moss grow under our feet."

"Yes. No ballyhooing and crying for months on end. Why suffer a lengthy betrothal? Short and snappy. That's what I like to see." Ridgemont rubbed his hands again.

Christine's strangled ejaculation was covered by Lady Ridgemont's crowing. "We can arrange the ceremony for midmonth. The vicar won't mind not posting banns. Such a dreary, dragging process, banns. Two weeks is sufficient time to plan a breakfast."

Too soon! Too soon! echoed in Margaret's head. Whose idea was it to take weeks of freedom away from her? Papa had mentioned May. Now they were talking March. Her father looked pleased as punch, as did Step-Mama and Mr. Treadway Senior. Her stomach churned.

Margaret did not want to keep company with James Treadway. Wedding him was unthinkable. Mucking out the stables would be more to her liking. Anything was better than watching her betrothed and her sister drool over each other.

Now Papa gloated over his triumph. She didn't want to watch. Her chair felt like nails protruded from the seat.

Christine's face twisted in what was surely a grimace of pain. She looked like she had been condemned. Though Margaret hated the feeling, seeing how Christine chased Mr. Treadway, a stab of pity went through her. *Poor Christine, Papa should have given him to her. They would have scandalized court with their raking and had a marvelous time doing it. Her life would have been much improved over what it is now.*

Good heavens, the thought struck Margaret like a boulder to the head. Did Christine entice Mr. Treadway to assuage grief at losing her husband? Did she miss Mr. Whitmill? Martin Whitmill had been a dreadful boor; eating peas with a spoon was the least of his offenses. Yet Christine had married him. She must have cared.

The idea her sister was trying to recover happiness lost when Mr. Whitmill died skewed Margaret's view of the past week. Deep in thought, she startled when Mr. Treadway grabbed her hand.

Treadway, prodded by his father with a finger in his side, produced a ring from his pocket. Raising her arm with so little grace her sleeve almost ripped, he said, "Then it's time for this. A sign of our union." He slid the ring on her finger.

She felt like a bystander, too numb to object to his crudity. The ring slid up her finger, over her knuckle, and settled. An emerald, crowned at the compass points with diamonds. Heavy gold band, large emerald, four diamonds twinkling like stars. Against her will, she liked the ring. It fit.

"Well, say something," Lady Ridgemont urged. "One would think you unwilling, Margaret."

She felt unaccountably shy. "Thank you." Out of the corner of her eye she saw Emma's look of scorn. Goodness, at whom was she glaring?

Treadway nodded. "I'll go for the license. There's business I need to tend in London."

"Have to prepare the townhouse, I imagine," Mr. Treadway Senior said. "It's been a bachelor establishment. You'll need maids, my boy."

"A shame for you love-birds to be parted." Lady Ridgemont rustled over. "But it will be a short separation. You will hardly notice him gone, Margaret, with all the preparations. We have an amount of work to do. Before the month is out, you will be wed." She patted her stepdaughter's hand. "Such a handsome piece of jewelry. It fits perfectly.

"Wait till you see the dress we have devised, gentlemen. Tiers and tiers of lace. Margaret will be a lovely bride. None of this nonsense about brides wearing satin or silk. Her dress will be of the finest lace, as it should."

As Lady Ridgemont rambled hill and dale of bridal concerns, Mr. Treadway looked over her head at Christine. Margaret could not divine his thoughts. Christine's were all too plain. She looked like she had swallowed a lemon. Poor Christine.

* * *

Clouds blew around the night sky like tea leaves tossed in a pot of boiling water. Not a breath of breeze shivered, but sleepy birds burst frantically from the dubious shelter of trees beginning to leaf. They cowered on the ground, tucking heads under wings.

Two clouds, larger and denser than the others, scudded over the horizon. One from the east, one from the west, they raced toward each other, gathering lesser clouds along their edges as the heavens roiled and heaved.

The massive clouds met. With a cataclysmic cascade of thunder, one cleaved the other in two. The fractured mass scattered, hurling splintered fragments into the treetops. Racing heedlessly on, the victorious cloud scattered minute pinpoints of light across the sky.

The lights twinkled like the aftereffects of fireworks. Drifting in the wake of a rising wind, they hung on the air until the rays of the rising sun burned them out.

With the dawn, nature righted itself.

* * *

And so they were betrothed. The Right Honorable Miss Margaret Ann Ridgemont and Mr. James Conner Treadway would wed as soon as may be.

His belief that Margaret was dull and impossibly countrified meant nothing. Her surety that he was a beast, icy of heart and incurably rakish of eye, also meant nothing. In the eyes of society, it was an eminently suitable match.

Carlton Treadway, father of the prospective groom, patted his stomach in satisfaction. He had been trying to settle the lad for several years, worrying one of those loose widows at Camelot would snap James up or his antics would land him in Newgate or worse. It wasn't only nobility who worried about the future; Mr. Treadway Senior had a family to perpetuate. He promptly sent the notice to the papers so the world would know of Miss Ridgemont's triumph and his son's defeat. An advertisement in the court news incised the engagement in stone—James could not back away and retain a vestige of honor or influence at Camelot.

When Mr. Treadway Senior returned home from the Ridgemont estate in Hertfordshire with the marriage contracts negotiated and signed, he found his wife in her favorite chair in the solar, a rosewood writing desk drawn before her. Paper littered the under-tier, held on the shelf by a pierced brass gallery. She laid a clean sheet of paper before her and glanced up as he walked in.

"Carlton," Mrs. Treadway said absently, immersed in the planning of menus. "I did not know you were here. Have you seen Constance? She lost a bit of pudginess, but is recovering. Nurse assures me her appetite is returned, voracious as ever. Ann is distressed over the loss of her favorite doll—it somehow went down the well. Susan looks too angelic not to be responsible. I do wish you would speak to her about it, and if you could comfort Ann—bring her smile back. I have been singularly unsuccessful."

Thankful none of their promising brood besieged the room, with or without dolls, Mr. Treadway Senior broke the welcome news to his lady. "It's all settled—he is to be wed at last."

Menus and children forgotten, Mrs. Treadway squealed. "All favorably, I hope! Do tell. There is none of this modern nonsense of the lady retaining her dowry, is there?" Paper scattered as she thrust the desk away and jumped to her feet. "Oh, Carlton, bless you. I wish I could have gone also. I should have made Miss Ridgemont's acquaintance immediately. I long to meet the darling girl. Nothing was said of my neglect, was there? I could not have left Constance, not while she was ill. I would have been frantic the whole time I was in Hertfordshire, you may be assured."

"No, my love," Mr. Treadway Senior reassured his wife. "I made your excuses, never fear. Lady Ridgemont understood you could not leave Constance to battle an ague alone." She bombarded him with questions about her eldest son's sweet fiancée.

"Is she lovely?"

"A pretty little puss, with manners to shame a duchess," he replied, recalling the stiff, punctiliously polite young lady who signed her name to the marriage contracts with precision and a glare. "Has a pole down her spine, that girl does. She will never turn into a hussy—never be like those London widows, crawling over every man they see. Not tall, dark hair and eyes."

"Is James content?"

He thought back to his son, gallantly turning the pages of

Miss Ridgemont's music as she played. "She played the pianoforte nicely, no off-notes or stumbling over the keys. He is perfectly fine," he mumbled, not telling his wife of the bump in the road of his plans.

He had recognized the sister's type; a great deal tiger and little lady. She made eyes at James, no denying. A Guinevere set to ensorcell. Not the sort he wanted for his son, not at all. Too bad if the boy felt drawn in Mrs. Whitmill-Ridgemont's direction. And he was drawn. The stupid boy's eyes nearly fell out of his head every time the widow's bosom hove into view.

Now he was betrothed, James could be rakish as he pleased—out of sight of Miss Ridgemont. The lad knew his manners. As long as the music continued, James had kept his eyes off the curvaceous widow and on his prim betrothed, as he should.

Miss Ridgemont had endeavored at all times to keep her eyes off James.

"Proper shy, that's what she is." Mr. Treadway Senior convinced himself, ignoring the lack of warmth between his son and his betrothed. That was fine, at least until after they stood before the parson. Then it would perhaps be a bit of a tangle, but nothing he could not clear up. The lad just had to be firm. And stay away from widows. *And* do nothing to further upset Bow Street.

"I do love weddings. I will hold a betrothal ball when we get to London. A dinner—"

"No you won't. The wedding is as soon as the license is ready and we can get to Hertfordshire. No sense wasting time." Mr. Treadway Senior succinctly told his wife the plan.

* * *

A few days later, Adrian Hughes paced the antechamber of the London office. Mr. Moneypenny offered a chair, but he shook his head. Stalking the perimeter of the good-sized room, he viewed the paintings, all landscapes. Not merely landscapes, but landscapes with vast reaches of sky. Clouds. How dull.

When he was a child, his nurse liked to look at the things. Pulling him to the ground, she would urge him to find shapes in the clouds. Fanciful shapes, like dragons, or humdrum, like sheep. He'd fooled her—Hughes would magic the sky and form bon bons, mounds of potatoes with rivers of butter flowing, lamb chops and cherry tarts. Tarts invariably sent Nurse to the kitchen, her stomach rumbling. Now, with nothing better to occupy himself, he looked for shapes in the painted clouds. He didn't know if painters had the imagination to shape tarts.

Well, may he be walled up in a crystal cave. Right there in the sky above a dull stretch of meadow. It was a woman. Seated, reaching for something. He moved down the wall and stared at the second painting. There she was again, just her torso, arms outstretched.

He viewed the paintings in order around the room. There she was loosely sketched—the sky was pink, the clouds faint. Hughes felt a tremor of excitement. In the next painting, she was less formed, but he found her diving, head tucked, arms straining forward. Finally, curled as if he viewed her sleeping figure from the foot of a bed.

A bell tinkled and the secretary rose to open the door to the inner sanctum. "He will see you now," Moneypenny murmured. Reluctant to abandon his scrutiny of clouds, Hughes stepped through the doorway and closed the door.

"Go back out," his grace called. "You have not finished. There are two more paintings to examine."

"It was only an idle pastime."

The Duke of Haverhorn wagged a finger. "You don't really think that. Now go. I have a pile of letters to sign. I can wait."

Thoughtfully, Hughes returned to the antechamber. Placing himself in front of one of the two paintings he had not examined, he eyed it, rolled his lip and frowned. Ah, there she was, in the classic pose of a sexually dominated woman, arms stretched overhead, elbows bent. He hadn't seen her at first because her lower body was hidden behind a tree. The lover was a dark seething bank of clouds, arms and head barely formed.

In the final picture, the woman was unmistakable. Center frame, hills rising as if to cradle her, she gave her back to the viewer. Hair tumbled and rolled. No more could be seen, but the impression of satisfied wantonness could not be missed.

No longer amused with the childish game, Hughes marched into the inner office and slammed the door. Ignoring the vast floor of polished hardwood, the opulent white and gold furnishings, and the expanse of ebony atop four veined marble pillars that was the desk, he demanded, "Is this your idea of a joke?"

The duke rose from the chair behind his massive desk. "I didn't create her," he said flatly. "She has been forming over the last week, as the person we seek creates havoc in our world. Moneypenny wants her out of his office—feels like a courtesan is looking over his shoulder."

"A sign."

"I fear so." The duke rounded the desk and shook Hughes's hand. "But only written in the sky, thus not permanent." Incongruously average in height, he paced in front of the desk. Haverhorn looked like fifty other men. But once a man looked in the hard gray eyes and delved into the agate honor of the duke, he would never underestimate his grace of Haverhorn. Title or no title, here was power, immutable and eternal. It was sobering to see his concern over clouds.

"If we act fast..." At the duke's nod, Hughes said, "I found him—at least I know where he is. In Puckeridge, Herts. At Sir Denison Ridgemont's estate. And he's a her."

"A female! By Merlin, women and magic don't mix. Act quickly, my lad." The duke turned his head to the side. "Puckeridge..."

"Do you know something?"

"Puckeridge. I know Puckeridge from somewhere. What's the family name?"

"Ridgemont."

"Doesn't ring my bell. Wait—" The duke swung back to his desk. "Moneypenny. Get me DeBrett's *Knights Register*."

In a moment he was flipping pages in a thick volume. "Ah, here it is. Ridgemont. Married 1788 to..." The duke groaned. "I should have guessed. Blood tells."

"Your grace?"

"Margery Laycock." As Hughes looked befuddled, he said, "Come now, you have heard the tale. Who hasn't?" The younger man shook his head dumbly.

"Margery Laycock was sister to William Pitt. They took to calling her the Laycock curse. Come, my boy, this must jog your memory."

"I am afraid not, sir."

"Where are you from that you've never heard of the Laycock curse?"

"The Antipodes."

A spark of interest lit in Haverhorn's eyes. "Sometime you must tell me of it."

"Yes, your grace."

"Bah. I was telling you of Margery Laycock. Pitt's sister. She decided to play a trick on him. Magicked a shipment of tea he was puffing off to a dignitary. Set the gaudiest seal she had ever seen on each and every cask. For some reason, no one noticed. A ship loaded and sailed for Boston."

Hughes cocked his head. "Seals?"

"Margery thought they were inspection seals. So she told me. But they were tax stamps."

"There's no tax on tea going abroad, sir."

"No? Well, I wish you'd been on that ship. Might have saved King George a bit of a fracas. The ship landed in Boston harbor. The Americans, fiery souls that they are, ogled the tax stamps and took umbrage. Dumped the casks in the harbor and near started a revolution. George was hard pressed to calm them. That was when, over all objection, he granted the colonies their independence from England. A matter of politics. After all, it wasn't the colony's fault the highest rate of tax stamp was on those casks."

The younger man shook his head in wonder. "But what does that have to do with Puckeridge?"

"Margery Laycock was Ridgemont's wife."

Hughes sank into a chair, his mouth hanging open. "Then it could be any of them."

"It must be one of Margery's get. The one born with the blood."

"It isn't so simple, sir. I have not been able to narrow it. I have three suspects."

Haverhorn ran his finger down the page of Debrett's. "Margery had four children. A boy and three girls. You said it was a female."

"My suspects are the three sisters." His grace heaved a sigh and cradled his chin with his hand. Staring at the wall, he was silent for some moments.

"They could all be blooded. Can't take them out of the way," he said with finality. "Farmer George had a fondness for Margery. Can you neutralize them?"

"I don't believe that is wise."

"What *do* you believe?"

"That something must be done at once. The phenomena is disturbing."

At the duke's nod, he elaborated. "Pinprick holes are appearing. So far, I have seen them in a carpet and on cloth. There is magical residue."

"The holes are tiny?"

"At least for now. Your grace, I need your advice."

* * *

From the Council offices, Hughes went directly to his rooms in Albany, entering the Rope Walk from Vigo Street. Everyone was sure to be at G1, his flat. As usual, he guessed correctly. Letting himself in, he found a motley collection of men draped around his not so commodious drawing cum dining room.

The rancid smell almost made him turn and leave. Empty bottles littered the floor and one man, Squire Charles Leighton by the tone of his snores, reclined on the dining table. Snuff, cigar ash, and sticky spots speckled the floor. A streak of brandy ran down the veined marble chimneypiece; shards on the hearth intimated a snifter had been thrown.

Ernest Chively announced on his entrance, "Silvester found the betrothal notice in the paper, Hughes. He's reading it for the umpteenth time because Stone can't believe it."

Fueled by a deep gulp of spirits and an ingrained distaste for the married state, Stone pleaded, "Tell me it ain't so. Can't we do something to save him?" Billy Johnstone would have been called 'Silly Billy' if that bloke over in Europe had not already taken the name. Instead his friends gave him the sobriquet 'Stone.' Not for the strength in his arm muscle and not for the weakness of his head muscle, but for the fact he couldn't swim, only sank like a rock.

"We should kidnap Tread and hold him till he comes to his senses. Can't we tuck him in Chelsea or somewhere? Put him in m'brother's love nest, if nowhere else. Not on the same floor as the skirt—Sloane would kill him. In the attic, if it has a lock. When he forgets her, we can let him out."

Chively scooped a Berwick cockle off the floor and popped it into his mouth. "Don't despair. Tread is Tread. He'll come to his senses."

"I don't think so. His father is forcing him to the altar," Hughes said, clearing a seat for himself by dumping a load of wrinkled jackets from a chair to the floor. "The wedding is in a few weeks."

Peter Silvester threw the newspaper on Leighton's head. "His father? Well, I say. That's a scurvy trick. Fathers are supposed to uphold a man, not drag him down."

When Hughes only took a deep pull from the bottle he grabbed away from Leighton's boots, Stone whined, "This means Tread'll have to escort the petticoat. Balls and the like. Won't ever be the same. Who's going to introduce me to Harriette Wilson?"

"Don't know why you want to meet her. She'd never look at you."

Stone raised his chin. "She's done with Leinster. Perfect timing."

Hughes grinned, imagining a twist of fate linking Stone with London's most discriminating courtesan. Half the nobility and all the monied men in Britain would have to fall dead before Harriette looked at Stone. London would be a lot less crowded.

"Worcester is sniffing at her heels." Leighton turned from his front to his side, pillowed his head on the discarded newspaper, and snorted.

"It's enough to make one lose faith," Silvester grumbled under his breath. "If you can't trust your father to protect you from petticoats, who can you trust? Thank Arthur mine is under the sod. He wouldn't have liked it when the magistrate threw me and Tread in Newgate for taking his daughter and her friend to the Cyprian's Ball. But he'd never have made me marry—"

Leighton lifted his head. "You didn't even get to enjoy them, did you?"

"No, I quit when mine cast up her accounts. Tread's girl left with Du Lac. Now, if Tread's Pater wanted retribution, there's the man to flay. Du Lac flashes his bankroll and connections at the ladybirds and they fly to him. It's immoral."

"He won't appear in the Green Room." Arthur, Lord Chively, heir to the Earldom of Wellwood, should be aware of the necessity of siring the next generation of heirs, but was not. His understanding of life was limited to horses and the demimonde. "Tread is a chump to get shackled when Merlin's Gardens has unearthed a promising new crop of beauties to chase. What a bore."

"We should do something to stop this madness. There's a skirt at the Garden made for him. Long legs, huge breasts, just what he likes. A lot like Sloane's doll, come to think of it. How could he pass that by? He's the only one can introduce me to the Wilson, unless you'll do it, Hughes." Stone moaned, overcome by the demise of his hopes for Harriette Wilson, the most notorious courtesan in the Isles.

Leighton rolled off the table, landing flat on his back at Hughes's feet. He groaned and opened his eyes. Leaning over to shove jackets under his head for a pillow, Hughes said, "Not on your life, Stone. Little Harry would eat you alive."

"Don't mention food," Leighton begged.

"Little Harry?" Stone asked.

"Harriette Wilson's nickname, you fool."

Silvester propped his boots on Leighton's hip. The bottle in his hand dribbled on the floor. Leighton closed his eyes again. "Won't be until after the first son is birthed that Tread gets back in form. What will we do without him?"

The meeting was devolving into a wake. Margaret Ridgemont's engaging face before his eyes, Hughes had to say something in her defense. His friends were entertaining drinking and gaming companions, but boorish otherwise. "It behooves us to prop our friend up in his undertaking," he lectured. "Pater Treadway is adamant and unless Tread knuckles under, the poor lad will be miserable. Probably lose his allowance and have to stay in Grassville. That would be worse than leg shackles. The girl's no fishwife—she won't be so bad."

"You met her. What's she like?"

"Agreeable. Shy. Not his type." That Treadway might be cutting off his nose to spite his father was left unsaid. Miss Ridgemont had a pleasant manner and the disposition to match her winsome face. She deserved better than her father had chosen for her.

Unhappy as they were with the thought of one of their own snapped in parson's mousetrap, the men were stymied. There was nothing they could do to save Tread, not with a determined father and the announcement already in the papers.

"Why does it have to happen so soon? Not like he compromised the chit—why wed so soon?"

"He won't have time for a last fling with a skirt from the

Gardens."

Hughes squashed a stabbing sense of guilt. "Oh, yes he will. If we arrange it, he can have one night."

Enthusiastically, Tread's friends planned the grandest bachelor's party ever conceived. "Harriette Wilson! Have her be hostess. She has a soft spot for Tread and I can meet her," Stone suggested.

"Brandy," Leighton whined. "More brandy."

Chapter Four

Margaret was aware of Treadway's flirting and didn't care—not much. She hadn't had a moment to herself in days. With all the simpering and smirking, her nerves were strung like a harp. She rubbed her forehead.

Step-Mama throws us together. Papa hides. It's a large house, where can I hide?

The attics were a good choice. Cold, drafty. Christine would never go there. Dusty, crammed with generations of discards. Mr. Treadway could have no interest in attics.

Shifting a bulky coverlet in her arms, she closed the hall door and faced the stairs. In honor of her hiding place, Margaret wore a dowdy calico dress. Ignoring the dust collecting on the hem, she stalked up the stairway and into the hall bisecting the middle of the attic. Past the box room, where luggage snoozed under Holland sheets, she debated where to hide. There was a miscellany of uncomfortable straight back chairs in the third room and crates in the fourth.

At the end of the corridor, in the room that held trunks of old clothes and a few discarded armoires, was a chaise with a broken leg. There was her desert island, her oasis. Several mildewed books propped up the legless corner. The chaise hadn't been covered; its pale blue satin felt gritty. She flung the old coverlet she had found in the linen closet over it. Why a maid had not appropriated the stained but cuddly cotton throw for her own bed was a mystery.

Not that she was interested in mysteries. The only mystery she would have welcomed was a search for the murderer of her betrothed, James Treadway. If there had been one, she would have knighted the villain.

Time had not eased her affront. 'Insipid.' Her skills did not matter, her feelings did not matter. Margaret did not matter. He liked Christine's 'lushness.'

Not for the world would she allow Mr. Treadway, a suave, experienced Londoner, know she had overheard him. She possessed a modicum of pride. 'Much too staid' he had said. That had been part of Papa's tirade since last year, when her season had come to nothing. Margaret was too timid, too staid to attract gentlemen. Little as she liked it, the description matched.

Yes, Christine was flamboyant. She was in mourning, but only the color of her gown reflected grief. Christine thrived on fashion and the boldness of gentlemen while Margaret yearned for comfort and a gentle knight. But did he have to ogle Christine?

Curling her legs, she leaned against the upholstered back of the chaise. To ward off the chill, the edge of the coverlet covered her legs. Christine would serve him right. She would nag and demand constant attention, jewels and adulation. She would drive Mr. Treadway up a tree. Yes, it would serve him right.

Margaret ignored the musty tickle in her nose and opened her book. Blessed peace.

Downstairs, Christine whispered. Her lip pouted and her finger passed his belly button. "Up there we can be private. Positively no one will think to disturb us."

"But it's dusty," Treadway objected. "Chilly."

"You will warm me, won't you? There is an old chaise. Someone propped up the broken leg. It won't rock. This will keep dirt from our clothing." She waved her free arm, over which draped a drab wool blanket.

Warm wasn't the word—he intended to send her up in flames.

The chill in the stairwell cooled his heated blood. A little dirt. Scratchy wool blanket. An attic was not the most romantic site for seduction. He prowled the roughly finished corridor, following the beguiling form of his intended victim. Her skirt swayed. He had a sudden vision of Margaret's skirt swaying the same way, but he pushed it from his mind. She was his father's choice, not his.

He snaked an arm around the widow's waist from behind. Pulling her against him, he lowered his head and raised a hand to the swell of her bosom.

Christine melted into him. His groin caressed her buttocks. The friction raised the temperature of his blood. Heliotrope rose above the smell of dust and made his head swim. The feel of her—firm, warm, enticingly rounded—made Treadway a god of love.

He sipped and tasted. The widow's neck was smooth, her hair silky. Her fingers were clever, playing with the bulge in his pants.

With a groan, he pressed forward and gave himself up to pleasure.

Thanks to the stimulation, he needed to get her prone. He raised his head to take a breath, to decrease the lightheadedness. *Where the hell is that chaise?* Scooping up the blanket she had let fall to the dirty floor, Treadway urged the widow on.

"The chaise is in the last room." She had a deal of experience, enough to slip her fingers through the opening of his inexpressibles. Christine squeezed as he opened the door.

A pool of light splashed across the floor. It illuminated the chaise and Margaret, asleep on the chaise. His betrothed, cuddled on his projected bed of passion. A coverlet glinted blue in the light, shifting with the movement of her chest. Eyebrows a fine arch, oval face calm in sleep, Margaret looked like a princess waiting to be awakened by her lover.

He pulled the fingers out of his inexpressibles and took a step back, dragging the widow with him. Without a sound, they retreated.

"Why?" the widow wailed when he closed the attic door. She beat a fist on his chest in frustration, then stalked down the stairs. He followed. Why, indeed?

Treadway didn't notice the wisp of lavender smoke curled at the base of the door, or the lacy holes, smaller than worm holes, that formed where the smoke brushed against the oak. His groin ached and throbbed, cheated of release.

By the desire of Lancelot, he wanted the widow but was stymied at every turn. Tomorrow he had to leave to fetch the license. He would lose his chance with Christine. The Pater had laid down the law. Either James wed Margaret or he was disinherited. Too bad the Pater had stumbled on evidence of his brief occupation of a Newgate cell.

Chapter Five

Lady Ridgemont extended a hand to be kissed. "James, it is good to have you back with us. And Mr. Hughes."

"Only a day later than Sir Denison requested," Christine said, *sotto voce*. Margaret buried her nose in her embroidery so far she almost dug the needle into her cheek.

Treadway flashed teeth at the three ladies. "I meant to return yesterday, but was unavoidably detained. Several friends required my presence. Would have been rude to say no."

"Charles Leighton put him in the way of a good thing," Hughes inserted, feeling his cheeks mottle.

"Business, I suppose," Christine said, dry as a Latin scholar.

"But of course. My friends arranged an introduction; my timely approach resulted in a vigorous new association." Treadway tugged his waistcoat. "We ended up at Merlin's Gardens. The meeting opened fertile avenues to explore in the future."

"What kind of business did you conduct?" Margaret asked, curious.

"Dolls and other amusements," Hughes said with an enigmatic glance.

"It is nice to see a young man wise enough to be active in the world of finance. Too many waste their fortunes at the gaming tables." Lady Ridgemont rang the bell. To the butler she commanded, "Craig, bring tea. The gentlemen must be thirsty."

"Tea would be welcome," Hughes said. "It is dry for this time of the year. The road from London was as dusty as late summer."

"We have had no rain," Christine said. "The clouds roll; we hear thunder, but not a drop falls."

Lady Ridgemont waved a languid hand. "Sir Denison is not pleased. There was a great disturbance one night; it must have been around the time you left, Mr. Hughes. A stand of oaks at the edge of the property was fired. A spot of rain might have averted the disaster. As we speak, Sir Denison and other landowners are meeting to discuss removal of the charred remains."

"How unfortunate," Treadway said. "It was the result of

lightning?"

"I don't believe so. Rather, it appears the fire was deliberately set. The thought of a malicious person in the neighborhood upsets my nerves."

Hughes noted a hole in the door frame. Looked as if a knot had fallen out, if one ignored the iridescence coating the wood. He frowned.

* * *

Upstairs, a maid jerked in fear. "What?" The noise came again and she craned her neck. The chandelier over her head tinkled, swaying lightly in a non-existent breeze.

"Cor." An empty bed warmer sagged in her hands. Suddenly, a crystal drop fell. It clanged against the brass warmer, exploded and spat slivers in an arc. She shrieked, dropped the pan, and fled.

* * *

If Christine was raking in dubious benefits in her effort to steal Margaret's fiancé, Treadway wallowed in the attention. The well-rounded widow flattered his ego, excited his libido, and kept a dull visit in the country hopping. Hughes could see why Treadway felt free to indulge. Margaret was Mr. Treadway Senior's choice; she was perfectly proper and ladylike, just what Treadway would despise. As he had done before, once Treadway rationalized his behavior, his Lilliputian conscience died a quiet death.

Embarrassed for his friend, Hughes made himself scarce, taking marathon rides and spending a prodigious amount of time sequestered in his room researching rogue wizards. Three days after their arrival in Puckeridge, he ran out of places to hide. Thus, he held back a curtain in the solar, scowling out the window. In a vile mood, he listened to the widow's aimless chatter and sniffed the enticing aroma of gingerbread clinging to Margaret's skirts. And breathed in the noxious fumes of the oppressive atmosphere in the room.

"With the return of the sun, it is almost warm. I begin to envy you the excursion to the Roman settlement of Verulamium yesterday, Mr. Hughes. I feel stifled by walls. Shall we go out?" Christine asked.

"Sounds good," he muttered, unwilling to abandon good manners.

Margaret took her eyes from her sewing. "I would welcome a walk. My finger has worn a groove from the needle. And somehow, I must have poked the needle into my nail. I have a tiny hole in it."

"Does it hurt?" Christine asked.

"No, but it looks silly."

"You should let the chatelaine do the mending," Treadway said.

"She has not found time for it," Margaret responded tartly. "There are holes to be darned."

"In my circle, ladies do decorative stitchery."

"In my circle, ladies do what needs doing."

The corners of Christine's mouth lifted. "A turn in the shrubbery will ease your finger."

The four decamped from the house. Since the oppressive atmosphere strangling Hughes was created by massive flirtation between the widow and her sister's fiancé and disaffection between fiancés, it followed like an ill-omened cloud.

"Why do you stink like the kitchens?" Treadway hissed at Margaret.

She frowned back. "I baked a batch of gingerbread biscuits."

"You baked—"

"Yes, I."

"Commoner." He sneered and she turned her nose up.

The awkward group moved through the gardens, looking for a sheltered spot. They settled to the east of the gazebo, where the wind calmed and hardy primroses heralded spring.

Christine said, "If we were in town, I would go to the modiste and order a new wardrobe."

"You are soon out of mourning," Margaret reminded her. "New clothing is a waste until July, when the year is out."

Treadway tilted his head. "Black becomes you, but I can see you in pink, or better, scarlet. Your beauty can carry a strong color."

"Mint is a good choice for an afternoon gown," Margaret said. "I prefer lighter hues."

He looked her over. "Why am I not surprised?"

Fighting an urge to violence, Hughes inspected the entrance to the gazebo. Holes in the elaborate trellis and swinging gate said bugs were going to be a problem—or some pesky shafts of magic had escaped from the house. Glowing embers buried in the beams told the magician which was more likely.

Margaret has a hole in her fingernail. By the crystal cave, is it the magic? Digging savagely at the wood with his own unblemished nail, he cursed the rogue wizard. *I must move quickly. If any harm comes to that angel, I'll never forgive myself.* His suspicion had born seed, rooted, and sprouted a cushioned patch of clover. Margaret Ridgemont wasn't one of those shallow society misses interested only in establishing herself as advantageously as possible.

Hughes moved beyond the gazebo. Through the foliage, he watched with thoughtful eyes as Margaret polished an apple with her handkerchief. Without bees, clover would wither. With a better man, would Margaret thrive? With, say, someone like him?

Wishing he could keep company with Miss Ridgemont, he aimed his steps to the outer gardens.

* * *

Sir Denison was barricaded in the library, working out the most advantageous way to spend the generous marriage settlement Carlton Treadway had authorized. Margaret was sure that was what he was doing. She tiptoed past the doors.

He probably thought he deserved a new carriage for his efforts. Not a high perch phaeton, which wasn't suited to rough country lanes, but something with a bit of dash. *He is Judas, selling me for thirty thousand pieces of silver. Or gold. Thirty thousand gold sovereigns. Pounds,* she fumed, trying to do the math in her head. *How many sovereigns make thirty thousand pounds?*

She entered the solar. Emma was at the round center table, gluing shells on a wood frame. Margaret leaned over her stooped shoulder.

"The frame looks nice, dear," she said. "I like how you grouped those star turbans at the corners. They look like full blown roses."

"There is nothing better to do," Emma muttered.

"Have you finished the corners, at least?" Her sister's nod wouldn't have disturbed a gnat.

"Emma is doing well with her shellwork," Lady Ridgemont said, not looking away from the fashion periodical she studied.

"Still, if she took the time to plan each shell's placement, it would be more becoming. The corners look like deadheads." While Emma hunched her shoulders, their stepmother turned to Margaret. "It is ever so. I do my best, but you girls will not listen. A wealth of experience lies in your grasp, spurned. Ah well, it is your loss.

"You look flushed, Margaret. I suppose you have been mucking around the kitchen garden again, gathering herbs. I shall never understand your unladylike pursuit of cooking." She raised a malicious eyebrow. "Though another possibility comes to mind. Was James with you—did he kiss you?"

"I walked to the gazebo. Perhaps the exercise accounts for my heightened color." She took up her workbasket and extracted the Florentine stitch fire screen she had begun after Twelfth Night. She admired how the shades of blue, coral, and yellow mingled as she tried to deflect Lady Ridgemont. "There are holes in the gazebo roof. I will tell Papa."

"Yes, yes," Lady Ridgemont said. "But was he with you?"

"You know he was. You ordered him to attend me."

"Ordered? Your imagination is disordered. I merely sought an opportunity for you to become more familiar with each other." Her stepmother continued with a coy air of discovery, "La, he overwhelmed you with passion."

"I would not allow that," Margaret protested, threading a needle. "In any event, Christine and Mr. Hughes accompanied us."

"It is perfectly natural, you ninny; betrothed ladies have more latitude than spinsters. Intimacy will allow you to know one another. James is no mealy-mouthed fop. If he wants to kiss you, he will make the opportunity. You mustn't be shy about it."

Margaret determinedly mangled her needlework. The wool pulled so tight on the flame stitch a crochet hook could poke through. Shy kisses, hah. They couldn't find a common interest for conversation.

Her dark hair slipping from a ribbon, Emma turned a shell in her fingers. She might not have been there; the girl did not speak or stir. She also did not appear to be working on her frame, Margaret noticed. No shells went from the pile to the wood. Her face was blank, as if she were miles away in her mind.

"I don't expect you to show gratitude for the match," Lady Ridgemont said, "but you will learn. A house in town and frequent invitations to court—what more could you want? And once the nonsense is done, your father and I may take a holiday. Florence is said to be agreeable—or Rome. Now the French have stopped thinking every traveler is looking to steal the Ark of the Covenant from under their noses, we can go overland. So much more pleasant than a sea voyage and we may stop in Paris.

"It is too bad I cannot have a Parisian gown for your wedding. Continental fashion is superior to anything to be found in London. Look at these clumsy sleeves." She tapped the magazine in front of her. "Well, I daresay there is no sense wasting a Parisian gown on your wedding. No one of any consequence will see it."

Lady Ridgemont's monologue continued. "At least it is *warm* in Italy. The damp is soaking into Denison's bones. He will love the sun. Margaret, look at this sketch. It is perfect for me to wear on your special day."

Yes, Margaret thought, glancing at the magazine. *I will look a clown in that grotesque pile of lace you are having sewn, despite my objections. You, on the other hand, will be coolly elegant.* "Very nice."

"It will do, at least until I can visit a *modiste* in Paris. I can have it made up with the blue silk. Yes, I know the blue was yours, but it will look much better on me. Chinese silk would emphasize the thickening of your middle."

Thickening? What thickening? Trust her stepmother to find a reason to steal the length of material Margaret had been saving for a special occasion. *If only it didn't feel like Papa is constructing my tomb. The only good thing to come from marriage is escape from dear Step-Mama.* Margaret gave the coral wool another vicious yank. It snapped and the threaded needle flew into the fire.

"My dear," Lady Ridgemont said sweetly, "Burning wool smells. You should take your frustrations elsewhere. Why don't you go find Christine?"

"She and Mr. Treadway are in the garden."

"Shoo."

There was no point arguing; Margaret put away her needlework. It was back to the garden, whether she wished or not, to play gooseberry to her sister and her betrothed. "Would you like to come, Emma? You have been in that chair for quite an hour."

"If I must," Emma muttered. The shell she held fell to the floor and broke. Margaret led the way out of the room, trying not to look at her sister. Sixteen must be a trying age. Lately, Emma had an uncomfortable aura.

Worse, she was beginning to suspect her sister was at it again. The last time, she almost died. Mama pulled her through. But now, Mama was dead herself. If Emma was doing it, what was Margaret to do? She didn't have a tenth of Mama's aptitude. Or Emma's.

Donning coats, the two went out a side door. Margaret tucked Emma's hand in her arm. "It is chilly, but the sky is clear. Before we know it, summer will arrive. When you were little, you would come home covered in grass from rolling down the hill to the pasture. Is it still your favorite time of the year?"

"I don't have a favorite time."

"Even Accolon is said to have loved the dawning of the year."

Emma loosened her cloak strings. "I don't remember who Accolon was."

"He was a—friend of Morgan Le Fey," Margaret said. "King Arthur gave Morgan Excalibur's scabbard to keep safe; she passed it to Accolon. The scabbard conveyed protection from wounds. Using it, Accolon fought King Arthur and nearly defeated him. Morgan tricked him into jousting with the king, hoping Arthur would be slain. She meant to take the throne for herself, the wicked woman."

"I recall now. Stop treating me like a child. Accolon was Morgan Le Fay's *lover,* Meggie. He allowed her to use him for her own ends. If someone hadn't taken pity on King Arthur, Accolon would have slain the king and been damned for it."

"It wasn't any someone; it was Nimue, the Lady herself. And your language is deplorable."

"I don't care," Emma replied, sounding mulish. "I'm tired of you lording it over me because you are older, as if I'm not as good as you. I am. In fact, I am better. You are the one Mama said didn't have talent." She pulled her hand away. "Even Christine has more. She just never learned to control it."

Eyes down, the girl headed toward the knot garden. Margaret did not call her back. The accusation stung; no, Margaret did not have the talent of Emma or Christine. But her sister had not meant to cut her. It was her distress speaking, not her heart.

Someone had to be a mother to Emma. Christine was too self-absorbed, Step-Mama uninterested. Margaret won the chore by default and shouldered it. The Lady willing, Emma would talk to her when she was ready. She trained her gaze on Treadway and

Christine, visible on the gravel walk in the east rose garden.

They made a handsome couple. Coatless, Christine bent over a plant. He admired the view afforded by Christine's bodice. From many yards away, Margaret could see the gleam in his eye. *Nauseating.*

At least I am warm, Margaret thought, with an enveloping pelisse buttoned to the throat. *Dear Christine looks a bit blue around the edges.* James Treadway should turn as black as his soul.

She decided she had obeyed Step-Mama's instruction to the letter. She had joined Christine in the garden. She turned her attention to inspecting the gardeners' work. They hadn't finished clearing the detritus of winter. A generous bed of needles made a carpet under the pines, but two dead weeds, ragged, holey leaves sagging, poked through. She scuffed the weeds with her foot. Oddly, they crumbled, but she paid no heed.

Moths had gotten at her cashmere shawl. She swallowed past a lump in her throat. The shawl had been her mother's. Memories led to her father and his perfidy. Why did Papa think Mr. Treadway was a suitable husband? *Mr. Hughes* was a gentleman, couldn't Papa have chosen him to wed her? He was every bit as handsome as Treadway—hair darker, eyes lighter, they could almost be brothers. Except for facial expression. Treadway kept a sneer on his face that Margaret actively disliked.

She turned on her heel.

The swinging garden was in the first sheltered roundel. Gravel turned to the left, went several feet, and separated into a circle planted with bushes and trees of varying heights. Two massive urns, empty at this time of year, stood at the beginning of the circle. In the summer, they would house orange trees. To Margaret, the best part of the garden was the chain-suspended garden seats lining the perimeter of the walk.

It was a good place to hide. Christine considered the swings childish.

She entered the swinging garden, admiring yews trimmed, topiary fashion, in a diamond shape. Around the curve of the path she spied Adrian Hughes. Slumped pensively on a swing, he swished back and forth, propelled by a careless toe. She swallowed a sweet spurt of pleasure.

He looked up. An elusive twinkle in his eye, he said, "I'm six. How old are you?"

She grinned, appreciating his sense of humor. "Four."

"That's not old enough to swing."

"Then I am five. Any self-respecting five-year-old can swing."

"Climb on. I'll push." He rose with a fluid twist and held the seat for Margaret. She slid on and centered herself. An expert, she tucked her skirts between her ankles and he pushed. Cold bit her cheeks and nose. Her hair flew every which way, sliding out of pins.

"I can see through the trees all the way to the stables. It's marvelous." Hughes pushed her high enough for the seat to bounce, then maintained a steady swish, back and forth, up and down.

"This is a fairy ring garden," he said. "You made the mistake of stepping in the enchanted ring. There is no deliverance."

"Then I must remain forever," whistled through the air.

"And never grow old and crabbed."

"I'll never be crabbed. I'm going to be dotty, like Miss Henderson in the village."

"What does Miss Henderson do?"

"She talks to her flowers."

"Is that all?"

"Nooo," floated on an upswing. "Miss Henderson crochets fingerless mittens for her mother and every forenoon consults with her on what to prepare for supper."

"Dutiful."

"Mrs. Henderson died in 1802 of the cholera."

"Yes, you will be dotty."

Finally, she sang, "Enough, I'll get dizzy," and he stepped back, allowing the swing to come to a natural stop. Sliding off, she asked, "Would you like a turn?"

"No, I had finished when you came. The chain is cold to the touch."

"Yes, but I am five. I can do anything." Peeping from the corner of her eye, she said, "I want a biscuit. Race you to the house." Hughes put back his head and laughed.

"No, you little hoyden. If I am six, I have begun lessons. I'm above racing with babies." He tucked her hand in his arm. "I will walk you back decorously *if* you help me get some biscuits."

"Would you settle for a gingerbread man?"

"With raisin eyes, yes."

They repaired to the house. Outside the kitchen door,

Margaret pulled her hand off his arm. His forearm went cold, missing the contact. The sensation reminded him of the completion of a spell, when his mind blanked and he felt like an empty ewer. Her mischievous, "You must distract Cook while I sneak the gingerbread out," chased the curling thought away.

Chapter Six

Hughes made a production of peeking around the door jamb at a beehive of activity. Kitchen girls carried bowls and plates to and fro, some pausing to proffer foodstuffs to a bony, apron-wrapped woman. She waved a spoon, issuing a stream of orders right and left. Here was the ruler of the kitchen, the cook.

"She doesn't look like a gorgon. Give me just a moment." He flashed a crooked smile and sauntered through the door, sniffing.

"Ahh, I smell a well roasted joint. Who do I thank for that?" Cook, her spoon suspended in the air, turned a frown his way. Hughes didn't give her time to object to his presence. He turned on the charm. "I made my way here to compliment the chef. He must be an old hand to have gained all that expertise. Dinner last night was rare." He kissed his fingertips.

"Who are you?" Cook asked. Suspicion smacked the spoon against her lips. "If you come from Squire's, you can turn 'round and go back. Tell Annie Fellowes I ain't giving her the receipt for them 'tatoes. She'll have to think it out—"

Planting a smacking kiss on the cook's thin cheek, he swung her till her back was to the door. "I don't know who Annie Fellowes may be. You, young as you are, must be the chef. I am Adrian Hughes, a guest of the manor."

"A guest—oh, my. Oh, dear."

"I wanted to tell you how much I enjoyed the meal last night." Out of the corner of his eye, he watched his conspirator tiptoe to the sideboard, where an overflowing plate of gingerbread resided. Several maids dipped curtsies to her. He returned his full attention to the cook, blasting her fluster with earnestness.

"The potatoes were mouthwatering. Is that the receipt you refuse to give Squire's cook? I don't blame you. Let Squire come here when he wants a taste of heaven."

Cook beamed, little apples dimpling on her cheeks. Behind her back, Miss Ridgemont had several pieces of gingerbread wrapped in a napkin. Laying a cautioning finger against her lips to quiet the maids, she whisked out the door. Hughes readied a quick departure.

"A good dish of potatoes on the table makes the meal. I don't suppose you would give me the receipt—no, my London chef isn't to your level." Doleful as a child at the seashore during a thunderstorm, he shook his head. "Gaston would burn them. He's just a Frenchie, not a good English cook like you. Thank you, ma'am, for the treat."

He reached the outside door in four long strides and had turned to close it when he heard, "My gingerbread! Drat him. That man stole—" He slammed the door and took off, running.

His conspirator was at the end of the kitchen garden, peering around the dry stacked stone wall segregating the beds from the more formal grounds. As he drew level with her, she hissed, "This way."

Cook burst out the kitchen door, yelling like an Antipodes native in pursuit of a kangaroo. The spoon flew from her hand and sailed over the herb plot. It buried itself in a chink of the garden wall. There it quivered like a spent arrow.

Cook's voice faded and their steps slowed as running, they rounded the end of the servant's wing. Miss Ridgemont collapsed on a garden bench. Hughes joined her.

"You did well," she said, throwing him an admiring glance.

Hughes shrugged. "I am six. I do many things well." She handed him a gingerbread leg from the cracked and crumbled pile in the napkin and he popped it into his mouth.

"Then I can't wait till I turn six." Not to be outdone, she took a bite of arm. Taking a good sized head from her palm, he got another bite in his mouth before he swallowed the leg. She wasn't more mannerly than he. Like the children they pretended to be, they munched rudely large bites of gingerbread, talked with their mouths full, and licked their fingers.

When the napkin was empty, he shook it out on the grass and brought the linen up to Margaret's face. "You are a messy five-year-old," he commented and casually brushed crumbs from the corner of her mouth. His fingers lingered.

She laughed it off, but Margaret was thrown into confusion. His fingers felt good. As if Mr. Hughes should be permitted to touch her. It went against her mother's teachings, against all she had learned of good manners. Gentlemen did not touch ladies.

Was he trying to seduce her?

She took an abrupt leave of temptation. Running her hand along the stone wall, she turned back towards the kitchen entrance and forced her mind to other matters. Step-Mama wanted her to inspect the larder. She may as well do it now. At the same time, she would return the napkin. Later, perhaps she would go into Puckeridge for a new shawl.

* * *

After parting from Margaret, Hughes ran to the stables to arrange his escape for the next day, this time to view the 'tree-tomb' and highwayman's post at Tewin. Getting away was doubly important.

This was out of his experience. At home in Lancashire, there had been only one female his parents would have approved as a match for him. She had not touched his heart; nor had any others. Not till he met Margaret Ridgemont had any female roused more than a pleasurable sensation of lust. Now, he ached.

Never one to delude himself, he admitted his feelings.

Every encounter with Margaret dragged him deeper. Tread didn't appreciate his fiancé. He was tempted to bloody Tread's nose. A fine line to walk.

Also, familiarity bred blindness. Too much time spent in the magic saturated atmosphere of the estate drained his reserves. Hughes found himself itching to cast wild spells to counteract the magic like a farmer burning a field to clear it of nettles.

He didn't know which was harder: controlling passion, or magic.

A mount selected for the next day, he wandered back to the house, avoiding walks where he was likely to meet anyone. He didn't plan to go in. If he walked around the house outside, maybe he could locate the room where magic was practiced. He lifted his nose. *It'd help if I could smell it, as well as seeing the aftereffects.*

There was nothing aromatic. Not unless he counted damp earth. Turning the corner around the end of the east wing, he smelled mold. He stopped. Would that be significant? No. It looked like the roof channeled rainwater to the ground at this spot.

With a huff of disgust, he scanned the wing. Window panes glinted, lines of red brick marched like rows of archers. He didn't see anything. Didn't sense anything. *How can this rogue effect the atmosphere and I not get a whiff of her? There must be something I can latch on to.* He ran his eyes over the windows, hoping to see fluorescence on a frame. Nothing.

He glanced at the sky. Clouds shifted. One streaked mass scudded past a chimney. It stretched and reformed into a hand, index finger pointed east. "Crystal cave," Hughes swore. "Bloody crystal cave."

"Did you say something?" A young girl peeked around a bush, her head cocked. Automatically, he checked, but the girl wore gloves and a simple brown cloak. It was flung over her shoulder as if in grudging concession to the chill in the air. If she would only pull the hood up and drape the cloak the way it was meant to be worn, she would look a proper lady, especially as she bore a striking resemblance to Margaret Ridgemont.

"Good afternoon." He sketched a bow.

"Sir." After a short pause, she said, "Can I help you? If you have lost her, I can show you where to find my sister."

Ahh, this was the youngest Ridgemont, Emma. He hadn't placed her for a moment. He studied her as she edged around the pine. Not as dark as Margaret, but taller, with a Madonna face. Oval, smooth cheekbones. She promised to be a beauty. If she smiled, which she hadn't. In mannerisms, who did she take after, delightful sister or wicked stepmother? His reply was slow, considered.

"I wasn't lost. I am inspecting the grounds." His eyes swept the house again.

"You were talking to yourself," Emma said, twitching hands to her slim hips. "Do you often?"

"Yes. I do talk to myself. Helps me to remember. Rain water pools here. Not good for the foundation. Sir Denison should correct this before it becomes a problem." Too bad she patterned herself after Lady Ridgemont. He could see her in a few years, nagging.

Her eyes dropped, then her nose wrinkled. "It smells damp."

"Precisely."

"Why would you want to make note of that? It isn't your house."

"Estate management is an art. I practice so I will be alert to problems on my own estate." Hughes turned away from the house and pointed at a distant clump of trees. "For example, I have larch

Thwarting Magic • 55

saplings like those planted in a rather boggy situation. Mine are not as well branched as these. If I move them to drier ground, they may develop better."

The sky was clearing over the larches. The cloudbank had moved over the house, drifting south, with no fingers, no figures, to be seen. He gave a short bow. "Nearly tea time. If you will excuse me." He turned and walked away.

It wouldn't do any good to talk to the girl—not while she had gloves on. Couldn't tell anything. More, there was something about Emma that made him uncomfortable. He sensed simmering resentment, or sullen disobedience, or...something. Whatever it was, Emma made him uneasy.

* * *

She got through dinner by concentrating on Mr. Treadway's good points—he was good with horses, both in the saddle and in the driving seat. And handsome. But Mr. Hughes's smile was infectious. When it was aimed her way, she tingled. *No, Margaret, don't think it. Papa is decided.*

Why Mr. Hughes should be Mr. Treadway's friend was a mystery, unless under that whimsical exterior, Mr. Hughes was a rake. No, he wasn't. And he wasn't trying to seduce her. She must have had windmills in her head to think that. Mr. Treadway, on the other hand, was definitely a rake. He was her rake, though. Perhaps he would settle down with marriage. Perhaps he would come to care for her. Perhaps, perhaps, perhaps. The spoon slipped and syllabub splashed the tablecloth.

She was not about to admit, even to herself, Christine had poor taste and the gentleman in question deserved her vulgar sister. He was her husband-to-be. Such thoughts were not conducive to a comfortable home.

After dinner was more difficult. Sir Denison and Lady Ridgemont retired early, leaving the younger set in the library. As often occurred, they drifted into two camps: Margaret and Mr. Hughes versus Christine and Mr. Treadway. Margaret's temper, burning for days, threatened to scorch her fingertips.

"You must tell me more of that fascinating collection." Christine threaded her arm through Mr. Treadway's, pressing closer to hear his assessment of the Dutch paintings Hughes had amassed. "I know little of art, but you are so knowledgeable, I am sure you can bring the subject to life."

"Hughes is the one with an eye. The prince has been known to seek his opinion of a van Olstade. Has one called 'Tavern Scene' that is rollicking, though it is pretty dark, if you ask me. Should ask him about it."

"He is occupied," Christine demurred. "If you think the work dark, it is. Your taste is impeccable."

"My taste is aroused by livelier subjects than art." His grin was wolfish.

While Treadway and Christine flirted, Hughes pored over a guide book to the southern shires. He also fiddled with the stone in his pocket, the one with a vein of green chrysotile running through. Chrysotile, according to the Germans, plucked magic from thin air. He hoped it would here.

Tamping down the desire to do her sister harm, Margaret said, "The Knebworth House gardens are worth viewing. Or if you prefer ecclesiastical sites, the church in Tring is pretty." *The Dutch and assorted others could go to Hades.* "It depends on whether your taste is for historic sites, fine views or industry."

"My taste is eclectic, Miss Ridgemont." Mr. Hughes tapped the guidebook. "Having never been to Herts, I find I wish to see everything. Do you think the cathedral and abbey church at St. Albans would be worth a visit? King Offa of Mercia founded a monastery there. The present church was built in 1077 with Roman brick from Verulamium."

Mr. Treadway sneered. "Since when are you interested in churches?"

"Since I cannot bear to see you acting like an ass," Mr. Hughes muttered low, but Margaret's hearing was acute. "How about Ashwell? Its springs are one of the sources of the River Cam."

To diffuse what could become ugly, Margaret said, "Ashwell also has architecture. The church dates almost entirely from the 14th century and is renowned for its tower. During the time of the Black Death, people wrote on the church walls. But you must avoid tasting the water. It is said to bring on illness." Mr. Treadway threw her a disgusted look.

Hughes defended the choice. "There's a fine brewery in Ashwell." His hand went into his pocket. The stone was quiescent.

"If you visit a brewery, you'll never find your way back,"

Treadway said. "If you want to go somewhere, Hughes, you should visit Abbots Langley. Pope Adrian IV was from there. Your namesake. He choked to death on a fly."

As Treadway baited him, Christine said, "We could drive over to Great Hormead and pay our respects to the Stables family. I have not seen Lieutenant Colonel Stables since before my marriage. They have a church you can view, Mr. Hughes, I am sure."

"You won't see him now. Lieutenant Colonel Stables died at Waterloo," Margaret said dryly. Hughes hid a grin. Smart girl, just needed encouragement to drop the shyness and she came up with flashes of a priceless wit. He fingered the stone in his pocket again.

"I'm for Ashwell," he said. He pushed the stone under his handkerchief. It hadn't done a blessed thing to identify his rogue wizard. "I will return in time for supper tomorrow, Miss Ridgemont. Good night."

* * *

Returning from Ashwell, Hughes glanced first at the house, three floors of four-square red brick, and then at the sky. Clouds scudded, some white and fluffy, others with a thin tone of gray. He was unpleasantly reminded of the paintings in the Council of the Mages' office, but could discern no shapes.

He'd gone to Ashwell, visited the brewery, and wandered the lanes. It was a bore, but he'd needed to get away. He was out of charity with Tread and distance kept the magical influence in prospective. Watching a friend transform into a boor and wondering when magic would take a lethal turn soured the spirit.

The butler opened the front door as the dust-streaked carriage pulled up. "Welcome," he intoned, ushering him into the hall. "The family is not in at present, but will return shortly."

"Where did they go?" Hughes stripped off his gloves.

"The church, sir."

"What—all of them?"

The butler busied himself brushing a speck of dust from Hughes's shoulder. "Lady Ridgemont, Miss Ridgemont and Mrs. Whitmill-Ridgemont are speaking with the vicar. While they mind business connected with the ceremony, the gentlemen intended to visit the inn. Mr. Thorpe brews a tolerable ale."

"Ahh, makes sense." *Good. Leaves me free to investigate.*

Warning his valet to ready his evening wear, he went for a walk through the corridors of the house. It took a mere five minutes to find it.

Fluorescence.

One door handle didn't just gleam, it sparkled. Phosphorescence slithered around the brass like a snake around a rock. Giving the door a knock, which went unanswered, Hughes entered. A quick glance assured he was alone. Wasn't difficult to verify ownership of the room. The bonnet hanging over the back of a chair, looped on one side with a pompadour Spanish brown ribbon, was unmistakable. He steeled his nerve.

Nothing magical in plain sight, he pulled open the double wardrobe doors. "Ta da," he sang softly. A box, writhing with tendrils of laid spells, shivered in response to his presence. He slid off the papered top. Inside, a rope coiled around a silver spoon and two black candles. Spices. The box stunk and he sneezed.

He stirred the mixture with his stick pin. Nutmeg, dried rosemary, thorn apple leaves.

Henbane.

Hughes swore. He slammed the top of the box, cracking it down the middle when it did not immediately fit properly. With another oath, he shoved it back in the armoire, knocking two other boxes aside. A stack of handkerchiefs fluttered to the floor.

Not bothering to close the armoire door, he stormed from the room. The makings of a love potion in wildly inaccurate amounts was not nearly as disturbing as black candles.

Black for death. And henbane, which could kill at a touch. Merlin alone knew what the rogue wizard was doing. If it was she, by no means certain despite it being her room, he was going to wring her neck.

Chapter Seven

Mr. and Mrs. Carlton Treadway arrived in Puckeridge after dark the night before the ceremony. "Rain-washed roads," Mr. Treadway Senior said, shrugging off his greatcoat. "The weather south of here is vile."

"Wish rain would fall here," Sir Denison grumped. "It's dry as Cicero."

"Not tomorrow," Lady Ridgemont said, firm as a backboard. "Rain the morn of a wedding is an ill omen." She motioned for the butler to assist Jane Treadway, who battled with a tangled scarf.

Mrs. Treadway waved the servant away. "No, I'll do it. It will tear if not handled carefully." She turned to Lady Ridgemont. "Ann's measles and Davinia's broken arm contributed to our lateness. I doubt it will rain here. The sky is clear. Lovely scenery." She tugged the scarf when it snagged her brooch. The fine silk ripped and she sighed. "Was that the church we passed in the village? Oh, what a charming mirror."

"Thank you." Lady Ridgemont tried to respond to multiple subjects in one breath. "You must be tired after such a grueling journey. All is now well at home?"

"Oh, yes. I could not have come otherwise. Davinia decorated the bandages on her arm with watercolors and Ann has stopped scratching. We left before another disaster overtook us. I wish I had a few days to recover, but Carlton didn't take the children into account..."

Lady Ridgemont nodded as if she understood the travail of parenthood. "Children can be a great inconvenience. Would you like to retire to your room? Cook has food prepared. It would be no trouble for you to dine there."

"It sounds lovely. I do want to be fresh for tomorrow. The children..." Mrs. Treadway trailed syllables up the stairs. "A bowl of soup and some bread—and a brandy to ease my aching back." She hadn't liked Lady Ridgemont's implication children were a bother, but contented herself with sniffing disdainfully at the décor of her room.

***

James swaggered into the parlor and dropped gracelessly into the wing chair closest to the door. "You commanded my presence?"

Mr. Treadway Senior sighed deep inside. The boy was still belligerent. *This could be easier, but I can't think how. Have to break him of it now, while I still have some control.* "I did want to speak with you," he said aloud. "I have the document drawn up. You must sign it before the ceremony tomorrow."

"And if I refuse?"

"Then I will tell Ridgemont he should keep his daughter from the church. Of course," Mr. Treadway Senior flicked his watch fob for luck, "I will also tell him why. In detail. If I am not mistaken, even your friend, Adrian Hughes, does not know. Don't mistake yourself, James. Once I tell Ridgemont, the tale will be all over England in a fortnight."

"You would sink my reputation."

"And disown you. You won't see a penny farthing."

"I'll sign." James leaned his head back. "I will never understand why you are making a business of this. It's not as if the man is important."

Though Mr. Treadway Senior knew his son wouldn't—or couldn't—listen, he tried one more time to explain. "It's unacceptable, completely unacceptable. If you persist in this, I will have no choice but to disown you." His voice thickened. "James, son. Taking a man's belongings and auctioning them off—he was in Portugal with Wellington, for Merlin's sake—it is theft. The act of a scoundrel."

James jumped from the chair. "Enough, enough. I'll sign your damned paper." He strode to the table. "I'll do as you order. I just wish to God you would leave me alone."

A quill slashed across the legal document, was thrown down, spattering ink, and James stormed from the room. Mr. Treadway Senior leaned against the wall, wondering if he had done the right thing.

***

"Oh my dear boy," Mrs. Treadway exclaimed from the

comfort of her bed when James poked his head around the door. Arms outstretched, she bade her son enter. "I am delighted to see you looking so fine."

"Wanted to make sure you were comfortable, Mama." James tucked the comforter closer around his mother's form. His finger poked through a hole in the material. "Shoddy housekeeping," he muttered. Distastefully, he shook his finger free and straightened her night cap. "I hoped you would arrive sooner, you know. You haven't had a chance to get to know Miss Ridgemont."

She sighed with the drama of a tragedienne. "I did wish to come sooner, dear boy, but Ann was misherable, wanting to scratch all over. She could have been scarred. Then your scamp of a sister fell out of the oak at the foot of the drive. The doctor set her arm and assured us Davinia will be fine, but I could not tear myself from her side for a time. The trip was abominable, what with the mudslide down that hill. My heart was in my throat, truly in my throat, when the carriage slipped. But your father assured me there was no danger. And here we are."

Overwhelmed by the spate of words, he said dutifully, "Just in time."

Her night cap slipped askew with her vigorous nod. "I intend to be fresh as dew tomorrow for your big day. Sir Denison and your father will stay up much too late drinking brandy and solving the country's problems. It will be left to me to uphold the decorum of the family." She pushed at the edge of the cap and twittered. "You don't shuppose something will go wrong?"

"Grandfather said things always happen in threes," James reminded her, gently pushing the cap back to the top of her head. "Ann, Davinia, and mud have done the bad luck in." If he'd been dealing with one of his friends, he would have taken her resultant giggle as a signal she'd imbibed more brandy than was wise. As it was, he attributed it to exhaustion.

She drained the wine glass on the bedside table. Leaning back against the pillows, her words slurred. "I shuppose, though the children wouldn't agree. Ann missed Ruth Dorsey's birthday party and Davinia moaned at being confined, the little hoyden. We may hope your grandpapa was right. But when he talked about threes being a dish-dishaster, he was referring to my brothers. They were a hellish lot. Your Uncle George sh'pecially.

"He took up with that hideous Harriette Wilson's vulgar

sister. Nearly married her. I thought Papa would have an apoplexy from the grave. Your father had to sit George down and talk sense into him. Then he married Shusan."

She paused to gather her scattering wits. "Though with marriage being a joyous occasion, p'raps one of the other children will create a dishaster to balance everything. Children are like that." She took a deep breath and cracked her son's composure. "Jamie, I am glad this is a love match. Just what I wished for you. Be happy, dear boy, as happy as your father and I. It's an adventure of the best sort."

"Mother," James began, his voice clogged with annoyance.

She stifled a yawn. "Marriage ish difficult enough without affection to temper the impatience, disappointment and ill feeling events thrust upon one. Not for my children the aridness of the fashionable alliance. I've known too many miserable people to want that for you."

"But—"

"Thank heavens you are shensible." Her eyelids fell. "Now go away, darling dear, so I can sleep. I wish to be fresh for your big day. I will steal a moment to become acquainted with Mish Ridgemont. But for now, I really need to rest."

The darling, dear, dumbstruck boy let himself out of his mother's room. She was overtired, sounded almost drunk, but her meaning was clear. What had his father done? His mother thought he had contracted a love match? Egads. She must have misunderstood the Pater.

He wandered the hall, pausing outside the widow's door. What he wouldn't give to turn the handle, climb on top of that luscious body, and take his fill. He knew he could satisfy Christine. He was certain she could pleasure him. But the widow would scream for the wedding ring to go on her finger, rather than her sister's. He could see it happening. Unholy crystal cave, the wedding was tomorrow. A pity he couldn't celebrate his last night of freedom with her—or at Merlin's Gardens again with a doll. He leaned his head against the door frame. Then he gave up and went early to bed.

* * *

"Emma," Margaret called. "Can I come in?" There was no

sound behind the door, but she knew her sister was inside. In her mind she could see Emma rushing around, hiding whatever she didn't want Margaret to see. After all, that was how she would have reacted to a visit from her elders when *she* was sixteen.

Whatever the girl was hiding, it was taking a long time. Margaret rapped on the door again. "Emma." The door opened a crack. Her sister's eyes showed, but precious little else.

"What do you want?"

"I'd like to talk." Margaret caught the faint scent of spirits. She tried to peek around her sister into the room, but all she could see was a strip of yellow and ochre-block-papered wall.

"I can't. I'm sleepy," Emma said. "Besides, there is nothing to say."

Margaret's mouth tightened. "I'm getting married tomorrow. I am leaving Puckeridge—I might not see you for months."

"So?"

"So I thought—"

"Margaret, I am sleepy. Good night." Emma closed the door.

Margaret closed her eyes to block the tears threatening to drop off her lashes. *Emma.* Her sister's unresponsiveness hurt. Now, when her life was to change drastically, she yearned to keep close.

She could smell spirits again. *Papa must have been here chastising her for a misstep. No wonder Emma is cross. Poor girl.* She wandered down the hall.

It was talk to someone or burst. *Don't fool yourself, Margaret. You are trying to put it off. Emma can't tell you what you need to know. Now, do it.*

Her stepmother wasn't in her room. Margaret bade the maid who answered the door a civil good night and turned away. *I must have lost my mind. True, Step-Mama is the logical person to ask, but I cannot imagine her imparting the information gracefully.* Her face burned.

Light showed under the door of Christine's room. Telling herself, *Don't think about it, just do it,* she knocked. There was a pause, then Christine cracked the door open. Like Emma, only her eyes showed. "I can't sleep," Margaret complained. "Please, may I come in?"

Her sister didn't budge. Margaret felt panic curl around the edge of her face. "Chrissy," she pleaded, using the childhood name that had gone unsaid since Christine painted Margaret's favorite doll with cosmetics stolen from the village shop.

"Why not." The door opened, revealing the glory of Christine's negligee. All lace and the thinnest orange silk, her every line was scandalously revealed. She risked inflammation of the lungs from the cold.

If Treadway had knocked on that door five minutes later rather than leaning his head against the wood in defeat, he might have escaped the clutches of matrimony. Margaret, perched on Christine's bed in her practical flannel nightgown and warm robe, pondered how to ask the question. *Fiddlesticks, might as well blurt it out.* She couldn't ask Step-Mama, and her sister was not the most delicate of ladies under the best of circumstances. Look at Christine's nightwear. This sensitive matter should be right up her alley.

"S-sister, what happens?" Margaret stammered, hoping Christine had not had the actual experience with Mr. Treadway. "On the wedding night, I mean."

"You have lived in the country all your life, Margaret. Have you never watched animals: dogs, sheep, horses?"

"Noo, I saw plenty of plants and flowers, bees and butterflies, but never animals doing anything odd. I haven't the vaguest idea what to do." Christine shook her head, orange silk rippling.

"I can hardly explain it to you. There is much involved. Why do you not wait and see? I am sure James knows all about it."

Margaret would not have taken a wager against it. Of course that libertine knew all about wedding night activities. "But what should I do? I know we will retire to bed, but beyond that all is mystery. Please tell me. I do not wish to be ignorant."

With a shrug, Christine obliged. "He will light all the candles in the room and suck on your toes. If it tickles, I suppose you may giggle. It never bothered Martin."

"That is all? He will suck on my toes?" Margaret was appalled. Her toes were not the prettiest. Stubby, with little hairs sprouting, two twisted to the side. She could not imagine him looking at them, much less setting lips to them.

Christine abruptly put a lid on the conversation. "I am tired," she said, fluffing the deep lace gathered at her elbows. "You should sleep also. Tomorrow will be a long day."

Feeling frumpy, Margaret slid toward the door. Her hand on the knob, she turned. "Christine, I wanted—you mustn't feel guilty—I understand. Mr. Treadway filled a hole in your heart." Christine looked as if she had swallowed a frog. Appalled that she had increased her sister's agony, Margaret blurted, "You will find a man you can love as much as you cared for Mr. Whitmill. It takes time."

"Don't be a ninny." Christine croaked as if a frog was truly lodged in her throat. She grabbed Margaret's elbow and squeezed. "I don't understand why he is marrying you. He wants me, I heard him say it. You heard him too. James is more manly than Martin; I deserve him for having tolerated Martin." Once begun, she didn't seem able to stop.

When Christine hissed, "Why should you take the prize," Margaret's store of empathy fizzled.

"I wonder I have never pulled your hairpins out and stuffed them in your ears. Goodnight, sister. Thank you for the advice." Margaret popped the door open and went to her room, where she spent more than a bit of time staring at her toes.

* * *

The weather was terrible, dripping cold rain, and the wedding dress didn't fit quite right.

"If Margaret had been sensible and eaten, she would not have lost the weight and the dress would be perfect." Step-Mama reached for the rouge pot. "It's only been a matter of weeks. What a ninny she is, dropping so much from her bust. Not likely that will please James, is it." The maid hummed a reply, hair pins stuck in her mouth.

"The dress will do credit to my taste, if Margaret does not." Lady Ridgemont sniffed. She arched her chin and dabbed color on her cheekbone. She paused to admire the creamy blue silk of her gown, then she picked up an elegant beaded reticule and slid a vinaigrette inside. It fell out the bottom and landed on the dressing table with a thunk. "Mordred," she swore, and flipped the purse over. A gaping hole rendered it useless.

"How did this happen?" Lady Ridgemont turned on the maid, waving the ruined reticule in her face. "What did you do?"

As Lady Ridgemont berated her maid in one room, Mr. Treadway Senior held his nose in another. Having drunk a bit too much brandy the night before, he took what he fondly called 'the hair of the dog'. Green-brown in color and smell, he gave it the traditional doubtful look and held his nose. The glass sloshed as it tilted too fast. A putrid mustache painted his upper lip.

"That's better," he announced to his valet after downing the restorative. "Wouldn't do to be under the weather today. No it wouldn't do at all."

"If I may be bold, sir," the servant answered, "the mistress ain't up to the mark either, according to her woman. She ain't out of bed yet."

Mr. Treadway Senior grabbed his discarded nightcap off the bed and dabbed at his upper lip. "Not surprised, not surprised. Her back ached last night. I know how she treats that malady. Tell you what, Fenton. You go mix up another glass of hair. I'll present it to Mrs. Treadway myself. It'll bounce her back." Tying his cravat, Mr. Treadway Senior forgot to caution the man. Hair of the dog didn't need quite so much bite to do for a lady what it did for a man.

Her abigail had not exaggerated. His wife moaned. "Carlton, I caught an ague. I feel dreadful; my head spins and my stomach...My ears are affected. The softest sound thrums in my brain."

After her husband forced the nasty drink into her mouth, she improved.

"Carlton, stop grumbling about ladies not having any sense. Would you prefer I be laid up for a week with my back? You could spend the time with Lady Ridgemont, hearing about her stitching and charitable interests." She giggled as she bumped into the bedpost. Mr. Treadway Senior caught her before she landed on the floor.

"How much did you drink?" he asked, forgetting he had watched her quaff a brimming mug of hair. "By Accolon, the dog has gone and bit you, Jane."

"Bit me—where?" She whirled in his arms, sagging with relief. "Carlton, there aren't any dogs here."

Sir Denison wasn't concerned with shrinking busts or dogs, but with his expanding waistline. Sternly, he ordered his valet, "Move the buttons over. I don't want to strangle. How did that vest come to be too small, huh? Fit fine when I wore it at Christmas. Demn, someone must have taken the seams in." He shrugged out of the offending garment and threw it at the servant.

Finally dressed, he descended to the dining room. It was going to be a long day; he needed fortification. A gargantuan breakfast crowded the sideboard. Platters of sirloin, ham, and kippers jostled chafing dishes with three kinds of eggs. Scotch buns warred with scones, plain bread, and toast. Inexplicably, a pool sat under a pitcher of ale.

Dripping ale into the kippers, he poured a glass. Sir Denison whistled as he sat to eat. No one else appeared, which suited him fine. He got to eat his eggs in peace, read the London paper (only three days old but there were holes in places) and contemplate the day. Eggshell crunched between his teeth. He shrugged.

Everyone bundled up for church, all except Margaret, who was to maintain fashionable style with a gauzy shawl and miniscule bonnet over a dress made of lace and not much else. Despite a fire in the bedchamber, she shivered as the maid assisted her into the lightest silk shift and petticoats. Her shivers escalated as the dress was drawn over her head.

"You look a treat, miss," the maid exclaimed.

"No, a treat is an ice from Gunter's. I'm merely an ice. Didn't Step-Mama think about the weather when she chose lace? It would be more suitable in July."

Obviously, a response was not required. Her maid laid a shawl around her shoulders. Margaret breathed a sigh. "Thank you," she said. Now she should shiver less, gauzy though the thing was. "Just the thought of a wrap is enough to generate warmth."

Then the maid arranged the shawl artfully, pulling it off her shoulders, draping it prettily over her arms. Margaret shivered more. "How can anyone find blue skin and goose flesh fashionable? Heavens, I don't want to do this." Buried in tiers of lace, her heart was in shreds.

"You look wonderful. No one will notice you're a tad cold," the maid promised. She jumped as Sir Denison bellowed through the door.

"Time to go. Come now, Margaret. I don't want to be late to the church."

"I'm coming, Papa. I need to find my salts. Where are my salts?"

"You don't need salts, girl," her fond father replied. "You ain't such a ninny that you'll faint at the altar. And if you do, all the ladies are bound to have vinaigrettes with 'em. Eulalie never goes without hers. Stupid things."

Margaret went to meet her doom, grumbling, "I really don't want to do this." Her courage had fled the country, perhaps for America, where ladies sent unwanted spouses to fight Indians. "It's a wonderful concept," she said, hooking her arm through her father's.

He gave her a confused glance and ordered, "Don't go talking to yourself. Carlton Treadway will get the idea you are bumfuddled and the fat will be in the fire."

"A fire sounds heavenly."

Chapter Eight

The sun shone watery, weak and worthless for more than lighting the sky. It did highlight the grayness of the rain-soaked landscape. It was one of those spring days when one wondered if spring would ever arrive.

Chatting with the Treadways on the arched church porch, Victoria Viceroy, the vicar's spinsterish sister, bent to pet a striped tomcat. He hissed and she confided, "Cook gives him the remains of the fish to gnaw. But he never sits on my lap—he growls when I try to pet him." She frowned briefly, and meandered her thoughts back to the occasion. "Seldom has my brother allowed me to work in the sacred precinct. I was delighted to do it for dear Miss Ridgemont."

"There are no flowers," Mrs. Treadway complained.

"Lady Ridgemont forgot to order blooms cut from her greenhouse. But there is no dust. Look how the wood gleams." They peeked into the building. Miss Viceroy had celebrated her usefulness by waxing the pews until they shone. Cleanliness and the nicely carved altar piece were the only concessions to comfort. Bare whitewashed walls and no cushions on the six pairs of pews, not a scrap of lace or embroidery in the building. Sir Denison's mother had drummed into his head that piety was not comfortable. A little numbness was good for the soul.

"You did a nice job, dear," Mrs. Treadway praised and tugged her husband up the aisle before he said something disgraceful. He was wrinkling his nose. "Come Carlton, it is time to be seated. I can see the carriage coming."

"Why does she smell like that?"

Mrs. Treadway gave a half amused, half irritated sniff. "Can't you recognize camphor? I imagine Miss Viceroy was so concerned with readying the church, she forgot to air her gown." She pointed her husband toward the front pew. "Oh, look, there is that sweet boy, Adrian Hughes. He looks elegant, doesn't he? As neat as Mr. Brummel."

"Don't know why James asked a fribble to stand up with him.

Those stockings are silk or I'll eat my gloves. What's a man want with silk stockings? Give me good sturdy wool any day."

Hughes wore his best Almack's togs, which were very fine indeed. Black silk breeches and yes, silk stockings with elaborate clocks delineating the calves, drew attention to his straight, well-muscled legs. More elegant than the Bishop of Camelot, their son's friend walked up a step and down behind the organ. He entered the door behind and was lost to sight.

* * *

Pacing around fusty piles of music in the tiny room off the sanctuary, Treadway needed a drink. Unfortunately, most of his drinking buddies were in London and he was in church. He did have Hughes. The oaf knew most of his secrets and could be trusted to keep silent. His friend was a brick, finding a toy to comfort him at the Merlin's Gardens bachelor farewell. The sweet memory of a doll wrapping her legs around his waist made him smile. Bless Lancelot, no hint of the carouse had wafted to Ridgemont's ear.

The door opened, admitting light into the cell-like room. "Tread, are you ready for this?" the brick asked, cutting off the brightness of the church proper as he closed the door.

"Not hardly," Treadway replied. "I shouldn't go through with the wedding if there were any way to escape with my name intact. This is the worst conceived marriage in Christendom."

"How so?" Hughes's eyebrow lifted. Dreading the amusement he would see in his friend's face when he admitted the truth, Treadway cracked the door and peeked out. The ghost of a ray of sunlight wavered in the dusty air. Hughes was at his shoulder.

"What are you looking at?"

"Rough plank pews. Can't they afford cushions?" Treadway slumped. "Hughes, Miss Ridgemont heard my remarks about her sister. She must have. She's making me pay for it."

"Are you certain?"

"No."

"She must not have," Hughes pulled him back and closed the door. "If she had, you would have been thrown out on your ear. The lady has too much pride to settle as second choice. She's shy, but not cobblestone to be walked on." Treadway, heartened by the thought, opened his mouth to thrash the matter out, but was not afforded the opportunity. The door opened, bumping his shoulder.

"It is time to take your stations," Vicar Viceroy announced. Treadway glanced wildly at the lone window. It was too small for him to crawl through.

Hughes gave him a long, clear look. Treadway swallowed and straightened his cuffs. The two friends strode to their places at the foot of the altar. Hughes flashed a white smile at Mrs. Treadway, who beamed maternally at him.

By Mordred, it is too late, Treadway thought, panicked.

"Ready?" Hughes whispered in a cheerful tone. "Your bride will be here any moment, unless she's late for everything. Won't matter if she is. Once the knot is tied, you'll be in possession of a sterling wife, one many a man would envy."

"Shut up."

The parish church had never seen such regalia. Adrian Hughes dressed as if for the most courtly of affairs at Camelot. Treadway had outdone him. His attire reflected the hope of spring: grass green, sun yellow, and the pure blue of a perfect sky. He more than made up for the lack of sunlight; James Treadway was blindingly brilliant. His tailor made the outfit for the occasion; Weston had threatened to blackball him from court for the insult of the order until he explained.

"If I must be shackled, it shall be as the jester." At Weston's indignant glare, Treadway begged. "If I look the part, perhaps Miss Ridgemont will think me a fool and forgive me. If she does not, I will have the fond memory of my attire to keep me warm at night." Weston finally agreed, but the tailor forced a promise never to reveal who had created the waistcoat, the coat, the inexpressibles. Especially the inexpressibles.

So Treadway reflected the hope of spring and prayed he appeared such a fool that Margaret would overlook his behavior at the time of their betrothal. It was too late for anything else.

* * *

The almost empty pews held a smattering of servants and locals who'd had a fondness for Miss Margaret since she was a tot. She was a bright little thing, caring about butterflies and such.

"Coo, he's a fine lookin' gent," old Sissie Brown whispered.

"Who, the black one?" her twin asked.

"No, the one all prettied up. I like all that color; jest like spring."

"I ain't never seen a man with lace bows at his knees."

"Must be fancy London fashion."

In the first pew, Mrs. Treadway turned to her husband. "Do you see James? He looks so...so..."

"Egad," Mr. Treadway Senior replied. He rose and half turned. "Arthur be praised, we have to get out of here." Before his wife could comment on his gaucherie, the narthex door banged.

Feet tapped like woodpeckers on the flagstone floor. The small congregation stood and turned. A few steps ahead of Margaret and Sir Denison, Victoria Viceroy marched up the aisle. There was no music; the tiny organ had given its last gasp at the second Advent service, and her heels assaulted stone. Mr. Viceroy coughed as camphor fumes from his sister's dress reached the altar.

Emma was next, a ray of sunshine in primrose muslin. Her eyes on the stone underfoot, she stumbled over a crack and hit the pew, nearly running over her stepmother's foot.

"Watch where you are going," Lady Ridgemont snapped. "It is bad enough it rained this morning. If you fall, the union will be cursed by Morgan."

The church was a blur. Margaret noticed two things: Lady Ridgemont's ill temper and Christine's dejected figure. Her sister, who could not be a bridal attendant, being in mourning, occupied the pew seat next to Step-Mama. Forgetting their altercation the prior evening, Margaret's tender heart went out to her sister. This must bring back memories of her sister's own ceremony, so tragically short a time ago. *How bitter for Christine to be a widow before she was accustomed to being a wife.* Then, if Martin Whitmill was as bad as Mr. Treadway, perhaps Christine had been blessed.

And Emma. I believe she is more nervous than I. She can't walk straight.

She caught sight of her groom. Margaret took one look at the impossibly bright inexpressibles, horridly bright coat, and awfully bright waistcoat and groaned. *Dear Lady, he is a fool. His taste is worse than Miss Viceroy's. And I am landed with him for eternity.*

No forgiveness for his sins entered her mind; her biblical training skipped the part about suffering fools. Nor was the Lord merciful. The heavy beams of the ancient steepled ceiling did not fall on Treadway's head. A combination of Miss Viceroy's camphor, Christine's tragedy, and recognition of her groom's inanity glistened in Margaret's eyes.

When she was stationed at the altar, the congregation sat. Lady Ridgemont slid. And fell to the floor. The vicar's sister had a heavy hand with the polish.

Fortunately, Lady Ridgemont's fall stole attention from the bridal pair. Treadway turned up his nose at Margaret—she turned to march down the aisle alone. Her father's arm twined with hers kept her still.

The ceremony proceeded without a hitch. Treadway knew his part. With his mother's words echoing in his head, he only hoped he could get through the thing without disgracing himself. A love match? His mother thought he had contracted the affection disease? Gads, his father had a lot to answer for.

He also had a lot to answer for. The vicar, smoothly reading the service, asked him a question and he did not promptly answer. He pulled his mind from the enjoyable vision of choking the life out of his father and attempted to look overcome with emotion to account for his delay in speaking. He came close enough to pacify everyone except Margaret.

She made her responses right on cue, unlike the chump next to her. Wearing a faint smile, she did her duty to Papa. Inside, hands choked the life out of harpy Eulalie for driving dear Papa to this extreme. *Do I have to go to Camelot with him looking like that? I will be a laughingstock.*

She almost looked forward to the reality of her life with James Conner Treadway. Death was too good for him. She would improve on the concept of marital bliss with feminine vengeance. She made her responses firmly. She would love, honor, and obey the chump when toads exploded.

* * *

The small party gathered at the Ridgemont estate for a wedding breakfast. Knotted by the door of the drawing room, they had remarkably little to say. "Lovely service, wasn't it?" The vicar broke the silence.

"The bride is lovely." Mrs. Treadway smiled at Margaret.

Her husband, close behind, said, "Yes, Margaret is a vision.

But you have never seen a bride you didn't think beautiful, my dear."

Mrs. Treadway dabbed the corner of her eye with a scrap of handkerchief. "There is something about her wedding that makes the plainest girl shine. Margaret, who is not plain, looks stunning. It's an important day for a woman, Carlton, though you are too thickheaded to realize it."

Vicar Viceroy frowned. "As momentous for a man, Mrs. Treadway, I'd say."

Hughes followed the vicar's thoughtless remark with, "Interesting architecture in the church."

Sir Denison grumbled. "Very Cromwellish."

"You say that because I forgot flowers," Lady Ridgemont said.

"Did you? Didn't notice." Sir Denison narrowed his eyes. Glaring at her husband, Lady Ridgemont regally moved to the end of the drawing room.

At Lady Ridgemont's frozen departure, the group came unglued. With four walls in the room, it must be coincidence that couples graced each instead of mingling. Carlton and Jane Treadway drifted east, looking unaccountably irritated, Sir Denison and James Treadway headed for the sideboard and the decanters. Emma disappeared.

Christine went in pursuit of James, and Victoria Viceroy took her camphor-soaked skirts after Lady Ridgemont. The vicar trailed the Treadways.

This is going to be dreadful, Margaret decided, stalking to a sofa. She smoothed her lace skirt with choppy, vengeful slaps, glared at an unoccupied portion of wall, and tried not to think. Or listen. The salon had the peculiar quality of rendering every sound audible. Every breathy whisper from Christine, every inane comment from Miss Viceroy came to her ears.

Step-Mama glared at Papa, who did as he usually did: he acted as if he were not aware the wrath of the Lady would fall on his head when the party dispersed. He had forgotten to bow to the vicar, Margaret recalled, failed to save his wife from falling to the floor and, to cap it off, pointed out Step-Mama's failure to deck the church as a bower. The bride couldn't find it in her heart to allot him an iota of sympathy.

Sir Denison gulped a finger of brandy and said to his new son, "Heard your family collects. Stunning pieces of furniture."

"Priceless to the family," Treadway said. "Collecting is a recurring hobby down the generations. My grandfather was most prolific." He also took a large gulp from his glass. Christine cooed. The conversation becalmed.

Lady Ridgemont and Victoria Viceroy commenced a determined effort to plan the village's spring celebration. The conversation pooled in a discussion of their pet peeves.

"I wish we could eliminate the May pole," Victoria said. "The green becomes unpleasantly littered during the dancing."

"The ale tent is what I would like to abolish."

"Perhaps both could be left out." With nothing to stop its destructive flow, the conversation flooded into every objectionable practice of the neighborhood.

Mrs. Treadway's eyes misted as her husband helped her to a chair. "Mind my back. It still aches from that horrendous carriage ride into Hertfordshire. Oh Carlton, a mother's dream is fulfilled. My darling boy has captured his one true love."

"In outrageous clothing."

"Perhaps Miss Ridgemont—no, Mrs. Treadway Junior—requested the colors?"

Mr. Treadway Senior shook his head in disgust and turned to the vicar. "Allies two fine families. I can't ask for more. Promises to be a fine marriage."

Mrs. Treadway filled the gap in her husband's comment. "James and Margaret will make their home in London. He is set up in Mount Street. The house has been in the family for years; many of the special furniture pieces are there. I flatter myself it's a jewel of a museum as well as a comfortable home." The vicar nodded.

Hughes fidgeted. Margaret looked lost. It was her wedding breakfast, made miserable by his own folly and Tread's loose tongue. He was the wit of his friends; hostesses facing dull dinner parties begged his attendance. Even government types enjoyed his conversation. His facile tongue could ease the awkwardness of this situation for her. As a gentle knight, he could do no less.

Sidling his elegant, black clad form onto the sofa by Margaret, he opened his mouth, expecting a fountain of sparkling conversation to pour forth. He couldn't think of a thing to say.

She must have heard; yes, she must. Poor girl doesn't deserve the grief. "Lovely ceremony," he blurted.

Hughes's banal effort broke in white caps at his feet. Margaret slid to the end of the sofa, crushed her hip into the arm, and stared across the room. "Your dress is lovely too," he resorted to a bare faced lie.

Stupefaction and umbrage pinched her nostrils.

Nice nose, he decided. *Not too short, but her expression hardly matches.* Hughes was drowning. It served him right. "Can't say the church was lovely, not without flowers, but it was clean. Why weren't there flowers? I thought they are customary. M'mother seems to think you can't do anything without them. Last time she held a ball, there wasn't a bloom to be got in London. She had them all. Roses, violets, some blue things—they were all over the house. Not that I am complaining," he tacked on.

"Nice room here. I like the combination of blue and green. Restful." His foot began jiggling. Pity was an uncomfortable conversationalist. No, not pity. Compassion.

"Nice flowers on the tables. What ones do you like?"

She didn't deign to answer. Maybe a change of subject would help. "I hope to see you at Camelot for the season. Tread spends April through July haunting Camelot." When she failed to respond, he sank beneath the waves.

Margaret would not crack more than a social smile. Her face seemed graven of marble though her eyes, which he had not noted before, failed to be icy. *Most unusual eyes,* he mused. *I have never in my life seen such eyes.* The color was pretty, if not remarkable, being a clear blue. The whites were the customary white, the black the normal black, he supposed. It was the blue between the blue and black that was different.

"Never seen the blue and black mix together," he whispered. "Can't see where one ends and t'other begins." He slid closer on the sofa, the better to analyze her eyes. "Misty, like the horizon at sea."

She pinched him hard just above the wrist.

"What'd you do that for?"

"You were nearly sitting in my lap, staring at me and mumbling like a bedlamite. What do you think I did it for?" Margaret snapped and went to stand by the drafty window in a swirl of summery lace. Around her, conversational waves hit breakwalls when she pounded the window frame with a fist.

"But I never did see eyes like that before," Hughes said to her back. "Wanted to look closer." He pinched himself in the same

Thwarting Magic • 77

spot she had nipped. *Once she is in town, I will find a way to make it up to her. For now, should be looking for signs of magic, not mooning over eyes.* He wandered toward Lady Ridgemont and the vicar's spinster sister.

Admiring the cold beauty of the bride—*Why is she banging at the window? And when will Lady Ridgemont get around to serving food?*—Carlton Treadway congratulated himself on saving his son from the clutches of some wanton widow. Or worse.

Mrs. Treadway, praying Margaret wouldn't break the window, grew perturbed. Carlton was thinking of his stomach, she knew, but there was a more serious matter to discuss. Much more serious. She needed to haul her husband into the library for a private chat.

"Excuse us, vicar," Mrs. Treadway said, twitching her husband's sleeve.

"What?" he inelegantly asked.

"We need to speak, dear. Privately." She swept from the room. He trailed her like a muddy dog promised a bath.

"You did it this time." Mrs. Treadway rounded on her hapless spouse as soon as the double doors of the library met the frame. "You told me he was happy, but you pushed James into this marriage. Explain yourself!"

Mr. Treadway Senior shook in his boots and then remembered he was the man of this particular marriage. He firmed his chin. "Yes, I desired James to make the match. Margaret is eligible in every way. What is wrong, my love?"

"I will tell you what is wrong, husband mine. You deceived me." She waved a finger in his face, back and forth like an irritated cat's tail. "James cares not a button for Margaret, despite your flaunting of her eligibility. He is more interested in her vulgar sister, the one making calf eyes at him. And that eligible young lady, the one with the manners of a duchess, seems to have developed a hatred of my Jamie. He will never make a comfortable wife of her, they will never give us a grandchild. And by the time he dies, an old, old, man, he will have lost every vestige of joy he ever had." Mrs. Treadway sniffed, nigh overcome with her darling Jamie's sad end.

"But he won't be hitched to a vulgar widow. Think how wretched that would make him."

"Widows! That is all you think of." Mrs. Treadway lost her woe in ire. "Just because Jamie was entangled with one widow when he first went to town, when he was green as grass, when he was but a sprig fresh out of Oxford. He untangled himself and has stayed away from widows ever since. But no, you have to have a ridiculous bugaboo of widows sinking their claws into him. Bah," she spat and stalked out of the library, her back straight.

Mr. Treadway Senior wiped his forehead with a shaky hand. He was in for it now. At least Mrs. Treadway didn't know all of her precious Jamie's doings.

* * *

In a corner, Hughes closed his eyes. The words of the spell slipped through his mind, knocking into each other and twisting into fantastic shapes. They wouldn't behave. He focused, going back to the opening sequence. Instead of invoking an atmosphere conducive to exposing the rogue wizard, the spell clumped like an adoring lap dog around Miss Viceroy's camphor-soaked chair.

A mental command to the spinster failed to move her from her seat. He hadn't thought she would; his talent didn't encompass suggestion. Hurst would have had her running from the house in panic, but Hurst wasn't here. He swiped damp palms over his knees and tried again. His stomach knotted. This had to be done perfectly. Hughes silently pronounced syllables rather than full words, hoping the spell would abandon the camphor and do its job. Digging nails into his palms, he fought to push his magic past intoxication and into working order.

Despite concentrating so hard sweat tickled his spine, the spell failed to crystallize either in his mind or in the air. It cavorted in camphor, metaphorically kicked its heels and rolled through the drawing room in an ecstasy of drunken abandon. With forlorn hope, he intensified the words.

Invoking the spell in pure Hebrew, he bathed the words in a plea to Merlin to extend his power to Hughes. *For England.* Rather than forming a pattern, the magic ran up the wall and crawled under the intricately gilded cornice board.

He opened his eyes, admitting defeat. Miss Viceroy's camphor blocked him from performing magic. It didn't appear she was leaving soon, either. He glanced up and swore. The gilding had melted off the cornice, running down the walls like Midas's blood.

To cap off a rotten occasion, Hughes became an unwilling

eavesdropper. From the looks of it, half the room could hear as well.

"Your poor flower is wilting." Christine touched a finger to the flawless rose on Treadway's lapel. "Let us go to the conservatory and choose another. I know where the best blooms are."

Treadway did not have much experience denying pleasure; a battle between nature and the elements of survival commenced. Which would win?

Survival lost the crucial battle.

Off to the conservatory slipped two reckless people with at least two other pairs of eyes watching intently. Mrs. Treadway swatted her husband sharply in the stomach and Hughes swallowed a mortifyingly hysterical laugh.

Chapter Nine

Finally, the nonsense was done. Tread and his new wife were in a carriage headed for town and Hughes was free for one evening to nail a rogue wizard. The next day he would leave Puckeridge. There was nothing to do to suit the purpose. The ladies had retired to their rooms.

The men holed up in the library. "Eulalie is breathing fire at me again," Sir Denison complained, sinking into a leather chair. "Next she will agitate to go to Italy, of all places. The people there don't speak proper. Don't wash either. All they do is drink wine and make love. Why would anyone want to go there?"

Hughes said, "The scenery is stunning."

"Who the hell wants scenery? I can see scenery just fine here. No one goes to Italy unless they are on business or in politics. Not likely I'm going to do either." Sir Denison peered suspiciously at Hughes. "Don't tell me you're one of them damned dilettantes what collect antiquities—like Elgin. Him and his broken pieces of marble. Reeks of the shop."

"Italy's the place to go to avoid the duns. There or Belgium." Hughes's stomach rumbled, distracting him from the feeling he had stumbled badly. He hadn't unmasked the rogue, curse Mordred. What was he to do now?

A spell popped into his mind. He examined it, reversing the words and listening to their resonance. Dangerous, but if it did the trick..."

"Belgium's where that court card, Napoleon, went to ground. We showed him. He lost half his Royal Guard in the tourney. Wellington trounced him good."

Mr. Treadway Senior asked, "Any hope for food? Lady Ridgemont never signaled the butler to serve the wedding breakfast."

* * *

"Damnable wedding," Hughes muttered. "Tread shouldn't

have done it. Should have told the Pater to go fly a kite." He pulled viciously at the rope.

Tugging the rope achieved nothing beyond relieving a bit of the magician's spleen. The rope wasn't attached to anything; it hung in the air, suspended by nothing. It hung so well the tug didn't cause the rope to go anywhere.

Instead, it quivered.

"Sorry," he said, abashed. "Ain't your fault. Shouldn't take it out on you." He began setting stones in a circle where the rope almost touched the ground. "It's put me in a foul humor—that and this rogue wizard." One rock didn't line up straight. He scuffed the ground with the heel of his boot until it was level and dropped the stone in place.

The ground was wet. Grass and dirt clung to his hands, his boots, stones, and a bag. This was a messy business. He cursed and a bird flew out of a tree, startled.

Checking the spacing of the stones, he mumbled. "Not that I don't fancy saving the world as we know it. Don't mind. Deuced heroic thing to do. Set me higher on the Council's list. Maybe his grace will gift me with that Arabian he keeps teasing he'll sell." He pushed one rock an inch further from the rope. "And it's a quest—if I succeed, I'll be knighted. Wouldn't mind.

"Hah. I won't get that horse. Shouldn't fool myself. Saving the world as we know it ain't worth a prime stud like his grace's Arabian. Still, I'll get a handle to my name. Sir Adrian."

Satisfied the stones were precisely placed, he pulled a shallow silver bowl from a soft felt bag. Polishing the etched rim with the bag, he told the rope, "All this effort to counteract henbane. I can hardly believe it. People who don't know what they are doing shouldn't dabble in things they don't understand. Should stick to the tried and true."

He reverently set the bowl under the rope. "Grinds my soul. Henbane." From another bag, he pulled a fistful of leaves. These he tossed into the air; they fell willy-nilly and speckled his boots.

"Well, are you ready?"

He raised his arms and uttered a stream of incomprehensible syllables. Anyone listening would have been flabbergasted at the complexity of sound. Only another magician, *if* the magician were trained in the arcane Babylonian style, could have made sense of it.

The syllables coalesced into minute bits of light. Smaller than a firefly's light, the twinkles swirled and danced their way into the silver bowl. When the bowl was overflowing with a heap of the sparks, when the sparkles sat glowing just below the hanging end of rope, he went silent. For a pregnant moment, the entire glade was still.

Arms stretched, Hughes spoke one word. One powerful word in a language not spoken in more than single words for countless generations. The word whooshed over the bowl. It sent sparks of light climbing the rope. Writhing up the twisting strands of hemp, the sparks smoldered. Spurts of smoke puffed from stray hempen hairs and sections of the rope glowed molten red. The first spark to reach the top twinkled like a star. Like the star which drew the wise men to Bethlehem, it drew more sparks up.

He waited patiently. When at last every spark was gathered at the top of the rope, clinging in a huge misshapen ball, he spoke another word.

The ball exploded. Sparks flew with the power of Congreve's rockets on a bad day, flinging themselves in all directions. The force of the blast flung the magician to the ground. He lay, his head pillowed on a tuft of grass, soaking damp from the grass and dirt into his clothes, and watched what his spell had wrought.

The sparks danced aimlessly in the air. Aimless with no discernable pattern. He cursed and beat his fists on the ground.

* * *

Margaret plowed through farewells to her family with a stiff upper lip, only seething when she embraced her deceitful elder sister. Now she faced hours in a carriage with her equally deceitful newly wedded husband. She scowled out the window, so streaked with rain and dirt there was nothing to be seen. Mr. Treadway lounged, a crisp red rose on his lapel. He fingered it occasionally and she wondered if she should press it into a book for him.

Contemplating crushing a single perfect rose in the heaviest tome available and then slamming the book and its contents over her groom's head was an amusing distraction from the dullness of the journey. It was so amusing, she went back to the scene over and over, embellishing and adding details. The most satisfactory version left Mr. Treadway crumpled and helpless at her feet.

After a very long silence, he spoke. "I do not recall seeing you in London. Did you enjoy the season?"

"Tolerably, sir," she answered. How was she to tell this jackanapes he had attended at least four balls in conjunction with her? Indeed, Lady Jackson had introduced them at a musicale at the Silvester residence. Mr. Treadway did not remember her. So much for any desire he'd had to pursue her, the toad.

"I hope we may go out often. Do you look forward to it?"

"I suppose." Margaret unbent a tad. "There are a number of people I will enjoy renewing acquaintance with."

"Ahh." He was glad to see her relax. At the start of the journey, Miss Ridgemont—Mrs. Treadway—had looked locked in mortal combat. Treadway rejoiced that the prickles were retreating and she'd left his hide whole. Maybe they could hold a civil conversation. "Perhaps I know some of them."

"Miss Honoria Silvester, for one. I met Miss Silvester at the Earl and Countess of Wellworth's ball honoring Lady Clarissa. We became fast friends."

"Oh," he replied, knowing full well he had been in attendance at the same event. He had danced twice with Honoria. She wore silver something with tiny dots on it. The sheep went back to looking out the window. Wasn't anything to be seen through the mud and rain. At least she didn't suffer from the motion of the carriage. That was small consolation for the dreariness of her conversation.

Another long silence served to bring the newly married couple to the inn where they were to spend the night. It did not appear they could hold a civil conversation.

By the time the carriage stopped, Margaret was ineffably tired. The strain of the day, a miserable drive, and lack of exercise or congenial conversation to offset the tension served to bring her to the edge of exhaustion. Swinging a massive volume of Shakespeare's compleat works over Mr. Treadway's head again and again hadn't contributed to her tiredness. Bashing courtesy into the dolt's head had been imaginary. The chilling silence in the carriage was real.

* * *

Silent men held torches as she swept up a length of stone steps, through a wide front door, across the cold tapping of marble flooring in a wider hall to a private room. Alone at last, though not for a sufficient time. Her croaking husband saw to the stabling of the cattle and arranged for dinner. He'd be back like a chill in January. Pulling off her bonnet, which seemed to have glued itself to her ears, she approached a looking glass.

Leaping frogs, she looked frightful. There was smut on her chin, her hair was matted to her forehead, and the blue merino pelisse looked wilted. Whirling to the maid waiting by the door, Margaret announced, "I wish to tidy myself. Could water be brought to my bedchamber?"

The maid curtseyed and silently backed out the door, waving her to follow. As they climbed the stairs, she roused herself to pay attention to her surroundings. This establishment was not a common inn; it looked like a private residence. The stair was broad, allowing four large people to climb it shoulder to shoulder, well carpeted, and polished silver sconces gleamed at regular intervals. The upper hall was equally pleasant, with a brass inlaid ebony table and a few chairs.

The maid, hushed as a maid in a proper household, quietly opened a door. "Your room, madam," she as quietly said. "I am Gert. I'll be glad to attend you." She bustled to the washstand and shook out a towel.

"This is nice, Gert," she complimented, referring to the soothing pale green décor. The maid unbent and together, amid lacey hangings, they worked to rectify the insufficiencies of her appearance. Warm water, fragrant soap, and a soft linen cloth did much to revive the bride. A vigorous brushing of her hair and a change of clothes completed the transformation. Gert proved herself an efficient lady's maid; Margaret told her so sincerely.

She now felt equal to a meal in the company of James Treadway.

Back at the blue-papered parlor, Margaret composed herself on the sofa, running appreciative fingers over intricate damask garlands twined on columns. Knowing her appearance was improved, she felt more in control. She was married, that could not be altered. If only to retain her sanity, the bride determined to make more of an effort with her groom. He had the manners of an untrained dog; she would still have to make conversation.

A small mahogany dining table waited at the other side of the room, two chairs pulled to place settings of silver, crystal, and cream porcelain. The room needed only one man and food to be complete. Both arrived at the same time.

Mr. Treadway, cleaned and brushed, entered a step ahead of liveried footmen carrying steaming platters and covered bowls. He nodded pleasantly and motioned toward the table.

"Are you as hungry as I? Can't wait to get at the roast beef. It's a specialty of Simpleton House, you know." He pulled a chair out and courteously seated her.

Margaret took a deep breath and commenced her campaign. "First you must drink your soup. Cook is awfully upset if her soup is shunned."

"All cooks are alike." He picked up his spoon. "My chef has been known to storm the dining room if a dish isn't sampled to his satisfaction. Once he came brandishing a knife because my mother left her jellied greengage plums untouched. 'Ze fruit, it iz not cookated? Madame does not care for ze Chablis jelly?' he demanded to know. Mother cringed, not daring to tell Armand she was too full for the plums."

He dipped the spoon in the shallow soup bowl and stirred vigorously. "She had two helpings of the Rockingham chicken with curls of ham; she felt she couldn't put another bite in her mouth. I thought Armand was going to take out the center of the table with the knife."

She smiled, ignoring the lack of table manners, and the tone of the meal was set. The soup was well seasoned, the side dishes imaginative and equally tasty. Tasting the beef, sliced thin with stock drizzled over it, she looked up, surprised. "This is good. I don't believe I have ever had such succulent meat."

"Yes," he mumbled around a full mouthful. "I always stop here just for this reason."

"This is not like any inn I have seen. It seems more like someone's home. My room looks a bit like Miss Silvester's, all soothing greens and lace."

"Because it used to be a private residence. Simpleton came upon hard times when his father took the gambling fever and decided to go into trade. Has a genius for innkeeping, I think. Kept the staff, even augmented it. Hosts private parties from town. The Mainwarings held their Christmas ball here last year. We are only an hour from London."

"You are right; he has a genius for hospitality. The maid who tended me is a wonder. Why did Papa never mention this inn?"

"Probably doesn't know about the place. Simpleton keeps it rather quiet and it's off the main road."

By the time Margaret and James had eaten their way through fig ice and rum cream pie, she felt comfortable. From his behavior, he had discovered she had wit. He smiled at her once or twice.

Nevertheless, when the footman placed the decanter of brandy in front of him, she became uncomfortable. Never in her life had any man taken his after-dinner libation in her presence. Being in his company without a chaperone was difficult enough. Would she have to sit at the table and watch him become castaway? Then...

If only the ceiling would fall on his head. He was going to come to her bed.

Mr. Treadway, more observant than she thought, spoke up. "Why don't you retire now? I will indulge in a glass, then be up."

She nodded and scurried from the room, trepidation making her clumsy. This business of marriage was complicated, but maybe she could handle it. Once he was done with her in the marriage bed, maybe...maybe...

No, miracles did not happen for Margaret. He wasn't going to choke on a bone and expire, as Christine's husband had.

* * *

After Gert helped her out of her dress and into her fine lawn nightclothes, Margaret dismissed her. Wandering restlessly around the room, she worried. How long before he came? Would he come to her room, or go to his bed? She shook her head. Of course he would come to her. Much of the companionship she felt at the dinner table dissipated. Sitting on the bed, she flexed her feet, encased in brown felt slippers.

Christine's words came back to her. Oh dear Lady, he would want to suck on her toes! And those same stupid toes had been in one set of footwear after another all day long. She jumped off the bed and raced to the washstand, grabbing a cloth. Wetting it in the bowl, she bent and wiped off the top of her foot.

Whoosh, rum cream pie and two glasses of wine rushed to her head. She swayed, nearly falling against the table. Grabbing the washstand, she righted herself and considered her options. She could sit on the bed or on the chair at the dressing table, but dirty water might spot the green silk covers. It would be a shame to ruin them.

Wetting the washcloth, she sat on the floor and pulled her nightdress to her calves. Scrub, not only the tops and bottoms of the feet, but get between the toes. *Do it well or traces of dirt will remain on whichever toe he wants to put his mouth on.* She shuddered at the thought. How strange. Could not God have devised a more dignified way to create heirs?

She scrubbed harder.

* * *

Treadway opened the door without knocking and stopped. Good God, what was she doing curled up on the floor? Had she had a fit? He looked more closely.

The chit was scrubbing her feet. He could not help it, his mind flitted to Drury Lane, to Mrs. Siddons performing a chilling rendition of Lady Macbeth. The parallels between the actress's hand wringing and his bride's behavior were unmistakable. The same rash movements, the same air of desperation.

Bloody hell, what had his father gotten him into?

Margaret had not noticed his entrance. She labored at the last small toe, forcing the cloth under the toenail with her finger. Then she saw him, leaning against the doorframe. She tossed the cloth up to the basin and missed. The wet linen plopped to the floor as she scrambled to her feet. It bunched under the high arch of her foot, squishing with a spurt into the rug.

"I did not see you, sir." She squeaked, swooped and captured the sopping cloth. She laid it on the table beside the basin of water, where it dripped on the wood instead of the rug.

"I did see you," Treadway responded. "Have you finished your ablutions?"

Margaret flushed to the roots of her hair and glanced away. "Yes."

He advanced into the room, cursing his father fluently, if silently. Tender virgins he was accustomed to; this tender virgin, with her maddened scrubbing and staid behavior, was not one he wanted to become accustomed to. Couldn't his father have picked a silly deb? A blonde, empty-headed chit, thinking of nothing more than lace and feathers. Ah well, onward into the breech. His father demanded nothing less.

"I expected you to be in bed, with the counterpane pulled tightly to your chin. I was prepared to allay your fears whimsically, perhaps with a glass of wine and lighthearted conversation. How do I proceed now?" He paused and contemplated his bride, whose blush had gone beyond any he had ever seen. "Do you have a suggestion? Merlin forbid, do you sleep on the floor?"

The stupid sheep looked embarrassed to death. With her eyes closed and her mouth screwed up, she said, "If you like, I shall get under the covers, but I think that would not be best. I know I have to submit to you, and I do mean to do my duty. I just don't know what I should do. I take it we are to use the bed?"

The innocent question induced an amazing response. Treadway's heart sped and interesting twinges darted further down his body. He stared boldly at the figure of his wife, covered well enough in vestal virgin lawn, certainly not flaunted. Definitely not flaunted. Pert breasts peeked and bobbed with each agitated breath under the ample white folds of her nightdress. Everything else was shielded, except her bare toes, which gleamed damply.

"Do as you think you should," he commanded. "I shall take my cue from you."

Chapter Ten

Margaret crossed to the bed like Accolon facing Excalibur as wielded by Arthur. Climbing to the edge of the wide expanse, she sat demurely, legs straight out, toes pointed to the ceiling, unsupported by the feather mattress from the knees down. The edge of the lawn nightgown fluttered, coming to rest on the side of the bed, pulling the hem up from her ankles.

She wiggled her toes.

Talk about vestal virgins! She looked as if she had placed her feet in the stocks. She clearly expected dire punishment. Then the possibilities of wriggling toes caught his imagination. Under his robe, ruby red silk with embroidered horses rearing, galloping, and standing at rest, he wore breeches, nothing else. Treadway was glad of the breeches; otherwise, the front of the robe would be disturbed and the sheep would run bleating from the room.

He moved forward, coming to stand in front of the slender feet hanging in the air. He put a hand under Margaret's heels, offering the support her legs lacked. He moved closer, setting one foot where he throbbed. If she had a fascination for feet, he would feed on that interest. He'd never done the like before, but the concept intrigued.

Under the guidance of his hand, her foot slid up and down. From the look on her face, she didn't understand what he was about. One of his hands reached out, his long arms allowing him to touch the buttons on the front of her nightdress. He unbuttoned one.

Her hands flew to resist, fluttered.

Quickly the nightdress was unbuttoned to her hips. Small pearl buttons went to the hem, but Treadway stopped when his hand hit her thighs and she flinched. His other hand, holding her foot with ease, continued the gentle massaging motion against his belly.

His hand dipped under the edge of her nightgown at her neck and pushed it aside. The lawn slid along her shoulder, fell off the rounded edge of arm, and fell. He repeated the motion on the other side and his sheep was shorn.

Her eyes snapped closed and an inarticulate protest issued from her lips. He ignored it. He took in her form; pearly skin, not as white as some would prefer, but with a pleasing glow, slender waist, and breasts. Oh, breasts a bit larger than fashion preferred, but softly rounded, firm. Breasts any man would delight in. Though he preferred larger, his mouth watered.

Treadway did what came naturally. He lifted the girl, allowing the nightgown to drift to the floor, then laid her back on the bed, legs dangling. He spread the legs, the better to stand between them, and lowered his mouth to a breast.

Margaret bucked, not understanding at all. *When is he going to suck my toes? Or are gentlemen different in their tastes, one sucking toes, another sucking breasts?* When Mr. Treadway held her down, she resigned herself to the strange behavior. *Martin Whitmill must have liked toes better than breasts, but Christine did not know what she was missing. Ohhh, heavens, this feels good!*

His lips and tongue played with the tip of her breasts, one after another, shooting spasms into her stomach. Nothing could describe those spasms; they hurt, making her back arch, but they didn't hurt. Noooo, they didn't.

While she mindlessly squirmed, he threw off his robe, exposing firmly muscled shoulders, arms, and a well-formed chest. Sweat sheened his skin and the neat vee of hair on his chest gleamed as he gulped for breath. Stepping back, he stripped off his breeches and crowded closer between her legs, bracing his thighs against the mattress. Margaret, lost in the world he led her into, was oblivious to the view. The arm he braced by her shoulder shook as he returned to her breasts.

Something swirled over and around her private place like a pestle grinding spices.

This proved more to her liking than the attention to her chest. She moaned. He slid his tool lower and began to push, pushed a little more, and then pushed harder.

Margaret stilled, wondering what this new sensation was. It burned. She protested, verbally by uttering a strangled noise and nonverbally by pushing back. Mr. Treadway jerked upright, holding her hips still with his hands. She gulped, astonished by the feel of something buried within her.

He didn't appear surprised; instead he looked as if she were torturing *him*. His neck corded, muscles bunched and twisted. Then something inside her twitched and set him off. He pushed and pulled, his thing going in and out of her, and she marveled that pain transmuted into something wonderful.

It was so wonderful she fell. Not off the bed, but inside her head, she fell off a cliff and flew. She couldn't feel her fingers or toes, but other parts of her, oh, my. They jerked, spinning like a windmill's sails in a storm, while she flew. He collapsed on her, keeping her from floating to the ceiling. He breathed heavily, his eyes closed.

When she could speak again, when Margaret could turn her head, she asked in all innocence, "Aren't you going to suck on my toes?"

"Not hardly," Mr. Treadway replied.

* * *

They were truly married, till death did them part. The next day Margaret sat in the carriage, such a short distance to London. She was sore. Her legs had not ever been contorted so. She had never had that pushing, and Mr. Treadway had done it three times during the night.

But she did not think to complain. She enjoyed the pushing; she also enjoyed the fact he was not to suck her toes. That sounded undignified. If he preferred to do it with Christine...well, as long as he only did the pushing with his wife. Margaret was not in the mood for recriminations. She needed a nap first.

In the carriage next to his wife, Treadway congratulated himself on his suitable bride and more, congratulated himself on his performance. He went so far as to feel smug. She might be a bedlamite, but she brought a fine dowry, had a pleasing way to her in bed, and he should be able to mold her into whatever type of wife suited him. Her lascivious interest in feet was titillating. Vestal virgins were a surprising delight.

The carriage twisted this way and that around London streets, first through the poorer areas of town, then through Mayfair to Mount Street. The cacophony of the bustling city drowned the silence in the cab. There wasn't anything to say.

When they arrived at the Treadway townhouse, he watched for her reaction. She oohed in an appropriate manner. The building was not remarkable for a London residence, being of average size and aspect, with a neat entryway. It looked much as its neighbors, a solid home for a solid man. The front door was spotless black-enameled wood with a massive lion's head knocker and lights along its length on both sides. Inside, Treadway knew people in the past (mostly his grandfather, feted as an original) had indulged a taste for unusual furniture; Margaret would become acquainted with the eccentric pieces rather quickly. His lips quirked.

On the whole, he was pleased with his home and its distinctive accoutrements, although he supposed if she found the furnishings too outlandish, he would allow her to make minor changes. She could move things around a bit; it would give her something to do while he went about his life.

Right there in the front hall, she made acquaintance with one of the Treadway atrocities under the critical eye of the butler, Craig, and the chatelaine, Mrs. Norris. A blackened wood chair sat in lonely state against the long wall opposite the stairs where it was immediately seen on entering the front door.

The chair was square with a flat wooden seat and plain legs connected by stretchers at the floor. Severe in style, it was not its primitive form that offended, but elaborate carvings rendered it most uncomfortable looking. Unsightly. A coat of arms was carved in high relief on the chair back. High relief did little to describe the carving; each detail was formed with ridges as sharp as thorns. The splintery carving carried around the apron of the seat and at the edges of the arms. Surmounting the back, two whittled birds, ravens judging by their size, with open beaks and outspread wings, faced each other. They appeared to be pecking at the bulbous mass rising between them.

The unwary person who leaned back in the chair would risk cutting his back, fingers, and legs to shreds under the baleful gaze of the birds, if he did not first remove the hair from his head on their wings.

Margaret blinked. The first genuine smile she had received from James burst forth and bathed her in its glow.

"Like the chair, m'dear?" he queried. "It's monstrous old. The coat of arms is for Nicholas Roope of Dartmouth, who had the wood carried from the Amazon—that's in South America—back around the time of the Conqueror. It's Brazilian bulletwood, most rare. One of our treasures. Came to the family with the marriage of...someone."

"Indeed," she managed to reply. "The chair is remarkably well preserved." If more than three people had sat on that eyesore each century of its existence, Margaret would eat her gloves. It would stand square and ugly until the end of time because it would never be used.

The new Mrs. Treadway steadfastly resisted throwing away the horrible chair. *A family heirloom, it's a deuced family piece,* she kept reminding herself. *Heirloom furniture is priceless and to be treasured, even if it's the most awful thing ever made.*

* * *

In the solar two weeks after her wedding, sharpening a quill preparatory to writing to her father and stepmother, Margaret mistrustfully eyed the desk. Carlton Treadway, with an eye for modern design, had purchased it. This elevated the desk to the realm of family treasure, forever to be cherished. Unfortunately.

She could barely tolerate the desk. The writing area of the mahogany piece was small—there was room for standish and paper, nothing else. Where her elbows were to go was a mystery; a candlestick to illuminate the paper was an impossible dream. There just wasn't room. Inches from her arms rose drawers a full three feet high. Whoever had designed the piece attempted to reproduce a castle, complete with corner towers. The mahogany was heavily grained with light and dark patches like stone blocks, ivy inlays swirled up the towers, and the top was crenellated with carved half shells at the corners.

How was she to write a cheerful letter imprisoned between dank castle towers? How could she tell Mr. Treadway the desk was ugly and unusable? She sighed, dipped the pen into ink, and wrote. Breezing through the customary opening sentences, her pen went dry as she sought words to describe her new life. It was impossible to explain the reality of her marriage. Not to Papa.

The Treadways managed to rub along. If he did not find Margaret enticing, Treadway hid the fact. She sensed nothing hinting at a preference for her sister. His eyes didn't linger on other ladies and he intimated he was fully satisfied with his marital status. At night, after the candles were snuffed, he was attentive.

To be fair, she should admit he did well as a husband. His enthusiastic pushing into her night after night pointed to warm feelings. It must. It had become routine. She was usually abed, sometimes he woke her. The hideous horse embroidered dressing robe shrugged off, he slid between the sheets naked. There would be a session of caresses, most of which felt nice. Then the pushing.

Perhaps she judged too hastily. Mayhap he had seen her worth. Belated acknowledgement of her charms was better than none. She brushed the quill feather across her lips.

But how to tell Papa the only place Margaret met her husband with equanimity was in the bedchamber? Other than there, she could not help watching for the crack that would ooze Treadway's true feelings. She was certain one of these days, sooner rather than later, he would indicate she fell below the mark. He hadn't given her leave to use his Christian name, for heaven's sake.

It wore on her nerves, watching for the inevitable setdown. Some days, she felt as if her head would roll off, her shoulders were so stiff.

She tried telling herself it didn't matter. The likelihood of Mr. Treadway spurning her for Christine was equal to the chance of her being crowned with strawberry leaves and being called Duchess. It wouldn't happen. How could it happen? Christine was at Puckeridge.

Nothing helped. She couldn't dissipate the fear any more than she could wave rain away. She could and did bottle it up. It was the only way to get through the day. Sighing, she dipped the quill in the ink and wrote about her new wardrobe, hoping Lady Ridgemont would appreciate the description. If she were lucky, mulled muslin would revenge Step-Mama's selection of a wedding dress.

She was unaware of his presence until he appeared in front of the desk. "Oh, Mr. Treadway," she squealed, dropping a blot of ink on 'Alencon lace.' "You gave me a start!"

He chuckled. "You were so intent, couldn't resist. To whom are you writing?"

"My father and stepmother. I am past time for news; Papa will be concerned." Flustered, Margaret used the blotter to smear drips of ink across 'cherry satin.'

"Tell them about the play last night—Sir Denison should enjoy hearing about that popinjay, Kean. Hughes said he was in top form as Shylock, strutting like a Bond Street beau." He juggled three unwieldy books from one arm to the other. *And show the old man I am upholding my end of the bargain. The theatre, bah.*

"I had chills when he threatened Lorenzo. Mr. Kean made Shakespeare's play come alive."

"I can't stomach Kean, I prefer watching the audience myself. Never did care for Shakespeare. The theatre people make a production of it. Too much Shylock for my taste. Portia should have had more presence on the stage. I like her wit and perception of the ridiculous."

"I found myself wishing she showed more mercy to Shylock, though he was unpleasant."

"Your tender heart. She should show less mercy, not more. Can you put off writing? Need to go over the accounts with you." Treadway hefted the thick books on top of her spattered letter. "The top is this year's; the others are the past two years. One book per year.

"Well, now you have the household accounts, I'm off. Won't be back until late. Don't need anything, do you?"

"No, I will be fully occupied."

* * *

Margaret rang for the chatelaine. If she must review the household accounts, it would be well to have assistance. If nothing else, Mrs. Norris might keep her awake.

An hour into discussing line upon endless line of expenses, she closed a ledger. "Mrs. Norris, I commend you. With a staff only marginally adequate, you have done a wonderful job maintaining the townhouse. The front door and hall—the first thing visitors see—is immaculate. Sets the tone."

Her face rivaling the sun, the chatelaine settled in her chair in front of the desk. "Thank you, Mrs. Treadway. It isn't easy, I will say. 'Tis near impossible to get good workers with the wages we can pay. Look at Molly. I had to discharge her Monday. She went to the cellar to fill a hob and screamed fit to rattle the china. One of the boys ran down the stairs to save her from whatever and ripped a hole in his best britches. Molly had the nerve to spin an outlandish tale about holes in the coal. Our coal comes direct from Newcastle; it don't fall to dust in the bin. Here I thought the girl was straight as a seam; she must have been in the cooking sherry. You never can tell." She wagged her head. "I had no choice but to turn her off. I'll have no nonsense in this house." She slid a piece of foolscap between the towers. "Do you want to go over menus now, madam?"

Shrugging off the chill climbing her back, Margaret squared her shoulders and looked over the listing. "You do a nice job of balancing meals. I see no need to change this. It would be pleasant to have less mutton, but I understand that hasn't been possible, given the monies available. Mrs. Norris, the ledgers show our problem is that the budget Mr. Treadway set for household expenses is not adequate. Your duties include making your master aware of deficiencies. Did you approach him about increasing the budget?"

"Yes, madam, I did. The master said to make do." The chatelaine pursed her lips.

"I imagine that is why there are not enough maids on staff."

"Decent maids demand more wages, madam. They won't work here, not when they can earn so much more any other house."

He was clutchfisted. It didn't surprise her. She rubbed the knot in her neck. There was a solution somewhere just beyond the tip of her tongue. What was it she had seen? It had been during her season; something about the Earl of Wellwood's household. Ahh, now she remembered.

"We must be creative." She leaned forward confidentially. "What about maids who cannot be hired in other houses?"

"They won't be worth having. Thieving and not doing their chores, that's what we would have. Better to make do."

"Surely there is any number of competent maids not employed in the better houses, not because of the quality of their work, but for other reasons."

"Those girls," Mrs. Norris sniffed, "tend to be pretty."

Margaret nodded. "No one will hire an attractive girl for fear of disruption in the household. I noticed it when my stepmother interviewed girls for my season. The Countess of Wellwood was as critical of her servants, according to her daughter. The quality of service is not in question, only their allure for the men of the house. It must be difficult for the girl, who begins in service at the age of twelve, after all, and grows to passable looks. She is well trained, willing, but cannot find employment. To work in a decent home, don't you agree that under those circumstances, a pretty girl might accept what we can offer?"

The chatelaine widened her eyes. "What happens in other households could happen here. Don't you fear the master—"

Margaret interrupted, "No, I do not think Mr. Treadway will bother them." She would see to that.

The next day, her plan was accomplished. Mrs. Norris, under Margaret's direction, sent to the employment agency and the house was properly staffed at the wage rate Mr. Treadway insisted upon. A handful of grateful maids and Mrs. Norris became her champions.

The butler was a harder nut to crack. As four passably good looking girls filed past him into Mrs. Norris's office, his mouth hardened, his hands fisted.

"Mrs. Norris," Craig said, "what is the meaning of this?"

"Mrs. Treadway hired 'em," the chatelaine said and closed her office door. He had no option but to approach the mistress.

Margaret was ready. She flew to a chair and arranged her skirts becomingly. Picking up her needlework in the assumption the genteel occupation would reinforce honeyed insults and threats, she trilled, "Come in," to the knock on the door as if she wasn't girded for battle.

Craig stalked in, on his dignity. More supercilious than the highest duke in the land, a good butler could rot one's toes with a glance. Craig was an exceptionally good butler. He looked like he'd eaten an apple to the core only to find it wormy, Margaret being the apple. She did her best not to cower.

"Madam, Mrs. Norris has brought in—"

"I know." Detecting a palsied hand, Margaret felt sorry for the old man, but not sorry enough to alter her course. The butler was an obstacle in her path; she would brook no interference. "Such a relief to see the house fully staffed," she said, setting a delicate French knot with blue silk in the center of a daisy. "You must be ecstatic. Having a sufficient number of maids will lift a burden, allowing you to finally perform your duties properly."

He stiffened, as she knew he would, but she hadn't expected him to sneer. "I was trained in the house of Kay. My performance has not suffered."

She dropped the embroidery in her lap and looked him in the

eye. "It is a pity the Kay's couldn't keep you." She paused to let the comment sink to the bone, then brought him to his figurative knees. "Conditions have been primitive, but I know you did your best. You need not fear I will take action against you for your lapses." The butler fisted his hands impotently.

Now he was cut to size, she imparted a warning. "I understand from Mrs. Norris the new maids are above average in appearance. I rely on you, Craig, to ensure the footmen do not take advantage. I will tolerate no rakishness in my household." She calmly wound silk around the needle for another French knot. "That will be all." She didn't look up until the door closed.

Margaret trusted that with her authority acknowledged, the butler would accord her the respect she merited. Clipping blue French knots out of daisy eyes ruined the needlework.

* * *

Margaret did her duty well, seeing to the household and preparing for the season in an unflustered manner. The washing water was hot, the dust balls that made James sneeze disappeared, and the kitchen produced satisfying meal after delicious meal. It was a pleasure to watch the staff at work. The maids were more than comely. One girl, Rose, had an impressive front end.

At night he had a sufficiently attractive bed partner. The sheep performed well enough in the sanctified setting, the marriage bed, he thought, being not too bold, nor experienced enough to notice if he lacked an overpowering ardor.

A wife; that was what he had needed. The Pater was wiser than one could ever have guessed to have known he needed a wife.

Driving to Ludgate Hill, Treadway congratulated himself on a marriage well-made. *When the season begins, I'll be able to return to my accustomed activities. Marriage won't put a crimp in my style after all.*

Chapter Eleven

Hughes carried the oddly wrapped package himself.

Trotting at his heels, his valet dithered. "I can carry that, sir," the man gasped. "Ain't fittin', you know it ain't fittin'."

"I don't want it damaged. Won't collect the magic properly if there are any splits or cracks," Hughes said over his shoulder. "If we stop in the tobacconist for snuff, you may carry that."

The valet screwed up his face. "Ye don't take snuff."

Imperceptibly, Hughes quickened his pace. "Friend, ho!" he called. A man pivoted, revealing the chubby countenance of Billy Johnstone, his coat buttoned wrong. The valet groaned.

"Old man," Stone said as Hughes came up. "Glad to see you. Was on my way to Jackson's."

"Not to box, I hope. Last time you did, they had to replace all those towels."

"Unkind to remind me." Stone slapped him genially on the back. "No, the Marquess of Brinston has accepted Sir Hurst Dunsmore's challenge. No holds barred, I hope. Should be a bang-up match."

It sounded promising. "Here," Hughes said to his valet, shoving the package into the man's arms. "Mind you take that straight home. Don't squeeze it." To Stone he said, "I'll be glad to accompany you. Need to talk to Brinston anyway. What is the challenge?" They crossed the walkway while the valet turned and headed in the direction of Albany. He held the package most gingerly.

"Not sure. Something about a piece of land Sir Hurst picked up a while back. Hurst wants to sell it to Brinston—the marquess says he don't want it. The winner of the bout decides who gets the estate. In Devon—it's called Whole Place."

Stone stopped to stare in a shop window and Hughes grabbed his arm. "Come on, don't want to miss the match."

As Hughes pulled him along, his friend said, "Did you see that waistcoat? I want it."

"No you don't. Scarlet won't look good on you."

"But I'd look like a Bow Street Runner. I'd like that."
"No, Stone."

As they cut through Ludgate Hill, Hughes saw Treadway's curricle in front of Rundell and Bridge. "Friend, ho!" he called again and Treadway turned his head.

"Well, don't you look self-satisfied," Hughes commented, stepping to the side of the carriage. "Stone, don't you think our friend appears content with his lot in life?"

"Looks all right," Stone said grudgingly. "I ain't seen you in the Green Room, Tread."

"And you won't," Treadway said. "Not for a while. Once the season gets under way, I'll be free."

Hughes's eyes flashed. "And in the meantime, it looks like you are going to drop a packet."

Stone blinked. "Huh?"

"Tread is going to the jeweler, Stone. If he don't have a skirt, he must be looking to sparkle up his wife with a geegaw or two."

"It's expected," Treadway said stiffly. "M'mother warned me."

"Want to go to Jackson's with us?" Stone asked eagerly. "Match between Hurst and Brinston."

Tread pursed his lips. "Better not. If I don't do this now, I'll forget." They parted, Stone remembering belatedly that the bout was set to go shortly. He didn't want to miss anything.

* * *

Wishing he were as free as Stone and Hughes, Treadway wandered into Rundell and Bridge to pick up a necklace for his wife. Not having looked at her fully, not once, Treadway would be hard-pressed to note the color of Margaret's eyes. The oversight gained significance as he eyed the long glass-topped case displaying brooches inside the door.

"Can I help you, sir?" Mr. Bridge himself smoothly slid behind the case Treadway faced, peering at jewels in all the colors of the rainbow. Treadway scratched his chin.

"I need something."

"For..."

"My wife." His eyes flicked at the man and returned to the case. "A necklace, I suppose." Bridge unlocked the cabinet.

"I have several spectacular sapphires. They are sure to please."

Treadway tried desperately to think what color Margaret's eyes were.

"They go with blue eyes, don't they?" he asked dubiously.

"Perhaps the lady would look better in green. These, though small, are perfectly formed emeralds." The jeweler reached into the case, pulling out a sparkling stream of emeralds set in shells like pearls. "Don't be fooled by the size of the stones, sir. They are the finest I have seen."

Treadway frowned.

What color are her eyes, damn it? "Topaz?" He looked around.

"Amethyst is popular this spring." Annoyed with the vacillating customer, Bridge stifled a sigh. "Rubies then. Unless the lady is of florid complexion or hair, rubies are stunning. This one here," he extracted a necklace and laid it on a velvet pad, "is in exquisite taste."

A blood red pendant the length of Treadway's thumb winked in the light from the window. "The chain comes from Madrid. Made in a monastery there with traditional tools. Notice the fine engraving on the links. It duplicates the border on an illuminated manuscript. Most detailed."

"I don't know." Mr. Bridge held his temper and contemplated the stock in the cabinet.

"I understand your hesitancy, sir. Come." He bustled around the counter and waved the difficult customer further into the store, determined now to sell him a necklace at all costs. "One's wife deserves jewelry out of the common way. I know just what you would like." From another display case, the jeweler pulled forth a necklace with a flourish.

"This is unique. It comes from the wilds of America; was traded by Indian savages for blankets or some such. Look at the stones—perfect for an English flower, don't you agree?" Treadway appraised the necklace. Unevenly round blue stones, mottled and veined, in an outlandish silver setting. They didn't shine; they didn't do anything but lay there. The setting twisted and turned, laying the dull stones in a pattern that reminded him of a falcon swooping on a mouse.

"It is turquoise," Mr. Bridge explained. "The setting compliments the stones, don't you agree? Hand wrought by savages, it's the purest silver I have seen in years. I would be proud to enter Almack's or any ball at Camelot as escort to a lady with this necklace around her neck. Distinctive, very distinctive."

"I don't think so," Treadway muttered. Whether her eyes were brown or blue, he didn't think Margaret would like a bird of prey hanging around her neck. From desperation, he said, "Diamonds. I want a diamond necklace." Diamonds looked well on anyone.

By Mordred, he wished he'd gone to Jackson's with his friends.

* * *

Men stood three deep, watching the bout. They found a corner with a view.

"Ouch," Stone said.

"He's in fine form," Hughes agreed.

The Marquess of Brinston and Sir Hurst Dunsmore were fighting. Shirts and boots off, they circled warily in the open area in the work-out room of Jackson's salon, surrounded by cheering men. John Jackson, the proprietor of the boxing establishment, watched critically.

Sir Hurst threw a punch; Brinston danced back. Hurst threw another, connecting with Brinston's chest. A rain of blows had both staggering. Separating, they circled again, assessing weaknesses.

The two engaged anew. With each swing, they came a step closer. When it looked like they were about to waltz, Brinston swung, grazed his opponent's chest and connected with his jaw. The sound of teeth clacking together made onlookers wince. Sir Hurst fell back, visibly shaken, and rubbed his jaw. "Mordred. Don't break it, Brin."

"I'll try not to," the marquess answered. Sweat gleamed on his shoulders; he wiped his chest with a towel. "Do you concede?"

"No. I don't want the place."

"What makes you think *I* do?"

"You know why," Sir Hurst said.

"Give it to your sister."

"She wouldn't know what to do with it."

"Then put your fists back up." Brinston followed the order with a resumption of the boxing stance. Sir Hurst shook his head and attacked.

They boxed around the open space, engaging and

withdrawing. Evenly matched, neither seemed able to fell the other. Brinston's eye swelled; Sir Hurst's ear glowed red. Both had bruises forming on their chests, arms, and faces. At last, Brinston landed a mighty wallop to Hurst's mouth. His lip split.

"First blood!" the crowd howled. Brinston grabbed a tossed towel out of the air and wiped his face. Hurst dabbed at his mouth and chin. Sweat rolled down their backs. Jackson, the boxing champion, stepped between them.

"Are you satisfied, gentle sirs?"

Brinston nodded. "I am. We agreed first blood would decide the match. Hurst?"

"I concede."

As they toweled their sweaty bodies, men drifted away. A few stayed, clapping the jousters on the back and congratulating them on a match well fought. Hughes kept Stone in their corner.

Sir Hurst made a last stab at unloading his unwanted estate. "Are you certain you won't take Whole Place, Brin? It's close on Sturminster Marshall. I thought you wanted to investigate the church tower there."

"I don't have time to amuse myself with that now or for the foreseeable future. It's been there since 1802 when the tower fell. It won't go away."

"But Whole Place is convenient—"

"No, Hurst."

Sir Hurst, helping Brinston on with his coat, indicated the last remaining spectators. "Hughes is giving you a look," he said quietly.

"Let's see what he wants." Brinston nodded to Hughes.

Leaving Stone in the corner, Hughes approached and immediately said, "It's one of three ladies, Lord Brinston."

"How are you going to determine which?"

"I bought a fishing creel."

"Interesting approach." Brinston turned to Hurst. "Your opinion. Given three ladies, one of whom is dabbling in magic, how would you go about discovering the malefactor?"

"I'd make myself indispensable," Sir Hurst promptly replied. "Free access to their boudoirs would turn up proof."

Hughes cringed inside. The ladies under discussion were not ones he could seduce. Or would. Lips tight, he said, "One relentlessly wed, another too young. The last is a man-trap."

"So you are going to go fishing? Audacious," Hurst said. Across the room, chorused groans heralded the end of another bout. They watched Gentleman Jackson wave a bottle of salts under a groggy man's nose.

"Might be a good way to go about it," Brinston mused. "Wouldn't set our wizard on guard. The results are generally reliable. But, with the disturbances in the atmosphere, it could set spark to tinder."

Holes in foreheads. Hughes grimaced.

* * *

A few mornings later, at a breakfast table littered with the remains of toast and tea, Margaret industriously opened her mail, mainly invitations to events. The season was in swing; scarce a moment was idle. She marveled she could go from the *modiste* in the morning to a Venetian breakfast, to tea, to a dinner engagement, and on to three balls, all without taking a breath. Wholly different from her season under her stepmother's aegis, when she'd enjoyed one and only one evening at Camelot.

"Mr. Treadway," she inquired, "would you prefer the Wellwood ball or two routs and the Opera? We have received so many invitations for the day, I fear I cannot decide."

He looked up. "Definitely the Wellwood invite. Chively would never forgive me if I left him unprotected at his mother's ball." He went back to his mail, a lighter but more officious stack.

"I forgot Lord Chively is the son of Lord Wellwood. He is unlike his sire. Imagine, at Almack's last week Lord Chively refused to dance with a single lady. He stood against the wall and sulked."

"Sulked?" Treadway rose an eyebrow. "Margaret, the man is nearly thirty years old. He doesn't sulk."

"What do you call it when his lower lip protrudes and he glares at everyone?"

"He was displaying displeasure."

"Well, I call it sulking." She opened another invitation, gilded at the edge. "Princess Esterhazy was all out of patience with him."

"What ho," Treadway exclaimed. "Here is a fine state of affairs."

"Hmmm..." She consulted the calendar at her side.

"This is from your father. Sir Denison and Lady Ridgemont

plan to go to Italy. Your stepmother yearns to see the canals of Venice. Sir Denison asks us to take your sisters in." Margaret lifted her eyebrows, her attention fully caught.

"Christine would like to enjoy the season once she is out of black gloves," he continued. "They arrive in a week or so and remain with us until your father and stepmother return from abroad. What do you say? There's plenty of room." She ran the tip of her tongue behind her front teeth.

What was she to say? "Of course Emma and Christine are welcome," she responded the only way good manners allowed. "I know my sister looks forward to coming out of mourning; Puckeridge must be dull now." She fiddled with the invitation in her hands. "What of my brother? Will Thomas come here?"

"No, your brother goes to a friend for the long vacation. At least I won't have to bear-lead him." Treadway folded the letter. "Your sisters will be company for you when I am not available to escort you around. I know how unhappy you are when I am occupied and it should be amusing to have them."

Amusing? To have her elder sister here day in and day out, when her husband had expressed his preference for Christine. Amusing. And Emma had been positively unsociable. If her younger sister's problem was what she suspected, dealing with the girl was going to be exceedingly difficult. Margaret would rather be banished to the crystal cave than balance three awkward relationships. Fate, destiny, or happenstance, she resented the position she was thrust in.

She gathered up her papers, trying to ease the crick in her neck. "I shall tell Mrs. Norris to prepare rooms. Knowing Christine, she will not await an invitation. They will be here within the week."

* * *

Five days later, they arrived. "Mrs. Norris," Margaret called, her voice echoing in the stairwell. "Call a carpenter. Oh, please, call a carpenter immediately. He must patch the frame. Oh, how did the window get a hole in it?" She wrung her hands. "All was going to be perfect. Now there is a draft in Christine's room."

Mrs. Norris rushed from the kitchen and the butler wandered to the hall from the silver pantry. "There you are. Find a carpenter," Margaret demanded, flying down the stairs. "There is a hole in the window frame as big as my thumb."

"Where, madam?"

"In Christine's room, of all places. And Papa's carriage just pulled up. They are here and there is a horrid draft in Christine's room. How did it happen?"

The butler, the malicious toad, ignored her and opened the door with aplomb. Then they were in the hall, taking off their bonnets and gloves and Margaret had to swallow her agitation.

"Dear sister," Christine oozed, "you look wonderful. Is that a new gown? But why are you wearing green? It is not your color." She grabbed Margaret's hand and twirled her. "If this is the latest, I must speed to the shops. I like those gauzy sleeves. Not that I need to conceal my shoulders as you do." Christine had discarded mourning early; she wore yellow-spotted India muslin with a double flounce around the hem.

Margaret nodded and flashed a desperate glance to the chatelaine, who, wagging her head, turned on her heel. Ignoring Christine's cattiness, Margaret turned to her younger sister. Emma, in plain white muslin, stood near the wall, about to set her bonnet and reticule on the ancient carved chair. "Emma, stop!" The girl froze, looking bewildered, as she had every cause to.

"Don't use that chair; it is a menace." Margaret hurried to her side. "The carving is wickedly sharp. If by a miracle you don't harm yourself, your attire will be shredded. Come, let's go into the solar. None of the furniture there is dreadful. Well, not much, at any rate. There is one table..." Explaining about the carved Chinese table with no flat surface to set a cup on, she ushered her family into the solar.

"Why do you keep these things about?" Emma asked. "If they are horrid—" She caught sight of the piece her sister had mentioned. Dark wood, embellished with exotic scrollwork in mother of pearl, and carved. Deeply, deeply carved. Houses, trees, and weird animals covered the tabletop. The relief was so pronounced one could search all day for a needle thrown on the table.

"I haven't found courage to ask Mr. Treadway about it," Margaret admitted. "I know nothing but it is from his grandfather's collection. My husband seems rather fond of it."

Emma's lip curled in the classic young girl's version of

'Eeeww.' "He likes it?"

"I don't think I would ask to remove it," Christine commented. "I would rather see there was an accident; preferably something involving a bonfire."

"That is not an option," Margaret said firmly. "Do as I do—don't look at it. I have found the ability to ignore what can't be changed leads to serenity." Sitting, she satisfied the conventions, discussing the weather, the journey, and again the weather. "Now, tell me, Emma—what would you care to do while you are in town?"

An owl's blink was more expressive. "I don't know."

"Impossible girl," Christine said. "She sat in the carriage and never said a word. Not one word the whole journey." She picked up a silver dish and inspected the bottom. "Emma's too young to do anything. Can't go to Court. I hope you have a slew of invitations, Margaret. It will be easier running into my friends at Camelot than having to write notes or make calls. Such bliss to be back to the social whirl."

"Emma," Margaret asked again, "There must be something you would like to do."

The girl scowled. "All right, how about the Tower? I'd like to see the Holy Grail ."

"We will go in the next few days," Margaret promised. She looked toward the door, where the chattelaine bounced from foot to foot.

"The problem is being dealt with," Mrs. Norris said with a curtsy.

* * *

Like a good hostess, Margaret gave Christine and Emma privacy. They would need to recover from the journey, arrange their personal effects, bathe, perhaps indulge in a nap. Christine could take all the time in the world, but Emma—an hour after her sister was ushered to her room, Margaret tapped on her door.

She didn't give her time to deny admittance either. With a bold hand, Margaret swung the door open and sauntered to the cheery corner fireplace, swinging her arms vigorously to loosen tight shoulder muscles. Emma was stowing bandboxes in the wardrobe.

"A maid can do that."

"I know." Emma shoved the last two boxes atop her shoes and closed the wardrobe door with a snap.

"You look tired." Margaret looked at her sister critically. "There are dark circles under your eyes. What are you up to?" Hands on her hips, Emma scowled.

"Stop treating me like an infant. I don't need you hanging over me. Pretending you care. You don't care. You left and went off to town to have fun without me."

Margaret ignored the tirade. She had heard it a number of times before. Emma had been furious she was not allowed to come out at the same time as her sister. With a fine display of logic, Emma maintained schoolroom lasses should be given the opportunity to become accustomed to society, as fourteen years was the ideal age to dance and attract a husband. 'Papa says gentlemen prefer malleable chits. Who is more malleable than I?' Emma howled.

She thought perching on uncomfortable ballroom chairs and evading the notice of fortune hunters and glossy dandies was fun. Poor optimistic girl.

Refusing to be drawn into the old argument, Margaret asked, "Have you been doing it again? That's the only thing I can think of that drains you so." She raised her brows when Emma stomped to the door. Margaret sat on a slipper chair and smoothed her skirt. "You can't avoid me, my dear. There is nowhere in this house you can hide. Outside is London. You don't know anybody. You have nowhere to go." Emma stopped with her hand on the doorknob.

She wasn't stupid. Margaret had her. "Now, tell me. Have you been performing magic again?"

Emma sagged against the door. "You know I have," she said, her face sullen against the wood.

"Why?"

"Because I want to."

With a soft exhalation, Margaret kept tears from her eyes, but sympathy softened her next words. "I can't believe you want to make spells. You hate magic. After Mama died, you said it was from magic and that you would never do it again."

"I have to," Emma murmured. A tear sparkled on her cheek.

The tear jolted Margaret's heart. Emma never cried. Something was seriously out of kilter, much more wrong than a young girl's pique at being shuffled to the background. *Thank you, My Lady, for having me approach Emma now, rather than later.*

"Oh, Emma. Come here, my dear." Her sister stubbornly shook her head and her arms open, Margaret repeated herself. "Come here." Emma's composure fractured. With a hurt moan, she flew to the floor in front of Margaret. Hugging, the elder rocked the younger as sobs choked the girl.

"Hush," Margaret crooned. "It's all right. I'll help you, whatever it is."

"You can't help. It's too much for you. I know it is."

"I will help in any way I can." The vow was made in a fierce whisper as Margaret's hands clutched the heaving girl close. "But you have to explain." The tears fell harder, the sobs grew deeper. Margaret could only hug, her heart breaking at her sister's distress. At last, the storm lessened and she mopped Emma's face.

"Feel better, my sweet?" Emma sighed, burrowing her fingers into Margaret's skirt.

"A little; not much."

"So tell me what is happening."

Leaning against her knees, Emma buried her face next to her fingers and said in a dull voice, "Once I started, I had to keep going. It is keeping her alive."

Margaret paled. Emma could not be alluding to *that.* Disbelieving, she asked, "Who? What? No, don't tell. I can guess. You are keeping Step-Mama alive?"

"Yes." The single word rocked Margaret's world. She stared at the top of Emma's head. What was she to say? "You don't like her."

"No, but you weren't there. Papa sent you and her off to London. You didn't see him." She gulped and tears marked her cheeks again. Margaret made a meaningless soothing noise and Emma sat forward, leaning her elbows on her knees. Despair etched lines into her youthful skin. "Meggie, you didn't know. You were gone. Papa was sad; I could tell he really likes her. I can't understand why, but he does."

"What caused you to start spelling?"

"It was before you left, before you had your season." Emma plucked at the rug. "Do you remember when she got sick? The doctor said..."

"He said she had a constitutional weakness and if God wanted her, He would take her. Emma, you know the rules. Mama taught them to us. She was most strict on the subject. You must not tamper with nature. Even Merlin, the greatest magician England has ever seen, hesitated to interfere with death."

The floor received a pounding. "You were with her. You didn't see Papa."

Margaret let 'Why' pass. If Emma disobeyed their mother's strictest injunction, it was done, she couldn't change it. Her efforts must go to understanding and smoothing over her sister's indiscretion. "Are you telling me you have been physicking our stepmother magically for three years?"

"No."

"Emma..." Her sister whirled on her knees.

"Meggie, she got better. Then you two went to town for your come-out."

"And Step-Mama was fine."

"She was sick again," Emma whispered. At her intensity, Margaret's hand froze on Emma's neck. "She was."

Margaret thought back. London and the sooty air did not agree with her, Step-Mama had complained, waving a languid hand at yet another invitation. Too many late nights, too many balls. She'd had little enthusiasm after the first month. Her stepmother had not been well?

"She improved when she returned to Puckeridge," she said thoughtfully.

"No, she didn't." Emma turned her face up. Tear-shot eyes and porridge-pale skin showed the depth of her emotion. "You and Papa went into Puckeridge, about a week after you got back. She collapsed. She stopped breathing. So I did the spell." Margaret stared at her sister in horror. Emma didn't blink.

"I said I was keeping her alive."

Margaret couldn't face her sister's stark look. Dear Lady of the Lake, Step-Mama had stopped breathing? Emma was keeping their stepmother alive with magic?

Here was disaster.

Chapter Twelve

After a full night of sleep, the three women met over the breakfast table. Cook had experimented; runny eggs and crunchy vegetables folded into a quiche drove them to the toast rack. Even the ham was dispirited, being dry around the edges. Margaret nibbled a piece of toast and followed it with a healthy swallow of tea, regretting that Cook's foray into the intricacies of French cuisine coincided with her relatives' arrival.

Hoping Christine would be charitable for once, she said, "I thought we could go shopping today."

"Oh, yes. I need a whole new wardrobe now I am out of blacks. I haven't a stitch to wear." Making a face at the eggs, her elder sister stirred a lump of sugar into her tea.

"And Emma deserves something pretty to mark her first visit to London." As Margaret had hoped, her younger sister's melancholy face lit up like fireworks at Merlin's Gardens.

"Can we?" Emma asked.

"You can't expect to be turned out as a debutante," Christine said.

"Something more decorative than white muslin," Margaret mused, shooting Christine a wicked look. "To show the difference between Emma's dewy youth and our advanced age, don't you think?" Christine firmed her chin.

"If you think it will improve her looks, dear Margaret, then by all means, Emma should have a new gown. Dimity is a sturdy fabric for playing in the garden."

"It has been such a long time since you were sixteen," Margaret cooed, "I daresay you have forgotten the activities favored at that age."

"I love picnics." Emma spread preserves on toast. "Colonel Gooding picked wild flowers with us at a picnic. Remember, Christine? You asked him to escort you to the meadow and the Colonel wanted me to come also. Such a gentleman; he helped me make a flower crown. The Colonel was trying to get violets to wrap around daisies and didn't notice your slipper stuck in the mud."

Emma is in for grief now, Margaret thought. Christine will never forgive her interference in a flirtation, not if Emma persists in reminding her of it. It would be better to leave them to fight the episode again without her. Forestalling Christine's next utterance, Margaret said, "I must see the chatelaine about menus. Can you be ready to leave for the shops at eleven?" She quitted the room for her desk.

* * *

Later, quarrels and housekeeping done, Christine ambled Brueton Street, purchasing gloves here, a parasol there. Margaret and Emma followed in her wake. After browsing a third shop, Emma said, "Oh, look at the mechanical doll." She pointed to a window display.

A child sat on a stool in the window, turning keys on a succession of figures, animating them. A butterfly spread shimmering wings, a rose bloomed, and a dog waved its tail and dropped a ball. Wondrous though these toys were, what caught Emma's eye was a doll, dressed in the height of fashion, twirling around a Maypole.

Christine turned her nose up at the display. "Stay and play," she said. "Madame Celeste's establishment is down the block. I am going there. I suggest you try Pierpoint's on the corner. Her designs are less expensive—and less exclusive."

"Oh, but Celeste's is the place to get a lovely dress for Emma." Margaret, with a hand on her younger sister's elbow, gave a demure smile. "This is to be special, as I said."

Christine sniffed and stalked to the modiste's door. Emma and Margaret followed. Inside, an atmosphere of privilege slapped them in the face. Their feet sank into luxurious carpet and their eyes feasted on a series of dolls dressed in examples of haute couture on tables around the room. Hushed voices made a cathedral of the place while attar of roses wafted incense from an altar table holding bolted silks.

"Margaret," Emma whispered, awed by the opulence. "Can you afford to get me a dress here?"

Overwhelmed by the lavish appointments herself, Margaret paused before she said, "Why not? I said I was going to get you something special. It can be your birthday present." With a twinkle, she continued, "Should it be from Papa and Step-Mama, do you think, or from my husband?"

Throwing herself into the spirit of the outing, Emma said, "Oh, let it be from Mr. Treadway. I like the thought of him spending lots of money on me." They shared a mirthful glance and glided into the room like swans to the waterfall.

Christine had gained the attention of a haughty woman. Already she was seated on a chair with a pattern book open on a table. Margaret caught the eye of another, less forbidding woman, who had just exited a room. The woman looked her up and down, then bustled over. Thanks to the smile on her narrow face, broadened by fashionable curls at her temples, Margaret felt welcomed.

"Can I be of assistance, *madame?*"

Margaret offered a gloved hand. "If you please. I am Mrs. James Treadway; this is my sister, Miss Emma Ridgemont. We would like a gown made for her."

Shaking her hand briefly, the woman turned to Emma. "You are not out? *Mais non,* of course not. *Trop jeune.* But I see great possibilities in you, Miss Ridgemont. You wish something *ingénue,* but with a touch of *finesse. Avec le temps,* when you do make your come-out, I will design a wardrobe to dazzle the eye. *Votre grande beauté mérite.*"

She turned to a girl standing against the wall, and snapped her fingers. With speed and grace, Margaret and Emma were ensconced in chairs, and presented with a pattern book. Out of the corner of her eye, Margaret noted Christine's scowl.

The woman seated herself opposite them. Tipping Emma's chin up with a finger, she pronounced, "You can wear the fashionable colors."

"Can't all ladies?" Emma asked.

"Certainement. Their complexions yellow." She waved that aside. "This book features *ma meilleur modèle,"* she said. "Of course, most are for *les mademoiselles plus âge,* but with a touch here and there, they can be adapted to the *demoiselle.* I would suggest this," she flipped to a page, "in muslin, *que peut,* with the *décolletage* raised. *Voila, une faire belle.*"

Margaret stared at the drawing. Not only would Emma look breathtaking in the style pictured, *she* would love to wear it. Paneled bodice, skirt liberally ornamented with fanning, the dress looked designed to be sewn in silk. It was the sleeves—a second drawing showed the genius of them. Layers of lace, each delicately Vandyked, dropped to the elbows. What lady could resist those silken cobwebs?

She glanced at Emma and was satisfied. The girl was so thrilled she didn't look to be breathing. Emma's eyes didn't blink as she said, running a finger along the lines of the sketch, "Oh, Margaret. Could I? Would you?"

"Bon, you like my *creation."* The woman beamed. Just then, the outside door banged open. A horse whinnied, breaking the hushed atmosphere.

"Madam." The booming voice belonged to a portly man in a murky green overcoat. From his less than elegantly cut boots to the bald pate shining through the thinning hair on his head, he exuded the air of a country squire floundering in a field of velvet. "Where's Madam Celeste?"

One of his companions, a thinner, more modish personage with an unfortunate florid complexion, peeked around his shoulder and gestured toward Margaret. "There she is, Sir George."

Behind the crude interlopers, Adrian Hughes hovered, a glint of hilarity in his eyes. When he saw Margaret, a broad smile creased his face and he bowed, but he remained at the door, one hand holding it. She straightened her spine, conscious of her posture.

Like a cow in a chicken coop, the 'squire' lumbered across the carpet. "Ah, just the person I want to see," he bellowed. "Madam Celeste, I need a job done."

"Excusez-moi," the woman murmured to Margaret. Standing, she faced the man. "Can I help you?"

Margaret's mouth opened in astonishment. She looked at the woman and at Emma. "She is Madame Celeste herself," she whispered. "I didn't realize." The knowledge they had been discussing a gown for her sister with the *première modiste* in London was drowned by the room's amusement at the intruder's antics and awareness that Hughes was enjoying the moment immensely.

"Yes. I'm Colby, Sir George Colby. Need you to make coats for my bitches."

Madame Celeste's back straightened. *"Pardon?"*

"I'm designing a new kennel. Brick, you know. Until it's done, I need coats to keep the bitches warm. You know what I mean." He waved a hand. "Good warm coats so they don't take cold."

"Il et pour comble," Madame said. *"Méprisable homme."* A flood of French in the most outraged tones left no one in doubt of her meaning. That Madame Celeste, the *modiste* whom the most eminent ladies begged for attention, should demean herself to make anything for a kennel of dogs beggared the imagination.

Sir George's companion stepped forward. "Not what you think, *Madame,"* he said. "Colby's pack, you know, not bitches—" He stopped, his face turning pinker. "Dogs, not women," he said. "It's a pack of setters, Gordon setters."

"I do not create for dogs," Madame Celeste said, lifting her chin.

Sir George looked dumbfounded. "You don't? Why not? Weston's doing the males. In tweed. Bring out the colors in their coats. Thought we'd go with a quality wool. Not velvet. Can't keep velvet clean. Least I can't keep my collars clean."

"Out!" Madame Celeste shouted. *"Sortez d'ici!"* She struck Sir George's chest. He fell back as she advanced, poking her finger at his breastbone. First he ran into his florid companion, then knocked a table holding a fashion doll wearing royal purple and miniature cottage bonnet. The doll fell into his arms and he convulsively clutched it.

"Give it up," Hughes said to Sir George. "I told you she wouldn't be flattered."

Sir George sputtered, "It's the best pack of Gordons in Sussex, if not all England." He waved the doll in Madame's face. Its cottage bonnet spun across the room. "Why wouldn't you want to make their coats?"

Madame Celeste snatched the doll out of his hands and swung it at him. Its head popped off and went over Sir George's shoulder, hitting the wall with the tinkle of porcelain shattering.

"Can't have them take a chill," he complained as Hughes adroitly opened the door and shoved him to the pavement outside. The other man scurried out, head down, ears crimson.

Hughes made a sweeping bow to the room, openly laughing. "My apologies." He caught Margaret's eye and winked. Then he closed the door. Madame Celeste's French imprecations petered out. She dropped the doll, made an expressive French gesture toward the door, and returned to Margaret and Emma.

Her hands stretched and curled while she stared at the sketch of the gown they had been discussing. "You like my *robe en dentelle?*" she asked, visibly calming herself.

"Very much," Margaret said. "It is perfect for Emma. But not in velvet or tweed. Also, I would love a gown of yours for myself. No one has better taste and fashion sense than you, Madame."

Across the room, a woman gave a shrill cry. "How dare you try to palm rubbish off on me? Look at it, just look at it!" She held up a length of lime satin. Margaret turned her head. From that angle, she could see sunlight from the front window through the material. It was riddled with holes.

Her fingertips prickled and Margaret looked down. As if an unseen needle punched them, holes popped onto the open page of the pattern book. Instinctively she pushed. The book flew off the table and the page scattered like *confetti fiori,* the candy coated almonds the Italians threw at weddings.

Madame Celeste covered her eyes and sobbed.

* * *

Margaret waited until the bedchamber door closed before she turned to her sister. "Emma, could your magic make holes in things?" Her sister blinked and her brow furrowed in confusion.

"Holes?"

"Yes, holes. I believe I first noticed them at home. There were holes in things. Now, with you here in town, I am seeing holes again."

"I don't understand."

"Madame Celeste's pattern book. I watched the holes form. The drawing was obliterated. Could you have made them?" Emma shook her head.

"Meggie, I didn't do it. Why would I?"

"No, dear, I don't mean did you do it deliberately. Could your magic—" she scratched her forehead. "Could holes be an—an effect of your spells?"

"I can't believe you are saying this," Emma spat. "I've never done bad things with magic. I won't listen to you—you are mean." She jumped up and brushed past Margaret, who grabbed her wrist.

"I'm not accusing you; I just don't know any other possible explanation." Margaret wrapped her arms around Emma's waist.

"Listen to me. The holes were in Puckeridge. The gazebo roof was full of them. So were the linens. There were none here, but the day you arrived, I found a hole in the window of Christine's bedchamber. Now the pattern book. There have been others; some harmless, some destructive. If you have anything to do with them—"

She shook Emma lightly. "If you are making them, somehow we have to stop it."

"But I am not."

"Could your magic be doing it without you knowing or realizing?" Margaret's urgency transmitted itself to Emma. She twisted to face her sister.

"Not that I know... Let me think." She wriggled away and went to the window, laying her fingertips on a pane of glass. After a few minutes, she said, "Meggie, I can't think of any way I could make holes. Mama never mentioned it." Margaret laid her head in her hand. Her fingers absently rubbed her hairline.

"Then what is doing it? Emma, I can't get it out of my head that you are connected to it. Your training is not complete; Mama's death cut it off. There may be something you didn't learn, some warning or prohibition about holes. If you don't know what to do, we will have to find help."

"Where?"

"A council... Mama mentioned it. A council of mages. We could ask them. Do you know—?"

"I don't know if it really exists."

"Neither do I," Margaret admitted.

* * *

Several days later, Margaret's eyes ran the length of the mirror, inspecting her reflected image. Preparing to attend her first formal Camelotian event as Mrs. James Treadway was unexpectedly satisfying, or would be if she were not concerned with holes.

Her introductory season, her wardrobe was frumpy. Tonight, her hair turned up behind with a bandeau and gentle curls at the temples, no one could say she looked off. Her gown, a deceptively simple ivory sheathe with a floating Chinese gauze overdress in pale green, accented her slender figure. Madame Celeste's seamstresses labored until every stitch, every fold in the silk gown was perfect. It slid over her curves, highlighting the best points of her figure and disguising a single flaw, a slight overabundance in the bosom. The only ornamentation was the lace on the sleeves.

Tonight, no one could call her dowdy.

She rustled, loving the feel of silk. "What's this?" She dipped her finger in a puddle of powder on the dressing table. "Agatha, when you are done there, please wipe the dresser. I spilled." Margaret nudged the powder box, turning it until she saw a cloud puff out three holes in the side.

Tensing, she flipped open another, larger box and considered the choice of jewelry. Dissatisfaction crept over her taut nerves like mold on bread.

What to wear? The sandalwood box held a strand of pearls and a set of garnets which had belonged to her mother. The garnets were delicately embedded in a fine tracery of gold, highly etched, but the stones did not flatter the gown. They were too red. The pearls were well matched, but she had worn them throughout her introductory season. Pearls were the mark of the *ingénue,* the newcomer to society. That was not the impression she wanted to make now.

She didn't want to be reminded of her previous experience in society.

Margaret sighed and picked up the pearls, wishing Papa had not seen fit to hand over most of Mama's jewels to Christine. Mama had been accustomed to wear a diamond pendant, cut in a marquis shape, which would be just the thing to flatter her toilette. Christine had taken to wearing it tangled with three massive gold chains, an overpowering display. Mama would have had the vapors.

Reminded of her mother's volatile temper, Margaret's lips thinned. Mama's rage would have known no bonds if she had caught Emma doing *that* spell. But she would also have been able to counteract the magic her guileless daughter unleashed. What could Margaret do? Margaret, with lesser ability, lacking a strong enough talent for magic to vanquish shadows, was at a loss.

She absently rubbed the back of her sore neck. There were enough worries on her plate to drive her to Bedlam. Between the spell keeping their stepmother alive and holes...

Stop thinking about it. She would not worry, not tonight.

She banished problems and handed the pearls to her dour maid, commenting, "I suppose it shall be these. I wish I had something new; I wore the pearls so often when I was in town before, I have no desire to lay eyes on them."

Agatha, from her lowly status as dresser and maid, wouldn't understand Margaret's discontent with the gleaming strand, but made no comment. The connecting door to the master's apartments opened and Treadway made an entrance.

Swinging around on the stool, Margaret faced her husband with composure. She was used to his presence in her chambers. He came in many nights, after all. He waved the maid away, took his wife's hand, and lifted her from the seat.

"You look nice," he said, "but do you really think pearls are quite the thing? You will look like a debutante, not the stylish wife of the dashing James Treadway."

Displeased, she bent one of those looks upon him. "Dashing? Try plodding."

"What! Your husband falling behind in his attentions?" He tsked, digging in his pocket. "Can't have that. Try these," he invited, laying a slim package in her hand. She opened the box. On a fine gold chain hung an elongated diamond flanked by baguette diamonds in the shape of a cross, the rage of the moment. They glittered in the candlelight.

"Oh, my, it's lovely. Just the thing to go with this gown!" She let it swing, admiring the flash of gems in the candlelight. Pure as the sea, the large diamond winked at the slightest movement while the smaller ones twinkled.

Treadway fixed the pendant on her neck in a no-nonsense manner. "Much better," he approved. "Look under. There is a second tray."

She had missed the looped ribbons at each end. Margaret lifted the top tray of the box. A pair of diamond earrings sat like robin eggs in a nest of blue velvet. She lifted them, one at a time, and threaded the wires through the small holes in her ears. She posed in front of the mirror, admiring the faceted shadows the jewels left on her skin. No, not dowdy in any sense.

He chivvied her out of the room. "We will be late."

Straightening her skirts in the carriage, Margaret said, "I have never attended a Tying of the Garter. I was at home when Papa was knighted in 1803."

"What was his quest?"

"He did a study on poor relief." She bent to untangle her hem as the carriage started forward and slid on the bench. Treadway caught her by the arm and righted her.

"I thought it would be something like that," he said. Ignoring her glare, the one that would geld a sultan, he continued, "I heard in the clubs mad King George will be in the hall to knight whoever has completed a quest. Hope he doesn't lop off a head."

"Is there a chance of that?"

Treadway shrugged. "Unless he's stark raving, it is the king's honor to slap a sword on their shoulders. If he does behead someone, you'll be far away, you won't see it clearly. It's going to be a crush, you know; always is. Everyone who is anyone, plus a great many who wish to be, will jam into the Great Hall."

"I have never been in the Great Hall."

"It's lined with tapestries, one woven by Guinevere herself. You won't be able to see much of anything but them, though you should make an effort to see the indoor fountain. It's in the middle of the hall.

"They were talking about it tonight at the club. King George or no mad King George, the Prince is in charge. Prinny named Lady Sefton Mistress of Ceremonies. *La* Hertford, who must have been his first choice, is ineligible." Margaret looked the question.

"No matter how besotted Prinny is, or how sotted with brandy, he can't flaunt his petticoat in the Great Hall. Besides being one of the exalted patronesses of Almack's, Lady Sefton is known as a fine hostess. She has the knack of designing an entertaining evening with decent refreshments, except at Almack's. No one will accuse *her* of cheeseparing."

Talking about mistresses, how vulgar. She turned her head to look out the window. The road was clogged with vehicles. If only the cream of society were invited, it still meant quite three hundred carriages were attempting to pull up under the brilliant heraldic pennants all at once and from both directions. The confusion of traffic was intimidating.

She started worrying her biggest problem, as if wiggling it back and forth would pop it out like a child's loose tooth. What to do with Emma? The girl was a brilliant magician. Mama said Emma was the strongest she knew. But she didn't have the training to control it.

When Emma overreached her capabilities before, Mama and Emma laid a spell that funneled the rioting magic into a basket.

Then they burned it. With the flames licking at the rush, her sister had sunk into a swoon. It had taken all of Mama's power to save her from death. Margaret didn't understand what had happened, but somehow, the basket had taken Emma's essence. It became part of her and in destroying it, they were destroying a part of Emma.

Mama had made it right. Both she and Emma had been drained and spent a week in bed, claiming to have taken a chill. When Mama died only a few weeks later, Emma swore it was the magic that killed her. No amount of reasoning had changed her mind. Her hatred of spell casting sank deep; calling magic forth in her stepmother's name must have been agony. Emma's magic was out of control again. Margaret didn't know what it could do, but it would be bad. How was she to counteract it? And she was neglecting her sister. She hadn't managed to take her to the Tower; she'd been so busy.

"There's Silvester's carriage. The Haverhorns have arrived and the duke don't usually come." Treadway dropped the curtain on the window at his shoulder. "Like I said, everyone will be here; no one wants to miss the event. They all want to see who will be dubbed."

The carriage turned a corner and the pennon-draped entrance to the Great Hall came into sight. Walking to their destination was gauche. They crawled forward, listening to the coachman's curses as he vied for a turn to discharge his passengers at the red carpet.

Margaret put Emma to the back of her mind. Something would occur to her. It must.

"Saw Silvester at Brooks. Amazingly, he may soon join me in the wedded state," Treadway mentioned. "Never thought he would take the step, but he is besotted. Charlotte Wentworth is the lady he has set his sights on. Do you know her?"

"Yes, I attended school with her a term or two in Bath. She was presented the same season as I."

"Ah. He's a particular friend of mine, you know. Hope to see him tonight. If Silvester does marry the lady, it's as well she already knows you. Bound to see a lot of them."

"I like Charlotte. She has a lovely singing voice. I should be glad to renew the connection." With a congenial acquaintance to look forward to, Margaret's face took on a glow which lasted until they were in the receiving line.

Arriving unscathed at the entrance of the Great Hall was

magic in itself. The *ton* prized a crush because a crowd signaled social success. This was more than a crush. A massive wave of people tumbled, rolled and crashed through the corridors of Camelot Castle, converging on the Great Hall in a flood of silk, satin and perfume. There, the tide of bodies slammed into the seawall of ritual and slid into a mannerly receiving line.

Caught by the tide, she heard snatches of conversation. "...Hole in the bowl of my pipe."

"The whole medallion came loose. The carpenter said it looked like someone had taken an awl to the edge of it."

Behind her, a querulous voice. "I want to know which of my grandsons punched the canopy. How else did it get a gaping hole? Find out, Manchester. Whichever, he is out of my will. That silk was embroidered by Lady Jane Grey."

Finally, the Treadways reached the receiving line. Lady Sefton extended two fingers, demonstrating her understanding that the new Mrs. Treadway was at the opposite end of the stratum from herself. Margaret had to smile; marriage had improved her lot. The last time she was in Lady Sefton's eyesight, the Almack's patroness found the awkward debutante totally beneath her notice.

The prince was more likeable. Around his stomach's rotundity, he kept an eye out for a pretty lass. Margaret evidently qualified for a tuppence of flirtation. He said, "Doubt I will have a chance to stand up with you, curse my fate. I will look to see you on the floor. The gentlemen should be falling over their feet to reach you." He pinched her chin and stared at her eyes before he turned his attention to Treadway. With him Prinny was direct.

"Keep an eye on the little dear," the prince warned. "She may not be a polished diamond, but there is something about her..." He actually winked as she and Treadway went down the receiving line.

The crowd surged into the Great Hall. Moving with the flow, Treadway introduced Margaret to a select few. The Duke of Haverhorn bent a keen, oddly assessing gray eye on her, the Dowager Countess of Harcastle fingered the lace on her sleeve, and the Ambassador from Italy clipped her shoulder as he drunkenly pursued a tray of champagne. Mrs. Drummond-Burrell, the haughtiest of the Almack's patronesses, sniffed disdain at her diamond pendant, but Lady Sally Jersey was kind. And voluble.

"Ridgemont, yes. Remarkable. Do you use drops in your eyes? No, that is for brilliance, not color." She blinked. "I recall your mother, Mrs. Treadway. She was gifted on the pianoforte. Much my elder, you understand, but I peeked through the door when my family held a musical evening. She quite cast the other young ladies in the shade." Chattering, Lady Jersey looked over Margaret's shoulder, nor did she allow time for a response.

"Oh, there is Mrs. Silvester. The elder, not the younger." She turned to Mrs. Drummond-Burrell. "I do hope she comes over, Dorothea," she shivered delicately. "The last time we spoke I was treated to the most horrid critique of today's manners. She can't complain about the waltz; that would be too plebian. No, Mrs. S disparages the orchestras." Her attention returned to Margaret and Treadway. "Now run along, or you shall be caught. She is deaf to all hints you wish to leave, and I am sure..."

A knot of elderly gentlemen scudded around them. Lady Jersey spun her head and accosted one. "Sir Sellair, a moment of your time, please." Waving her hand to shoo them off, Lady Jersey turned her back.

Treadway took Margaret's arm and led her into a corner. "Stay here, my dear. I see Silvester in the distance; let me bring him to you." Not waiting for a reply, he melted into the press of people.

Miss Elizabeth Cheleav, a meek dab of a woman whom she knew slightly, and a sharp-eyed chaperone bore Margaret company. "I am endeavoring to complete a fringe before my sister's marriage; I wish to edge my reticule with it," the faded lady confided. "It would lend a touch of elegance to my outfit. If I cannot finish it, I do not know what I shall do." Miss Cheleav was not the most sparkling conversationalist. Her chaperone humphed.

"They don't make things the way they used to," the chaperone said. "There is a hole in my shoe."

"Don't be indelicate," Miss Cheleav whispered. Her companion made a face.

"It isn't you must stand around all night in such a state."

Miss Cheleav pursed her lips. "The fringe is black silk, quite elegant."

Trapped by Miss Cheleav's fringe, Margaret turned her eyes to the crowd. Was it her imagination that the spangles on that shawl were moth eaten? Nonsense, spangles were metal. They couldn't have holes all over. The velvet collar next to the spangles was threadbare in places; as she watched, snippets of nap fell to the man's shoulders.

Gulping, she tried to peek over the wall of shoulders without taking in details. If another hole appeared in an item of clothing, she might scream.

Treadway was correct; the Great Hall's beauty was obscured. Under her feet lay polished Italian marble and the wainscoting at her back was carved and gilded. Shoulders and heads filled her line of sight. Above them, all she could see were tapestries—long lines of woven historical scenes lined the huge room. She had little interest in tapestries at the moment.

Lady Clarissa, daughter of the Earl of Wellwood, whirled into sight in a frothing skirt of the finest snow-white gauze. "Margaret Ridgemont," she cried. "It is you! I had no idea you were in town. Come, why are you standing here in the corner? You must meet Sir Perth—he is with my crowd. And wait until you see Janice and Charlotte—they dressed as twins for a lark. If you will excuse us, Miss Cheleav."

Lady Clarissa tugged Margaret's hand, pulling her through clusters of people. The monologue on fringes faded. They were moving too quickly to look for holes.

"Clary, not so fast." Margaret laughed. Thank heaven Clarissa had found her. Her company was livelier than Miss Cheleav's and Margaret's imagination would not run rampant. "Take me back, please. Mr. Treadway will not be able to find me."

"Mr. Treadway—who is he?"

"James Treadway, my husband, silly. I am married."

Clarissa stopped in her tracks and eyed her friend. "But it was not in the Gazette, was it? I would have marked the notice if I had read it. When were you married, Meggie mine?"

"Not a month since. If you wish to meet him, you must come back to my corner. I was waiting while he searched out a friend."

"I already know him. He had the gall to abandon you with Miss Cheleav. It is typical of a man to expect you to meekly wait on his convenience. Hah." Clarissa tossed her golden curls. "Let him come seek *you*. Besides," she towed Margaret again, "you positively must meet Sir Perth. I am determined on him!"

"But you had a *tendre* for..." Margaret trailed off. Her friend obviously had not settled on Lord Shelton. Instead of meekly waiting for James, she followed her friend as Clarissa wove through the crowd like a skiff through a busy harbor.

They becalmed. Clarissa smiled coyly at a man in the center of a large group of younger people. "Here we are," she said. "Gentlemen and ladies, you remember Miss Ridgemont, do you not? She has returned at last, only now we must call her Mrs. Treadway." She turned limpid blue eyes to one man, seeming to see only him. "Margaret is the veriest angel. We must see she enjoys herself this evening. You will dance with her, please? I know I can trust my dear friend to you, Sir Perth." Margaret noted with amusement that Clarissa had not lost one iota of flirtatiousness since their first season.

Sir Perth was tall, dressed most properly, yet with a mop of untamed hair waving about his head. He bowed with an ungainly swing of his arms. He could have been bumpish, but casual elegance overlaid the awkwardness of his movements, and nary a hole in sight. Tiny lines crinkled around his eyes.

"What a nice man," Margaret thought. "If this is who Clary set her sights on, her eyes have sharpened."

Clarissa's friend glanced at her and looked again, as if compelled. His intense regard made her nervous, but the cluster of fashionable young men and ladies fit Margaret in the middle of their set and continued their gay chatter. She listened to the conversation, replied to comments and made a few of her own, trying to ignore Sir Perth staring her in the eye. Finally, Margaret turned her back, only to meet the startled eye of a dowager in puce. That lady did a double take and stared at her just as Sir Perth had—as if she faced the Sphinx.

Janice Jackson and Charlotte Wentworth, old friends, greeted her warmly. Sir Perth Sullivan—beyond him, Margaret could hardly fit name to face. Clarissa's enthusiasm had infected the group.

"Did you hear about Lord Shelton?" one young lady whispered. Behind her, two older men discussing dogs raised their voices and she raised hers accordingly to be heard. "He was going to divorce his countess, then they made it up. My brother says they may attend this season. What should we do if we are introduced to her?" The group pondered the dilemma.

"We need a good scandal; it has been dull lately."

"You forget Enid Foster getting foxed and falling over a palm at her own betrothal ball."

"I would have if I'd been engaged to Franklin. He drools."

"Shelton don't drool."

"But his mother..."

Clarissa replied coldly. "For myself, I intend to cut her. Lady Shelton is utterly scandalous."

Sir Perth shook his head, sending his hair swinging over his ears. "No, m' dear Lady Clarissa, you are out there. Kate is most unjustly maligned. Be glad Alex opened his eyes 'fore he made such a mistake as divorcin' her. Sweet lady."

"If you say, Sir Perth." Clarissa's frown showed skepticism. "I suppose, under your influence, I shall wait until I meet her before judging."

"That's m'girl." He gave her cheek a fond tap, and glanced at Margaret again, a tiny crease between his eyebrows. Then he devoted himself to a whispered conversation with Clarissa.

While Clarissa preened under the indulgent attentions of her swain, the others rehashed what was known of the Earl of Shelton's marital affairs.

"Did she not kidnap the earl and force him into wedlock?"

"...tried to seduce..."

"He buried her in the country..."

"She probably compromised him."

Sir Perth's head came up from Clarissa's ear. "Who can believe such nonsense? As bad as when everyone said Burdick murdered his wife. She was sitting at Brighton, buying an inn and havin' a gay old time. Makes me dread havin' to inquire, anyone have the time?"

At Margaret's glance, the knight elaborated. "My stomach is growlin'. I was hopin' the supper dance is comin'. I need a lobster patty or four."

"Did you forget your timepiece, sir?" Charlotte Wentworth asked.

"Supper is always served at midnight."

"Yes, I know," Sir Perth replied gravely. "Dropped my watch nigh two years ago. Haven't managed to get it repaired." His eyes twinkled as they moved to Lady Clarissa. "Not much call for the blanged thing. 'cept when I'm places like this. Home, would just eat when my stomach insisted."

"Most sensible," Clarissa replied. She took his arm complacently. "I trust my credit with Lady Sefton is high enough to peek into the refreshment room. Shall we see if food is available?"

"Ministerin' angel." Sir Perth escorted Lady Clarissa from the group.

Janice Jackson and Charlotte Wentworth, in identical gowns of white satin with sky blue ribbons and scalloped hems, began a running commentary on reactions to their toilette.

"Madame Justine said t'would be a disaster, but the earl! He will not soon forget us."

"He couldn't decide which of us to dance with."

"Simpson coerced Captain Rogers to make up a set."

"Lord Dutton is such a gentleman, offering to spill wine on my skirt so we wouldn't match."

"Byron bowed acclaim."

"Lord Alvanley *smiled.*"

A man whose name Margaret had not caught, only that everyone called him 'Say', curled his hand around Charlotte's arm and said, "Alvanley should smile. You are the brightest candles in the room."

That moment, Treadway strutted into the group. Visibly peeved Margaret had not remained in the corner where he left her, he shouldered his way to her side. Another man trailed behind.

With no desire to face her husband in a disapproving mood, Margaret studied his friend. "Sis," the stranger acknowledged one of the 'twins'. Sister and brother? This must be Peter Silvester.

His eyebrows would improve with a trimming, but his smile was genial. What caught one's eye was bright silver. His coat buttons, engraved with hunting scenes, were as large as the saucer under a teacup. An intricate cravat and mushroom-colored velvet coat put Silvester in the forefront of the latest style. Padding inside the jacket brought his shoulders into line with a protruding stomach, making his head appear absurdly small atop a bloated body. Black satin breeches tight over ample thighs stretched down to black dancing slippers adorned with silver buckles fashioned into bows.

On the whole, Peter Silvester was a dandy.

Dandy he was, but never would he be taken for a diplomat. "Tread," the man exclaimed, looking Margaret over as he spoke. "Expected her to be rabbitty. She ain't, but she's no diamond. Got strange eyes. Sure it's worth it?"

"Why ever not?" Treadway said. "I'm shackled, not executed."

Margaret steamed. Shackled, was he? Was she worth it?

Drowning in twitters of amusement, she strove to be gracious, all the while fuming at the lack of gallantry. He could have defended her to this oaf. She would show him, she would.

"It is pleasant to meet one of Mr. Treadway's friends," she cooed.

Silvester preened. "Tread and I go a ways back. The best companion around town. Miss having him..." He blinked hard. "I say, Miss C, do you know you got Saybrook tucked tight in your arm? Not done, not done! Let him go at once."

He swung around to the man called Say, whose arm was indeed entwined with Miss Wentworth's. Silvester gave her a look of reproach, and she paled. This seemed more than he could bear; his voice rose, along with the color in his face. "Desist, Say. You ain't going to poach... Owff."

Disgusted with the lack of grace, Margaret had aimed an elbow into his midsection. Silvester bent, trying to get his breath back, as she artfully flew her hand to her mouth in horror. "I am sorry, Mr. Silvester! I stumbled a bit and threw my arm out to recover my balance. I never thought to strike you."

Janice tittered again and Baron Saybrook jumped back a foot, jostling another man. "Lord, Silvester, apologize for my indiscretion. Meant nothing, you know."

Charlotte Wentworth said, "Dear Peter—" The rest of her speech was unheard as trumpets blared and the crowd shifted. Margaret found her arm in an iron grip.

"The dubbing begins," Treadway gritted out. "Once it is done, we leave." Her lips curved in a frozen smile, Margaret nodded.

Chapter Thirteen

The assembly quieted with the silencing of the trumpets. Peering over shoulders, Margaret watched an alley form down the center of the room. Finally, she could see a few details of the magnificent Great Hall.

Not far from where they stood, also in the center of the alley, was a fountain. She had heard of it, but with the press of people, she had not seen it before.

It was small for a fountain, which made sense, it being in the middle of a ballroom. The bowl sat on a marble plinth with a base smaller than the basin, plainly designed, except for the dolphins ringing the bowl. At least she assumed they were dolphins. They were sleek creatures, like a dolphin she had seen pictured in a book. Eight leaned against the rim of the bowl, facing inward, blowing streams of water.

Oh, those dolphins. Each had its own personality. One laughed, another pensively dipped a fin in the water. The dolphin with an open book under its belly wore a scholar's cap sliding over one eye. The tassel tickled its nose.

But the miracle of the sculpture was the statue dancing around the central pillar. With a triton in his raised fist, marble Neptune floated airborne. The dolphins burbled streams of water to keep the bearded god suspended. How was it accomplished? As far as Margaret knew, magic held Neptune up.

Movement at the end of the room tore her attention from the fountain. King's archers in dress uniform, forest green coats sporting two rows of gold buttons from collarbone to waist, marched from the wide front doorway the length of the hall. The glittering progression widened the alley and the polished pattern of the floor was displayed.

The drum cadence accompanying their march, while not loud in the crowded room, beat in her blood so she did not study the floor as she would have wished. Her eyes stayed on the archers. One by one, they came to attention under an empty dais. Matched in height, the tops of their heads were even with the floor of the platform.

From her vantage point, the oval carpet on the dais looked like a lake. Its clear blue stopped at the horizon of a tapestry. Her eyes went to it and she forgot the splendor of the archers. Sometime in the distant past, someone wove a glorious scene.

A vast assemblage of nobility, knights and common people swarmed the weaving. Ladies in a wealth of brocade splashed rich color through ranks of plain garbed males. The central figure, larger than any other, was King Arthur, Merlin at his elbow. Straight and tall, Arthur held a cross of gold.

It was Guinevere's tapestry. Some historians doubted the queen wove it, citing her known aversion to and lack of skill with a needle. Others pointed to the detail of the story—how Queen Guinevere, banished to a convent for her sins with Sir Lancelot, spent the remainder of her life creating the tapestry as a penance to her liege. Tales of her burial, of scarred and roughened fingers, supported the legend. The tapestry could have depicted a dubbing ceremony if the imposing figure of Arthur held a sword and not a cross.

Age muted the colors of the scene to a hazy dream. The hall in front of the tapestry blazed with color as if it had leached off the wall. With green archers in a martial line like wind screening trees in front of the blue of the lake on the stage, the king appeared. As regal as on a paper pound note he made his way up a short flight of stairs to the carpeted dais, in court robes of purple with a glittering silver crown banding his white hair. This was Farmer George. He had fits of madness which sent him running through the countryside before dawn, but tonight he didn't look ill, only tired. Behind him was Prince George, his dissipated heir.

Prinny held a sword, the pommel in his crossed hands, aping the woven figure above his head. With ceremony, he brought the tip to the floor and a herald stepped to the front of the platform.

"Hear ye, hear ye, the tale of a knight's valor."

The king interrupted. "Brin," he yelled, cupping his hands around his mouth, "Get your arse in here." From the entrance to the hall came a response, like an echo of Priamus' plea to Gawain for help in converting to Christianity.

"Sire, please. No."

Margaret craned her neck in the other direction to see who was so bold as to deny an order from the king himself. Treadway murmured, "It's Lord Brinston," as she caught sight of him. He was a tall man, dark haired and well dressed in the stark style made popular by Beau Brummell. The assembly seethed at his appearance. Brinston paid no heed to stares, pointed fingers, and waves of whispered comment. He bowed from the doorway, making deep obeisance to his liege, but didn't move into the hall.

"Lord Brinston." The king put his hands on his hips. "We are doing this whether you like it or not. Present yourself front and center." As the audience muttered, a woman in shimmering burgundy pushed him and the man stepped forward. His chin jutted proudly, his fists clenched, but the stride that took him to the foot of the dais was firm measured.

King George boomed, "There, there, my boy, that wasn't difficult. Proceed." Lord Brinston climbed the steps as if he were going to the scaffold while Prinny huffed. The king laughed with amusement and the atmosphere lightened. People murmured. Trumpets blared and the herald lofted his scroll.

"The tale of a knight's valor, unsung to this day. This is the story of Richard Shipley, a brave soul who insinuated himself into the smuggler's den, overcame all odds, and saved the realm." As the herald extolled the deeds earning the man a knighthood, Margaret's attention wandered.

Adrian Hughes was buried in the crowd. When she saw him, Margaret felt a stir in her stomach, like the beat the drums produced. She approved the way his hair brushed neatly back from his forehead and his dark jacket molded his wide shoulders. When his eyes wavered from the stage, his nod and smile of greeting was like the sun breaking through the trees and warming an isolated pond.

She smiled back. It was too bad Mr. Treadway had taken a snit. She would love to dance with Mr. Hughes, but it wouldn't be tonight.

Her attention was pulled back to the dais when the herald finished his tale and the king's voice filled the hall. "That'll tell them, m'boy. Silly asses mumbled you were a spy when you were doing as we asked. Get up here, Brin, where I can reach you. Got to brain you with the sword." The king turned to the prince. "Hand it over, George. Steel don't make you look noble, what, what?"

Prinny looked peevish, but thrust the sword toward the king, hilt first. England's illustrious monarch wrapped a hand around the chased silver pommel and brandished the sword.

He dropped it. It clanged and Margaret, remembering Treadway's callous comment about beheadings, flinched. "Crystal cave, forgot it was so heavy." The king picked it up, using both hands, and peered at the man standing at the top of the steps. "You ready, Brin?"

"If you insist, Sire," Lord Brinston said, sounding resigned. Back straight, he knelt in the pond in front of the king and lowered his head theatrically.

King George lifted the sword and poised it over Lord Brinston's right shoulder. It wavered and Margaret gasped. What if he dropped it again? The powerful shoulders were rock still.

Prinny asked, "Did you pick a name?"

Lord Brinston wriggled like a lad caught snitching a tart. "No, Your Highness, I did not. My mother did. She thought Sir Brinston would be nice."

The king cocked his head. "What, what?"

"Her grace has a firm purpose. My lady mother wishes me to be Sir Brinston again, Sire." Lord Brinston's smile stretched a shade more brilliant. "When I misbehave, she can refer to me by my titles, 'Brinston, Brinston, Brinston.'"

A rumble of chuckles shook the sword in the king's hands and Margaret crossed her fingers as if a childish ward against the devil would keep Lord Brinston safe. The king's voice was mirthful.

"We've even heard it. She shakes her head most sadly when she says it too. That's because you're incorrigible. For the record," King George paused and glanced toward a steward, who balanced a ledger book and quill. "It's Brinston for Lord Brinston, the title he carries courtesy of his standing as heir to the Duke of Haverhorn, Brinston for Sir Brinston, the title we dubbed him with after that escapade he performed in Ghent, and now Sir Brinston again, again, again."

"If it please you, Sire." Margaret laughed. King and subject turned guilty faces toward the doorway, where the woman in burgundy stood. *She must be Lord Brinston's mother, the Duchess of Haverhorn.* She looked fully capable of scolding an aristocratic man, but nice, very nice.

For all he said the sword was heavy, King George swung the blade most competently from one side to the other of the kneeling man's head as he intoned, "For the shenanigans you perform in our service, we hereby dub thee Sir Brinston. Long may you honor the memory of Arthur and praise Merlin, long may you please us. And take good care of her grace. We don't want her wearied shaking her head at you."

Prinny tossed a garter to Lord Brinston. The grouping on the dais broke up. Brinston stood, bowed grandly and backing down the stairs, disappeared into the crowd. Margaret was sorry to see him leave. She would have loved to meet the duchess.

With the culmination of the ceremony, the crowd disposed themselves for revelry. Treadway took Margaret's arm in a firm grip and said, "We will enter this dance. Once it is done, we leave."

She acquiesced with an apprehensive nod and spent the set listening to a lecture on proper manners. Sadly, it was one of those dances where the couple stayed mostly within each other's orbit, no passing to another partner, no facing away, no escaping an irate husband.

"What were you thinking?" he said in a low, mean voice. "You struck Silvester deliberately. Unheard of. I shall send you to the country if you do not mend your ways. To offer insult to one of my friends..."

His invective droned on and Margaret sighed. Was there no relief?

* * *

Adrian Hughes leaned against the dolphin named Horatio and absently patted its snout. The misted stone of the fountain was cool against his fingers and droplets sprayed his arm. Oblivious to water spotting, his eyes were glued on her.

Murmurs rolled around the hall, lapping at ears like wavelets on the shore. The *haute ton* was intrigued by her eyes, fascinated by the fading of blue and black in mystical gypsy orbs. One rake vocally wished to dilate the black with passion. He wanted to see if black would obscure blue, the ass.

In the dowager's row, set up in front of the dais after the dubbing ceremony, old Mrs. Silvester, in a hideous shade of puce, was having the time of her life reminding staid ladies the daughter had inherited her mother's eyes. "This one seems to have skipped the fatal flaw," she trumpeted to Mrs. Pelcher. "Hasn't a feather of perversity. The mother's fits and starts—you haven't forgotten Margery locked you in the salon with that ramshackle captain that Christmas at Castle Du Lac. What was his name?"

Mrs. Pelcher giggled. "Captain Montforte. Heavens, I haven't thought about him for years. After we were discovered, he applied to my father for my hand. I thought Papa would have an apoplexy; the captain was a gazetted fortune hunter. Margery apologized later, you know. She was jealous because Denison Ridgemont kissed me under the mistletoe."

He itched to whisper a spell. Mrs. S's squawking would be more amusing covered in feathers. *Can't change her into a kookaburra. Ain't ethical. Haverhorn would wring my neck.* He couldn't do it, though Mrs. S was maliciously reviving old gossip about the flamboyant Margery Ridgemont, nee Laycock.

Alternately shocked and titillated by memories of Margery's mischievous antics a generation before, obscure grandmothers joined the doyennes of Camelot swanning memory lane. Their titters sounded like a bevy of debs ogling a Corinthian's muscular thighs.

Hughes rubbed Horatio's forehead and did what he could. Mentally he told Mrs. S to shut up. His eyes swiveled to her, dancing with her husband. That they took no pleasure in each other's arms was evident. Tread had a pole up his arse, Margaret's head tilted away.

The nape of her neck caught his attention. With her head arched away from Tread, the line of her neck evinced breeding. Finely molded bones sheathed in alabaster, with wisps of hair dusting the sweeping length like wisteria blooms on a sensuous vine. If Mrs. S was a bird, Margaret Treadway was a swan.

He clenched a fist. *Has me mixing metaphors. Not alabaster, but something watery. A serene lake with night cascading over it. I'd be the lake and she a nightingale.* He immersed the forbidden thought in efforts to produce a fitting description of the lady's attributes, but the intellectual exercise didn't block Mrs. S's remarks.

"Those eyes tell me she inherited much from her mother," Mrs. Silvester laughed, a call reminiscent of the kookaburra's maniacal call to Hughes's sensitive ears. Angry at the world, his resentment at Tread's slighting of his delightful wife coiled tighter.

* * *

Treadway slammed the front door as he rushed out of the house into the night. Gads, he was heated; he felt the top of his head might come off. How could he have thought having a wife would improve his lot in life? Here was one of his closest friends, good old Peter Silvester, treated like a blasted mushroom. What was a man to do? Bow before his wife and cut his friends? Sit at home, henpecked, because his wife did not like the man he had gone through school with? The man who had cleaved to him throughout life? No! No mere female would dictate his friends or their behavior. He would not be put under the cat's paw.

Treadway went to the opera instead. To be more precise, Treadway went to the Opera's green room, where the gentlemen of the *ton* mingled with the dancers. To his intense satisfaction, Silvester was there ahead of him, tucked into the corner with two of the new crop of girls.

"Share and share alike," he announced.

Chapter Fourteen

Later that night, in the Albany rooms designated G-1, the Marquess of Brinston shrugged out of his coat. "You can't do this solo. The Duke feels it is too important for slap-dash."

"I work better alone," Hughes objected. "You'll break my concentration."

"You know me better than that." Lord Brinston advanced further into the hall, stripping off his gloves and stuffing them into his hat. "Where are you set up?"

"In the dining room."

Throwing the hat on the hall table, the marquess laughed. "In honor of the man-eater?"

Hughes snorted. "Not hardly. I can handle her. No, it's in honor of my meal. Haven't had it yet. I can offer you a beefsteak." He dropped Brinston's coat on a chair and led the way down the short hall. "Cook's left. My man's off to hobnob with his fellows. We have the place to ourselves."

Passing through the drawing room to the section furnished as a dining room, Hughes waved to the small oval table. Two place settings gleamed. "My arrival threw you off your stride," Brinston commented. "Who were you expecting?"

"You or Sir Hurst."

"Really."

"Of course. Neither of you can resist examining this type of spell. Never could. And," Hughes poured wine from the bottle into two stems, "the council would never permit this to be done alone."

"But only two plates?"

Hughes gave a tight smile. "Two's company and three's a crowd." He waved Brinston to a chair and they sat. Serving dishes littered the table; he passed one to his guest, taking a heaping portion first. "I had Cook do up a pile of fried potatoes. Rather like them." They set with a will on the beefsteaks and side dishes, knowing a hearty meal would prepare them for the rigors ahead.

"By the Green Knight, I see why you like these potatoes," Brinston commented, reaching for the bowl and dolloping another spoonful on his plate. "I'd steal your cook just to have them again."

"She got the receipt from America. After the Round Table voted to allow the colonies to form a separate nation, her brother emigrated. He became chef for one of their senators."

"That is one place I would like to visit. They had the courage to threaten rebellion."

"Thank the Lady it didn't come to war. Blood aside, I doubt I would have tasted fried potatoes."

"When this is all over, the duke wants to speak to you about your background," Brinston said between forkfuls. "He wasn't aware you hail from the Antipodes. If you don't consider the question intrusive, how did you come to be there?"

Hughes grinned. "I don't mind talking about it. It is a story in a nutshell. I'm from Lancashire. My brother irritated our father no end. There was an explosion over something or other and my father threatened to send Christopher to the Antipodes. Flaming, my brother decided to oblige. I couldn't let him go alone. We packed up and left on the next boat."

"How old were you?"

"Eighteen."

"Where then did you receive your final training?"

"The natives. They are more accepting of magic than Europeans. For example, when I made a dingo speak in their native tongue, they laughed."

"What's a dingo?"

"A wild dog." As Brinston blinked, Hughes added, "It was a jest. The shaman was nursing a dingo pup with a slashed paw. I figured it should say thank you." As content as tradesmen comparing suppliers, they discussed the state of the art on the other side of the world for the remainder of the meal. Finally, spoons scraped bottom in the serving dishes, a single wine bottle stood empty, and the moment had come.

Brinston cleared the remains of the meal to the sideboard while Hughes bore a common wicker fishing creel to the table. It looked new, the wicker the color of wheat in the field. From the way he hefted it, the creel was heavy. "I stocked it already; thought it would benefit from soaking up atmosphere."

"Standard items?"

"Some." Hughes chuckled. "You haven't met the ladies."

"Tell me about them. It will help me focus."

"Lady Ridgemont. Bourgeoisie, with feathers in her brain. She's stepmother to Treadway's bride."

"Ever come to town?"

"Not that I am aware. She's the type to mushroom around—she'll be here next season, I assume. The second is still in the schoolroom. Sixteen."

"A dangerous age. In females, magic more often manifests itself as an ability to throw things around a room."

"She shows signs of ability—and the sullenness to work at it."

"The other lady?"

"You've met her." Brinston raised an eyebrow.

"Mrs. Martin Whitmill-Ridgemont, nee Ridgemont." Brinston groaned.

"The man-eater."

"Yes." Hughes continued, "She is Treadway's wife's sister. That is why I could not divine which lady is our culprit. They were all in residence in Puckeridge. I saw no residue on their hands, but my meetings with the young girl were limited."

"My wager is on Christine," Brinston said. "Wouldn't be surprised if Whitmill's death is attributable to magic. How many succumb to choking on a bone? He could not have been a congenial husband and it conveniently left her with a sizable fortune to play with. But why do you not suspect Treadway's wife?"

Hughes felt warm, thinking of Margaret. "She is a darling; not a tuppence of vice in her. And I found supplies. They were in her room."

"She is guilty as Mordred."

No, she is Geraint's Enid reborn. A selfless and pure angel. "So you would think. But they were in a hatbox stuffed at the top back of the wardrobe. Covered with dust. I believe one of the others put it there."

The marquess leaned his head back and traced the cornice with his eyes. His next words were gentle. "You are not allowing sentiment to influence you?"

"No," Hughes said firmly. "Meet her, Lord Brinston. I wager you will find she is the proverbial white rose. It is one of the others, but she is still represented in the basket."

Brinston rubbed his chin. "Forgive my thinking aloud. You have the full confidence of the duke—he says you are more level-headed than I—if you are not blinded by feelings for the wife, we need not concern ourselves with her." He swung the creel around. "Hopefully we will soon name the culprit."

No further setup of the scene was required. Hughes and Brinston pulled their chairs back to the table and sat. The vague sounds of life seeping into the room now muted to utter silence. Staring at the basket, they concentrated their minds.

Into the basket. Weaving back and forth, in and out, following the reeds that wove the pattern of the fishing creel. Seeping deep into the pores of the material, soaking into the creel. Stains appeared in the rushes, mottling followed the pattern of the weaving.

Hughes began a low chant. His voice swirled inside the basket, passing over and around but not touching its contents. The words made deep primal sounds, deeper than the roots that grew the rushes, richer than the earth that nurtured the roots. They swelled and ebbed, dripping strangely patterned sentences deep into the creel, merging with the fiber.

The mottling spread, soaking like wine into a tablecloth, coloring the rushes with ochre and blood. His voice intensified, battering the creel with oddly formed syllables and cadenced words. Ancient, poetic words called to the rushes, rang with the authority of ages, seduced with the appeal of mysteries that must not be divulged.

On the table, the creel quivered. Its staining was complete; the formerly wheaten color of the rushes had transmuted to earth, dark and glistening with power. Hughes uttered a single word.

"Gratiae."

He reached his hand over the creel and curved his fingers as a child asleep. Minute bits of light drifted up, catching in his hand, sparkling along his fingers. They winked, a spate of lampyrid sparks. Following the whorls on his fingertips, the lights crept over his nails. Glistening bits of nothingness tracked along his skin.

Time passed. The hand could be marble. Brinston glanced at his companion. His eyes were closed, breath light and even stirred his chest. But gradually a change came over Hughes. His skin whitened and seemed to stretch over his cheekbones. Tiny dots of frost tipped his hair. His eyes, still closed, fixed on nothing.

Brinston frowned. It was dangerous, this spell. A strong magician could become lost in the weaving. He could wander the strands, twisting and turning, until his psyche dissipated into the atmosphere.

"Aglaia, Thalia, Euphrosyne," Brinston whispered, light as light, again and again, echoing himself, calling upon the Graces to guard the magician at work. Light continued to flow, clumping in the palm of Hughes's hand, but the frost melted from him in drips. His breathing strengthened audibly until he no longer had the look of marble.

Brinston relaxed and returned his attention to the creel. Light was pouring in a steady stream, pouring up into Hughes's cupped hand as spring water for drinking. It mounded, the excess leaking through his fingers to drip up from the back of his hand. The drips flickered in the air, dancing with the joy of creation.

"Aglaia, suppetoivi." Whispering, Hughes closed his hand, capturing the light. Opening his eyes, he bowed his head. Brinston tensed again. Stretched over the basket, Hughes's hand shook. His hair hung limply damp.

Slowly the light shining on his hand darkened, twinkling in flares and dying back, only to spark again and shroud. The last bits, those in Hughes's palm, puffed a steady beat, defying the command to cease until, with a puff of a word, they extinguished.

Hughes held a perfume bottle in his hand. Uncorking it, he passed it under his nose. His eyes twitched and watered as he inhaled. A grim look settled around his mouth, he recapped the bottle and thumped it on the table. "I know who she is."

The creel, now the color of plucked rushes, fell to pieces, riddled with holes.

* * *

Treadway dragged her from Camelot before Lady Sefton officially offered lobster patties to the party. Pray no one noted how he had taken her arm—Margaret had bruises where his fingers gripped, a ring of green and pale blue above her elbow.

Patting cream on the mottled area, she contemplated her marriage. The brute was as boorish as Geraint. Delivering her home like an unwanted snuffbox, Treadway promptly went out again, slamming the paneled front door resoundingly.

No calmer, Margaret paced her bedchamber for two hours. How dare he treat her so? First, to abandon her in a corner while he wandered off, secondly to allow his friend to speak slightingly without correcting the impression he made. Hauling her from the festivities was the final straw.

He was angry, but she was wholly unrepentant. Peter Silvester was a bore, a dandy, a boor, and a fool. No wonder he was such a good friend to her husband. Like called to like.

Where was he now?

"Just like Papa," Margaret muttered. "Mr. Treadway ran away rather than have it out with me. How am I to make my position clear to the lout when he doesn't have the courtesy to stay and fight?"

She spent time punching the pillows, dreaming they were husband, father, and stepmother. Ooh, why could she not have been wed to a gentleman more to her liking? A gentle, kind, considerate man? One who consulted and cared about his spouse's wishes? Adrian Hughes, she was sure, would not be crass.

Pummeling pillows was not satisfactory. The only other acceptable outlet was pacing. She walked the room from door to window, bedpost to wardrobe, grinding her heel in the carpet to change direction. Her arms swung to a beat more martial than that of king's archers.

She came to a decision, and satisfied, prepared for bed.

All the pacing and emotion wore her out. Margaret slept late. Enjoying a cup of tea the next morning, propped decadently against the pillows, her maid bustled in with the Note. The one Treadway dashed off sometime in the middle of the night. The one telling her in no uncertain terms of his disapproval, as if she was not already aware of it.

She unhurriedly fluffed pillows that showed no sign of the abuse they suffered the night before and straightened her nightgown before opening the missive. *'Madame Wife,'* the note began in the curt terms making sure she knew her husband's displeasure. *'I find I must absent myself for a time.'* There was no need for further details; Margaret had the gist of the missive right there. Indeed, he had not bothered with further details. His signature flourished over the remainder of the page, aggressive and aggravating.

"Poor downtrodden wife, her with them witchy eyes," the maid whispered, fueling Margaret's resolve to revenge the slight Treadway gave her. "Married to that 'ere-'n-there blood, bullied and mal-treated. Next he'll lock her away and starve her. Men are devils, every last one o' them."

In the absence of her devil, Margaret hummed over tea, reread the note, and smiled brightly at the wiry maid. "I think I will wear the pink muslin today, Agatha. Would you please find the striped slippers?"

The butler was taken aback by the cheerful look on his mistress's face when she descended the stairs for breakfast. In the kitchen, waiting for a steaming plate of eggs and a muffin, he grumbled to the chatelaine, "Didn't the master storm out the door in the middle of the night? Doesn't she understand Mr. Treadway hasn't returned and what it implies?"

"I don't know what the end of this will be, Mr. Craig. The household is atiptoe, fearful of the master's annoyance," Mrs. Norris said. "Cook thinks the poor lady will spend the day weeping."

At the table polishing silver, the footman had no question as to the outcome of the contretemps. "I know what my response would be to a mulish wife—lock 'er in a closet till she were cowed," he said. "The master being gone all night is warning her. Is the mistress proper sorry, do ye know?"

"Mind your own business," Craig barked. "You missed a spot. There on the handle."

The footman grabbed the sugar bowl in question and scrubbed at it. On the third swipe, the handle broke off, falling to the table with a metallic ping. He stared at the handle in horror and the butler boxed his ear.

"Now look what you've done." Craig picked up the pieces and fit the handle and bowl together. A line of holes pricked around the tube showed why the silver had snapped. "Who punched holes in it?"

Emma and Christine failed to make an appearance in the dining room. Margaret ate a solitary breakfast of eggs and a scrumptious berry muffin smothered in clotted cream, dreamily gazing out the window toward the mews. Hunger satisfied, she spent an hour in the solar concocting menus with the chatelaine. A color-washed sea of tulips and lacy clouds drifting across a sun drenched sky urged her outside. Bless the Dutch for cultivating tulips.

"We are finished here. It's such a nice day, I believe I will go out," she mentioned to Mrs. Norris when the chatelaine had noted what meats needed to be purchased.

In the hall clutching her pad of paper and a shopping list, Mrs. Norris shook her head dejectedly at the butler. "The poor, dear lady, showing such a brave face to the world when her husband is drifting. And them just wed. That's the mark of a true lady; never show your despair."

* * *

The tulips were as lovely up close as they looked from the solar window. Margaret knelt and drifted a finger gently over nature's velvet, admiring how the individual petals layered around the stem to form perfect blooms. Her muslin gown, the same hue as the tulips, was now a favorite—comfortable yet stylish, it made her feel like dancing down the path to the mews. She should ask Madame Celeste to make up several more in a similar fashion.

Like Hamlet, the decision to take arms against the slings and arrows of outrageous fortune gave Margaret strength. Whether or not her actions would end in tragedy remained to be determined, but she no longer cringed at her husband's disapproval. It simply no longer mattered.

Later she would visit Lady Clarissa. First, she had an arrow of her own to fire. She followed the path to the mews.

The groom's mouth hung crooked. "Beg pardon, ma'am," he stupidly muttered. "I don't think I unnerstand."

"Of course you do, my good man," she said. "I dislike the animal and wish to be rid of it. I want it gone this morning. Take it away. I suppose Tattersall's is the proper place."

"But...that's Mr. Treadway's new stallion, ma'am," the poor groom nearly stuttered. "He spent a lot o' quid to get 'im. Had to outbid half the gen'lemen in Lunnon to do it."

"Then Tattersall's should have no difficulty disposing of the animal. *Now,* Todd."

She watched the confused groom saddle a second horse and lead the magnificent stallion out of the mews. A single tear bumped over the furrows in his weathered cheek. Satisfied, she went to change. She and Lady Clarissa had a lot to talk about.

* * *

The crowd grew louder by the second. Today was one of the days set aside for the famous Tattersall's auction, when the gentlemen of the *monde* bid and overbid, all to obtain the best horseflesh. A surprise entry had everyone agog. The crowd swelled greatly as word spread to the clubs of what was happening and gentlemen hied hither to not miss the excitement or the bidding.

Some of the gentlemen frequenting Tattersall's were out to find the best horseflesh money could buy. Prepared to bid and bid high, their exhilaration knew no bounds. Others were more interested in scoring over rivals and enemies. Those men mentally checked their bank accounts, hoping to bid. Some were avid purveyors of gossip. Rather than bidding, they eyed the crowd. Their minds calculated relationships. One relationship in particular was being dissected by all.

"Why is he selling the beast? Is it something to do with his wife?" In varying construction, the words echoed in the barns, around the ring, and through the rooms of Tattersall's bloodstock auction house.

The stallion was famous no matter how one parsed its bloodlines. Sired by Sorcerer of the venerated Matchem line, it won every race it entered. Magnificently formed, marvelously healthy, and a proven stud—what more could the avid horse lover want? If the steed had been fashioned of gold, if it came with the Grail tied to its bridle, it couldn't be more valuable.

Pandemonium reigned. Most of the men lusted after the horse; many would have given a mistress her *conge* to afford such a beast. Whoever bid highest was going to be a happy man.

Of the men milling around Tattersall's premises, a few—a very few—were intimate friends of James Treadway. He was the target of the gossips. One or two of his friends had seen Tread in the Opera green room last night; they knew he was back to his old haunts. Thank Merlin leg shackles hadn't kept the man down. What they did not know was why old Tread was selling off that stallion. Hadn't he been delirious when he topped Sir Hurst's bid? Hadn't he bought a round for everyone in Cribb's Parlor to celebrate? Hadn't he vowed the stallion would be the pride of his stable, raced and bred? Why was it being auctioned off two months after he won it?

Still white and shaky after his labors with a fishing creel,

Adrian Hughes did his best to take the horse off the block; he knew there was something wrong. But Tattersall's proprietors refused to cooperate. The horse was delivered by Tread's groom; everything was on the up and up. With the taciturn servant's doleful acknowledgement the horse was meant to be sold, Hughes had to back away. The crowd would have mobbed him if he interfered further.

He sent a frantic message to his friend by way of a loitering lad.

Late that morning, Sir Hurst was a very happy man. He actually paid less for the stallion than he had bid two months before. As he left to pay a delayed visit to his club, modestly accepting congratulatory slaps to his back, Sir Hurst wondered why Treadway had changed his mind about the thoroughbred. He had been determined on owning the stallion.

Hughes's lad was still running around town, looking for Treadway.

* * *

The people enjoying the sunshine on the banks of the Serpentine didn't care about horses. They were governesses, nurses, nursemaids and children from nearby homes out to catch what fresh air was available in soot-laden London. They did care when a cloud formed. Out of the clear blue sky, over their heads and no others, a dark, nasty cloud popped into existence. It blotted the sunshine.

Tommy Rowe, wheeling a hoop along the grass, squinted against the sun one instant. The next time he blinked, he was squinting to see through the gloom. In confusion, he stopped running. His hoop teetered.

It started to rain—big, fat globs fell in an area only about ten yards in circumference. Tommy wasn't in the magic circle of rain, but his hoop was. A drop splashed, then another. With a sizzle, his wood hoop broke into pieces.

Women screamed, children cried. They ran, all except babies, who were snatched up and jolted to safety. Once everyone scrambled far enough that no rain drops spattered, they jabbered. Where a blue blanket had been spread for a baby to lay, now a woolen rag, full of holes, sagged in the grass; a pram's rattan hung in tatters off a metal frame.

No one was harmed, barring faces and arms splotched with small burned areas resembling freckles. Tommy broke into unmanly tears at the loss of his hoop.

Meanwhile, in a discreet private dining room in an obscure hotel in Greenwich, James Treadway flicked sweat from his eyebrows. Still, he was pleased, indulging in a little healthy exercise. His powerful muscles, nurtured by years of holding back restive mounts, never trembled as he held her over his seated body. The minx had lost her clothing willingly. Now she squirmed, positively anxious as he clamped his lips over her protruding nipple. He wafted her gently over his exposed member, sucking hard, teasing himself and the little flirt with the merest taste of what was to come.

This was the umpteenth encore; Tread tested his endurance with an undemanding partner, willing to do whatever he liked to earn her coin. No sass, no problems.

Minnie squirmed, trying to lower herself on the poised rod.

Finally, he took pity on her excited whimpers and set himself to the task of satisfying them both. Releasing her nipple with a final lick, Treadway lowered Minnie by degrees, sliding his throbbing length into her sleek, dampened depths. His view of the room faded—he concentrated on hennaed hair, painted face, and voluptuous body. He rocked in the chair, pushing deep, taking pleasure from his opera dancer.

Minnie was perfect. She didn't know how to please, but worked at learning. It was an unexpected bonus that Treadway, rather than just taking his ease, did his utmost to ease her also. It was not an easy chore, it being yet another encore, but he finally managed. Eight times in eight hours wasn't easy.

Rocking, rocking, rocking finally brought Minnie to a burst of pleasure and with a sigh, he followed. Brow dotted with perspiration, he pumped his seed into the convenient receptacle.

After, he closed his eyes. How he loved the feel of breasts against his chest. She wasn't bad. If he could get her to tone down the cosmetics, perhaps Minnie would be a good choice to fill the little house on Spring Street. Thank fortune he had not disposed of the *pied-a-terre*. Many gentlemen felt the need to divest themselves of their mistresses when they wed, but just as many found it convenient to rejoin the game after the nuptials.

By gad, he would show Margaret who was in charge. His rod stirred. Thank Merlin—or lusty Lancelot—he was good for another go.

Two hours later, after he finally tore himself away from Minnie, Treadway was white around the mouth and red in the ears, but he didn't sack the groom. It wasn't the poor sod's fault. Todd's eyes were red from weeping. It broke his heart to lose that horse. Besides, Treadway knew whom to blame.

* * *

At the same time Todd cried into his master's shoulder, Clarissa set Margaret right after laughing until compelled to clamp a hand over the stitch in her side. "Positively *everyone* was green with envy when Treadway topped Sir Hurst's bid for the stallion," she chortled, spilling the tea. "That's the one you ordered sold, Meggie, in case you didn't realize. Seeing the steed on the auction block raised a frenzy of speculation—the gossipmongers are out full force, racing from house to house to spread the tale. I've heard from no fewer than three friends within the space of an hour."

She mopped tea from the tray with a handkerchief and handed Margaret a cup. "Adrian Hughes was at Tattersall's, trying to stop the auction."

"By the grace of the Lady, Treadway's stable is full of horses. I selected the stallion only because it was in the back box," Margaret said, pulling out her own handkerchief to mop up the tea her friend splashed in her saucer. As she unfolded it, her finger poked through the middle. With a shocked blink, she inspected the hole her finger had made in a new handkerchief. Hiding a frisson of fear, she blotted the spilled tea, balled the handkerchief up and threw it on the fire. "I didn't realize the horse was special."

Clarissa laughed harder. "I would hope not. Your husband might strangle you for this." Her teacup tilted, bathing the tray and table again. Then she sobered. "I'm sorry, but you did go too far, dear. Firmly tamp down your pride, Margaret, in a higher interest. If you don't do something conciliatory, and right away, Treadway is likely to send you to the Antipodes, wherever they are."

Margaret sighed. "I know. I'll have to eat humble crow, dusty though the taste is. I intended to teach him a lesson, not send myself to Coventry. Nothing is going right. I neglect Emma, also. I wish she were of an age to attend events."

"I thought you took her to see the sights."

"I am supposed to take her to the Tower. Every time I ask when she would like to go, Emma makes an excuse. My sister wants to stay home. It is worrisome."

The butler opened the door and announced, "Miss Honoria Silvester, my lady." She followed on his heels, swinging a beetlewing embroidered reticule.

"I am glad to find you at home," Honoria said. "Lady Clarissa, I need your assistance." She turned her eyes to Margaret with a snap. "It is good to see you back in society, Mrs. Treadway."

"Oh, please do not be formal. You never used to." To Margaret's dismay, Honoria donned an air of reproach.

"You left the Great Hall without saying goodbye. I thought you meant to cut your old friends."

"I never meant such. That was Mr. Treadway's fault."

"Come have a cup of tea," Clarissa said cordially. Dropping the frosty attitude, Honoria patted Margaret's hand and fussed her skirt into the last remaining chair at the tea table.

"Thank you, dear," she said. "Tea is most welcome. I have been out and about these last three hours."

Clarissa raised her eyes to the butler. "Another pot and cup, if you please," she murmured. The butler bowed himself out of the room and she directed her gaze at Honoria. "What are you up to, Honoria?"

Margaret could not help but smile at Miss Silvester's response. "I have been visiting," Honoria said grandly. "I left cards at the homes of no less than five of the *ton's* most avid collectors of art. Lord Alvanley received me in the breakfast room. He wasn't interested," she said with a pout. "But Lady Blackwood thought Lord Blackwood may be intrigued. The stupid man is in Vienna. I doubt he will be useful."

She turned a brilliant smile on Clarissa and Margaret. "This morning has been fruitless. I decided I need your assistance." She sat back on her chair with an air of finality. "I meant Clarissa, but you may help, Margaret. We must plan a campaign."

"Plan what? You are being as mysterious as Lord Brinston." Clarissa played with the spoon in the sugar bowl. "What do you need us to do, Hon?"

"Why, sell Peter's paintings."

Margaret passed a plate of cakes, noting with surprise that her neck didn't twinge. For the first time in many a day, her neck did not feel like an anvil hung from it. She turned a blessedly loose shoulder toward Honoria. "Peter's paintings?"

"I did not know your brother was an artist," Clarissa said.

Honoria simpered. "Of course you didn't know. He has kept it a great secret. My brother is on a campaign of expanding his horizons. Painting in oils was his project last year. The year before, he made a walking tour of Camelot. Poor boy, he won't be comfortable until those paintings are gone. If our grandmother should see them, she will be most irked."

"But why should you sell them?"

"Peter hasn't been able to. Someone must." The butler interrupted, carrying in another tea tray. The ladies waited patiently until he arranged the offerings on the table and removed himself from the room.

Clarissa poured a cup for Honoria and passed it over. "I like the thought," she said. "I can think of any number of places to sell art work."

"You have not seen the paintings," Margaret pointed out.

"It is of no moment." Honoria waved her tea cup. "I bow to your superior knowledge, Clarissa. Where were you thinking of?"

"Ackerman's," Clarissa said promptly. "Failing that emporium, there are a slew of eclectic shops scattered around town. One of them should take your paintings. It is but a matter of approaching the proprietors. There is one..." She giggled. "You would enjoy going there, both of you. It has a stool made from an elephant foot."

Honoria smiled. "Excellent. I knew you could not fail me."

"I am not sure I should," Margaret said. "If Mr. Treadway objects..."

"Then you sell another of his horses," Clarissa said.

"Old news," Honoria said lightly. "There is much more interesting gossip to impart. Did you hear of the disaster in the park?" She was delighted to pass on a new *on dit*.

Chapter Fifteen

He never mentioned the thoroughbred to his wife after all. When Treadway stalked into the solar, stopping only to change from his crumpled evening wear, ready to blast the chit to hell and beyond, he was confronted by a pixie in Nile green muslin. Confound it, she threw her arms around his neck and wept. What was a man to do? He wrapped his arms around her and kissed her forehead. For Arthur's sake, he could have wrapped his arms around her twice, she was so small.

"I am sorry," she wailed, but he had forgotten the subject. His wife leaning against his chest did funny things. His member, sated by Minnie, stirred again. Rubbing helped. He rubbed.

Mayhap having a wife would do him well in the long run. He only had to teach her what to leave be, where her place was, then Margaret would be the ideal wife. Especially if she had no objection to a bit of lovemaking in the middle of the day. Treadway closed his eyes as he tasted her mouth, sweet as honey straight from the hive.

A stallion he hadn't had time to race no longer seemed important. An overly made-up opera dancer faded from his thoughts. Sex was his avocation; it took precedence over everything else.

Loving the feel, he rubbed his genitals against her again.

"I freely admit I was wrong to cut your friend at the Great Hall last night," Margaret cried into his cravat. "Will you forgive me? I don't know what came over me." She stretched to pepper tiny kisses along his jaw line, then dragged her breasts across his chest. Her belly crushed the lengthening rod in his pants. Sometimes crushing wasn't bad.

Standing was difficult with blood running high and legs weakened by desire. He moved her to the sofa, seating her on his lap where he could better explore the tantalizing figure.

Savoring the aroma of aroused female, Treadway forgot his horse, the unlocked door, and the butler's name. Other parts besides his heart ached, reminding him of the prime benefit of wedlock: instant access. The marathon efforts of the past hours with Minnie might never have happened. Margaret's bodice was rearranged, his cravat half undone. He itched to loose more tabs, unbutton more buttons. There was entirely too much material between them.

Unfortunately, social obligations allowed no time for a spot of sex.

The butler stood in the doorway, hopping from foot to foot, face red, eyes darting from disarrayed clothing to the window. Chances were he did not need to use the chamber pot. From the look of it, he was more likely to announce the house was afire. Skirts around her knees, her dress off her shoulders, James' flap was at half mast, what the flap hid was fit to fly a mainsail. Besides, a massive fire was the only excuse acceptable for the butler's interruption.

"Go away," Treadway ordered in a thickened voice.

The butler nervously cleared his throat. "Mrs. Silvester, the elder, awaits you in the drawing room." He stepped back and closed the door on his finger. Everyone winced and the butler mewled.

"Thank you," Treadway mumbled. "We will be right there." He ran a hand down his face. It bounced off Margaret's bosom and bellybutton before it reached the trouser flap. As he fumbled with buttons, he bellowed, "You, there—see the lady is served tea immediately. You know her views on hospitality."

Taking a deep breath, he used both hands to try to straighten the mess he had made of Margaret's hair. "Mrs. Silvester, the elder," he muttered. "She is Peter Silvester's grandmother and a fiercer dragon you will never see." He gave up on tangles and tugged at the rag around his neck that had been a starched cravat. "She is called the elder to distinguish her from her daughter-in-law and her granddaughter-in-law, who is the 'younger'. Autocratic as Mord...anyone. Silvester warned me she was to call. Slipped my mind."

Margaret, not accustomed to squelching the fires of passion, attempted to uncross her eyes. She was to meet someone *now?* She reached to tie tapes and button buttons, which threw her pelvis firmly against Treadway's groin. They groaned in unison.

Five minutes later, he ushered her out of the solar, rolling his eyes. "You would not believe how that *grande dame* rules. No, your dress is fine, she don't care what rag you sport. She'll cut up about it no matter what you have on. One of her specialties. Offered only one compliment in the last decade. She was pleased Sir Perth Sullivan didn't burn Oxford. Furthermore, that is the highest compliment anyone expects for the foreseeable future."

"Yoo hoo." Christine's voice floated down the stairwell, warning them her feet were floating down the steps. "Someone has arrived."

"I know," Treadway said. "Mrs. Silvester."

"The younger?" Her skirt still floated, but Christine froze in an attitude: young maiden caught by fear.

"The elder."

"Oh. Well, I don't want to see her." Christine didn't float up the stairs, she stampeded.

Treadway watched, hoping ankles would flash, then turned his eyes on his wife. "Mind your tongue. She cuts them out and eats 'em for dinner." Craig opened the drawing room door.

"What ho, Mrs. Silvester, we come as commanded." Treadway was at his most dashing. "You order and I leap to obey." He grabbed the lady's claw, lightly kissing the gnarled knuckles.

Margaret was not as ignorant as her husband seemed to think. Her husband was sucking the knuckles of one of the dreaded doyennes of the English nobility. Never mind that she had no title; Mrs. Silvester was intimately connected to every one of the families claiming twigs on the heraldic tree of Arthur Pendragon's Round Table. Her antecedents encompassed the vastest fortunes in the land. She was the only lady in all of England who could claim to be on a first name basis with the queen.

The week before, she had tweaked the prince's ear in the Park. In front of the entire *ton* she scolded him for slighting her in favor of Lady Hertford. Prinny, self-indulgent hedonist that he was, apologized humbly for his misbehavior and creaked a farewell to *La* Hertford. He stuck out one coat-covered sausage arm for Mrs. Silvester to hang on and escorted her to Hookham's as she commanded. Never mind it was after hours; the doors of the closed shop opened for the dragon and her rolly-poly St. George. Mrs. Silvester wanted a book about birds.

Margaret, who could barely string two thoughts together after Mr. Treadway's sexual play, teetered in *the* presence.

Grinning at having her hand slobbered over, the prince slayer chided Treadway for neglect. "I am most displeased," she pronounced, looking an inch more majestic than the queen. A black bonnet, edged with silk flowers in eye popping red and topped with a two foot long ostrich feather, threatened to slide over the crow's feet slashing her cheekbone.

"I should have known you would neglect to present your wife to me. That I should have to come myself to make her acquaintance—shame on you, young man, neglecting your elders. My grandson told me her name. Margaret Ridgemont. Humph. I know the family."

This dire pronouncement held Margaret still when she would have curtsied prettily. "I am sorry if you are disappointed, ma'am. I was under the impression Sir Denison is well regarded."

"He is, he is," Mrs. Silvester grumbled. "But Treadway could have done better. And your dress is creased.

"Well," she continued with a sniff, "it only goes to prove my point. I ate my beef at the Amboy's. They dragged out their children to sing for us. Can you imagine? Children are not to be brought into decent society. Most vulgar." She settled her reticule at her side and reached for the teapot cooling on the table at her knee.

"Of course, when my children were young, it was perfectly proper to parade their virtues. They sang like angels. Duke Kay had tears in his eyes. Nowadays, people should know not to do such a thing."

Treadway glanced at Margaret, indicating the chair to the left of the sofa. She sat poker-straight as if her mother's backboard was strapped under her arms. He casually took the matching chair to the right and crossed his legs, hiding the excessive bulge below his waistcoat.

She hoped he suffered. Her blood still thrummed unpleasantly.

"There was an occurrence in the park this morning. "Mrs. Silvester poured as if she were in her own drawing room, handing Margaret a cup of tea with cream. Margaret detested cream. "A strange story of burning rain. Hysteria, that is all it is. No one has ever heard of rain falling in only a few square feet—and for it to burn holes in blankets? Mere delirium, no truth to it whatever.

"Treadway," she changed the subject, "Have you taken my advice yet? You should have quite a collection now." She turned rheumy eyes to Margaret, who squeezed her thighs together, trying to ignore the message of her deprived body. "He collects buttons. Everyone should collect something; gives them an interest in life." She poured him a similar cup of creamed tea. "Have you found any interesting specimens? Or are you so busy with your new wife that you neglect buttons as you neglect me?" Margaret prayed the old lady's knowing glance didn't mean she guessed what she had interrupted.

"I did not knowingly neglect you, my dear Mrs. Silvester. Silvester did not tell me you were in town. I thought you were still in Bath, else I would have been on your doorstop, as well you know. How are the upper rooms?" Treadway adroitly turned the conversation.

"Aha, it is my scapegrace grandson who led you astray. I came to town a week since. General Amboy took the waters. Which is why I had to bear with those tuneless tots. As for Bath, my friends are become bores. All they do is sit around and discuss their aches. Who wants to do that? Everyone gets aches. They would do better to go to the shops and forget their knees and backs. They attend nothing but the concerts in the lower rooms. Except the two who died. Lost two of the girls I came out with. Wait until you are my age; you will have plenty of pains, but if you have interests, you can forget them and do better than concerts." She fastened a gimlet eye on Treadway. "Buttons? How goes your collection?"

He shrugged. "I had my valet pull buttons off some old coats. They are around somewhere."

"Do better," the old lady ordered, passing Margaret a plate of macaroons. "Check the trunks in the garret for your mother's old clothing. She dressed well enough in her youth, though her wardrobe never made the most of her figure. Your father's things you can ignore. He had no eye for fashion." Mrs. Silvester made a face as she bit into a macaroon. "Too dry.

"You need an interest to carry you if you are to live as long as I. Or General Amboy," she chuckled. "He still has the quills I suggested *he* collect; uses them too. Says you can't find quills like you used to. They don't sharpen as well as when he was young. Must be the way the animals are raised. Fed differently or something."

Mrs. Silvester set down her teacup and began drawing on her gloves. "I shan't stay, just wanted to let you know I had not died, not like Persis Naughton and Hermoine Butler. You may come for tea on Thursday." Rheumy eyes fastened on Margaret. "Sally Jersey will be there. It won't harm you to become acquainted. With that hair of yours, you should do well enough. More, I will take you up in my carriage tomorrow at five. Make certain your maid does better with the iron before then."

"Thank you, Mrs. Silvester," Margaret managed. The old lady may be a dragon, but she was a true eccentric. One mustn't take offense at the commandeering of one's drawing room or time.

Margaret opened her mouth the minute the door closed behind Mrs. Silvester. "Mr. Treadway," she croaked.

"I know. I tried to warn you."

She cleared her throat. "You will attend when I go for tea. There is no way I am going to brave the dragon's lair alone."

"No, the invitation was to you."

"She knows your family..."

"Tea is for ladies..." Across the room, a candle fell to the floor, leaving a stub in the candlestick. Neither noticed.

"The *ton* will note your neglect. It will reflect badly..."

"Shall I yap through town as your lapdog?"

The argument was in full force when Christine walked in. She looked straight at Treadway, like a collector finding a Rembrandt in a second hand shop. Treadway's answering smile made Margaret burn. If they were going to flirt, she would...she would...

Like any good collector, Christine got close to the object of her fascination as she asked, "Did you enjoy your visit?"

"You know Mrs. S," Treadway replied. "All noise. You dodged an invitation to tea."

"Thank my lucky star." Christine brushed an imaginary speck of lint off his arm.

Another candle fell out of a candlestick. Margaret noticed and stalked to pick it up. Rolling the beeswax taper in her hands, she contemplated throwing it, but she couldn't decide who she wanted to hit. Instead, she laid the candle on the table and watched her husband drool over dear Christine.

Slings and arrows—she had a quiver full. Margaret would paint the library. Like the undertow of the waves on the beach at Brighton, her mind began debating colors while she watched her sister's fingers climb her husband's sleeve. The look she sent Treadway promised the issue of the tea party was not abandoned.

Gilt on the brackets of the walnut shelves would brighten the room.

"It was delightful to meet Mrs. Silvester," she said.

"Oh. Well, to each her own cup of hemlock. I am glad I missed her." Christine smiled intimately at Treadway. "She does not approve of me."

"She approves of very few," he consoled.

Margaret rose and brushed at one of the worst wrinkles on her skirt. "I will be in the garden. There are vases to be filled. There must be something suitable in the tangle behind the house."

"I saw a blooming bush or two." Christine wove her arm through Treadway's. "I hope you don't mind if I appropriate your husband. I have a question." He lifted a brow, but didn't object. Margaret closed the door gently. Definitely, the library must be painted.

* * *

Treadway leaned against a convenient chair back and rolled Christine in front of him. Locking his arms around her waist, he asked, "You need me for something?"

She laughed lightly. "Yes, I came to London for a purpose. It has yet to be fulfilled."

"And that was?"

"You." She coyly slid her arms around his neck. "Kiss me."

"As long as you ask. A gentleman likes to be asked first." He covered her lips with his and began a leisurely exploration. She wanted it to go further, he could tell, but after Minnie sated, Margaret heated, and Mrs. Silvester dashed his desire, Treadway was not in the mood for a tussle. He nipped, licked, and allowed his hands to wander, but kept the mood light.

"I think I love you," Christine whispered. His response was automatic.

"Dangerous words. You shouldn't say them." She pouted and slid her palm down his front. Self preservation fell out of bed and yelled, *"A moi."* He stepped back out of danger.

He had enjoyed the kiss immensely, but did not like her confession nearly as well. The widow loved him? That was not good, nor was it the impression he wanted to make on the delectable lady. Tickles and frolics, that's what he was after. He backed further away from cuddly Christine and made a neat escape.

Punctiliously, Treadway retreated to the miniscule garden, where he offered his arm to Margaret.

"Done?" she asked, straightening up from a bed of something spiky. "I thought my sister would hold you for hours."

"She only wanted to ask about a horse," he lied.

Rattled. He was definitely rattled. Gentlemen discussed horses. Christine wasn't sure which end consumed hay. With a gracious smile, Margaret handed her husband the basket. The chump almost looked glad to hold it as she cut branches to arrange in a vase and slid the unwieldy stalks past the curved handle.

She managed to poke him in the face twice, the first time accidentally, the second taking a bit of doing.

Chapter Sixteen

They came into the drawing room like twin cyclones, dropped their hats on the Chinese table and swarmed over Margaret. "You liven up a dull day," she said, laughing at the air of suppressed excitement clinging to her visitors.

"Emma, may I make you known to my friends, Lady Clarissa Chively and Miss Honoria Silvester. They are kind, but you must beware they do not draw you into mischief. Clarissa is a firebrand. It was she who smeared blacking on the balcony rail when I played Juliet in the school play."

Emma curtsied and Clarissa enthusiastically spun her in a circle. "You remind me of your sister, though I'll wager you can do Juliet and not forget Romeo's name."

"I am pleased to meet you, Miss Treadway," Honoria said, pulling off her gloves and waving them. She was like a bubble of soap caught in the breeze. "You look like you could do with an outing. We have come to make you go with us. Charlotte Wentworth and a number of gentlemen are coming also. Her brother has gone for her in another carriage so it isn't a squeeze, but Perth is waiting outside. He stopped to talk to your neighbor."

"Explain, Honoria," Clarissa ordered. "You sound like Maria Wentworth, all half thoughts and sentences."

"No, Maria does worse. Don't you remember her explanation to Squire Michael of why she had the key to my brother's flat? Not one word out of three made sense." Honoria spun to face Margaret. "Maria is the sweetest creature but even Michael admits she is a ninny. And they are to be wed, if Maria can ever convince her father Michael is eligible. Well, he is eligible, since his father is a duke, but Maria's father doesn't see it that way. Michael finds her perfectly delightful. His devotion is inspirational."

"Why did she have the key?" Emma asked.

Honoria blinked, as wise as a wren wrestling ravens for a worm. "I gave it to her. It was an excellent place to hide from the Bow Street runners."

Clarissa interrupted, "That is not important. Can we get on

with it? Poor Perth has been left outside forever."

"True. We want you to come with us, Margaret." Honoria ticked on her fingers. "Let me see, the party is Charlotte, Ernest, Adrian Hughes, Sir Perth, and us. We are going to the shop I mentioned, the one with the elephant foot stool. You will come? You don't want to miss it." She draped her gloves over the carved dragon's head. "Miss Treadway, the invitation includes you."

"Please, call me Emma," she said shyly.

"Of course, no formality is necessary."

"Emma, I daresay you will like the African dolls. Their heads are shrunken. Positively ghoulish. Come Meggie, don't dally." Clarissa took Margaret's embroidery and folded it. "Today is gloomy enough without toiling over sewing."

"Give me a moment to neaten my hair," Margaret said. She looked forward to seeing Mr. Hughes. "Emma, do you wish to come?" Her sister nodded.

"I'd like to see an elephant foot."

Clarissa flicked the dragon's talon on the table. "Get your bonnets. Honoria and I will wait for you. But hurry. We don't want to keep Perth waiting."

* * *

As the Silvester barouche stopped in front of an old warehouse fitted with a broad window and weather-faded door, Margaret asked, "Is this about your brother's artwork, Honoria, or are we only to enjoy the curiosity of an elephant foot?"

Honoria straightened her bonnet. "I do plan to ask the proprietor if he would like to purchase the paintings. But that need not concern you, Meggie. Coming to an agreement on price should only take a few moments. Emma, take your sister in hand. She is making this excursion a conspiracy."

"I see the others," Clarissa interjected. "Their carriage just turned the corner." She pulled her head back in the window and reached to open the door. "Oh, Maria and Squire Michael are here also."

Ten people crowded the pavement.

Judging by embraces, Honoria and Charlotte Wentworth had not met for years. Sir Perth and Lady Clarissa revolved around them and Emma, greeting Lord Chively, Maria Wentworth and her beau, a gentleman named Michael who looked a great deal like Lord Brinston, the man knighted at Camelot. In the melee, Margaret found her arm taken by Adrian Hughes.

Introductions were breezy; Honoria pulled Emma forward and ran through names. "There," she finished, "now you know everyone. Can we go inside, please?"

Charlotte was distracted from thoughts of exotic wares. "Lord Michael, what do you know of the rain that fell in the park? It burnt people."

"Ith it a thign from the heaventh?" Maria Wentworth's lisping question brought a frown to Lord Chively's face. "I mean, like manna. Manna fell from heaven, didn't it?"

"Manna was good. This rain sounds evil."

Sir Perth said, "Been thinkin'. The rain made holes. Anyone noticed holes in odd places?"

"My mother's orphanage committee discussed holes yesterday," Clarissa said. "Lady Du Lac had to throw away her Wedgwood teapot. She was serving Princess Lieven and dribbled tea down her skirt. The pot had a hole in the spout."

Uninterested in holes, most of the group turned their attention to the windows of the shop. Hughes could have kicked Chively when he said, "Mrs. Treadway, your husband's tack fell apart t'other day. Riddled with holes."

"I didn't know." Margaret shared an alarmed glance with Emma.

"Not to worry, dear lady. He was outside his—" Chively stopped abruptly when Hughes growled.

Margaret wondered what he had been about to say, but Hughes, his hand on her elbow, diverted the group's attention. "What, are we to stand on the pavement all afternoon?"

"Yes," Honoria said firmly. "Let us enter. I wish to speak to the proprietor." The Wentworth sisters tucked Emma between them, but perversely, no one made a move to the door.

Maria nodded with enthusiasm. "I brought the remainth of my pin money. Mith Ridgemont, you mutht look tharp. I require a brooch to go with my new eau de Nil paithley thawl."

"It is Pomona green, Maria," Charlotte corrected.

"Ith it? There are tho many greenth thith theathon; thea foam, apple, olive, pea—and that one that lookth jutht like turtle thoup. How am I to keep them thtraight without getting hungry?"

When the man named Shipley said, "Leave it to me," Chively's face went from cranky to devilish. "What do you know of fashion, Squire Michael? You been outfitting a ladybird?" Maria looked alarmed, but her beau laughed.

"No, I escorted my sister to Pierpoint's. Lady Coletta wanted my advice." Squire Michael turned to Maria. "Letta got a pelisse in eau de Nil. I'll recognize something goes with that color."

With Squire Michael to supervise, Hughes didn't think Emma would get into trouble. Not wanting to share her attention, he unobtrusively pulled Margaret out of the group.

"The shrunken heads are to the left," Clarissa said.

"And the foot—the elephant foot?"

"In the window." With oohs and ahhs, the ladies crowded the store front, admiring gray wrinkled skin and mottled nails as big as a man's hand. Spying an intriguing Chinese screen with red lacquer panels farther in the building, Margaret whispered, "I don't wish to stand on the street staring like an urchin. Let's go in."

"After you," Hughes said. Leaving the others to enter or not, he pushed the door open. It creaked and a bell tinkled. Aisles stretched in three directions. Straight ahead was the screen, but Margaret was no longer interested in it. The counter facing the door, piled with a range of curious objects, caught her interest.

"What is this?" She picked up a long stick with of all things, a hand at the end. "Look, Mr. Hughes, it has rings on its fingers."

He didn't stand as close as he wished. "A Chinese back scratcher. It calls me Adrian, as I wish you would."

She raised mirthful eyes and he was lost in misty blue. "A back scratcher speaks to you, A-Adrian?"

"Inventive, ain't it." Taking a deep breath, he broke the link of their eyes and gestured at the wall to the side of the door. "I like the mirror."

"In the shape of a violin. It would look handsome in an entrance hall."

"The scroll is lopsided." Adrian's eye fell on a glass case a few steps down the right hand aisle. "What is this?" He took Margaret's elbow and moved her forward.

"Bizarre," she pronounced.

He crouched, bringing his eyes level with the case. "Bizarre, yes. But look, my dear. The scales are clear." On a velvet pad lay a skeleton perhaps the length of a forearm. Blackened as any set of old bones, with sharp teeth and beaklike nose, the monster was a wizened creature with bulbous head on a thin neck, sinewy arms ending in thickened talons, and emaciated rib cage. What was most fascinating was that below the ribs was the scaled body of a fish. "It is supposed to be a mermaid, I suppose."

"Mermaids are pretty. That is gruesome."

He flashed a grin up at her. "You mean the romantic tale of mermaids is pretty. This...I wonder, is it wood? It looks like a real skeleton. You know, I might purchase this."

"You have not progressed much beyond the age of six. Little boys have atrocious taste." She wandered to the next case, ignoring his, "I've improved with age—I collect snails."

"Now, that is more attractive." A jewel box, in the oriental style, with simple flowerets bordering the lid, teetered atop a domed clock. Fronting the box was a foo dog with a fanned tail and a silly red nose.

"You have refined taste. Too bad the corner is damaged," Adrian commented. "Look in the back of the cabinet. You may like that." Margaret breathed out a delighted sigh. Another foo dog, this a creamy stone, poised in profile. Its head turned to the front with an impish expression. The coloration of the stone slashed a darker line into the mouth, from which the dog's tongue lolled.

She smiled at him, turning Hughes's insides to mush. "You are getting older by the moment," she said. "But there should be another, shouldn't there? Foo dogs come in pairs."

"So they don't get lonely, like the mermaid. She looks like she wasted away without her merman. He reached out and touched the tip of her nose. "Keep looking. You will find a treasure worth the keeping." Inside, rolling in the mush, his heart expanded and contracted, thumping with love, though not for a mermaid.

They walked deep into the shop, hearing peals of laughter and the mumble of the others, but not crossing paths with them. Everywhere they looked, they saw amusing, interesting, or gruesome items, though he swore up and down the mermaid at the front door was the worst.

Suddenly Margaret stopped. "Look," she said. "Adrian, come away from those swords and see what I have found." She reached up to a shelf, then turned the object like a jeweler appraising a priceless ruby.

When Hughes reached her side, he saw she held a midnight

blue beaker, rimmed in gold with an etched tracing of bluish leaves. Monkeys climbed, tumbled, and played among the profusion of leaves. One audacious creature hung from the delicately wrought golden vine circling the cup's middle. Below the hanging monkey, a gold bangle circled the beaker, this one beaten nearly flat and scalloped like a crown. The base was another band of molded gold, with simple piercing and a richly detailed golden vine below.

"My word," he said, stunned. "Let me see, sweetheart." Margaret handed the vessel to him, and he turned it around and around, admiring the intricate adornment. Inside, he cringed. He had called her 'sweetheart.' It slipped out, natural as rain. Bless whichever god protected fools she didn't take him to task for it, as if endearments from his lips were a matter of form.

The mush around his heart lumped. The subtle aroma of violets made him breathe deep.

"It is old," she said. "It reminds me of the drawings in illuminated manuscripts."

"Yes, but in pristine condition. The rim is unscratched." He ran a fingernail around the beaker. "No dents, either. This is a real treasure." He looked from the piece to Margaret. Leaning an inch or two, he could lay his lips upon hers. He ached to do it, to kiss the woman he had come to love, but he couldn't.

She was wed. Margaret was wed to his friend. Former friend, he reminded himself. He had determined to abandon a friendship that stretched more than half his life because James Treadway didn't appreciate what he had. Tread had fallen into a bed of violets, if he would but stop and think. But, no matter how Tread acted, Hughes would never violate the sanctity of the marriage vow. Not even to possess Margaret.

"Would you like it?" he asked, soft as a kitten's mew. "A memento of this afternoon." Misted eyes turned to him like lotus blossoms turning to the sun. She nodded, her face pure. He couldn't help himself. He lifted the finger he had run around the rim of the beaker and swept it across her lower lip, along the darker edge, from corner to corner. *Delectable.* And damnably innocent, despite marriage.

She froze inside. It wasn't his offer to purchase the beaker that made her uneasy. It was the knowledge he was close enough she could feel the warmth of his breath wafting across her lips. She *wanted* him to touch her. She wanted a kiss. As if she had commanded it, Mr. Hughes—Adrian—stared at her mouth.

He ran his fingertip along her bottom lip. It was a whisper of a touch, a lover's promise of delights to come. She would give her soul to press a kiss to that fingertip, but she didn't dare.

It was wrong. No matter how heavenly his caress felt, it was wrong, wrong, wrong.

May the Lady strike her. She was no better than Guinevere, lusting after her husband's friend. It wasn't just wrong: it was wicked. As wicked as Guinevere's passion for Lancelot, nearly as wicked as Mordred's attacks on King Arthur. Margaret's life had not been entirely blameless—she had behaved badly on rare occasions—but this was different. Wanting Adrian surpassed thinking bad thoughts of her stepmother. It rendered meaningless the theft of gingerbread from behind Cook's back.

Want him; dear Lady of the Lake, she needed him. Her heart quaked. He would not denigrate her for disliking his furniture. He wouldn't permit his friends to insult her. Rather than callously taking her in the marriage bed, *he* would love her...

It was wrong in every way.

She wanted his kiss so badly she ached. Calling on every precept ever learned, Margaret didn't kiss Adrian's finger. Instead, she froze. Though she didn't respond in any way to his touch or to the desire she saw dancing in his eyes, her soul leapt the gap between them. It settled in his heart, there to remain for eternity, leaving her bereft.

She stepped back, a tiny step away from heaven. Taking his cue from her, his finger dropped. He stepped back also. They turned toward the front of the warehouse, paying no attention to the jumble cramming the shelves. She was silent, grieving.

At the case holding the mermaid Adrian handed her the beaker. "I think I need a souvenir as well." She knew what he meant without asking before he leaned over the counter and fished the statue out. Lifting it, he turned it back and forth with a bemused half smile.

"This is something to collect. I'll have to find more. A whole lot better than a pail of snails."

"The maids won't dust it."

With a shrug, he said, "I'll toss her in the Thames to get her clean."

It jolted her senses when Perth and Clarissa emerged from

behind a massive cabinet, both chuckling. "Hughes, Mrs. Treadway, look at my find," Perth called. Margaret didn't glance at the man at her side. Wrapped in the silence of despair, she waited for the other couple to come abreast. Perth cradled something in his arms.

Chuckling, Clarissa complained, "Meggie, Sir Perth is mean. He saw it first and insists he will keep it. Make him give it to me."

"What is it?" Margaret crinkled her nose when Perth waved another mermaid in front of her.

"By Avalon," Adrian said, "You have my twin." He held his mermaid up next to Perth's.

"Marvelous," Clarissa breathed. "Mr. Hughes, you should give yours to Sir Perth. He would have matching bookends."

"And nightmares," Margaret murmured. Inwardly, she howled with pain. She shouldn't have come on this outing. She should have stayed home and mended sheets, or worked in the account books. Drat Papa and her stepmother; she was married to the wrong man.

She would have dusted the mermaid herself.

Sir Perth and Clarissa's commentary on the shop and its contents masked Margaret's quiet to all save Hughes. Keeping an eye out for a salesperson to complete their purchases, he mentally kicked himself. *Too forward by half. She is not Harriette Wilson's sister, you ass.*

Slowly, he became aware of Honoria's voice. It echoed along the corridor. As she was a lady, he hesitated to say she yelled, but her voice was not well modulated.

"...never been so insulted. All you need do is promise to take the blasted things. I would give you the funds to purchase them. It is simple. If you do not wish to cooperate, fool, you need only say. But my brother is a fine artist, not a—a forger. It is his initials on the paintings, PS, not PS. Vile slanderer." She swept out through a door to their left, her color high with outrage.

"Miss Silvester's errand does not prosper," Hughes commented. Margaret nearly touched his sleeve, but she drew her hand back as if he were unclean.

"Poor girl. She only wants to help her brother." Honoria sailed down the aisle like a frigate ramming a pirate's prow, waving her arm wildly when she saw them.

"There you are. Come, I want to leave this instant." She

marched toward the front door. "Meggie, this was a dreadful idea."

"But—" Margaret protested, hurrying after.

Hughes called, "Wait in the carriage. I will collect the others." Sir Perth paused, the ladies hurried after Miss Silvester. He shook his head at Perth and calmly turned into the office, finding a little bandy-legged man wiping his brow. "I wish to purchase these items. Wrap them separately—I will take them with me."

In the carriage, Honoria beat a fist against the door frame. "That monster, that vile man," she spat. "If he is not interested in Peter's art, he could say so. Meggie, you will not believe what he said. He accused Peter—my brother—he accused him of signing Paul Sandby's initials and trying to pass his paintings off as his own. As if Peter would do such a thing. Peter is so honest he drove all the way to Sussex to return Sir George's toothpick. Now I ask, is that the act of a man who would steal someone's initials?

"I should lay a complaint with the constable." She flounced on the seat. "Just because Peter and Mr. Sandby have the same initials. Oooh, I could call the worm out and put a hole in his heart."

The others streamed out the shop with little ceremony. Lord Chively's breeches were ripped at the knee. Squire Michael dragged a large package to the carriage, saying, "I say, Honoria, you don't mind taking this in with you, do you? I'll put the other in our carriage." He unceremoniously opened the carriage door and hefted the bulky package up. It barely fit the width of the car. Honoria eyed it with disfavor.

"What did you buy?"

Michael grinned boyishly. "It's a guillotine. This package is the base. I've got the blade and stand in the other." At Margaret's faint "Oh," he said, "Not for me; for my brother, Brinston. A group of the farmer's wives at the Castle make quilts to sell in town; this should do a dandy job cutting the material."

"Rather than smashing our toes," Hughes said, "You should arrange for a carter to pick it up."

Michael braced himself against the roof. "I would, except something's put the proprietor in a filthy mood. Said to take it with me or I couldn't have it at all. Dashed disobliging. What else am I to do?"

Maria poked her head under Michael's upstretched arm. "Did Michael tell you? It ith tho exthiting. A guillotine. It wath behind the tree fort. Lord Chively climbed all the way to the top. He caught his breeches on a nail and tore them."

Emma danced up, a becoming flush in her cheeks. "We should come again. I could get all my Christmas presents here; there are enough gold chains to bring Christine to her knees, Meggie."

"I saw a tiger rug," Charlotte announced. "I dug my fingers into the fur. It isn't very soft, but the tiger's skin is striped."

"I wonder if someone went on safari." Clarissa, on Perth's arm, glowed. "In the back was an elephant saddle. I vow three horses could have been strapped to it. Gold braiding went along the edge and it had tassels as long as my arm hanging from the corners. Above the braid were jewels. From their size, they had to be paste. No self-respecting horse would wear such a gaudy thing."

"Don't know," Perth drawled. "Tame for Prinny's cattle." Hughes clapped him on the back.

"You are certain the jewels were paste? The Indians mine incredible stones. With his extravagance, some Maharajah might have had beauties from his treasure chest set in the saddle."

Perth shook his head. "One was loose. Foil on the back. Sorry for it; would have bought an elephant. Love to have an elephant."

"What would you do with an elephant?"

"Ride to hounds."

* * *

When they returned home, Margaret ran upstairs and put the beaker on the mantel in her room, moving the clock so her gift from Adrian could take pride of place. He was thoughtful to purchase the beaker for her; as he said, it was a memento of the perfect outing. She would never tell and he couldn't know she would treasure it above a tiara of rubies and gold.

What a shame he could be no more than a friend. He would be an excellent husband.

Adrian was handsome; nothing clashed, nothing put one off. What would his hair feel like under her hand? She closed her eyes and imagined. Hmm, silky. Thick. Her fingers ran along his temples, where two or three strands of silver promised aging would be kind. When he went completely gray, Adrian's head would shimmer like a merman's scales gliding through the water. She thought of his mermaid and smiled. When a knock came on the door, it startled her.

"Yes?" The door opened and Emma came in.

"Meggie, you have been sequestered in your room for half an hour. I expected you to come down for tea. Christine is in the drawing room, queening it over some of her friends and I don't want to face her alone." Emma walked to the fireplace. "Why do you still have your bonnet on?"

Half an hour? Margaret sighed and pulled on the bonnet ribbons. That is what she got for building air castles around Mr. Hughes. Time slipped away.

"Are we going to do the spell now, or do you insist on tea first?" Emma fidgeted with the ribbon at her waist. "I'd rather get it done with."

"Certainly. Let me put my bonnet away." Margaret moved to the wardrobe. "Where is best, Emma? Here, your room, the library?"

"In my room. I have everything there already." Emma hurried her along, tossing her pelisse and gloves on the bed rather than allowing Margaret to put them away. "I am anxious to get to it," she mumbled, pushing her sister out of the door.

It took a chair for Emma to reach the shelf. She pulled a hat box from under the others, risking an avalanche of clothing out of the wardrobe, handed it to her sister and roughly shoved the other items back on the shelf. Her agitation was plain.

"Meggie, I don't know this will work." She climbed from the chair and dragged it across the room.

"We have to try." Margaret set the hat box on the tea table. The box lid was cracked; when she touched it, it fell to the table in two pieces. She waved a hand under her nose. "Whew, these spices are rather pungent, aren't they?"

"No, they are old. I gathered them after your season. Don't touch—there is henbane. You can't touch it, it is bad for you." They shared a look, then Margaret lifted two black candles from the box and set them in the holders she had waiting by. A rough bit of heavy twine coiled in the box. Emma removed it and wove the length around the candles, forming a circle.

"What else?"

"Thorn apple leaves, nutmeg and rosemary."

"And henbane." Margaret sighed. "You are the expert, Emma. Do we need the spoon?"

"No, not yet." Emma pulled the chair to the table. "First, I am going to lift the spell. Then I will do what I can to close the holes." She raised worried eyes to her sister. "I don't know what this will do to our stepmother."

"We won't know until she and Papa write or come home." Margaret pulled the second chair forward. "That is the benefit of this situation. Step-Mama might die; she might be fine. What will be, will be and you will not have to watch. You took on a far greater task than you should, dear. At least, with her in Italy, undoing whatever damage you did will be beyond your sight."

Emma's shoulders hunched. "I'll worry."

"A spot of anxiety is better than continuing this course."

"Thank you," Emma said scathingly.

"Do not speak to me so." Margaret slapped a hand on the table. "You were the one disobeying Mama's directives. If you had behaved as you should, there wouldn't be holes popping up all over."

"Shut up, Meggie, or I won't do this."

"Fine." Margaret fisted her hands. "Exactly what are you going to do?" Giving her sister a dirty look, Emma lit the candles from a plain beeswax taper.

"I don't know if having Step-Mama in Italy makes it harder to affect the spell. I am going to use the candles to focus. Otherwise, it is spelling like I always do.

"Don't interfere," she warned. "Your puny magic skills would only muck me up."

"Get on with it." They did not speak again. Emma lowered her head in an attitude of prayer, her lips in a thin line. Margaret watched intently.

Nothing happened—at least nothing seemed to happen. Emma sat, Margaret watched. After a period of perhaps fifteen minutes, Margaret bit her lip, fighting the urge to make a comment.

She happened to glance up. Smoke from the candles wreathed the ceiling. There seemed to be more smoke than two candles could account for. Not only that, smoke never wreathed in quite this way. Smoke didn't form a wreath, not a wreath one could reach up and twirl.

Emma did. She raised her head, stuck a finger in the air, and twirled the wreath clockwise. It darted away from her, sliding to the window. There it hovered. She followed. The wreath tried to slide around her, but Emma hooked it with her index finger. She walked to the table, the smoke wreath writhing around her hand. Setting it down, she whispered, "Meggie, put the candlesticks on the smoke."

Shaking, Margaret did as she was told. The smoke flattened and lay on the table. Emma bowed her head again.

Margaret blinked and the smoke was gone. There was nothing on the table. Emma reached into the hat box and using the silver spoon from it, sprinkled brown crumbles on the table where the smoke had been. She picked up the box and tilted it to get all the aromatic bits. When she was finished, there was a layer of organic matter in a circle. She sprinkled a bit of liquid from a flask on the circle; Margaret caught the tang of brandy.

The clock chimed the quarter hour. Emma took the silver spoon, and with a deep breath, began crisscrossing the circle, dragging clumps of henbane into the center. There, they piled up and glowed, not the orange red of fire, but golden, with bits of sky blue streaking through. Emma's spoon hovered, she cocked her head, and sketching a sign in the air, whispered a word Margaret could not catch.

The gold became bronze, the blue a thin, uneven spattering of white, like fine sugar unevenly sifted over a cake. Margaret's stomach clenched when, wielding it like a hammer against the anvil, Emma banged the spoon on a cluster of white. Particles flew into the air, forming a cloud. A cloud, a real, honest to goodness cloud, hung over the table, casting a shadow on the henbane.

Emma methodically hit the white areas and they transformed into clouds. An unfelt breeze drifted them over the candles. As they passed over the candle flames, one by one, the clouds puffed into nothingness. Fascinated, Margaret watched them disappear. When the last was gone, she looked at the table and gasped.

The rope circle encompassed liquid bronze. A storm raged. A fury of molten metal crashed waves over the candle bases and licked at the rope. It seemed the spume would fly over the twine; deftly, Emma swung her spoon to block it and the wave subsided into the sea of bronze. Again and again Emma set the curved bowl in place; again and again the waves fought to escape their bounds.

It was a frightening spectacle. Margaret shrank back in her chair, afraid the bronze would splash her. Her eyes darted back and forth, following Emma's movements for an endless age. Her sister's face was tense, the muscles in her cheeks pulsed with effort while her body swayed, hand sprinted. It was primal battle, Margaret realized.

Emma, the creator, commanded. The sea, disobedient as any child, squalled defiance. Who had the greater strength: the bronze sea, immutable in its chaotic churning, or Emma, a half-trained, immature nursling of a magician?

Slowly, the waves subsided. They crashed against the rope sea wall marginally lower, the center of the bronze sea calmed. A tide sucked bronze away from the twine and the sea gathered itself. For a moment it swelled, then the bronze whooshed in a wild effort to escape the rope. Margaret's breath caught; Emma would be defeated; there was no way for her to stem this wave. A wall of bronze five times the length of the spoon's bowl surged to the rope. Dear Lady, her sister would fail.

Emma held the spoon out, bowl up, like a beggar seeking alms. Bronze leapt the rope, flew through the air, and splashed into the spoon. Miraculously, it clung, filling the bowl, not a drop overhanging the silver rim. The wizard's mouth moved silently and the bronze shrank into itself. Slowly, unwillingly, the bronze formed a pearl which rolled gently off the spoon onto the table.

The pearl sat in the middle of the rope circle on the wood. Not in the middle of a bronze sea, not floating in a molten cauldron, but on the wood table. Emma pulled the black candles from the candlesticks, blew their flames out, and threw them in the hat box, following them with the candlesticks. Gingerly, she made a neat coil of the rope before tossing it on top of the candles. Excepting the pearl, the table was clear, but not clean.

Henbane, thorn apple leaves, nutmeg and rosemary had disappeared as completely as the clouds and bronze sea. The table's wood surface, smooth and nicely polished before Emma began her spell, was pitted in a circle where the rope had laid. The bronze had taken a toll after all. Holes much larger than pin pricks went around the circle with random gouges thrusting splinters up. Stabbing the table with an awl and beating it with a chain would have done less damage.

Emma sighed and sat in the chair. The spoon clattered to the floor. She looked like she had swum the sea with wisps of hair plastered to her forehead, sweat streaming over her cheekbones, and a white line around her tightly closed lips. She looked exhausted.

"What do you do with the pearl?"

"Throw it away." Emma pushed hair from her forehead. "There is always something left over; as a duck dinner leaves the duck's carcass. It is worthless."

"So is the table." A tentative finger swept around the circle confirmed the table was ruined. Rubbing one gouge which could have been made by the kick of a horse, Margaret glanced at the clock. How much time had elapsed while her sister beat back the waves? Her back was stiff and sore as if the waves had battered her more than the rope.

As Margaret turned her eyes to the mantel, the clock chimed the quarter hour. No time had passed.

Chapter Seventeen

Good riddance to her, Treadway thought as Emma slipped out the drawing room door. He didn't believe for a moment she had the headache. She probably had been in the brandy. The brat looked flattened, a sure sign she had imbibed more than was wise. That would be a knock for his oh-so-uppity wife, to learn her precious sister tippled. The pair of them was worthless.

Come to think of it, Margaret didn't look much better. Her hands still rested on the pianoforte keys. A key tinkled; had a tremor in her fingers, did she?

"I suppose the rain has Emma bedeviled," he said. "With the heavy downpour, all London's plans for the night are blasted."

Margaret's voice was low. "Perhaps it will be over by morn."

Christine gave the throaty laugh that made him instantly stiff. "It may rain all it likes. This is cozy, just the three of us. How shall we amuse ourselves?" Oh, he could think of a thing or two to amuse the little widow. He opened his mouth and caught Margaret's eye.

The witch. The look was naked; either he stayed away from Christine or his wife would go crying to Papa. Turning to gaze out the window at the rain-washed street, Treadway carefully tucked his fist behind his back. Until he came up with something to spike her guns, he must beware. There was more involved now than momentary pleasure with the widow and punishment for the sheep his father had thrust into the fold. Treadway had found another mark.

Eyes on the rain, he turned his mind to his latest scheme. This year, with Wellington's men pouring into England, footloose from the end of the quest for the Ark of the Covenant, there were plenty of opportunities for a man sharp enough to snatch them. Look at the chump he had stumbled over, Captain Frampton. What funds Frampton had left after financing a captaincy in the ranks of questing knights were sunk in speculations. He couldn't finance the life of a man about town. Creditors snapped at his heels. In short, the man was ripe for plucking.

Frampton had given up the lease on his townhouse and moved his most precious possessions to lodgings on Cannon Street not far from the docks. Not a nice location, but Frampton had fine art. His father purchased the paintings, he told Treadway. If auctioning them would gain him some coppers, he could immigrate, probably to America. Coppers? The chump wouldn't recognize a Fra Angelico if someone hit him over the head with it. Any fool should know it instantly: the figures surrounded by fire, the soldiers fleeing in fear, the wall with the seated red figure of authority.

When Treadway conducted the auction for Frampton, *Cosmas and Damian Are to Be Burnt Alive* would sell for a few coppers. To himself, via an agent. Then he would resell it. The painting was worth a bloody fortune.

For now, he required peace at home.

A rainy evening with the widow thrusting her bosom to his notice, not to mention the finger a wedding ring would encircle, firmed his resolve. He wouldn't put it past Christine to create a scandal to force him to divorce Margaret. Wouldn't the Pater love that.

"Shall we play cards?" he asked. Christine took up the invitation.

"We can play whist. Margaret, you could use the practice. Your game is not what it should be. Perhaps you will finally learn the difference between spades and clubs." Treadway laughed and Christine gave her sister an arch glance. "I will win. I always win against Margaret."

"I don't care to play tonight. I promised crochet patterns to Miss Silvester." Margaret politely declined. "Why don't you play backgammon." She was encased in ice; he wondered how he had offended this time.

"I adore backgammon," Christine averred. "You may have black, James."

Margaret rose to leave the room as his body rose to the occasion. "The patterns are in the sewing room. It is too much bother to bring them here. If you need, I will be upstairs." He made to stand and she waved him down. "No, don't interrupt your amusements." The door snapped closed behind her.

Ten minutes later, Treadway had convinced the widow to *count,* rather than guess how many pips the dice allowed her to move. "You should try to keep your checkers in pairs, my dear. It's too great an advantage to me to have your blots on all the points." He slid a black onto the space occupied by one of her singles, and moved the red checker to the bar.

"Ohh, you put me in prison, you naughty man. When I get out, I will have to do the same to you." She leaned over the board and he stared where nubs pushed against the thin muslin of her gown. The nipples of the widow's breasts were hard and thrusting and he hadn't even touched her.

Two moves later, five red checkers sat on the bar. He tried to avoid capturing more of the widow's blots, but was hard pressed not to. His home board was rapidly filling and Christine was fated to lose. Badly.

"You will have to claim a forfeit," Christine whispered, again leaning over the board. Her bodice sagged and the barest hint of rosy pink appeared, the rim of what he knew was luscious strawberried womanhood. "We neglected to set a wager. Would you like to do so now?"

Those nubbins were there, just below the edge of the muslin, pushing like fingers against the material. Fingers, that's what they needed. Fingers to roll them, pinch them, worship them. To hell with Margaret and the Pater. "A kiss. What else would I wish?"

"Now, James, before Margaret comes back." In accord, they rose and stood before the fire. A checker fell from the table and rolled across the floor. Its rattle thumped in the otherwise silent room until it came to stop with a clatter against the edge of the Turkish rug. His mouth descended hot over the widow's curved lips. Working to hold back the desire flooding him, Treadway nibbled and sucked at the same time his fingers delved into the bodice barely concealing Christine's charms. Yes! Her breasts were taut, the tips furled and begging to be touched, as they should be.

Her arms stayed at his waist, allowing him to push muslin off her shoulders. He bent his head; fingers weren't the only part of him aching to touch her nipples. As his lips slid over one quivering breast, Christine's fingers found their goal. A groan wrenched out as the widow squeezed the hardening rod in his breeches. She wrapped her hand nearly all the way around, stretching the knit, and leisurely slid up and down. Up and down, down and up. Each down stroke pulled fabric across the sensitive head of his rod and her clever hand squeezed at all the right moments.

The caresses nearly brought him to his knees. He nipped Christine's nipple and ran his tongue up her chest, under her chin, and back to her mouth. There, he imitated the moves he wanted to make. In and out, hard and fast. By Arthur, to lay her on the floor and crawl under her skirt...

Treadway froze. On the floor. In the solar. They were in the solar, where Margaret could enter any moment. His wife. Her sister. The widowed sister who claimed to love him. What the hell was he thinking? He pulled back like she was a column of fire. The gilt mirror on the wall opposite the fireplace flashed candlelight in his eyes; he blinked hard.

"Come." Christine sighed like a siren, reaching again for his breeches.

"Uh...no." His brain felt like mud. He shook his head. "We c-can't do this," he stuttered hoarsely. "Not h-here."

"Come to me later. Tonight." He shook his head and hurriedly pulled the material of Christine's gown back over her shoulders.

"I have to go," he said awkwardly. Just as awkwardly, he quitted the solar, nearly falling over the low table to the right of the door.

Treadway's rod was so sensitized, it was difficult to use the stairs, but he managed. Christine may have a magnificent body, but Margaret was his wife. He couldn't seduce her sister under her nose. His father would disown him. He'd ruin him in society.

All the effort of marrying and putting up with a wife would be wasted. The auction might be cancelled and he'd be out a fortune. A bloody fortune.

If he tried hard enough, he could find more to admire in Margaret. *Lovely hair, not black, with glints of amber buried in it. It is always in a knot, with only a few of those irritating curls around her forehead. Shows some small amount of taste. And her complexion is clear. No spots. Well, that should do it.*

With the thought, he eased the material around his still eager nether parts. He had two options: Margaret or Minnie.

Minnie, definitely Minnie. He didn't want to touch Margaret.

Chapter Eighteen

A boy in blue livery swung his legs from a tree branch. "What you doing?"

"Go away," Hughes said. He peered toward the distant path, lining the sights on where his intended victim would be. A brougham was so high, she was so tall.

"That's magic you're going to do, isn't it?" He was faintly scruffy, the brown-haired boy in livery.

"I said to go away." *That should hit her smack in the middle.* He braced the tripod legs with dirt. Digging in a burlap sack, he pulled out a fringed silk sash.

The boy swung his legs again. "I wouldn't, if I was you."

Irritated, Hughes snapped, "Wouldn't what?"

"Mrs. S don't like magic. She sees you doing that, she'll take your head off."

He straightened. "Who said I was doing magic?"

"I can tell," the boy said, his chest swelling with pride. "You're getting set to do it. Not a good idea. Not with Mrs. S around."

"Firstly, if I was going to do magic, what makes you think I would permit you to watch?" He endured the time honored glare of youth disgusted with adult thick-headedness. Freckles ran down the lad's nose, smeared like beauty marks laid on with a pencil.

"Mrs. S don't like magic. And no one had better do what Mrs. S don't like."

"Then it would be infinitely safer for you to leave," Hughes suggested.

"Don't want to. It'd be something to see magic. You a magic maker?"

"Magician."

"They say magic makers are bad. Are you bad?"

Hughes wrapped the sash around an apple on top of the tripod. "If you won't go away, you might as well make yourself useful. Hand me the knife. In the sack, boy."

"You aren't going to stab me, are you?" When he didn't respond, the boy said, "Right. Didn't think so." He slithered off the branch, dropped to the ground, and rummaged in the bag. "I'm Tom."

"Can you handle a knife, Tom?"

"I can help?" Hughes grinned at the boy's enthusiasm.

"Dig a round hole in the middle of the apple. In about the depth of your fingernail." Hughes knotted the end of a rope; this he stuck firmly into the apple, using the hole Tom obligingly dug.

"What's next?"

"Now I wait. You get lost." But Tom didn't leave. He climbed back into the tree and arranged his gangly legs along a branch. Hughes leaned against the trunk and kept an eye on the path.

Perhaps half an hour later, Rotten Row came to life. Gentlemen on horseback, strolling ladies, laughing parties in carriages: the *haute ton* took its daily airing in the park. Hughes came to attention. He watched the path.

He muttered, low, so the boy couldn't catch the words. Tom did catch his breath. The rope, hanging from the apple, swayed. It rose, ending stretched in a perpendicular line from the apple, pointed at the path.

A rig came into view, rumbling along the path behind the Countess Du Lac's landau. Riding in state in the forward facing seat was Mrs. Silvester the elder. Hughes was relieved to see, squeezed into the back facing seat, Christine Whitmill-Ridgemont, Margaret Treadway and Emma Ridgemont.

His target was in view.

Sharp and clear, the magician said the final word activating the spell. *"Lehabah."* Like a burning coal, a ball of sparks catapulted from the rope. Straight as the flaming spear Hughes invoked, it flew toward Rotten Row. When it reached the crowd, the mass of embers skipped along heads, bouncing like a demented puppy seeking its master.

It reached its target. Coming off a high bounce, the embers dropped like a stone into the open carriage containing Margaret Treadway and her relations. It exploded.

A plume of smoke rose, Christine screeched, and the ladies began flailing at the feathers on Maud Silvester's bonnet, which had burst into flame.

Hughes swore. "Missed."

The carriage rocked and activity on the crowded path halted. Horses snorted, gentlemen sawed at reins, and one lady swooned, draping over the side of her carriage. The flash of countless vinaigrettes waved under delicate noses was balanced by the stamp of groom's boots racing to control cattle.

Mrs. Whitmill-Ridgemont shrieked like a debutante denied permission to waltz. Margaret, sphinx-like, watching the feathers in Mrs. Silvester's bonnet flame. Emma, the minx, legs braced like a naval captain on the bridge, swiped at ribbons and swung her arm.

Mrs. Silvester's bonnet bounced and was on the ground, trampled by grooms. She looked toward the tree and shook her cane.

"Hoo, look at old lady S—never seen her hair mussed before. Oh, oh, that's her sword cane." Tom swung from the tree branch. "She's going to kill you. Don't say I didn't warn you." He took off running.

* * *

Lady Wellwood's carriage drew alongside. As Clarissa's mother regally nodded her head to Mrs. Silvester, a ball of flame flew through the air. Margaret saw it from the corner of her eye and gasped as the feathers on Mrs. Silvester's bonnet caught on fire. They flamed and spat. The queen's bosom bow turned into a human candle and Emma stepped on her foot.

Christine batted at sparks raining off Mrs. S's feathers into her lap. Muslin billowed as again and again she slapped her legs. Emma bolted out of her seat. Exhibiting great presence of mind, she pulled the ribbons under Mrs. Silvester's chin and knocked the hat out of the carriage. Throwing sparks in all directions, it arced over Lady Wellwood's horses and plopped on the ground. The horses backed, neighing.

"I have holes in my skirt," Christine whimpered. "What rapscallion did it? He burnt holes in my skirt." Giving up on her clothes, she twisted, looking for the source of the attack. "A ball of fire came out of nowhere. What was it?"

Lady Wellwood fainted. She hung over the side of her shuddering carriage, one arm tangled in her hair, which had come unbound and streamed over the lacquered wood. Her companion pulled her arm, achieving nothing beyond tearing Lady Wellwood's sleeve half off.

Emma peered over Margaret's head at the grooms, stamping

on the bonnet, feathers, and each other's boots. "It still burns," she marveled. "They can't put out the fire."

What had begun as a towering French bonnet of a style popular several years before, with lace beading and ribboned plaiting matching that on Mrs. Silvester's scarf-cloak, was a smear of brown and green satin on the ground. Ostrich feathers, still attached to the massive knot of lace at the brim, smoldered and sparked. The smoke of burning feathers made their eyes water.

"Look, Margaret," Emma said, wiping her eyes and poking her sister in the side. "The feathers are still alight. Every time one of them tromps on them, they spark back to flame."

Her sister paid no heed to the trampled bonnet. Her awed stare was directed at Maud Silvester, risen from her seat and shaking her cane in the air. The old lady's hair was disheveled from Emma rudely knocking the flaming bonnet off, but her dignity was unimpaired. The only sign of agitation was the cane waving back and forth like an orchestral conductor's wand.

"You will pay for this, Adrian Hughes," Mrs. Silvester said as calmly as if she were speaking to a card partner over a games table. "By Nimue, I will have your head."

Adrian set her feathers on fire? How? Margaret craned her neck, fruitlessly seeking a glimpse of him. She scanned men on horseback and peered in as many of the carriages she could in the direction Mrs. Silvester pointed. She was gravely disappointed when she failed to spot him.

* * *

The next morning was sublime. She was as powerful as the Lady in Her lake. Craig sniffed, of course, but Mrs. Norris took her word as law from on high. Two of the footmen were respectable painters; they went to purchase brushes and cloths to cover the floor. Promising to give the chatelaine a color sample before luncheon, Margaret took Emma to the drapers to choose fabric.

"While we are out, Mrs. Norris," she said in the hall, drawing on a glove, "I trust you will personally supervise packing of the books. Would you prefer to have them dusted before they are put away or when the maids return them to the shelves?"

Mrs. Norris said absentmindedly, "Both, madam, both." She transferred her gaze from one sheet of paper to a second. "Mrs.

Treadway, the picture should be cleaned. It's been in the attic a good long while with spiders crawling over it."

"We will stop at Ackerman's Repository. They refer that work. And if you would have the two chairs in the room when we return, I can decide which will fit better." With Mrs. Norris's nose buried in her lists, Margaret and Emma left the house.

In the carriage, Margaret consulted her list. "The window coverings dictate the wall color, so we must decide that first. My dear, please remind me we need a sample for the footmen to match the paint. My head is full of information; it will go clean out. The chairs will need redoing and if we see a carpet, I may change the floor also. Oh, and Lady Clarissa told me the draper Lady Wellwood frequents. That is where we are headed. We shall see if they suit, though they may not carry the material I have in mind."

"You are doing the library top to bottom," Emma said, surprised. "I thought you were only going to paint, Meggie."

"Oh, no. Paint alone will not achieve what I have in mind."

"Pray, what may that be?"

"An eye-opener." With the cryptic comment, Margaret tucked the list in her reticule. "Thank you for coming, dear. It was generous of you to postpone our outing to the Tower again. I rely on your artistic eye."

"I don't care about seeing the Tower of London. When you asked what I would like to do in town, seeing the Grail was the only thing I could think of. You had me at a disadvantage; I was out of temper. Christine had nagged like a fishwife all the way to town, wanting to stop at every inn and visit castles."

Wisely, Emma switched back to décor. "Meggie, why this sudden interest in decorating?" The carriage swayed on a corner and they both grabbed for the straps. Emma missed the undoubtedly mischievous smile Margaret could not suppress.

"It is not sudden; I merely decided what I want to do. The library is dated. Mrs. Treadway had it done years ago. It reflects my father-in-law's taste rather than my husband's."

Emma nodded. "Mr. Treadway often wears gold with blue. Shall you choose those colors?"

"Wait and see."

The draper produced an ocean of material. Weeding through it, Emma quickly learned to bypass the cool blues and rich greens, concentrating on the hues her sister favored. After an exhaustive search, Margaret flourished a striped satin sample. "This is the drapery."

Emma wrinkled her nose. "That is not a color combination you like."

"No, I suppose it isn't." Margaret held it to the light and turned it this way and that.

"Then why choose it?"

"It's not my library. It doesn't have to please me. I think Mr. Treadway will appreciate it, don't you?"

"No."

Margaret rubbed the tip of her sister's nose. "I didn't promise he would like it, dear. I said he should appreciate it." Emma grew a devilish glint in her eye.

"The library will look terrible."

"Oh, but I am not done. This is only the start. Judge when it is complete."

The choices made in the drapers, they left the shop. Margaret observed, "There is an amazing variety of fabric available in London, unlike at home. For an hour's labor and a few days annoyance, the chore will be done."

Her sister's tone was dry. "You could redo the whole house."

"I could, couldn't I." They laughed. "I told the driver to have the carriage wait at the end of the street. Come, dear." Margaret took Emma's arm. As they walked, she quietly asked, "You have disposed of the potions?"

"Yes."

"Good. I have not determined what our next move should be, but..." Margaret broke off. "Good day, Lady Jersey." They exchanged bows and moved on. "Emma, can you—"

"Oh, look, there is Mr. Hughes." Heart pounding, she waved her hand at the gentleman paused in front of a shop. He saw them and waved back. Watching him weave around passersby, she said, "I have a thought. It will hold."

Glancing at Emma, a nagging question swelled to certitude. Her sister's look was unwelcoming. Emma didn't like Mr. Treadway; she wasn't going to be sweet to Mr. Treadway's friend.

Margaret lightly pinched her sister's arm, gaining her attention. "I like Mr. Hughes," she said calmly, if a trifle breathlessly. She had to leave it; he was too near; he might hear. She prayed her opinionated sister would be polite.

A placard advertised the shop before them had received a shipment of Angola trimming fur, an item Margaret would have been interested under other circumstances. With Adrian to distract, she hardly glanced in the window. They mouthed the conventional greetings and she mock scolded, "We have not seen you, Mr. Hughes. Do you intend to be a stranger?"

"I haven't seen you since we toured that shop," he acknowledged. "I left my card yesterday. I think you must be a butterfly, Mrs. Treadway. Fully caught up in the season, flitting here and there and never stopping for a moment."

Gentlemen did not care for butterflies. Wrapped in the nuance of his behavior, it did not register in Margaret's mind that leaving a card meant Adrian had visited the house. She searched for a way to dispel the illusion she was a flighty society miss, darting from engagement to engagement, too busy to nurture friendships, even friendships which threatened to rip the fabric of her life.

Intending to show just that, she said, "Not I. Mrs. Silvester is the one who cannot alight for more than a moment. She bespoke my time. We toured Lord Elgin's exhibit and drove through the park. She said she saw you there, but I could not find you."

With an eloquent shrug, Adrian accepted the excuse. He took her hand and placed it in the crook of his arm, where it nestled as if it belonged. Offering his other arm to Emma, they walked past shop doors.

"I wondered if the mermaid fit on your bookshelf," Margaret said.

Adrian dropped a social mask over his feelings. She could see it happen. By the Lady, he must be repelled. She held her breath, expecting a set down. Instead, he said, "The mermaid fits the empty space by Byron's works. Lends him a bit of respectability."

"Your maids didn't give notice when they saw it?"

"On the contrary, Lily adopted the mermaid. Begged some Gowland's Lotion from my housekeeper. Said the mermaid's skin must hurt, it is so dry. She dusts her every day and rubs the lotion in. I have not seen any improvement, but she says it's early days yet."

"It will take an ocean of Gowland's to improve that skin," Margaret observed.

"Just so." He turned his head. "Tell me, Miss Emma, do you also flit around London?"

Emma's response was breezy. "I have done my share."

"And you have seen all the sights—Astley's, Merlin's Gardens, the Tower and the Grail ?"

"I have not been to the Tower."

"No?" Adrian sounded surprised. "The Grail is not to be missed. For those who have an affinity for it, being in the presence is a..." he paused. "The Grail is a true treasure. It has watched over our island and kept Englishmen safe for untold centuries. Its power is not to be feared. You really must see it."

"There has not been time," Margaret said.

"You should make time. I'll escort you. Mornings are better; there are fewer people milling around." Emma made a noncommittal noise and he turned back to Margaret.

"You did not wish me to come to your home?" His voice was soft. Emma did not hear.

With a start, Margaret recalled his earlier words. Oh, this meeting was going all wrong and it was her fault. "I am sorry, I did not know you had been to visit. I imagine the butler gave your card to Mr. Treadway."

The sun came out with his smile. "I can find Tread in the clubs. You and I, we seem fated to meet only in passing. I saw you in the park yesterday, but from a distance."

"Did you see Mrs. Silvester's bonnet catch fire?"

"That I missed. From what I heard, there was no harm done."

Margaret sighed. "No, but it was unsettling. I haven't a clue what happened. One moment she was greeting Lady Wellwood, the next Emma knocked Mrs. Silvester's bonnet to the ground and the feathers were burning. It caused quite a ruckus."

"I can imagine. Unfortunately, I was occupied; couldn't come over."

"I am sorry. Your assistance would have been welcome." He pressed her hand. Suddenly, he lost the gentle look and his face drew stern lines.

"I have a serious matter to discuss with you. Could I arrange an appointment?" She blinked.

"I—I will be glad to see you. Tomorrow at two? Is that—"

"Margaret, we have passed our carriage," Emma said. In confusion, she pulled her hand from the safety of Adrian's arm.

"So we have. Mr. Hughes." Flustered, she nodded.

All the things she wished she could say, but with Emma at her side, it was impossible.

Who was she trying to fool? It was impossible, with or without Emma. With a bow, he handed her and her sister into the carriage while Margaret wondered how her heart had wound into this coil. His clothing was conservative, his appearance nothing above the ordinary. Adrian Hughes was merely another of the endless stream of gentlemen whom she knew, Margaret reminded herself. Still—*Perish the thought,* she told herself. *Stop wishing for the moon.*

Chapter Nineteen

In the afternoon, Margaret found time to visit Wellwood House in Kay Square. After she greeted a room of middle-aged matrons, visitors of Lady Wellwood, Clarissa promptly found a reason for them to adjourn from the drawing room. "Mama, Margaret has come to help me trim my old cottage bonnet," she called across the muted autumn colors of the Kidderminster carpet. Lady Wellwood looked up from her conversation with Mrs. Sessions and gave Margaret a piercing stare as she waved them away.

"Come, Meggie." Clarissa grabbed her hand and steered her into the hall.

"The Countess gave me an odd look," Margaret said as they climbed the stairs.

"She thinks you are going to make a scandal," Clarissa replied in a breezy voice. "She doesn't want me caught in it."

Margaret stopped with one foot on the stair above. "Should I leave?"

"Not on your life." Clarissa whisked them to her sitting room, where a chaise and two armchairs sat in front of a low bookcase jumbled with marble-covered novels. A charming tripod tea table overflowed with fashion periodicals and bits of lace.

Clarissa shoved a cacophony of handkerchiefs off the chaise and pulled Margaret down to sit. "Tell me all. I have been on thorns, waiting to hear if relations between you and Mr. Treadway have improved."

"You refer to that wretched horse. Miracle of miracles, he never scolded me," Margaret confided, folding a rumpled handkerchief and setting it on the table. "I thought he would, but we were interrupted. Then he was too busy fending off Mrs. Silvester's invitation." Margaret didn't add, *"Then* he was too busy not fending off my sister." She wasn't going to think about it.

"You were so meek during your first season," Clarissa said smugly. "You have become a lion." The description was absurdly pleasing. Margaret reminded herself the improvement was scarcely laudable.

"I must be careful, Clary—it would not do to go beyond tolerance. Just think if your mother refused to admit me to the house. But I will *not* be a compliant lamb. If Mr. Treadway thinks he can go on as he has, gadding about and ignoring me, treating me as a glorified chatelaine, he will have to be taught otherwise." She strangled another handkerchief.

"Goodness, such furor." Clarissa bounced to her knees in front of Margaret. "You act like the woman scorned. What have you not told me?"

"Nothing."

"Nonsense. There is something. If you do not tell, I shall discover your secret another way. There is a deeper reason for you to harass your husband than a dislike of being treated as nearly every lady we know is treated. Why should your situation be different than any other? Husbands wed and go their own way. You know this—we used to giggle at the comical way spouses ignored each other. Do you not recall when Sir Ahern had a highflyer in his curricle and his lady drove by with her gentleman? You nearly fell out of the carriage laughing when the lightskirt threw a kiss..."

Margaret's cheeks darkened but Clarissa would not leave the subject. "Should I ask Mr. Treadway?"

"No!"

"Tell all, dear friend, else I shall be unable to aid you."

Stumbling over words, Margaret told the history of her engagement and marriage. It was difficult to describe the latter without bringing Adrian Hughes in, but she endeavored. Clarissa must not be given a hint. At the end of the convoluted explanation, her friend laughed.

"How dare you. There is nothing amusing about this situation." Lemon dripped from Margaret's tongue. "All my life I did as my father demanded. Act the lady, show proper reserve. I was quiet and mild. Whenever Papa frowned, I reined my smiles in further. During my season, I dressed as he preferred. If a gentleman cast his eye upon my bodice, Papa had me tuck in a bit of lace. No rake was to develop an interest in me. Never did I attract any gentleman, much less a rakish one. Papa was pleased.

"What is the reward for reticence? A gentleman who cannot care two pins for my feelings. Papa refused to suffer another season and I suppose he tired of my stepmother's harping. No wonder my husband has no respect for me. I am devalued by my family and can expect no consideration from others."

"A more cold-blooded marriage contract has not been signed in years," Clarissa agreed, dimples fading.

Margaret tossed her head. "I showed contempt for the match. They did all but pat me on the head and send me to the nursery. If Mr. Treadway is lackadaisical in his regard, I shall disturb *his* comfort. That is why I disposed of his horse. What's more, I shall continue—I have already made my second move. You must come see the library when the work is done."

"The library?"

"Yes, his wretched horse is nothing to what I have devised for his library. He is not a total nodcock—eventually he will realize it is to his advantage to hold me in respect."

It was none of Clarissa's business he had been absent from the townhouse the last three nights. She would most likely advise Margaret to give an eye for an eye and set up a flirt. That she could not do, if only because no man seemed inclined to flirt. Adrian was more than...No. How many times would she have to tell herself it was impossible?

"I agree with you, dear friend," Clarissa soothed. "I laughed only because your situation rivals mine when I thought Lord Shelton was going to offer for me. He turned around and wed a complete unknown. I felt I was the only scorned and disregarded woman alive." She took Margaret's hands and shook them. "The lot of women is terrible. Is there not a one of us who has not been misused?"

"Poor Clary, did Lord Shelton wound you?"

Clarissa sighed. "I thought so at the time. He gave every sign he would offer for me, but he had a woman in his house. Shelton assured me he held me in the highest esteem, but *on dit* was he had wed. Still he kept company with me. I saw her on Bond Street—he behaved like a bear. It was humiliating, but the ache passed from my heart. My pride took the heavier fall, I believe."

She tweaked Margaret's hair. "Your dilemma is harder, sweet Meg. You are tied to the scoundrel."

"I will not let him treat me poorly. He ignores me," she whispered, forgetting she meant to keep the secret. Her need for sympathy was greater than for discretion. "You know, in the evening. He goes out—you can guess where."

"The cad. Nor should you allow such without protest. We shall have to plan carefully though, so Mr. Treadway does not bury you in the country and forget your existence."

"Clary, that is why I am decorating his library."

* * *

Ravenous hunger, generated by nightly physical exertion, drew him home. Treadway was at the breakfast table, digging enthusiastically into a beefsteak. No one could sear a steak like his cook. The meat oozed as he slid a knife along the edge, just as he liked it. Life was good.

He had not seen his wife for three days. He had returned to Mount Street with the dawn, changed his attire and immediately escaped into the daytime activities of the fashionable male. He smiled at the mug of ale.

Spring Street was a powerful draw. Minnie satisfied his natural inclinations without demand. She'd left off the cosmetics and to his surprise and delight, found a wardrobe equally unnecessary. Never had Treadway heard of a mistress running naked around the house; it was a delightful conceit.

He felt reborn when he rolled off Minnie—sated, yet emotionally detached. A profound feeling of sovereignty followed him throughout the day.

The door opened and the Pater's choice breezed into the breakfast room. By Merlin, he had meant to be away before she came down. Hysterics with breakfast was worse than Almack's. He chewed.

"Good morning," Margaret trilled. Above an apricot lawn gown her skin glowed. Lace concealed and hinted at the curves of her breasts.

"Ah, good morning," he responded. "Aren't you a bit early?"

"No, sir, I believe you are a bit late."

"Ah," he said again and sliced another bite of beef. *Now she'll start complaining.* Silence descended, interrupted by Craig's delivery of a small plate of eggs, half a slice of ham, and a muffin.

"Another new dress?" he asked, thinking it best to be conciliatory. To his disgust, Margaret thought it was a conversational gambit, not an evasion.

Halving her muffin with a deft twist of the knife, she said,

"Yes, this is new. I have yet to wear everything in my wardrobe. Finally, I hit upon the idea of wearing frocks in the order they are hung in the cupboard. My maid has orders to replace each at the end of the row after I wear it. I must have purchased too many gowns, though Lady Clarissa assures me my wardrobe is only adequate."

"Go to the *modiste*. I dislike to be seen as miserly. The *ton* expects to see you well dressed."

"I did not mean to complain. Clary has a jaundiced view of the season—I am content with my wardrobe. I shall ignore any who consider it wrong to wear the same dress twice. My consequence was never so fragile."

"Good, good." Another silence fell over the table.

"I am having your library painted," Margaret mentioned. "It is almost done. The smell will dissipate. I hope you do not mind. The room was shabby." At the sideboard, Craig dropped a spoon. Ignoring the butler's clumsiness, she cut a bite of ham and moved to the next topic of conversation. "Today we are invited to the Silvester's for tea. Do you go with me?"

"I told you no." At the thought of Maud Silvester, Treadway fisted his hand. If the old dame had heard rumors, she would not hesitate to speak, even bellow, her condemnation of his behavior. That would set the cat at the pigeons and since he didn't have any say with old Mrs. S he took the cowardly route. "Have appointments I cannot postpone." Rising, he pulled at his waistcoat. "In fact, have to do some research beforehand. I should be gone."

Without a farewell, he quitted the room. Margaret abandoned her muffin in favor of an abstracted gaze at her husband's empty chair. *He is afraid of me. I do believe I have the upper hand.*

* * *

Mrs. Silvester's strictures on her attire stung. Margaret donned a wrapping dress fresh from Madame Celeste. Fine cambric, trimmed at neck and wrists with double borders of light mull muslin, the sleeves were confined at her narrow wrists with gold bracelets and a snap so they should not interfere with movement.

She had splurged on an opulent Wellington hat of blended straw and white satin, tied under her ear with grosgrain ribbon. She loved the wreath of violets around the crown. The colors whitened her skin, a fashion triumph.

Lastly, against the chill spring air, Margaret donned a blue satin pelerine, trimmed with broad black lace over the shoulder. A sky blue sash of figured ribbon passed over the lace, tying in front of her waist, finishing a very Parisian look. Admiring the Roman shoes of buff kid, she pulled on gloves of the same color and asked the maid for the blue shot silk parasol. With a last detailed appraisal in the looking glass, she twirled the parasol to make the deep Chinese fringe swing and set forth, confident she looked her best.

Maud, the dowager Silvester, had called forth an intimate coterie of tea drinkers. Lady Sally Jersey was chattering to Peter Silvester and his mother, Matilda, Mrs. Joshua Silvester. With a characteristic lack of affectation, *La* Jersey held forth on the season's crop of debutantes being admitted to Almack's.

"Oh, there are plenty of the usual girls, milk-faced and above all, young," she twitted Silvester, whose silver gilt buttons glinted in the light from the ceiling high windows. "Enfield's youngest is out this season. Big brown eyes and all those curls! Lively little thing, Mr. Silvester. You could not do better; she has a hefty portion to balance all that hair. She would welcome your attention; I noted her making eyes at you at Sefton's. Can we hope you will make the lady an offer?"

His beet red face contrasted with the chartreuse of his waistcoat. His indomitable mama added, "She has such an original name: Nevada Rue. I found her manners perfectly delightful. And the family is well regarded; one cannot fault their rectitude."

Silvester pulled on his neckcloth. "Don't need to choose a lady," he sputtered. "Miss Wentworth..." Matilda would not allow her son to finish.

"Charlotte Wentworth. I wish you would come to your senses, Peter. The family is not suitable to be united with the Silvester's. Oliver Wentworth was nothing but a loose screw when I was young. He has not improved in all the years since. Constance Dearling has nothing but grief from that man. His son, Charles, is just like him. The moonling is enamored of the gaming table. He will run through the family's money soon enough, if his father does not do the deed himself, and then where will Miss Wentworth be?"

Sally interrupted the tirade. "I cannot agree, Matilda. Oliver Wentworth is an amusing rattle. His son promises to exceed him in charm. You should not allow Oliver's youthful behavior to influence you now." Ignoring the warning in Matilda's narrowed eyes, Sally delved further into Mr. Silvester's preference.

"Wentworth; there are two sisters. Squire Michael Shipley is courting Maria, though he is taking his time offering. She is as flighty as any, but sweet. I do not know Charlotte as well, as she sees fit to whisk into alcoves and behind pillars when I am around. Why does she do this, Mr. Silvester, do you know?"

Silvester wished he had gone to Tattersall's with Chively rather than obey his grandmother's command to come for tea. A bit of brandy splashed in his cup might make the conversation more bearable. He glanced toward the decanters, all the way across the room within reach of Grandmama's sharp tongue.

The butler opened the door and stood aside to allow Margaret to enter. "Ah, Mrs. Treadway," Maud Silvester greeted her, "So nice of you to come. Where's that husband of yours? Afraid to face me, I'll wager. Over here," she waved her finger, "Sit by me. D'you know everyone?" Watery blue eyes, faded from years of keeping the younger generation in check, peered through lines which radiated to the bridge of Mrs. Silvester's nose.

Introductions made in a ring around the room, the old lady pointing and naming each individual for Margaret to bow her head at in acknowledgement, finishing with Honoria and Sir George Colby on brocaded chairs in front of the fine marble fireplace with the dowager, who held court from the center of the sofa. Three Mrs. Silvesters was a bit confusing and Margaret wondered if she should call them Elder, Younger and Dowager, like titles. It seemed a rude thing to do.

Mrs. S shoved a creamed cup of tepid tea in Margaret's direction. "Have a cup while I finish with my granddaughter. I was about to explain to the chit why her Aunt Emily goes to church every Sunday. Imagine, in this day and age. Takes the servants with her. She leaves but one man at home to guard the place. Positively popish.

"It started after she had that accident, when everyone thought she was dead. Emily maintains she saw God and he sent her back. Joined a prayer group, of all things. They meet every Tuesday to discuss the Bible. When one of the group falls ill, she visits daily with comfits to console them. She don't make the comfits herself; half the time she wants my chef to do the cooking, but she enjoys playing Lady Bountiful. And she holds long conversations with the parson on the nature of heaven and man's sin." The dowager shook her finger in Honoria's face. "Mind you don't follow her lead!"

"No, Grandmama, I would not dream of doing so." Honoria swallowed a giggle. Sir George waggled his eyebrows.

"Don't try that around me, young man," Mrs. Silvester scolded. "Godliness is next to cleanliness. I recall your baptism; it was done most properly in church at the font. I gave you a silver rattle. There is nothing wrong with religion, long as it is kept in its place."

Maud's cheekbones, high and sharp, harbored the only skin on the lady's face not scattered with wrinkles. They held Mrs. Silvester's eye sockets in place and supported a jaw line lacking padding. She turned to Margaret. "You would never be so hurly burly as to bring a Green Knight to the dinner table, I hope," she admonished. "I suppose it is all right for my Emily to be intimate with religion, if it brings her comfort, but it would never do for you."

"No, ma'am," Margaret said.

"By the by, Maud," Lady Jersey said, "I heard the prince escorted you from the park to Hookham's. What did you want that could not wait?" Mrs. Silvester lifted her regal nose.

"A book, Sally. What else would I want at a bookstore?"

"Now, don't be difficult." Mrs. Silvester's lips twitched.

"If you must know, it was a book of bird drawings. Once I had it home, I found I had no use for it. I sent it to the Naval Hospital in Greenwich. Charitable of me."

"After all the trouble you put our prince to, shame."

"Yes," the dowager said complacently.

Nodding in accord with the old lady's bedevilment of their prince, Lady Jersey turned her attention to Margaret. "Mrs. Treadway, Maud asked you here to tell us how you came to be wed." The room fell silent. Everyone awaited an answer.

"The marriage was arranged by our fathers, ma'am," Margaret said, hoping this prosaic explanation would satisfy the gorgon.

Mrs. Silvester nodded. "As it should be. The young think they know better than their elders, but it is rarely true." Her curiosity assuaged, the dowager moved to a theme dear to her heart, that of ordering the lives around her. Matilda Silvester elbowed Sir George out of his chair.

"You should hold an entertainment as soon as may be," the dowager instructed Margaret. "Show the *ton* what you can do. Until you do, the biddies will be on pins and needles. They need to see your mettle, gel. Am I not right, Sally?"

"Most wise, Maud. A Venetian breakfast would be pleasant—not as confining as a rout, but an opportunity for everyone to meet you, Mrs. Treadway," Almack's patroness decreed. "You could invite those acquaintances of your husband's who seldom, if ever, grace a ballroom with their presence. Adrian Hughes, for one. He is monstrous attractive. And Lord Chively, though he is not apt to be an ornament to society, I fear."

"Chively is a fribble," Mrs. Silvester stated. Lady Jersey accepted the truth of the dowager's contribution with a nod.

"The Treadway townhouse is not well situated for entertainment, however. Where could the breakfast be held? It must be someplace new..."

She tapped a well-groomed finger against her cheek. "Why, I have just the thought! Could not the London Gallery be persuaded to open their doors to Mrs. Treadway? The rooms are large enough to hold the tables required, and the atmosphere so refined with pictures on the walls. Would the gentlemen be content in such a setting, do you think, Sir George?"

Colby cleared his throat. "It sounds delightful, my lady," he commented in a tone indicating the opposite, "if Mrs. Treadway would consent to provide more substantial fare than is generally offered. A man is like to starve at these breakfasts."

"You could prevail upon the Gallery to put away pictures not conducive to good digestion," Mr. Silvester murmured.

"Or only put out those matching the color scheme I choose," Margaret opted dryly, wondering what was wrong with the Treadway townhouse. She hadn't noticed anything forbidding guests, unless Lady Jersey referred to the torturous chair in the hall.

"Hang the pictures in a theme," Honoria chimed in. "Perhaps the four seasons—like Peter's paintings he is trying to sell."

A deadly hush fell over the room. Her eyes rounded, Honoria clapped a manicured hand over her mouth. Lady Jersey's well-kept figure swiveled to eye the young man of the house speculatively.

"What did you say, gel?" the dowager spoke in an awful tone. "Peter selling pictures? What nonsense is this?" She turned a dire eye upon her grandson.

Silvester twisted a button on the front of his coat. "Don't know what Hon is talking about," he blustered, staring in dismay at the button as it fell into his hand. "See what you've made me do."

"Unfair," Honoria cried. "It is not my fault."

"No, just you cannot keep your mouth shut. Never tell my sister *anything,*" he complained to Colby. "She can't keep a secret for all the diamonds at Rundell's."

"I can. I never told Mama you wagered her landau against Sir Perth's dog walking backward last October."

Matilda Silvester stiffened. "I thought the landau was damaged beyond repair when a dray struck it."

"It was, Mama," Silvester howled. "Hon don't know what she's saying."

Feeling bludgeoned by the squabble, Margaret wished to leave, though Sally Jersey looked highly entertained. Matilda swooned and Maud Silvester pounded an emaciated fist on the tea table.

"Peter, stop nattering. What this is about?" the dowager demanded. Silvester fell silent, leaving Honoria to make bad worse.

"Peter painted with oils, Grandmama, and he is trying to sell the most dreadful set of paintings. He calls them the Four Seasons, but I cannot understand why. They are hidden in the attic. Make him show them to you!" Matilda Silvester moaned, slumping back on her chair and trailing an arm on the floor.

"Honoria, you do not know what you say," Silvester scolded. "They are excellent paintings."

"Let us see, that we may judge your efforts," Sally Jersey said, for once the voice of reason.

Sir George, who had been vacantly staring at the portrait hung above the fireplace, said, "It's time to leave. Been here longer than I'm supposed to. The conventions, Mrs. S."

"Not a word about this, Sir George," the dowager growled.

"Must write my manager and ask if the roof for the new kennel's been installed yet. Want everything done and the dogs calm before hunting season..." Colby took his mind from brick arches. "Huh? Not a word? Don't know about what."

The dowager looked long and hard at the baron. "Never mind," she finally said, and reached for the bell pull.

Mrs. Silvester wished her gone also, so Margaret moved to

take her leave. The dowager grasped her hand painfully. "No talk of this, young lady, lest you find your way in society hampered. My grandson's idiocy isn't fodder for the gossips."

"Oh no, I would not dream of it. Everyone has private matters they do not wish exposed."

"If you say anything, I will expose *your* private matters. Don't think I won't. I know all."

And that was that. Margaret knew if she told anyone about Peter Silvester's paintings, Mrs. Silvester would make her miserable. What the old lady thought she knew was a mystery, but whatever it was, it would be unpleasant. She didn't much care if Mr. Silvester made a cake of himself, but she did care if society cut her. Meekly, she left.

Once the butler escorted Sir George and Margaret Treadway from the room, Maud grumbled, "Now, let us see about this upheaval."

Four footmen tromped to the attic storage room, led by an indignant Peter Silvester, and returned to the drawing room bearing four good size oil paintings, which they lined up along the wall. Four pairs of female eyes inspected the artwork and pronounced judgment.

Sally Jersey wasn't nicknamed Silence for nothing. "Heavens, you call those the Four Seasons. I would have said Four Mistresses. Why are their gowns so unconventional?" Pacing back and forth in front the paintings, she waxed voluble. "I mistrust the lady in the winter painting. Her cloak, with the fur trimming, at least I think it is meant to be fur, looks warm. But a bare leg thrust through the slit—it presents the wrong image, Mr. Silvester. I presume this one represents autumn, what with the hunting scene in the background. That part is well enough. The lady, with dogs jumping and tearing the skirt of her gown, ahem, she just doesn't look right. Is her wrist supposed to be bent like a poker?"

She gave Maud a tart look and moved closer to the last painting. "Mr. Silvester, why is the summer lady so scantily clad? The heat of July and August may be oppressive, but that does not excuse a lack of covering." She bent to examine a detail. "May the Lady have mercy. You *signed* them?"

His grandmother offered the most decided opinion. "You are trying to sell these daubs? Who would be looby enough to hand over the ready for them half naked whores? Selling outlandish paintings would put you beyond the pale, young man." Maud looked down her nose. "I want them destroyed."

Cutting short his impassioned defense of his art, Matilda dragged Peter and Honoria to the library to scold them and the salon cleared.

"So much for Peter," Maud said ruefully.

"Her eyes are remarkable," Sally Jersey mused. "Did you notice, Maud? They look baffling and misty, otherworldly."

"Margaret Treadway? They are like her mother's. Forget her eyes. You dare not reveal Peter's secret, you know." Lady Jersey left off twirling her gloves and dimpled at her hostess.

"Why not? Your grandson is quite proud of his accomplishment. With Byron's example before him, Peter may find himself a lion of the artistic set. Not many gentlemen dare to take brush to canvas, much less sell his work."

"Or he could end an ostrich with his head buried in the country sand. Peter ain't no Byron, he's got no mystery to him. And the ladies aren't going to fawn over his silly waistcoats. No, Sally, you are going to have to keep quiet."

"My dear Mrs. Silvester..."

"No." Maud was firm. "If you breathe one word about my grandson's idiotic aspirations, I will go to the queen. Charlotte will sympathize with me."

Chapter Twenty

An unearthly howl caused Mrs. Norris to drop the Minton sauce boat. It landed on her toe and exploded, spraying shards of gilded porcelain far and wide. Cook squealed, dropping the long meat fork on the stone flags in front of the soot stained hearth. One of the tines crumpled. The juicy steak speared on the fork splattered her apron, skirt, the floor, and the good linen tablecloth a maid had just finished ironing.

"Lands, is a dragon got in the house?"

"Oh, not a dragon—please don't let it be a dragon." Massive thuds rattled the crockery.

At the second shouted snarl, wilder than the first, a footman threw his hands over his ears, accidentally tossing the knife he held over his shoulder. It sank into the potato a kitchen maid was peeling. She screamed and fainted. The scullion dived under the work table, rocking it. A pot of peas tilted and fell atop the shattered sauce boat. It was followed by a brimming pitcher of ale. Potatoes rolled. Another maid cast her apron over her head and screeched.

"Pray Merlin save us, it's the Questing Beast. The Questing Beast is come to destroy the house." To the occupants of the kitchen, it sounded as if that dread creature, which made the unholy sound of forty baying hounds, had been unleashed upstairs. The offspring of a girl and the devil himself, the Beast was the most fearsome of creatures. King Arthur had quailed before it; a kitchen populated by humble servants was undone by fear of it.

"Lordy, it's the devil. The house is possessed by the devil Questing Beast!" Another eerie roar made the hairs rise on Mrs. Norris's arms. "A *magic* devil!"

Devils were one thing, but magic devils were the stuff of primal nightmares. The Questing Beast—they were about to die. The knife boy curled into a ball in the middle of the floor and sobbed. Maids ran back and forth, seeking hiding places where none existed and the footman quaked. The scullion wrapped quivering arms around the table leg.

Porcelain shards glittered and green peas floated in a sea of ale as the chatelaine dashed up the service stairs to the hall, following the bloodcurdling sounds. Reaching the landing, she slapped a hand over her frenzied heart as the baize door swung open and the butler pounded through the doorway. They collided.

Both reeled; Mrs. Norris would have gone back down the stairs on her head if Craig hadn't grabbed her arms. Another prolonged roar, accompanied by the sound of furniture smashing against plaster, echoed in the stairwell.

Mrs. Norris flinched. "What is it; is it the Questing Beast?" Craig curled a hand tight around her arm and started for the kitchen, dragging her with him. "What is wrong?"

Craig bellowed to be heard above the pounding noise. "The master is in the library."

"Oh, my stars. It isn't the Questing Beast. We are safe. I take it he does not like the drapes?"

"Lime and orange stripes? I doubt it."

"Nor the tables Mrs. Treadway purchased? He does not approve of gilded cupids?"

"No, I believe the first howled comment pertained to the tables." Another crash shook the floor and the butler winced, his eyes rolling to the ceiling. "If I am not mistaken, that is a tribute to puce and yellow damask cushions."

"The celestial blue walls?" There came a great rumble, as of books and lumber crashing. Safe on the flagged kitchen floor, they exchanged horrified glances.

"Perhaps not." A drawn out, guttural yell heralded the smash of slammed doors. Blessed silence fell over the house.

Mrs. Norris cocked her head and smiled, a slow tilt of the lips upward. "Mr. Treadway must have liked the rug. I thought Mrs. Treadway's choice was inspired with all those red and blue dragons thrashing around the edges eating each other."

The scullery maid, her nose pressed against a leg of the work table, suddenly bolted to her feet, screaming fit to kill, "A hole. Right in front of my nose—a hole. Oh, my gawd, it made a hole. Somebody save me!"

The leg the maid had anchored herself to—the leg of the massive oak work table, thick as a man's wrist—broke. The table slowly tilted, sliding bowls, potatoes, knives, and the ham, studded with cloves in a star pattern, to the floor. The table followed. The crash rattled china nearly as much as the master's response to his wife's decorating of his library.

* * *

Brooding, Treadway pushed Margaret's management of his stables to the back of his mind. Likewise, he blanked out her nerve redoing his library, though he shook with rage. He had dismantled the damn room. By Mordred, for two pence he would rid himself of the twit. To hell with the Pater.

If Frampton's auction brought in as much as he thought it would, he'd thumb his nose at them all.

With the auction scheduled for the following week, he took a less stressful step than demanding his due from the Pater; Treadway ordered the phaeton brought around and snatched up the case containing the papers for the sale of Frampton's artwork.

He'd made a run to the docks the day before. That fool, Frampton, signed his soul away with a fervent prayer the auction would net him at least a thousand pounds. So it would, most likely. The items to be sold were under lock and key at the auction house he had set up. All but the valuable one.

The Fra Angelica was in a safe place. He'd arranged for a friend of his, one who'd worked for him before, to 'buy' the painting before the auction began. Balger was a good actor. He was going to saunter in, fall in love with the colors of the painting on sight, and pay an inflated price so as not to lose it at auction. Frampton would be pleased as punch to sell a piece far over its estimated price, Balger would appreciate the fifty pounds he would earn, and Treadway would be free to sell the Fra Angelica. *Twenty thousand, maybe it'll bring as much as twenty-five.*

First, he would deliver the signed papers to his solicitor, then be in Spring Street in time to take Minnie to the park.

On the street in front of the townhouse, he threw the case under the seat of the phaeton and turned to his head groom and butler. "Disregard any orders Mrs. Treadway makes," he ordered. "If she asks *anything,* don't do it. Just let me know." He swung to the bench. Craig nodded, ponderous acknowledgement of the superiority of his master.

"Cain't we get the stallion back?" the groom bleated. "Mebbe Sir 'urst would sell 'im back."

Treadway gave him a look of disgust and said, "Todd, let it go. There'll be other horses."

"Not like 'im."

"Release the grays and stop whining." The phaeton clattered over the cobblestones. He guided the cattle at a brisk pace through the streets, impatient to get the auction business done.

* * *

As wheels clattered over cobblestone, Margaret slipped into Emma's room. "Are you hiding again?"

"Yes, from Mr. Treadway," Emma said bluntly. "I thought he was going to bellow the house down when he viewed the library."

"He had difficulty assimilating it all." Margaret grinned and handed her sister a dingy little book. "I found this stuffed behind the encyclopedias on a back shelf in Hookham's. The clerk looked at me oddly when I purchased it, but I gave him a royal eye and he didn't say anything. Maybe it will give you a clue."

Emma opened the cracked leather cover. "A grimoire. Oh, Meggie, I have wanted one forever. Thank you." She scanned handwritten pages with eager eyes. "Ariadne du Kay; do you know who she was?"

"No." Emma turned the page, paying little attention.

"I can't wait to try them all. I'll learn more by practice... Here is the first spell. Whew, it is a love potion." Margaret laid her hand over the page and Emma looked up, a spark of mischief in her eyes. "I could make Mr. Treadway love you. Would you like that?"

A goose walked over Margaret's grave. "Don't be silly. Love potions don't work and besides, nothing could make my husband care for me. He is too involved with himself. Emma, be a dear. Before you get immersed in any one spell, go through the book and see if you find any reference to holes. We must do something quickly; a hinge came off the carriage door. The coachman said something about the holes for the nails enlarging." She patted Emma's shoulder. "I have a visitor coming at two so you have the afternoon to work with the spells in the book. After I am finished, I think we should discuss it further."

Her sister settled, Margaret went downstairs. She had checked the calendar—Christine was invited to Lady St. Cyr's Venetian breakfast and Mr. Treadway was out, as ever. She had privacy for

Adrian's call. Surprised that she felt no guilt at meeting a gentleman alone, she informed Craig she was home to Mr. Hughes when he arrived and sailed into the drawing room, smoothing the shell pink trim of her gown.

"You here! Christine, I thought you were going out." Margaret was unable to hide a dismayed recoil.

Her sister gifted her with an indifferent glance. "Yes, well, the breakfast was going to be a bore."

Realizing she stood in the open doorway like a block, Margaret moved to the sofa on rubbery legs. How was she to meet with Adrian if her sister did not leave? They would have no privacy. "Louisa St. Cyr is one of your closest friends. Failing to attend her is a cut indirect."

"The breakfast is fated to be a disaster. Even St. Cyr would not have attended. He is laid up." Christine accompanied the casual statement with a malicious titter. "St. Cyr is going to be cut by everyone and he richly deserves it. Can you imagine, Margaret, he jousted with Parmeter this morn over Louisa, of all people. Parmeter put a hole in his shoulder."

"How distressing. How is Lord St. Cyr?"

"The man is fine, though he doesn't deserve to be."

"How can you say that?"

Christine played with the curl over her ear. "Don't be a ninny. Louisa has given him his heir and two spares. What more can he ask; she did her duty. The fool man went into a towering rage because Louisa and Parmeter took a jaunt to Brighton to dip in the water. They stayed overnight at the Old Ship; separate rooms, all perfectly innocent. I daresay St. Cyr is a laughingstock for challenging Parmeter over it. He certainly deserves censure."

Margaret threw up her hands, appalled. "It would be in his right to demand a divorce."

"Perish the thought. A divorce would ruin Louisa; I would never forgive him that."

"Christine, why don't you go purchase all the feathers in Sutton and Meeks's emporium? Or better, take Emma to the Tower?"

By two o'clock, she would have said anything to get Christine out of the drawing room. Adrian Hughes would arrive any moment and there her sister sat, impervious to all hints, drat her wizened heart, lackadaisically turning the pages of *The Ladies Journal* and nibbling Turkish delight. She could imagine what construction her cynical sister would place on Adrian's visit.

"Christine," she began, "I wish—" but Craig opened the door.

"Mr. Adrian Hughes," he announced tremulously and it was too late. Christine's eyes lit like Perceval's on beholding the Fisher King. Margaret sent a quick prayer skyward that, like Perceval, Christine would fail to ask the right questions.

"Mr. Hughes, you are a sight to gladden the eyes," her sister said. "You find us filled with ennui; do relieve our suffering."

"I doubt I can offer any *on dits* that have escaped your attention, Mrs. Whitmill-Ridgemont. You are seen everywhere and know more scandalous doings than I, to be sure. I hear much of you in the clubs." Adrian bowed over both their hands and took a seat on another of the Treadway treasures, a chair with a crossed fretwork back. As he stretched his legs and leaned back, Margaret distinctly heard a crack. He sat forward, a carved piece of wood fell to the floor, and he tugged at his coat, caught against the splintered break in the fretwork. Christine, oblivious to his dilemma, preened.

"I can't be that well known," Adrian said, face beet red. Margaret covered her mouth and coughed, strangling on mirth. Christine gave her a killing look.

Manfully, Adrian ignored the broken chair. "I assure you, your name is on everyone's lips. Du Kay raves of your beauty and grace. It was your appearance at Crompton's rout brought it on, if I am not mistaken. 'Twilight hair,' I think Du Kay said." His eyes moved slowly over Christine, lingering on the elaborate braids woven into a bun at her crown. "I wouldn't have said 'twilight'. A fawn glimpsed through the forest trees at misty dawn, mayhap."

He sounded so...so enraptured, Margaret's heart bumped. She peeped, expecting to see the same dumb adoration other men lavished on her sister. He bore the half quizzical, half amused smile he had worn for the bizarre mermaid in that odd shop. She let out a breath, one she hadn't realized she was holding.

After a discussion of the Crompton rout, complete with detailed analysis of Lady Crompton's choice of wall covering for the main salon, Adrian rose to his feet. "Much as I would like to stay, dear Mrs. Whitmill-Ridgemont, duty calls. Mrs. Treadway, are you ready?"

Christine gasped. "The two of you—you are going out together?"

He picked invisible lint off his sleeve. "Treadway desired it. I am to assist Mrs. Treadway in choosing new draperies for his library. He likes mine, you see, and since Mrs. Treadway cannot visit my rooms to view them, he asked if I would escort her to Millard's. That is the only place for drapery material, as everyone knows. The prince redid the public rooms at Uther House through Millard's." He slapped his gloves against his thigh. "Since we must go all the way to Cheapside, it won't do to linger here overlong."

"I need only fetch my bonnet." Margaret swallowed a giggle at the look on Christine's face. After the drama of the morning, her sister could not doubt Mr. Treadway did not trust her to choose drapery material.

"After you." Adrian bowed and swept his arm toward the door. She dashed up the stairs to grab a bonnet and was back at the front door before Christine marshaled her forces to demand she play duenna.

Margaret chirped, "Ta," to her seething sister as he handed her up to a seat in his curricle. He quickly followed, gathered the reins, and snapped the horses to.

"I hope you don't mind a spin," he commented as the curricle bowled along Oxford Street. "Millard's was the only excuse I could dredge up that wouldn't arouse Mrs. Whitmill-Ridgemont's hunting instinct."

She resolutely admired the paving in front of the matched grays. "Your contrivance was apt. As it turns out, the library is in crying need of enhancement. But must we go all that way? John Wood carries a full selection of velvet and Bow Street is closer than Cheapside."

"Perhaps we need not go that far, but I do need to speak with you without interruption. A drive will afford us privacy."

"In effect, you are kidnapping me." With that inflammatory remark, she dared to glance at her companion. His mouth was grim, but she couldn't tell if it was at disapproval of her comment or for another cause. Her eyes back on the road, she said, "I don't mind. When you asked for this meeting, you indicated it was important. Indeed, had I been able to dislodge my sister from the drawing room, we could have spoken there. Had your visit proven dull, Christine would have excused herself."

His chuckle warmed. "Instead, I threw the butter boat over her head. My error. I must say, I'd rather compliment your gown. I like that shade of rose; it brings out the color in your cheeks." The curricle turned onto Regent Street, where they were met by the tangle of a stopped barrow, three barking lap dogs, and a tiger striped cat which had taken refuge from the dogs on the barrow man's head.

Brought to a stop, they watched dogs growl, bark and do their best to scale the human mountain to reach their hissing prey. A milling crowd laughed as a lad in Etonian garb managed to latch onto one dog's collar and the cat took its chance.

Flicking its tail like a whip, the beset feline leapt on the back of one of Adrian's horses, visibly gathering strength for the next challenge to its lives. A pert head swiveled, seeking asylum. Then, realizing the dogs could not jump high enough to reach it, the tiger sat on its haunches and licked a paw. The startled horse shied, but Adrian pulled gently on the reins and it subsided.

The bewildered barrow man rubbed where the cat's efforts had left a trail of reddening welts across his forehead. He snatched up the handles of the barrow and marched to the alley, loudly complaining "They ought to set up a 'unting season, that they ought. Don't 'old wif them devil's creatures, no I don't. And see if'n I bring apples ta them Armstrongs agin. No, they can gets their apples from the Garden, like decent folk. Devil's street, this is Devil's street." He turned on to Great Marlborough, accompanied by half the jeering crowd, shaking his head and grousing with every step. "Devil's cat, should 'unt it down."

The curricle swayed with Adrian's laughter. "Get those dogs," he ordered another boy, and threw a coin. The lad quickly swiped the lap dogs up, one under each arm, and he gently clucked the horses into motion. They walked the street with an orange striped jockey astride the leader. Half way to Conduit Street the cat jumped and whisked down a stair. The horses moved into a trot.

Margaret wiped tears from her eyes. "Was it a good omen or bad?"

"Good, definitely good. Only the Devil's own tabby could have saved itself so. It took the bad *nous* away. But Hurst was in the crowd; I'll take a drubbing over it later." Relieved by the comedy, they spent a few blocks joshing each other, then Adrian turned serious once more.

"Margaret, I need to talk to you about Emma. I do not know if you are aware of your sister's activities. She has been doing magic.

She must stop."

She gripped her reticule like an anchor to save her sweeping out to sea. "How did you know?"

"That I cannot tell. My dear, you must get her to cease spell casting."

She blinked and met his steady look. "But how did you know? No one knows but me." Adrian looked back to the reins. He didn't answer. She sighed and fiddled with the string of her reticule. "I suppose this is about the holes."

"Holes?"

"How could anyone fail to see holes coming up all over the place? Of course I notice them. I darned them in three bed sheets at home. I have already spoken with Emma. She doesn't know how she makes the holes happen, but she undid the spell."

His voice was sharp. "When?"

"A while ago..."

"Margaret, try to remember. What day was it?"

She wrinkled her forehead. "I have never been good at recalling events. They jumble in my mind. Let me think... It was...it was a day or two before we went through the park with Mrs. Silvester." He looked blank. "You know, the day Mrs. Silvester's bonnet caught afire. I told you about it."

"Ahhh." Adrian's voice indicated comprehension; his face showed bafflement. The hand holding the reins lifted to rub his chin, but the well-trained grays did not break pace. "There has been time for it to dissipate, but the effects on the atmosphere are as strong as ever. The magic has not ceased. She must be lying to you." The utter conviction in his voice chilled.

"No. You are wrong," she cried.

"Hush. Lower your voice. People may hear." She looked around; the road had narrowed and they were passing a flock of stores. People crowded the pavement and a man glanced at her with curiosity written on his face.

"I am sorry..." She lowered her tone. "But Adrian, you are wrong. I know you are. Emma would not lie to me about this. I explained the immensity of her error; I helped her undo the spell."

His arm tensed. "Are you a magician?"

"No, I don't have talent. Emma inherited the ability from our mother. I got only a drip." His arm relaxed and he leaned against her as he guided the curricle around a corner. Margaret found the pressure of his arm comforting, but once they were on the Holborn road, he moved away.

"Describe the spell," he ordered.

"I don't know..."

"You were there. What happened?"

"Emma set it up on the table. She made clouds disappear in candle flames, a bronze sea of the tabletop, and ended up with a pearl."

"What did she do with the pearl?"

"I think she threw it on the fire." He nodded.

"What about the henbane?"

"How did you know?" His smile was the sun warming a flowery field.

"I knew." Accepting the statement, Margaret decided to confide in him fully.

"Emma does not believe she is causing the holes. We thought to go to the Council of Mages for advice, but neither of us is even certain it exists. Mama's mention of it was so long ago, I scarcely recall what she said."

"I agree with your sister. That spell should not make holes. Rein in your imagination, my dear. In the meanwhile, I will find help." Adrian veered off Skinner Street onto Hill and made a left on Snow which brought them back to the Holborn road. She held silent in deference to his need to concentrate on the horses.

"Let us head back," he said. "We can make a circuit of the park before I return you to Mount Street."

"No more kidnapping?" Margaret thought wistfully of an afternoon's drive, the two of them barreling down the road to Chelsea in a temporary escape from James Treadway.

"No," he whispered. "We can't. But we can enjoy the sunshine by the Serpentine." By the time they halted along a side path in the park, both had put holes to the back of their minds in favor of a spirited argument about the search for the Ark.

Flipping a coin and the reins to a stray boy with the admonishment, "Don't go for a ride, just walk them, if you would," Adrian jumped from the curricle and lifted his arms to assist her. "You are wrong," he said, swinging her to the ground. "Without Wellington's genius, England would have been in an impossible situation."

"It was impossible from the start. Using knights in battle

twisted the quest. It was to be a peaceful search for a wondrous gift from God. Shedding blood in the name of the Ark is blasphemous."

"We did not start the wars. Napoleon Bonaparte was the aggressor. What was Lord Wellington to do, stand aside and allow Boney to slaughter Englishmen? It could not be allowed."

"Lord Wellington did naught but heighten the acrimony." They set off across the lawn toward the Serpentine. The grass was a bit long in places, but was dry and fragrant. Ahead, several ladies grouped near two carriages. Their gowns laid a splash of color against the dun of horseflesh as if Mr. Turner had used a brush to paint them into the scene. Behind all, the Serpentine glinted like a flow of jewels in the sun. Margaret absently enjoyed the artistic vista while she executed a tiny bit of devilment. Adrian was becoming heated in defense of England's actions against the Corsican upstart.

"You can't reason with someone whose arrogance takes them so far from common sense," he argued. "Napoleon's search for the Ark was but a ploy. That was clear. His intent was to annex all of Europe without regard for the lives he sacrificed. He crowned himself Emperor, blast it."

"Like the people who control church committees without compassion for those they lead, Napoleon may have been correct in his vision; he might have been the person most capable of leading, but he did not employ finesse to soften the blow to sensibilities."

Adrian turned an incredulous eye on her. "Do you mean to say you think Napoleon should have overrun Austria, not to mention Russia, Spain, and all the other countries around him?"

"One big country," Margaret mused. "Adrian, think. Europe as a single entity. No more petty squabbles over who gets what or who is more important. It would take the world out of the schoolroom. Instead of fighting against each other, we could work to eliminate the evils around us."

Stunned by the radical statement, he almost missed the spark of amusement in her eyes. When he saw it, he exclaimed, "You minx. I thought you were a Bonapartist. Lord, that would put you in the suds. They hang..." Margaret's laugh drowned the remainder of his sentence. Then a footman approached, tugging his forelock.

"Excuse me," he said. "Mrs. Silvester asks if you would join her."

"Oh, is that Mrs. Silvester?" She eyed the ladies by the Serpentine. "I could not recognize her from this distance. We must pay our respects."

They spent time with Lady Jersey, Mrs. Drummond-Burrell, and Mrs. Maud Silvester. The ladies were disposed to be gracious; when Adrian said it was time to return Mrs. Treadway home, they parted with regret.

"Dear Mrs. Silvester," Margaret said as they moved toward the curricle. "I feared I would never think well of her. She is forceful, but has been all that is kind. Imagine her urging Mrs. Drummond-Burrell to invite me to tea."

"It sounded more as if Mrs. S was planning a rout. I've never seen Silence so quiet." He glanced at the sky and frowned.

"Adrian, what is it? You look perturbed."

"Clouds moving in. Doesn't look good." Margaret looked up.

"Yes, it looks like rain."

"Looks worse than that. Do you see anything, my sweet, do you see anything in the clouds?" Smoothly, he turned her to the west.

"What do you mean?"

"You recall I mentioned the atmosphere earlier." She nodded. "Well, I have to contend with clouds." Apprehensive, Margaret scanned the heavens as he explained his concern. "The clouds are a sign of the havoc magic is wreaking on the atmosphere. Emma's spells are more potent than she is aware. It has been my observation that clouds herald an increase in the magical effect. Whenever they form in this manner, the magic takes a virulent turn."

She gave him a weak smile. "I told you Emma has ceased making spells."

"Then I must determine why the magic has not dissipated." The gravity of his countenance revealed how serious the problem was. Instinctively, she laid a hand on his sleeve.

"I have faith," she whispered. "If anyone can solve this problem, it is you." They had paused, now they exchanged a clear, long look, full of the love that had grown like ivy around them. For Margaret, it was like drinking from the Holy Grail ; a wash of warmth flooded from her heart to the tips of her fingers. She felt inviolable; nothing could harm her, not clouds, not holes, not even her husband. Adrian's love was a lighthouse guiding her past the rocks and shoals of life's stormy seas into the haven of Avalon.

Her love could not be expressed, not while James Treadway lived, but she would no longer deny it. She glowed, an inner light winked.

Adrian set a gentle hand under her elbow and steered her to the curricle. "I had better return you to Mount Street."

* * *

Treadway was taking Minnie, dressed for once, driving in the park. In a breezy pink confection that clashed with her hennaed locks, Minnie bounced back and forth on the phaeton seat. There was little chance passers-by would miss the necklace around her neck. A gift, its heavy gold links dripped diamonds down her chest. The necklace was meant for evening wear.

"I hope Chickie and some of the other girls see us," she said with a giggle. "I want to show off this bang-up rig. And my necklace. You too." She slid her hand below his waist and squeezed the lump nestled in his pants. "I can't wait to show you off."

The horses jerked through the turn into the park. Part way around the circuit of Rotten Row, Minnie squealed. "Look, James, there's Mr. Silvester. Let's talk to him." Treadway obligingly pulled up.

"Hoy, there. What're you doing here, Sil? It's the fashionable hour."

"Staying out of m'grandmother's hair," Silvester responded, coming alongside. He glanced at Minnie and quickly averted his eyes. "Made me bring her—wanted fresh air. She's by the Serpentine, jawing at her friends. She spent fifteen minutes with your wife, Tread."

"Doing what?" Treadway asked sharply.

"Introducing her around. M'grandmother's taken a liking to your wife. Lady Jersey too. They were talking her into holding a rout. You're in for a pother; your house is going to be inundated with invitations and what not. I'll wager you'll be dragged into escorting Mrs. Treadway to balls and all. Where the Jersey and Mrs. S lead, the remainder of the *monde* will follow like lemmings, you know."

The report of his wife's burgeoning friendship with the Silvester dowager gave Treadway pause. If Mrs. S extended her umbrella over Margaret, doors would open. The upper ten thousand doors. He could indeed find his time spoken for if he didn't take measures.

Grown bored with talk not about her own self, Minnie said, "And you brought her to the park? That's sweet. But I was hoping you'd have brung Chickie. She ain't seen my James yet."

"Chickie had to practice. Are you for the show tonight, Tread? She's in the chorus," Silvester said.

"It's Wednesday. Almack's. I can't get out of it."

"Aren't you going to come see me?" Minnie pouted like the child she was. "I got an idea I wanted to try. I'm going to hang from the drawing room doorway and let you..."

His cheeks darkened as he interrupted. "No, I promised m'mother."

"Well, off I go," Silvester said, looking ill at ease. "Can tell when I'm *de trop*. Get it while you can, Tread. Your days are numbered."

It was sunny, no wind, a perfect outing if one ignored the knowing glances cast his way by various members of the intrusive ten thousand. Treadway ignored the censorious. Tooling the paths, Minnie cleaving to his arm and describing in rousing detail the circus-like antics she wanted to explore, he fought the urge to turn back to Spring Street. He wanted in the worst way to relieve his spiraling desire—and the spleen Mrs. S had kicked. Since that wasn't an immediate option, he wished Minnie would hold her tongue.

"Oooh, there's your friend, Adrian Hughes. Let's talk to him, James, let's. I can't show you off, he already knows what you look like, but I can show him my necklace."

It was the shock of his life. Margaret. A pink gown, much the same shade as the one Minnie wore, swirled down the graceful line of her hips, fluttered around her trim ankles. A spencer hugged her bosom. Unbuttoned, it framed Margaret's face and fragile neck, exposing nothing, but promising everything. Treadway's eyes caught on her décolletage and slowly moved upward. Her cheeks bloomed delicate rose. He recalled the feel of her skin, satiny and warm.

An excuse of a bonnet, a tiny confection of white satin with a profusion of pink trimming, and a plume of white feathers...curls peeping from under the absurd hat caught the sunlight and flashed, showing all the colors of the night. Damn his father.

Glued to Margaret's side was Adrian Hughes. Hughes the Apostate.

He felt primitive instinct rise. Bloody hell, the woman belonged to him. What did Hughes think he was doing, poaching on Tread's preserves? Gentlemen kept the agreement—hands off each other's skirts. Treadway almost leaped from the phaeton, but caught himself before he exhibited such cawkish behavior in front of Minnie. Bile rose in his throat.

He stopped the team, jaws grinding. His wife, Mrs. James Treadway, was flirting for all she was worth. She smiled, fluttered her lashes, tilted her head just so. With Hughes. Where in blazes had she come by feminine wiles? How dare she use them on his friend?

Hughes, the traitor, lapped it up like pap. He ought to give him a facer—couldn't the man find his own lady? Did he have to poach? Treadway's hand clenched.

A bawled "Move it over, clunch," finally penetrated the haze in his mind. Men were shouting. He was causing a jam-up of carriages, sitting in the middle of Rotten Row, watching his wife disport with his turncoat friend. He cow-handed the horses along the path.

The insidious devil, male ego, insisted he have his freedom, but not Margaret. She was not free to flaunt flirts all over London, to plant horns on his head. *She was his wife.*

Treadway asserted himself manfully. Back at Spring Street, he stripped Minnie and bade her perform her circus trick.

Chapter Twenty-one

Sally Jersey, one of the exalted leaders of the ten thousand, seen as the most human of the patronesses of Almack's club, was an acknowledged light of society. She also was such a nonstop chatterbox the *haute ton* freely called her 'Silence.' No other lady so clearly fit the picture of English womanhood; she possessed the ideal mix of what men admired in women, namely looks and a dimwitted mind, and what women envied in each other: power. Tonight, her urge to lead warred with her ninnyhammerish base.

Sally sank down on the bed. "I cannot go," she moaned to her maid. "I know I will say something. Emily Cowper will drag it out of me if Esther Latimer does not, and I will be ruined. It is impossible. I am going to climb into bed and stay there."

"My lady," the maid soothed, "I have a new gown from Madame Celeste ready. His lordship awaits you in the salon. Please, you must get dressed."

Sally dragged herself up on the counterpane. "If I retire to Middleton Park..."

"What nonsense is this?" a male voice boomed. "Sally, I've had two brandies waiting for you. We are going to be late."

"George, I cannot go! I held silent for a sennight, but I fear I can do so no longer." She buried her head in a pillow.

"Yes you can," George, Lord Jersey returned, not flummoxed by theatrics. "I don't know what bee you have in your bonnet, but tonight is Almack's night. You have to go. It's your turn to keep the rabble from the door. If you're lucky, Wellington will show again in trousers and you can turn him away. What's more, you dragged a promise from me to attend. I have the damned breeches on, not going to waste them now."

"But I will say something, and the queen will put me in the Tower!" She wiped a tear from the corner of her eye.

"What are you blathering about? There ain't any reason for you to be put in the Tower. That's for traitors. Come, get dressed. I don't want to wait for dinner—my stomach is rumbling and if I drink any more, I'll be cast away."

Lady Jersey did as her lord demanded, wringing her hands all the while.

* * *

With Spring Street and the park weighing on one side of his mind and her interference in his life tugging at the other, Treadway was pleasant, but every time he contemplated sex with Margaret, desire wilted under a rainfall of resentment.

Margaret lay alone in her bed night after night because he had a niggling feeling he could not have his cake and eat it too. Not if he wanted to keep from having his ears flailed by his father. But he would go Mordred's way before he allowed Adrian Hughes to nibble at the feast either.

One more infraction, just one more, and I will send her back to Puckeridge.

For the nonce, his sleeping arrangements were hintermost in his mind. He handed Margaret a glass of sherry and leaned against the mantel in the drawing room, to all appearances relaxed, but ready to beat his wife into submission. She wasn't going to take a lover, not if he had any say in the matter. She would behave properly if it killed her.

"Where's Christine?" he asked, twiddling his thumbs behind his back. A maid came in with a fresh decanter. It was the one with the chest. He smiled at her.

"She was invited to dine with friends. They go to the Paxtons." Margaret's finger traced the intricate carved molding at the edge of the sofa table. "Could you tell me about this? It is...unusual."

He grinned. That was a good wife, taking an interest in family heirlooms. Perhaps she was not straying. *Don't allow her to make any changes and she can stay.*

"Chinese," he stated. "M'grandfather brought it from the East. Like it?"

She nodded hesitantly. "I have never seen such a piece."

Treadway said affably, "It is teakwood. The shiny part is mother of pearl. Grandfather said the carver was China's premier woodworker. I can believe it. Look how realistic the dragon's scales are. See how the claws are exposed? I stabbed myself on one when I was young. Was sure I could lift the beast off the table. Course, I was only a nipper and didn't understand." Her head bobbed.

"The high relief is a marvel of craftsmanship; it is all one piece of wood. The belly of the dragon curves like he just ate a big meal. I especially like how the pearl is dug under the relief. Fancy it makes the figures look like they are rising out of the water." She nodded again.

"Those there," he pointed, "are foo dogs or some such. They sit at the door of the temple. Grandfather said they were to scare demons. My favorite is here in the other corner: the toad. It protects wealth. Looks noble, don't it?"

"But how is one to set anything on the table? The carving is extensive, there are no smooth places to set anything. Glasses would spill. It seems rather useless."

"You wouldn't want to use the table! Might break off a bit of the carving. It's to be admired, like a painting, not used."

Why had he thought she would be a good wife? The woman hadn't an iota of poetry in her. The way she did the library proved it. Curse his father for saddling him with an unsatisfactory female. Didn't appreciate treasures the family spent centuries collecting. Wouldn't put anything past her.

Treadway glowered. "Shall we go in to dinner? Can't be late to Almack's." Silently, he promised himself a visit to Minnie. There was a girl as the Lady meant her to be: appreciative of what she was given. Maybe she would sit on his face again. After he made sure Margaret made no scandals at Almack's, of course.

* * *

While Treadways, Jerseys, and countless others converged on Almack's assembly rooms in King Street, fire burned merrily in Treadway's bedchamber. In the grate, a coal fire gleamed, banked until the master should return and desire a blast of heat. On the rug in front of the marbled fireplace, sparkling droplets of fire played leapfrog. One drop nestled on the center of a ribbon of the border. Another drop jumped the first, landing in the center of the next ribbon. Around the perimeter of the rug they bounded, landing accurately, until the ribbons of the border had perfectly round holes burned in their centers.

Inside the border, a series of fiery drops rolled around the repeating field of stylized fleur de lis, one drop per element of the design. They traced the leaves, sizzling through wool, burning through jute backing until they touched wood. Then they promptly blinked out.

Treadway's valet elbowed the door open, a stack of crisply ironed shirts in his arms. Closing the door with his foot, he headed towards the clothes press. In the middle of the room, he stopped and wrinkled his nose. The aroma of burnt wool hung like a miasma.

Depositing the load of linen on the bed, the servant looked around suspiciously. He strode to the fireplace, sniffing. Taking the poker from its stand, he raked it through the coals, spreading the neat pile.

Seeing nothing out of the ordinary, he rattled the poker back into the holder and knelt on the hearth. His palms flat on the floor, he peered up the chimney.

Then he did a curious thing. He dug his fingers into the rug. He leapt to his feet and grabbed the rug, jerking it up. His eyes widened and he screamed. Like a girl, the valet shrilled terror in a prolonged "eeeek" that screeched 'calamity.'

A footman arrived first, skidding around the doorframe. A housemaid peeked in, eyes wide with fear. The butler pushed past her, puffing with the unaccustomed exertion of running. "Merlin's cave," he shouted, "is the house burning?"

Wordlessly, the valet waved the rug and the maid fainted. The footman leaped backwards into the hallway, crashing into a hall table. It splintered as his head hit the wall.

Mrs. Norris ran from the stairs. "My stars and garters. How could you be so clumsy? Mr. Treadway is going to kill you," she yelled at the footman. "That is his Queen Anne table." She picked up the skirt of the piece and fingered the carving along the rail. "You broke off half the swords." The table was in ruins. The top was split, one leg crushed. The skirt, detached and dashed to the floor, was a ragged line where a craftsman had had the innovative idea of carving delicate swords instead of scallops.

"It's magic," the footman said dumbly. "I know it is. I ain't staying where there's magic."

"It is not magic, it is your stupidity," Mrs. Norris yelled, swinging the broken table piece into the footman's chest.

"Naw," he yelled back. "That's magic!" A finger pointed dramatically into the bedchamber.

On the floor fronting the fireplace was a balanced design of fleur de lis in ashes, surrounded by a neat border of precisely spaced circles, also in ashes. The rug the valet held in shaking hands was missing its design.

Outside, clouds hung lower in the sky.

* * *

Almack's was enjoying one of its most successful nights in anyone's memory. Neil Gow and the orchestra were in top form. The refreshments, generally stale bread and butter with weak lemonade, were enriched by Princess Lieven's donation of crumpets. Her chef was experimenting with a new recipe and had turned out dozens of the things. He had not yet achieved the perfect flavoring. Almack's assembly benefited.

An exceptionally fine gathering of debutantes lined the room. For a miracle, none were crying—no one's nerves had drawn too tight under pressure, no flounce tore under masculine feet. Unlike many balls, where one dowager's green clashed with another matron's puce, the selection of gowns was pleasing to the eye in all directions.

What made the night perfect, beyond the fairy tale perfection of the details, was the number of extremely eligible unattached gentlemen who chose to attend. Adrian Hughes danced down the line. The charming auburn-haired twins, Gavin and George Latimer, dragooned by their mother, Lady Esther, stood against a pillar, a matched set.

William Johnstone, Lord Chively, and Peter Silvester all danced with worthy young ladies. If Johnstone was considered a bit dim, his healthy account at Childe's Bank made him acceptable. Chively's position as heir of the Earl of Wellwood brought him instant popularity, and Silvester's grandmother, as everyone knew, was *someone.*

Most exciting, the heir to the Duke of Albany was in attendance. Lord Anthony was a mystery, being from the island of Jamaica. No one knew him; everyone wanted to, though his looks were nothing wonderful. The dukedom was a rich one, the current duke, Anthony's grandfather, was ill, and every husband hunting lady in the room prayed his eye would fall upon her. It wasn't often the soon to be elevated heir to a dukedom was younger than Moses *and* unwed.

Icing the cake, Lord Anthony's younger brother had entered Almack's rooms. Now there was a man to end all men. The figure of Apollo, an income derived from not one, not two, but three healthy inheritances, a puckish grin, and connections to the Albany dukedom; Squire Conrad had it all.

The room hummed. No one fell asleep, no wallflower drooped, and the gentlemen seemed disposed to dance. A perfect night.

Alone of the company, Mrs. James Treadway and Lady Sally Jersey seemed dispirited. Mrs. Treadway's problem clearly was her husband, who escorted in, then promptly deserted her. After her ill-advised remarks about the Chinese table, Treadway had taken a snit.

Margaret was both steaming and cool as ice. His friends—a disreputable gang—clapped the chump on the back and made him welcome. That his snit caused him to eyeball the prettiest girls made her steam all the more.

"Meggie, love, isn't he a dream?" Lady Clarissa kept her eyes on Squire Conrad and raved.

"More a nightmare," Margaret replied. "Men are horrid. No one will dance with me—wait and see."

"How can you say that? You are in looks tonight." Clarissa sighed. "His looks are perfection and he dances well. What more could any lady want?"

"The point is you shouldn't want. If Squire Conrad looked your way, Sir Perth would slide out of your fingers. You would be back where you started your first season; trying to attach a gentleman who has too many ladies falling over him to care about any one. Men are fickle."

"You are a spoilsport."

"And Squire Conrad is poison to you. Be satisfied with what you have." Margaret frowned displeasure at the male of the species and noticed her husband glowering. She turned her back.

"Sir Perth is perfect for you. Would you throw him away? Though maybe you should. Gentlemen are selfish. Above all, they are unreasonable."

"He is still a dream." Clarissa ignored her friend's sour grapes and smiled at Sir Perth, who entered the room a coattail ahead of the closing of the doors. "I will consider your advice, my dear.

Perth is sweet."

Margaret glanced over her shoulder—there was Mr. Treadway, staring at her with narrowed eyes, chasing away any man interested in dancing with her. A bustle at the door indicated more arrivals. She swiveled her head. Christine swept in, dressed with careless elegance in well-dampened petticoats and a bodice markedly lower than her sister's. She filled the bodice remarkably well. The man at her shoulder licked his lips.

Christine caught Margaret's eye and gave a barely perceptible nod before turning to display her charms more fully to the slavering man. No, Margaret was not having a pleasant evening.

The other lady not enjoying herself was Sally Jersey. She and Emily Cowper were in charge of the rooms; Sally had been approached no less than twenty times for introductions to the Albany heir and spare. Each introduction required her to make conversation. She had bit the inside of her mouth till it bled.

"Hsst." Lady Jersey spun, confronting Lady Esther Holden.
"Oh, go away."

"What is the matter? Why is there blood on your lip?" Esther did not wait for a reply. "Only look, look who just came in. I am glad I was delayed; I was going to tell you it is eleven. Time to bar the door." Sally turned to the doorway.

Framed in the wide opening was the cream of the cream, Lady Coletta Shipley with both her brothers, Squire Michael Shipley and Richard, the Marquess of Brinston. Behind them, still shrugging out of an overcoat, was the Duke of Haverhorn, their exalted father. Sally rushed forward to welcome the group.

"How delighted I am to see you here, your grace," she gushed. "It is too seldom you come to town, much less Almack's. And to bring your family also. We are delighted. Lord Brinston, I am especially delighted to see you. Delighted." Sally's tongue was greased as she forgot the secret that must be kept. "I did not expect you to come to Almack's, Lord Brinston, with a cloud still over your head. Imagine, consorting with smugglers and putting your life in jeopardy. Did you not wish to crawl into a hole for safety? Oh, no, I know you really were not a spy, but many still believe it. I hope you are not cut. If you are, let me know. Jersey is here—he will set whomever straight."

The duke stepped forward. "Lady Jersey, I doubt I need you or your husband to protect my own."

She colored. "Your grace, I meant no disrespect. But these are my rooms, you know. As your hostess, it is my place to..."

"Yes, yes," the duke interrupted. "I am sure you are equal to all occasions. We are here because Coletta wants to dance. Shall we enter?" He took Sally's arm.

"You will be particularly pleased to meet Albany's heir," she confided. "Lord Anthony and his brother are here. They seem gentlemanly, though they were raised in that outlandish place. It hardly shows. The younger, Squire Conrad, dances exceptionally well."

Was this a perfect Almack's night? Now it was elevated to the realm of dreams. Adding Brinston and Michael to the lists, debutantes fluttered frantically. The Marquess of Brinston, but a short while ago under suspicion as an accused traitor to the crown, was one of the premier eligibles of the realm. Recently exonerated from charges he conspired with smugglers to sell secrets to England's enemy, Napoleon Bonaparte, the lingering scandal elevated his romanticism for naïve debutantes.

Then, as with the Albany brood, there was the younger brother, Squire Michael, more handsome than the ducal heir, suave, and precisely the man to set a young lady's heart pounding.

Older ladies primped. The Duke of Haverhorn was a fine figure of a man. With the duchess nowhere in sight, many a middle-aged matron sought to catch his eye. It was how society worked; while the cat's back was turned, the tom was expected to chase another bit of cheese.

Squire Michael slipped Miss Pelcher from Gavin Latimer's side and ushered her to the dance floor. Lord Brinston attached himself to the knot in front of a window and enjoyed a heated discussion of the Prince's Cottage, which renovation had the Treasury up in arms. Did his highness need a conservatory seventy-five feet long by almost forty wide supported by freestanding columns and paved with hexagonal brick tiles?

Lord Jersey spat, "At the price of 52,000 pounds? Demn, no house is worth that much. Not even my principal seat." Re-thatching the roof was the only expense the group supported.

The Duke of Haverhorn settled on a chair among the dowagers. Deliberately, he put himself next to Maud Silvester, anticipating the lady's dry commentary.

"Can't you walk into a room like any other person?" Mrs. S

said. "Sweep in as if you were the king, Haverhorn."

"Ah, but I threw Sally Jersey into a tizzy. That's worth any bit of pomp," the duke replied. "Don't throw stones, Maudie, I heard you all but took Prinny by the ear in the Park."

The old lady harrumphed. "You shouldn't gossip. It's unbecoming. You heard about those two?" She inclined her head in the direction of the Albany pair. "Word is the younger dabbles in voodoo. It's some form of Indies magic."

* * *

Lady Coletta wafted around the perimeter of the room, greeting friends. At Brinston Castle until a few days before her brother's dubbing, she was then confined to bed with a chill. This was her first chance to renew her acquaintance.

"Esther," she enthused. "It is good to be back, my dear. I was going to pay you a call tomorrow. I need you; not one *on dit* has reached me for weeks."

"Precious little of interest has happened," Lady Esther Holden replied. In a mist of lavender, Coletta sat with Margaret Treadway, whom she did not know, on one side and Lady Esther, one of her most intimate friends, on the other.

"Her Grace returned to the country," Coletta told Esther. "Her roses have spots."

"She will probably dust them, but won't know if it solves the problem for weeks."

"I may return to the Castle next month to help her pack for town. In the meantime, I am hostessing a dinner for the ministers at the duke's request. So bring me up to snuff." They began an intensive review of the beginning of the 1814 season.

Against the wall far to Lady Coletta's right, an acquaintance of Margaret's, Charlotte Wentworth, frowned at the floor. Her whole attitude bespoke anguish.

"Don't look happy, my dear," Peter Silvester commented.

"No, Mr. Silvester. Look!" Charlotte made a sweeping gesture at the dancers, almost spilling the glass of lemonade she held.

"Look at what?"

"Sir Saybrook. Just look at him. Connie Marwick has stolen his affections."

Peter narrowed his gaze at the couple Charlotte indicated. Say was dancing, a rare enough event to draw comment, but his partner was a dewy young thing with soulful brown eyes. In a typically white muslin gown, she simpered, and Arthur above, Say simpered back. "Egads, there must be something in the lemonade," Silvester exclaimed.

Charlotte gave him a pitiful look. Though his heart fell, he said, "I'll fix it for you, my angel." Her look of wonder made his chest swell, the better to accommodate sagging *amour*.

"Would you?"

Silvester laid his hand on his cracked heart. "If your divineness is determined to have Say, I will do my all." He took the lemonade glass gently from her hand. "You won't need this watery mess. I shall put it to better use."

Lady Coletta looked up at the shriek, wondering who had lost their decorum in the sacred halls of Almack's. Fairly running along the wall was a debutante, curls flapping against muslin clad shoulders, hands grasping air. Behind her sprinted Peter Silvester, a glass of lemonade in hand, followed closely by the Baron Saybrook. The girl shrieked again.

Saybrook stopped with a look of pain. Charlotte Wentworth came swiftly up behind the baron and spoke to him. He went off with her toward the refreshments room. Silvester continued the chase, evidently prepared to toss the lemonade at the girl.

Coletta swung her attention between the characters in the drama and decisively stood. The girl dashed past her, looking over her shoulder in horror. Silvester passed Lady Coletta and lost his balance. His arm wove in the air, drops of lemonade flying, but the agile man recovered. Watery lemonade cascaded down his front.

Lady Coletta stepped back from the lemonfall. "Mr. Silvester. Were you planning what I think you were planning?" He stared dumbly at her then at his clothes. "Do you not ever accost a lady in such a fashion again, sirrah," Coletta said sternly, albeit in a whisper. "I could see what you meant, if no one else did."

"You, you stuck your foot in my path. What did you do that for?"

Her eyes flashed, accentuating the resemblance she held to her formidable brother, Richard, Marquess of Brinston. "If you ever do such a nasty thing again," she enunciated carefully, "I shall tell the world about your painting."

Silvester's eyes popped. "What do you know of it?"

"Never you mind, bacon-brain. Remember. I shall be vigilant." Coletta turned on her heel and resumed her seat next to Lady Esther, who, if one only knew it, was a bit deaf. She looked a question.

"Merely a small mishap." Coletta laughed. "I imagine the gentleman thought he was going to collide with me. Mr. Silvester will surely recover with no ill effects."

Unnoticed on Coletta's other side, Margaret marveled. She heard the lady's words, soft but vehement. Responding to disgraceful intent, she had added brilliant retribution. Margaret wished she had the lady's acquaintance. She would know how to bring a recalcitrant husband to heel.

Speaking of husbands, Margaret noticed hers again. Mr. Treadway stood with Adrian, arms folded menacingly as he lowered his eyebrows at her. Disapproval radiated from him in waves. No wonder she was invisible to the company; who would dare approach her in view of his obvious censure?

If she could do magic, she would devise a spell switching men as ladies traded ribbons between bonnets.

Dowagers whispered, nodding their heads knowingly as they swiveled their eyes between Mr. and Mrs. Treadway. Lady Marmont summed it up perfectly. "Let us hope relations improve over tonight's exhibition. I never thought Treadway would settle so well, even showing sagacity in choosing such a sensible little thing. Jane Treadway must be pleased. She caught him before he sunk far into depravity."

Lady Phillpot cautioned, "Let's hope his wife keeps him on the straight and narrow."

"Did you see her eyes?" Sir John Galwin said, picking up Lady Marmont's dropped fan for the third time.

"No, what about them?"

"Look at her eyes sometime."

Meanwhile, in the hall, Peter Silvester mopped futilely at his drenched inexpressibles, coat and waistcoat. Lemonade was sticky, even watery lemonade. Charlotte Wentworth, joined by her sister, Maria, and Janice Jackson, commiserated with him. A young Connie Marwick, in ritual white, dripped tears from cow-brown eyes to her mother's shoulder.

Leaving ducal heirs, spares, and the Latimer twins to the dangers of a rapacious crowd of debutantes, Sir Saybrook slunk out of Almack's to the safety of the open street.

"By Accolon," he whispered. "That was a close call. When Miss Marwick shrieked, she sounded just like Mama. Crystal cave, I could have been shackled to her."

Inside the hall, under the last arch of the ballroom where gimlet eyed patronesses seldom ventured, the coterie Treadway acknowledged as his closest friends ducked duty.

"Tread!" Chively exclaimed. "Ain't seen you for days, m'boy."

"He's gone to ground in Spring Street," Charles Leighton drawled. "Luscious strawberries to pick, don't you know. Knew a paltry wife wouldn't keep our lad down."

"I have a bone to pick with you. You set m'mother thinking." Stone shoved against Treadway's shoulder. "Decided if you were ready to tie on apron strings, then I should too. She dragged me to this marriage mart and is throwin' debs at me right and left."

Treadway laughed. "Duck, Stone. Instead of sticking to you, the debutantes will roll across the room." Glancing beyond Chively's shoulder, he noted Margaret had moved to a chair tighter against the wall. By the Lady, was she going to be a wallflower all night?

"Easy for you to say—you ain't got cross-eyed Angeline Bradley crawling on your sleeve," Stone grumbled. "She wants me to get permission from the Jersey to waltz."

"Mama explains Stone's presence, what about you?" Treadway asked his other friends.

"We came to support him," Chively said, proud in a dim way. "Mothers shouldn't waylay a man. He needs all the help—"

"I want an intro to the strawberry," Leighton broke in. "She must be something. Got to see her." As Treadway shook his head, Leighton pushed. "I have a right to vet your connection. I took that spavined bay off you when your Pater was going to burst a vein. Remember?"

Leighton and Stone were disparaging Treadway's eye for horses when Hughes wandered up to the group. "Traitor," Treadway mouthed to him.

Hughes's eyes looked strained. "What boil do you have on your—"

"Poaching."

"Ah, the park. I shudder to think what would have happened. Right over your wife's shoulder was a certain couple. I distracted her until you could whisk your, ahem, carriage away."

"I'm for Spring Street," Leighton drawled. "Introduce myself to Tread's skirt."

Hughes jammed his nose in Treadway's face. "Your brain box must have been swaddled in cotton to chance meeting your wife with your mistress preening at your side. Rides in the park during the fashionable hour are not advisable. Not with muslin decorating the seat of your chariot."

"We are going to Spring Street, Tread," Chively prompted. "Leighton wants to meet your skirt."

"Not that that is your only sin. I hadn't seen her before. She's young," Hughes whispered, his eyes dark. "Too young. You promised—"

"You don't go by yourself." Treadway turned his back and clapped Leighton on the shoulder. "After I get out of here, I'll take you to meet Minnie."

Hughes walked away.

Chapter Twenty-two

"I don't know how them holes got in the pans. The pot boy—he could have dug the middles out with a knife," Mrs. Norris said with a frown. "I'll send a man out to purchase new ones on the instant, like you say, Madam."

Margaret agreed. "I think you must. Cook can't possibly do without utensils. But Mrs. Norris, the pot boy cannot be blamed any more than another. I haven't a clue how holes came to be in perfectly sound iron pans, but no one dug them with a knife." She unlocked the strongbox. "Here is two pounds. Let me know if it is not sufficient for a full set."

"The staff says it is magic," the chatelaine mumbled. "With all the doings, we've lost a footman and the scullion, not to mention all them pretty maids. They all up and left."

"Then hire new," Margaret said, digging in the strongbox again. "Offer a bonus to the remainder if they will stay." She passed over the funds and the chatelaine bowed herself out of the little office behind the library. Margaret didn't see her go; determined chin in hand and blind eyes on the desk in front of her, she attempted to solve a problem.

Holes in the cooking pots. Not just the pots, but the sheets, a rug, a window and no less than three doors. The worktable in the kitchen destroyed and the chestnut period table, the one her husband insisted was made by Daniel Marot, reduced to kindling. Last night, leaving Almack's, she found a hole in a glove. The gloves had been whole when she entered Almack's. They were new, not worn before, and nothing had occurred inside the hallowed hall to pierce the finger of her left hand. It was as is if magic...

The snapping of fingers brought Margaret back to the office with a start.

"Margaret, pay attention." Christine, pelisse over her arm and bonnet on her head, snapped her fingers again. As she raised her eyes to her sister's face, Christine said, "That is more like."

"I am sorry, did you want something?"

Christine pulled the pelisse over her shoulder. "You looby. I am packed. The least you can do is give me a proper sendoff."

"You are going somewhere?" Margaret blinked, sure she had missed something.

"Belinda Judson asked me to come to her. Her husband was called to Norfolk. We will do the season together and remove to Brighton at the beginning of July."

"This is sudden." Thorn number one was leaving? Margaret tried to hide a surge of elation behind conventional expressions of dismay. "I hadn't a notion you were thinking of going anywhere." Banging a mental poker over the imp demanding she exhibit better manners, Margaret failed to request Christine reconsider her decision to leave. "We will miss you, sister. Our house is always open to you."

Christine tossed her head. "I wager you will miss me," she muttered darkly. Exchanging an insincere embrace, they made their way to the front hall, where stacked baggage threatened to topple a white-faced maid.

From the small mountain of bags, boxes and trunks, her sister was taking all her worldly goods. At least one portmanteau belonged to Emma; Margaret guessed Christine had not bothered to buy baggage to hold her recent purchases. Stepping around a trunk straggled from the group, one that had surely carried part of her trousseau from Puckeridge, she added, "You will be gone some time?"

The front door's swing made the footman on duty jump nervously and the maid squeaked. She frowned at them and the moment for objecting to Christine's appropriation of luggage passed. Margaret didn't think she would have said anything. If she did, Christine might take it into her head to remain, just to be contrary.

Treadway strode in the opened door, bringing a shaft of sunlight, fresh air, and a swirl of dust. It sparkled. "What's this," he asked, dropping his cane on a table which seconds before had gleamed and tossing his hat to the butler.

"I am leaving," Christine said bluntly. Margaret held her breath. Her husband would be displeased. He would find a way to blame her for the departure of his inamorata. There would be another row. She was tired of rows; the mental poker that silenced her good manners swung at his head for what he would say.

He stuck a hand out to shake Christine's limp one. "Well,

well. Shaking the dust of London off your feet?" With a disdainful toss of her head, Christine ignored his hand and buttoned her pelisse.

"No, I will suffer the dust in Upper Woburn Place. The Judson's have invited me."

Treadway could have lied better. He only said, "We'll miss you," and turned to Margaret with a whine in his voice. "My cravat has holes in it. What did your laundress do?"

"If it has holes in it, why didn't you notice before you put it on?" Margaret threw up her hands and turned to the butler, who had developed a tremor. "Craig, Mrs. Whitmill-Ridgemont is ready to leave. Have you called the carriage?" *I can't believe it. He doesn't care she is leaving. The chump must be wearied of her demands.*

Her husband bounded up the stairs and Margaret saw her sister out with grace and a sense of righteousness rewarded.

* * *

The next, a dreary rainy day, passed. Dinner, served by jittery footmen, came and went. Spending a dull evening home, Treadway hid from his wife behind a wine bottle. There was good reason for gentlemen to remain at the table after ladies adjourned to the drawing room. He couldn't articulate the reason, but it was there.

He traced the vintner's label with the tip of the cheese knife. *Quinta de Vargellas.* The finest in his cellars. No sense pouring it into a decanter. The bottle would be empty before he left the table. Only a fool would leave a vintage port for the butler to guzzle.

Tipping the bottle, he poured another measure. Rolling port around his tongue, his anger at Margaret faded. She didn't have to like the family treasures, as long as she accorded them the respect they deserved. Irritation with Adrian Hughes took center stage. *He's planning to put horns on my head. The woman wouldn't say boo to a goose but he's got no compunction.*

Another three fingers of port mellowed his nerves. "Chattered about nothing at dinner," Treadway mumbled to the wine bottle. "As if I care about Wellwood's rout." His eyes sidled over the elaborate silver epergne the Mater's uncle had sent from Madras.

Uncle John had outlandish taste—this was worse than the cobra head table. Worth a fortune and his father took great delight in its intricacies, which was why it sat in the middle of the table, but those foreigners didn't have the idea right. Should have baskets or plates to hold food, not the open mouths of fish. Never saw a carp with its mouth so wide. Grapes and comfits spilling out of open jaws gave him nightmares when he was a sprout.

The Treadway collection was famed in the *ton*. His wife had better learn to like it. At least she behaved at Almack's. Not that she danced. He had kept his eye on her; she didn't dance, not once. Nor did she spend much time in conversation. Instead, she warmed a chair against the wall. Wallflower, nothing but a damned wallflower.

Good thing the widow left. Her charms palled beside Minnie's. Treadway couldn't recall what he had found enticing there. Damn female just wanted a wedding ring.

He sat with his good friend, the wine glass. As was proper, Margaret removed to the drawing room. The dining room was too demned quiet. The night before nagged and the clink of his teeth against crystal echoed. He hated drinking alone—with silver carp spitting up fruit and nuts, it was a dead bore.

Minnie wasn't available for a week. *Women and their courses. Thank Lancelot she is almost done. If it weren't raining, I'd go to the Gardens. Find a doll.* At the thought, his rod stirred. *Well, that's one use for a wife.* He abandoned a half-full glass of the finest *Aguardente* and headed for the drawing room.

She was doing a needlework something or other. He could see her, placid as Igraine, retiring to the country rather than enjoy the hustle and bustle of society. She filled him with ennui, but there were compensations, compensations he intended to avail himself of. Tonight.

"Would you play for me, my dear?" Margaret nodded mutely and moved to the instrument.

The sonata faltered when Treadway sidled behind the bench. Her skin rippled, sensing his nearness. "Keep playing," he whispered. He caressed the nape of her neck and she skipped three lines of music. When his hands slipped into her gown, she forgot the coda. Her hands stilled on the keys.

"Lay back against me," he suggested in a husky voice. When she did, she discovered the wicked man had tricked her. The fastenings at the back of her dress were undone. He slipped the sleeves down her arms, trapping her, and played with her chemise covered breasts.

Treadway knew what to do. Soon she was squirming on the bench, which creaked and groaned. "They'll hear," she moaned, her head rolling feebly in protest.

"Who?" her husband breathed. "Who will hear what?"

"The bench. The servants." Her husband laughed and scooped her up in his arms. With her sleeves pulled down, Margaret felt trapped. "Can't have a footman barging in." He breathed out as he spoke; the aroma of wine, trout and beef passed sourly over her face.

Crossing to the door with long strides was a bumpy, dizzy, moment. He stooped to turn the key in the lock. Then they were in front of the fireplace. When he laid her on the hearth rug, her hair caught on his arm and pulled. Untangling the strands, Treadway knelt with one leg on either side of her hips, pinning her to the floor. He leaned over and kissed her. It was a wild mating of lips, his aggressively demanding, hers compliant. With a swift move, he raised her and swept the gown off, tossing it aside.

The rug prickled like a heat rash, but she did not protest. The look in his eyes silenced her. He swept his tongue over her breast, the tip of which skimmed the top of her chemise. He moved from breast to stomach to the thatch of hair between her legs. The chemise, wet from his mouth, clung to her skin where he sucked and nipped.

She forgot the rug, forgot the servants. Indeed, Margaret forgot herself. His breeches came off as quickly as his cravat. He wore nothing but his skin and she was still hampered by shift, stays, and stockings.

"Do you want me to remove my clothes?" she asked, studying the erect nature of his penis.

"No, you look delectable as you are. Spread for me, sweetheart." He swooped, covering her. "Spread your legs wider," he said hoarsely. "I won't split you in two. Promise." Margaret obediently stretched her thighs and without a pause he surged in, beginning the pushing process.

To start, he pushed evenly, not quickly. His eyes focused on the rug, his body glided over hers. Soon the tempo increased. Sweat sheened his chest and the glide became a sticky jerk. Her nipples caught in his chest hair, pulled and bounced. Margaret felt the sensation of floating begin. Her stomach cramped. The cramp meant soon she would feel free. Free of her body, free of the earth.

Her fingers tingled.

Treadway pushed faster. Harder. Sweat beaded his forehead and chest. The smell was vaguely unpleasant. She turned her head to the side.

His rhythm faltered. His eyes unfocused and his arms, holding his body braced above hers, shook. This was the time she liked best. He rocked, pushed, and jiggled inside her. The movement rubbed him against the supremely sensitive part of her. In response, she closed her eyes and flew to Heaven. He groaned.

Later, in her room, Margaret toyed with the comb on her dressing table. Scraping the teeth lightly over the lid of a pin box, listening to the rhythmic ping, she reviewed the session in the drawing room.

On the rug. Not dignified, but at least it felt good. She sighed. For all the closeness of their skin, she hadn't felt a connection between the two of them. With his thing inside her, they moved together, but they weren't *together*. It was disappointing.

* * *

White's Club was quiet. Treadway felt bilious. What had possessed him last night? To take his wife on the drawing room floor—gads. He didn't understand himself. He rubbed the cool glass against his forehead and then swallowed a healthy dose of brandy.

His thoughts swung to his mistress. Now, there was a satisfying chit. He took another swig.

To be met at the door by dancing bare breasts. It was a man's dream. She wasn't so vulgar he wanted to shut her mouth either. He'd trained her well. She combined polished skill with a natural exuberance for bed work. Making love to Minnie was sublime. What more could a man ask? He poured from the bottle into his glass and tried to wash away memory of the night before.

Bloody crystal cave. Listening to Margaret play the damned pianoforte—watching her sway back and forth, imagining her swaying impaled on his rod—he hadn't been able to resist taking her then and there, the prim, passionless ninny his father forced him to wed.

Though he'd had her any number of times, every time was like her first. She was small. It was like taking a chit from the schoolroom. Another swallow of brandy loosened his suddenly tight throat. Tight like her sheathe. By Lancelot, he'd melted in her heat, had experienced the explosion of pleasure he only got from virgins. That was why he'd wanted her, but he didn't want to desire her.

Treadway tilted the bottle. Empty. He waved his hand; the waiter, bless him, had another ready. He tossed a coin to the man and filled his glass. His hand shook.

He left the half empty bottle on the floor and made his way towards the door. Minnie. Had to get into Minnie. She would make him feel better. Curse it, her sheathe was looser than Margaret's. If only he could have Minnie sewn up like a virgin again.

"Friend ho," a familiar voice halted him.

"Stone." Treadway rolled his shoulder around the door frame until he was leaning against it. "Thought you'd sworn off White's."

Billy Johnstone shook his head. He'd been drinking, more than Treadway. When his head shook, his shoulders did also and he nearly fell. "Wouldn't never give up White's. Only place to escape debs. Come, bend an elbow with me."

They reeled across the salon and Treadway settled back in his still warm chair. "You've been hiding your skirt," Stone accused. "Saw Hughes and he swore you haven't had her out of Spring Street but once."

Treadway grinned. "Would have to put her in a dress to do it." He listed in the chair, but Stone shot straight and true.

"Is she hideous or are you afraid someone'll steal her?"

"Is that a challenge?" Treadway asked, taking no offense. Stone wasn't known for tact or charm. His friend sagged down in the chair so he could stick a hand in his pocket. It was a struggle to get it back out. His fist was full of pound notes and guineas.

"Bet you won't take her out tonight. A pony on it. S'still early. Take her somewhere where she's seen. Poke her there—lay claim like a man." He threw paper and coins on the table and grinned lopsidedly.

"Stone, you're foxed; you can't count. That's a monkey—is the bet a monkey or a pony?"

His friend owlishly pawed the money. "Aww, give over. A pony'll have to do." He plucked half of the notes up and shoved them into his pocket. "Got to buy m'mother a present; is her birthday. Thinkin' of getting her new harness for the carriage and the good stuff don't come cheap." Stone shook a finger. "Don't change the subject. You 'cepting my challenge?"

"Why not?" Treadway's eyes gleamed as he hauled Stone out of his chair. "What was it? I take her out where she's seen and poke her good? You want to watch?"

"T'night. You got to do it t'night. Or I'll spend the money on m'mother. She'll think I'm making up for bein' bad some way."

"Where shall we go?" Stone looked at the ceiling and staggered into Treadway. They flailed and righted themselves.

"The Opera. Get a curtained box and keep 'em closed. Poke her there. You can only make her squeal when the soprano shrieks."

Chapter Twenty-three

"I adore the opera," Honoria Silvester said. She settled on the velvet covered seat. Margaret, Charlotte, and Maria Wentworth nodded with varying degrees of enthusiasm.

Clarissa concurred. "I would like to have a magic flute."

"I care little for the music." Charlotte spread her fan. "The audience inspires me. I have learned more watching boxes than I ever gleaned from the lending library."

"What do you mean?"

Charlotte said slyly, "Lydia Norton."

Clarissa crowed. "I know what you refer to, you wicked girl."

"Do tell."

Charlotte leaned close to Honoria. "You remember Lydia Riggs. She wed Mr. Norton the year we came out. He was not the grandest catch, but they were well suited, everyone said. Both possessed of modest fortune, both enjoyed modest success. Margaret, you were in her set. You must recall how in alt Lydia was when she caught Mr. Norton's eye."

At her friend's nod, Charlotte continued. "I met Lydia not a week since. Here. At the opera with her Mr. Norton."

"You never told me," Maria objected.

"No, Lydia asked me to keep her presence in town quiet."

"Why would she do that?"

"Her mother-in-law," Margaret guessed, as Honoria's forehead wrinkled in puzzlement. Charlotte giggled. Clarissa interjected a more conventional explanation.

"Mr. Norton's mama is hardly enthusiastic at Mr. Norton's choice."

"They wed at the end of the season." Margaret picked up the story. "Mrs. Norton made Lydia miserable for two months. She tried to ban the poor girl from Almack's. But how does that apply to a night at the opera?"

"His mother finally convinced Mr. Norton to retire to his estate," Clarissa said. "To hide his shame, I believe she thought. But now they are in town. Lydia is hiding from her."

"There was a moment I thought they must come face to face," Clarissa said. "Lydia cleverly stepped on the hem of her gown and spilled a glass of wine down Sir Burley's waistcoat. He jerked back and bowled over Adrian Hughes. Hughes fell against Princess Lieven and ripped the lace at her bodice in a most immodest manner."

"Lord Burley was faulted," Charlotte chimed. "Princess Lieven warned him away from Almack's on the spot. We will not have to suffer him dancing on our toes—not for the remainder of the season."

"And dear Lydia did not have to speak to her mother-in-law. Mr. Norton looked highly irritated with her clumsiness and whisked her out of the theatre immediately."

"How does she look?"

"Well, but she has gained flesh. Give her a few years and she will have a double chin."

"Poor Lydia."

It was a refreshing change for the ladies to be without male escort breathing down their necks. Charlotte and Clarissa had conceived the idea of snubbing men for a girl's night out. Margaret appreciated the opportunity to solidify her friendship with the Wentworth sisters and Miss Sylvester. More, it was dizzying to know there were ladies in town who did not speak, eat, and breathe the opposite sex. For this night at least, the marriage mart was closed.

Not that they had been permitted to find their own way to the Opera House. No, Mrs. S had sent Honoria's brother to see them settled in their box. But the deed done, Mr. Silvester made himself scarce. There was no disapproving male in the gilt chairs behind them. No stultifying man tsked at their conversational topics. And no infuriating husband made her feel ten years old as she and her friends mulled the plight of Lydia Norton, nee Riggs.

"Did you see Lady Jersey in the lobby?"

"No, I missed her."

"She was directly in front of us. The funny thing is, I didn't hear her say a word."

The curtain drew back on the stage and the coterie of ladies turned their attention to the first act. To their delight, Tamino was handsome.

* * *

Maud Silvester frowned across the theatre. "Haverhorn," she said abruptly. "Do you know what is wrong with Sally Jersey?"

"Hmmph?"

"Sally Jersey. She hasn't opened her mouth."

"That's good," the duke responded absently, opera glasses to his eyes.

"*Not* good. Something is wrong."

Haverhorn lowered the glasses. "What are you talking about, Maud?"

"Sally Jersey," she said impatiently. "She is as silent as Merlin in thought. Something is wrong."

"Well, if you think there is something wrong with that, you should do something about it. For myself, I think it is a pleasant change to have Silence silent. It is such a rare event."

Maud chomped down on her response. Haverhorn was only a man, elevated title and all. "Well, I am going to go see her," she grumbled. "You stay here. Don't let anyone steal my seat."

A few minutes later, she was in the Jersey box, where Sally sat, alone and unattended.

"Where's Jersey?" she asked, stomping to the vacant chair at Sally's left.

"He has gone to Inman's box." Sally twisted her fingers in the satin covering her lap.

Maud cocked her head. "What, that is all you are going to say? Five or six words?" Sally turned her head away. Disgusted, Maud charged into the breach, sword swinging. "What is wrong with you? The last weeks, you have been as mealy mouthed as Maria Wentworth. You have hardly been seen in public. People are starting to say you are ill, or that Jersey has tumbled to a major indiscretion. What is it? Out with it, girl."

Her response was a single tear trembling on a lash, not even bold enough to slide down a paper white cheek. "Oh, for Arthur's sake." Maud dug into her reticule for her handkerchief. Thrusting a scarlet bandana into her friend's hand, she repeated her demand. "Tell me what is wrong this instant."

Sally sighed deeply. Closing her eyes, the tear finally escaped her lashes. It wended down her cheek, sticking in the corner of her mouth. "Maud," came out as mournful as a ghost in an unoccupied house. "Maud, I cannot bear it any longer."

"Cannot bear what?"

"I am going to tell someone."

"Sally, make sense. What are you going to tell?"

"About your grandson." The words were faint.

"My grandson? Peter?" Sally nodded. Maud sat back, flummoxed. "What would you tell?" she finally asked, wondering if bees had got in Sally's belfry.

Sally's chin dipped all the way down to the cabochon ruby centering her necklace. "His painting."

Maud's chin dropped also, but since her head didn't dip, it exposed a dark cavern below her nose. Her eyes roamed the audience, seeking enlightenment. It came when she beheld Margaret Treadway in a box across the way with her granddaughter, Honoria, and a few of her friends. Memory, of a day earlier in the season when the Treadway bride had come for tea, romped down the stairs of her mind, dusty from hiding in the attic of the unimportant. The memory dragged along a tattered blanket of understanding.

Maud clenched her hands into fists. "Good God, Sally Jersey, if you aren't the biggest goose in town. Do you mean to say that you are afraid you are going to reveal that my idiot grandson painted four of the ugliest paintings ever daubed?" Sally rubbed her chin on the ruby.

"That is old news," Maud said flatly. "No one cares."

* * *

After the interval, the ladies squeezed the chairs together at the rail so they were in a row. Margaret was on the end with her chair against the wall separating their box from the next. Her feet tangled in the floor length velvet curtain. It could be pulled across the front of the box to gain privacy, but was pushed to one side, partially obstructing her view. The neighboring box had its curtain pulled.

As a portly Sarastro bellowed Act II's opening aria, Margaret found that curtains, while obstructing vision, did little to obscure conversation.

In the adjoining box, "Kiss me, Min," a man crooned drunkenly. "Didn't come here to listen to the cacophony. Stone bet me a pony I wouldn't."

An uncultured female voice answered. "I'll do better n'that." Margaret did her best to ignore the groans, breathless coos and rustles seeping from the box next door. The curtain proved no barrier. Papageno's stage utterances didn't drown the unmistakable sound of lovers wooing. Heavily.

The Wentworth sisters tittered. "I've never heard the like," Charlotte whispered. Maria blushed. The other ladies could not hear, but Charlotte filled them in.

The sounds increased. "To Mordred with the wager. Why don't we go back t'Spring Street. Y'can get out of that blasted dress and I can feel what I'm getting," the man growled, sounding frustrated.

"Aww, it'll be all right, Jamie," his companion responded. "Suck in yer gut; let me get them buttons undone. Yer pantaloons is too tight." She giggled shrilly. "Now, ain't that a sight better? Coming to the Oprey was a fine idear. Don't need no bed for this."

The man groaned. Again. "Minnie," he slurred, "Use your tongue. Ahhh, thas right."

Margaret narrowed her eyes in disgust. The licentious groans and giggles distracted from *The Magic Flute*. That man and his doxy were ruining her enjoyment of the evening. It shouldn't be allowed. She shot an angry glance at the curtain.

Honoria leaned over. "Shocking, is it not? I wonder who it is?" Her flushed cheeks and glittering eyes indicated less horror than fascination. Margaret gritted her teeth and did her best to concentrate on the Queen of the Night. But the lovers were less quiet as their activity increased.

"Jamie," the female squealed.

"Spread your legs wider," the drunken man said hoarsely. "I won't split you in two. Promise." Margaret froze.

"I don't believe it," she whispered. Her teeth gritted. Her hands clenched. "Unprincipled...lecherous...monster." Abruptly, she stood.

"What is the matter?" Maria asked. "Margaret, why do you look so?" She closed her eyes. Dear Lady, the Opera House. She couldn't scream or throw anything. It would cause a scandal. Heaven forbid there should be a scandal. She closed her eyes and amended the thought.

More of a scandal than she already faced. In the name of Guinevere, she was going to kill him. What did she care about scandal?

"I will return in a moment," Margaret whispered. She turned on her heel and left the box, closing the door gently behind her. She moved to her right and regarded the door facing her. How could she dare? It took less than five seconds to find the courage. It was bolstered by the sounds from beyond the door. A particularly evocative groan curled under the sill, wafted through Margaret's bones, and chilled her blood.

She opened the door, strode forward, and closed it carefully. When she reached the man, she drew back her foot as far as her fashionably slim skirt allowed and kicked. Her aim was true. The man groaned again, this time in pain from the satin slipper connecting with his ear. He rolled over, his breeches flap flapping, and gaped.

"Wha...?"

"Get out of here." Margaret kicked his chest.

"Ahh..."

"Get clothing on that...that... Get out of here," she whispered, kicking him in the arm.

"Ohh...m'god..."

She kicked him somewhere below the waist. Unfortunately, she did not aim low enough to strike the wilting rod that sprang from his open breeches, but the man's abdomen contracted visibly. "Get yourself and your...your doxy out of here. And if you dare come near me, James Treadway, I will find a gun and shoot you between the eyes."

She stormed from the box, almost bowling over a smiling Lady Jersey, strolling the corridor, chatting with Mrs. Silvester the elder.

* * *

Margaret shifted the damp cloth covering her eyes. She would be skinned alive before she allowed that profligate to see she had been crying. At least with the cloth soothing the redness around her eyes, she could not see the morning light flooding her bedroom from the undraped window. It was humiliating enough to have Lady Clarissa and her other friends aware of his betrayal, but to lose sleep over it...

"That libertine," she said low. "He doesn't have the courage to face me." She dropped the cloth on her dressing table and regarded the pair of jousting pistols. They were vaguely handsome, she supposed. The case was elegant against gold velvet lining, but there was a bewildering array in the box. There were no less than three long things with polished wood handles, a pair of pincers, and a number of long thin metal parts. Most curious was the metal button thing with a prong sticking from it. She could make no sense of the paraphernalia.

If she was to shoot Treadway, she would first have to ask him to load the gun for her.

"He didn't come home. I would have heard if he had. He is probably still with his doxy. The Lady have mercy, she was young. No more than a child. How dare he. Wait till I see him. Just wait," Margaret muttered as she dressed. The indigo cotton was simple to fasten. In deference to the presence of jousting pistols, she did not call her maid to assist her. The stupid girl was useless, mumbling about magic curses and starting at her own shadow.

"No more. I will no longer be a complaisant wife. That man may find every woman in the world more attractive than myself; I do not care," she growled to the carpet as she descended the stairs to the dining room. "But I will be treated with respect. Or else."

Entering the room, she finished her thought aloud. "I am not going to stand for it anymore." A startled footman goggled at her.

"Don't just stand there," she snapped. "Pull out my chair and fetch a plate." The servant performed as ordered and fled the room. She leveled her gaze up the table. The view of her husband's empty chair was obscured by the hideous silver epergne Mrs. Treadway's uncle sent from the East. Why did he bother? Treadway inherited atrocious taste. It explained the cheap trollop he'd been with last night.

"He has no discrimination," Margaret said with finality. The butler entered the room with his accustomed tread. He flashed an unfathomable look. She watched him, seething as much as she had the evening before at the Opera House. The decision was instantaneous.

"Craig, remove that ugly thing." She waved her hand at the table.

"Madam?"

"That hideous epergne. It offends me. Put it in the attic." He goggled, much as the footman had done. She raised her eyebrows.

Back ramrod straight, Craig picked up the massive epergne and headed for the door, only to be stopped facing the raised panel. He shifted the silver piece in his hands; it was obviously too heavy and unwieldy for him to hold with one. He couldn't open the door. Nuts dropped from gaping fish mouths.

As he turned away, the door opened and the footman rushed in, balancing plates and pots on a serving tray. Her breakfast had arrived.

The footman didn't expect the massive epergne to be blocking the doorway. The butler didn't expect the footman to be in a tearing hurry. With a clash as of swords, the two serving pieces met in desperate combat.

The epergne lost the battle. A fish mouth slammed into the edge of the sturdy tray. The mouth closed, dented into non-service. Never again would the bounty of the kitchen and garden spew from the fish mouth, not unless the silversmith achieved a miracle.

Margaret was hard pressed not to laugh. The butler looked so outraged, the footman so intimidated, and the fish mouth so crumpled. She poured tea while the footman babbled.

Bolstered by the smooth, uncluttered expanse of the dining table, she calmed enough to come to a more reasoned decision. It was her house. She would not live with furnishings which did not please. As she ate, so did she plan.

The hall chair would go in the master's bedroom, the oriental carved table belonged in the attic. The Dresden porcelain mirror, with its overly elaborate edging of white and pastel flowers, birds and leaves, with gilt ribbon twined through, did not belong in the drawing room. It could grace the wall of a guest room. Not that it was hideous; but every time Margaret used the mirror, she was conscious the flowers had faces in their centers. Faces that leered, laughed, even impudently stuck out tongues.

The African masks, most particularly the one with misshapen holes for eyes and mouth, could hang in the library. Let Treadway—if he ever dared come home, drat him—stare at the dried red seeds and grotesque dangling stones framing a nightmarish asymmetrical visage.

Margaret mentally rearranged the contents of the house, unaware her agitation was increasing. With each mouthful of food, each banishment of bizarre heirloom, she wound tighter. Her fork stabbed kippers, the knife slashed toast.

Emma entered. Her cheery "Good morning," was answered by a growl. A mass of bundled nerves, Margaret rose from the dining table.

"I have finished," she told her sister. "This is a busy day. I hope you can amuse yourself." She swept from the room while Emma's brow crinkled.

Gliding into the drawing room, she summoned the butler and gave him his orders. He paled.

"Madam," Craig gasped. "You cannot..."

She raised a supercilious eyebrow. "I cannot?"

"The master...Mr. Treadway..."

"You have your orders," Margaret said dismissively. "I am mistress here. If you don't like it, complain to your master, *if* you can find him." The butler stood stock still for a full minute, then turned on his heel and left.

* * *

Treadway woke on the couch in Adrian Hughes's back room. His brandy soaked head ached, his icy feet poked from under the quilt crookedly covering him, and his arm flung into space, straining his shoulder and elbow. Worst, his chest was constricted. A dead weight pressed his breastbone, forcing him to labor for breath. Tiny needles repeatedly stabbed his collarbone. A demon perched on his chest, plucking his life away.

He cracked one eye open. "Off, Ganymede," he croaked. Hughes's cat, fifteen pounds of solid mouse hunting muscle, with another pound of spiky gray and white fur that didn't know the meaning of nap, purred. And dug claws in harder, kneading his chest.

"I said off," he repeated, rolling to dislodge the cat. In response, Ganymede dug in four sets of claws. Needles stung his stomach as well as his chest.

"Arrrgh." Treadway raised the arm hanging off the edge of the too narrow couch and pushed his hand into Ganymede's side. Warmth and the softness of down caressed his fingers. He gave up and massaged the cat's shoulder. It purred louder, the cannonade of an approaching storm.

As the cat drove thunderbolts of purrs into his sore head and flashed lightening of claws into his skin, he thought back on the night before. He won a pony off Stone. He had the funds in his pocket; they would make a dent in the bill he was going to run up at the jeweler's.

Minnie was going to need a flashy diamond bracelet or some such. She had not appreciated Margaret stomping into the box in the middle of her climax. She would not like being turned off either, but that was first on his list of things to do. There was a serving girl at the White Horse Cellars who intrigued him. She looked about twelve, but was well developed in the chest.

Second, Margaret required something. Something ladylike but spectacular. Something to thaw what Treadway knew was going to be a glacial snit. The sinking feeling in the pit of his belly must be the dregs of the wine he had drunk, not apprehension. He wasn't afraid to face her. It wasn't guilt.

May he be immured in a crystal cave, what made him take Minnie to the Opera?

When Hughes walked in, Treadway was sitting, Ganymede on his knees. He had his head in his hands, feet on the floor, and stomach somewhere around his knees. "Well," Hughes said, "I haven't seen you as foxed as last night in years. What happened?"

Treadway peered through his fingers. "Not so loud."

"You couldn't walk straight. Talked and talked about your skirt and your wife. Didn't make sense."

"Because it didn't make sense," Treadway mumbled. "Still doesn't." He peeled his hands from his face and pushed the cat to the floor. "Hughes, men all over London have mistresses. Why can't I have a harmonious visit with mine?"

"Probably because you don't deserve it."

Chapter Twenty-four

Due to Treadway's condition, it took him two days to return to the townhouse on Mount Street. The first he spent making himself presentable after Hughes banged out of the house. There was something wrong there. The man was angry. Then he spent hours in the jeweler's finding a presentable peace offering for his wife. At least this time he knew the color of her eyes.

"Blue surrounded by teary red," he snapped at Mr. Rundell. "Not that my wife's eyes are any concern of yours."

"I was attempting to determine what stones would enhance the lady's beauty," the jeweler protested.

"She looks good in anything."

"May I suggest something unusual?"

"You may—not that I'm going to like it." When Mr. Rundell led the recalcitrant customer to the display case of American Indian turquoise and silver, Treadway drew himself to his full height and spat, "I said my wife's eyes were blue, Rundell, not a washed out, damned insipid excuse for blue. Bridge tried to foist this tripe off on me before. Where the hell are the diamonds?"

He left the jeweler's shop with two boxes too large to fit into a pocket. Minnie first.

* * *

As master of the house, Treadway did not attempt to sneak through the kitchen. He boldly knocked on the front door of the property in Mount Street. A punctiliously correct footman opened the portal and he strode in, divesting himself of hat and gloves. He ignored the footman.

"Is Mrs. Treadway in?" Barely registering the servant's garbled, "Yes," he made for the stairs. She would be in the drawing room. All ladies spent the afternoon in the drawing room, unless they sallied forth to visit other ladies in *their* drawing rooms. Seeing as this was the second afternoon Margaret would have spent in the drawing room since their disastrous meeting at the Opera,

Treadway trusted she had donned an attractively muted gown, a miniscule lace cap, and icily polite demeanor. That's what shrewish spouses did.

At least she was at home and not on the road leading from London to Hertfordshire and her father's house. Or off to pour her troubles into his father's ear.

Stopping only to adjust his waistcoat, smooth his hair, polish the toe of one boot on the seat of a side chair, and adjust the bow of the box he carried, he opened the door and confidently strode into the drawing room. Ever alert, he ducked before the vase struck his head.

It sailed into the hall. As it crashed into the wall and shattered, spraying chips of meticulously hand painted Meissen porcelain, he closed the door gently.

"Good afternoon, my dear."

"Do not 'good afternoon' me," Margaret said.

"Would you prefer to wait another week before I come crawling?"

"No, I would prefer you fell off the face of the earth." Her nose rose as she tipped her chin up with a belligerent huff. By Merlin, her snit was worse than he thought it would be. The Grail must have guided him when he overruled Rundell and bought the flashier necklace. A delicate string of tiny, perfectly matched diamonds wasn't going to surmount this bastion.

"Sorry, I can't oblige." Treadway braved the miniscule wyvern in muslin and tossed the package on a chair. "But I hope you will accept my apology." She leaned over, sweeping the box to the floor with a flick of her fingers.

"Unlikely. I don't take bribes—especially not pitifully obvious bribes." She stamped her foot. "How dare you? It is bad enough you have a mistress, but to flaunt her in front of me..."

"Many men of my station sport ladybirds," he started.

"But they don't indulge in *that* at the Opera." Margaret vibrated. The hem of her gown shivered. He was going to have to listen—and grovel abjectly—to get through this patch. He consciously tried to relax his shoulders.

"Do you know what I mind the most?" Not giving him time to reply, she tumbled into an angry tirade. "It's not that you humiliated me in front of my friends. Indeed, all of London could hear what you were doing, if they were inclined to listen. Lady

Clarissa knows what happened. She was right there, for the Lady's sake. In the next box! She could hear every sordid grunt, every nauseating moan.

"She undoubtedly thinks I am the stupidest twit in England. The Misses Silvester also. And Miss Jackson." She paused for breath.

"No, it is not that you hold me up to ridicule. What matters most, what is most disgusting, is that you stick your thing into me and then you stick it into that whore." She shuddered. "And you come home and stick it into me again. Merlin only knows what you have on it."

Treadway towered over his wife and gritted his teeth. "That thing, as you call it, is a penis. A rod. My manhood. That which brings you great pleasure in lovemaking."

"Well, how was I to know what it is called?" She was beyond heeding her words. "It is not as if my stepmother gave me a primer on the subject. And for you to call it lovemaking—the only way it could be termed love is if you pretend it is my sister rather than me you are sticking your...your manhood into."

Appalled, she clapped a hand over her mouth. Hot carmine flashed across her cheeks and forehead and crawled down her throat. It faded, replaced by pallor hinting of the grave. Still covering her mouth, she stormed to the door.

He let her go. What else was he to do? Slowly, as if his bones hurt, Treadway picked the bulky package—his peace offering—off the floor.

By Accolon, she *had* heard what he'd said about her sister. His peccadillo with Minnie was nothing to that. If his father found out, he'd be disowned for sure.

* * *

Margaret barricaded herself in her room for hours. Finally, an inconvenient hunger forced her to send to the kitchen for a tray.

Thinking on her failings, then her husband's, she absently called, "Come in," when the knock came on her door. "Put it on the table," she instructed as she wiped her eyes once again. The tray clattered. She turned. Treadway righted a spilled wine glass.

"Well, it didn't get into the food," he said. "I'll just pour more."

Margaret stared in astonishment, then let her eyes drop.

"May I sit?" he asked. He didn't wait for a reply, but pulled two chairs to the tray laden table, and sat. "Come, eat. There's nothing worse than quarreling on an empty stomach."

"We are going to quarrel again?"

"No. I think we've done enough of that. You are going to eat. I am going to grovel."

Stiffening her spine, she moved to the table. "I can't see you groveling," she commented as she inspected the tray. What was he up to?

Chicken, stewed apples, and two slices of thick buttered bread nestled on a plate. Side dishes held glazed carrots and Cook's special green beans with horseradish sauce. Wine made a sea of the tray.

"Comfort food," he said, waving his hand. "Come, my dear. Don't be shy."

"Do not call me 'your dear'. I am not and never have been." She darted an unfriendly glace at him. Treadway looked relaxed, his legs akimbo under the table and his hands waving gracefully in concert with his words. It was irritating; he should be upset. After what he had done, he should... She looked at his eyes. No, he wasn't relaxed. Straightening the chair, she seated herself and nibbled at a slice of bread.

He nodded, satisfied, stupid man, and began his grovel. "I have things to say. Generally conversation at meals is light, but as I said, I have things to say. Nothing to upset your meal, I trust."

Wiping wine off the fork and knife, she cut a miniscule bite of chicken. He looked polished, with a coat in the tweedy brown green that made his eyes brilliant. Not to mention what it did for his shoulders; if nothing else, she was married to a fine figure. Bully.

"Well," he drummed his fingers on the table. The wine glass shook again and he flattened his hands. "You did hear what I said to Hughes. About your sister. That was unfortunate." Chewing, Margaret couldn't respond as she would have liked; she bridled and he pointed his finger at the plate. "Eat.

"Yes, it was unfortunate." His eyes wandered to the wall. "I told him I preferred your sister to yourself. That was badly done and I apologize. Shouldn't have said it."

Writhing inside, she dropped her eyes to the tray and kept

them there. May the Lady save her, she wanted to slide under the table. No, slide the buffoon under the rug. Did he think oily apologies would make her forgive his behavior?

"I shouldn't have said it, not just because it was rude, but because saying it made the comment more than it was." Treadway took a deep breath. "Yes, I was intrigued by your sister, but not to your detriment. Not really. It wasn't so much your looks, as what your looks represented. What m'father wanted me to have."

Her eyebrows drew together. What her looks represented?

"Yes, my dear," he said ruefully. "I said I was going to grovel. Now, where was I? Oh, yes. What I thought of you." He frowned. "Can't lie, can I? Didn't think much of you. Weren't my style—widows and...erm." He pursed his lips. "No, you weren't my style. But I shouldn't have said it. I am sorry."

It was a bald apology. He sounded as if he meant it. Sincerely. He was desperate to appease her. She dipped the fork into the stewed apples. She liked stewed apples. He shifted uneasily in his seat.

"Well. Glad you ain't going to bite my head off. As for the Opera and Minnie..." He heaved a sigh and Margaret coughed.

"You all right?" Treadway asked. When she nodded, he continued. "I don't have a good excuse. I can only say I regret it—in every way." Distantly, she registered the apples were delicious. The more active part of her brain seethed.

"I'll leave you to your meal." At the door, he turned. "Oh, and Margaret? Hope you don't mean to tell anyone about it. The Pater would take it amiss." The door closed.

She lifted the wine glass and took a deep draught. The Pater. His father. He apologized so she wouldn't whine to his father. She contemplated the next forty years or more. The remainder of her life. It was to be spent with a brute, a contemptible, philandering lout who made Lancelot look like a schoolboy playing charades with Guinevere.

Untying the tapes to her gown, she prepared for bed. She would take a nap to subdue the headache throbbing behind her eyes. Then she would search out Emma. Surely there was a way to extricate her sister from the coil magic had spiraled her into. There was no escape from her own.

* * *

Whistling, Treadway sauntered from his wife's room. He handled that well. Shut the shrew's mouth. Now he'd apologized, she couldn't complain about the business with the widow. Same with Minnie. She couldn't go to his father about Minnie.

He paused, frowning. She could still go to the Pater. Women didn't have a man's sense of honor. Margaret wouldn't care that snitching impugned hers. And if the Pater got a sniff of Minnie, two years younger than the age limit he had set on his son's mistresses, the hullabaloo would be worse than when Arthur caught Lancelot sniffing around Guinevere's skirts.

He'd be disinherited. Cut from income, left to drown in River Tick. The Pater had been clear as a watchman's yell through the fog. 'If I hear of you consorting with children again,' was how he put it. Children, hah. Minnie might be young, but she was as old as sin.

The sense of ill usage grinding, he slammed the door to his room and rang the bell pull. When his valet entered, he ordered two bottles of brandy and a glass.

Hours later, bottles sat empty and he listed at the window. Propping his shoulder on the frame, he stared out. The people across the way were out to a ball or something; a carriage waited at the curb. The light from the open door illuminated the face of the sweet young thing Lord and Lady Finch had thrown into the marriage mart this season. "Another blonde, just like all the rest," Treadway thought. "Won't look at you unless you've got a title. Mordred knows how or when they learn it, probably in the schoolroom. For certain they have it absorbed before they come to Camelot."

His glass was empty. He tossed it in his hand, then, with an impulsive gesture, he threw it against the wall. The crystal made a satisfying crunch against the plaster. The urge to do violence slashed his psyche much as the shards of glass stabbed the carpet. He strode to the wardrobe.

A dark coat for night dimmed streets; Merlin's or Covent Gardens. Both held plenty of women, but Drury Lane sheltered the type of female he preferred. Refolding the coat collar, he exited the room.

Closing the door, a metallic sound came from Emma's chamber. He cocked his head. *Margaret's precious sister. She hardly gives me the time of day, the little snob.* But she was young, with perky little apples where Margaret had melons. A virgin. The tightening in his groin told him he could find pleasure there.

Would she be pliant in his arms or a tiger? He preferred rough, but even if she fainted, he would enjoy Emma. Treadway moved from the door. A whore would have to do. The way he felt, tonight it'd better be Covent Gardens. It was closer.

He didn't see anyone, man, woman or beast. There wasn't even a beggar rolled up like boneless rags in the shadows. No dog skulked in the alley. Murky fog drifted through the Gardens, turning signposts to wraithes and fluttering chill fingers against his skin. It was eerie, how alone he was. His forehead misted; his gloves wiped away sooty fog. Finally, he leaned against the rough corner of a doorway, waiting for someone, anyone, to pass by. Splinters from the paint blistered wood caught at his jacket.

Peering through the gloom, a spark of light dazzled his eyes. Didn't seem to be a torch; did someone light a candle or strike a tinderbox? He couldn't see. Even after he blinked, a blob of bluish white danced in front of him. Another light flashed and he winced. It was brighter than the gas lights they'd put up around town. Damned unpleasant lights. Gads, even with his eyes closed, he could still see them. Lifting a hand to shield his face from further flashes, James realized tears were streaming down his cheeks like rain down a windowpane. He swiped at them blindly, jabbing his shoulder into the splintered doorframe.

By Arthur, he couldn't bear it. It wasn't the deserted street that was too dreadful to face; it wasn't the lights that hurt his eyes. It didn't matter that he hadn't found a woman to ease his desire. This was deeper, darker. Like the blasts of color that assaulted his eyes, the desolate sensation flooded his soul. He was a gamester gazing at the turn of the card that loses a fortune, the knight speared on a lance. The truth darted into his brain and crippled all thought but one.

I love her.

He had recklessly shoved her away, but he loved her. He lifted his face to the heavens and opened his mouth to howl the pain. Before he could make a sound, agony bloomed in his chest. James clenched a fist over his heart and closed his dazzled eyes.

* * *

The table at his hip rocked on uneven legs, the creak loud in the hushed room. A grizzled seaman moaned, "Nor any drop to drink," like the spectre of Coleridge's ancient mariner, and another elbowed him still, the better to hear the fearsome tale. As if they could smell elemental fear, the patrons at the bar gave Ollie wide berth, crowding the wall of the narrow tavern. His dread soaked the air. Tankards and glasses abandoned, ears strained to know what ghastly apparition had brought the old cutpurse low.

"What'd it mean?" Ollie Hawes scrubbed his hands on stained buckskins in agitation greater than that of a hostess faced with a dearth of champagne at her ball. "It was queer, I don't know what it bloody means. Gawd, I hope never to see the sight again. I came to you because of the lights, yer honor. You said you'd pay for telling about tiny lights doing things." The odorous tallow candle on the deal table lit the whites of his eyes and painted grotesque shadows over the listening crowd. Ollie, who kept body together picking pockets and scrounging the grounds of Covent Gardens for odds and ends of turnips and cabbage, was scared witless.

"I don't know what it means either," Adrian Hughes said. His calm demeanor sent shadows slithering; the crowd responded with a collective sigh. He sent his eyes around the room, a warning and a comfort. "Yes, I'll pay. But not until you tell clear what you saw, old man. I can't make head nor tail of your story." While Hughes quaffed ale with contrived nonchalance, Ollie clutched the frayed hem of his scarlet and celery striped waistcoat and made a visible effort to calm himself.

"I bloody told you."

"Tell me again."

Ignoring the glass of blue ruin a slatternly girl had slapped on the table earlier, Ollie mumbled, "I was on Adelph, hard on by the river. 'Tis south of Covent Gardens, you ken. The press gang took Wimpole's boy to the wharf. Bloody bloke was sotted. Didn't tell 'em who he was. Got a crack up the head for it and they dragged him off to the ships. Wimpole's gonna bloody screech at having to part with the ready to get him back. He's as tight fisted as a sinner's ass."

"I don't care about press gangs."

The table rocked again as the thief braced against it to lower to a stool as if his legs could no longer hold his weight. "Well, as I said, the press gang was gone by the time this toff came down Adam. A swell; all in black, he was. A bloody stickpin with a sparkler big as my fingernail, he had. Winked real pretty against that black cravat. Gawd, he was grim as the Reaper. Didn't make a sound."

Apprehension spicing his ale, Hughes swallowed and turned his attention back to the noxious piece of humanity in front of him. It would take patience to get a round tale. The old man was still shaking. The magician coaxed details from Ollie's spare narrative. "Have you seen him before?"

"Sure, I have. Who hasn't? He's that bloke likes girls bloody young. Comes round enough." Ollie spat on the floor, his contempt palpable and temporarily drowning the fear. "Didn't find none this time, I ken, the bloody toff. The press gang scared everyone off."

Under the table, Hughes's fist shook. *It must be Tread—the diamond cravat pin he won at faro—and young girls.* Like Minnie. What other reason for him to prowl Covent Gardens? Not satisfied with Minnie or Margaret, Tread had gone hunting. All his efforts hadn't weaned Tread from his vice, from his perversion.

"If the press gangs sent people scurrying, why were you still there?"

"Me and the gang are old friends," Ollie boasted. The glimmer of a smile lapped at the aversion on the thief's face. "I went to them a couple years ago. Offered my services, I did. Told them how old King George put me in charge of tending the Grail . I run the whole bloody Tower. Everything I know, I'd be good on a boat. I know where the Ark of the Covenant be. Saw it when I was flying around one night. Told 'em too. Their captain said as how I was more valurble where I was. See, I've got an important job. Someone's got to keep the Grail away from the bloody frogs."

"Tell me again what happened to the toff." Ollie's face closed and his eyes darted to the door.

"He fell down."

"He was drunk or set upon," Hughes said, pressing a finger over his eyebrow. The old man's sketchy details weren't enough. He had to know more. Was it magic or footpads who attacked Treadway? "A man doesn't just fall down. Come now, you must tell me everything you saw if you are to earn the reward. How did he fall?" He jingled the guinea-stuffed purse. The lure of coin prompted the thief better than any other goad.

"I was just watching idle-like, wondering who was going to get the bloody sparkler off the toff. He was right there, just as far away from me as I am to the bar." He waved a palsied hand toward the long shelf where the girl stood ready to pour ale from a tap. "He stopped at Sutter's. Just stood there, lookin' around. Him and the bloody sparkler." Hughes waited. Ollie shuddered, but continued his tale.

"He was black as a damned nightshade. I could see clear. That bloody sparkler... Gawd, it were the strangest thing I ever seen. Little lights started up on his chest."

Hughes stiffened. *Finally the fool gets to the important part.* "Lights?"

"I guess, if you say so, yer honor. Lights. Looked like the fireworks they do at Merlin's Gardens all twinkling. They showed clear as stars against the toff's black coat. Twinkling in the dark. Went round and round like a St. Catherine's wheel, a big glob of them. They come out of nowhere and starts twinkling. Gawd, I ain't never seen the like." Ollie rocked, the table rocked, and the crowd shuddered in fear.

"I was just minding my own business. I wasn't gonna take his sparkler. There's a pile of sparklers at the Tower; don't need his. And I didn't make them lights. I swear, I swear on my mother's grave, yer honor, I didn't have nothing' to do with them lights."

"How many?"

"How many? What? How many lights?" Forgetting his fear, Ollie bristled. "How would I know? You think I can count?" Hughes stared and Ollie backed down. "I don't know how many. They covered his chest about like this." He held his fist up and twisted it around. "They just kept going round and round, like fireworks."

"The man—how did he react? What did he do about the lights?"

"He didn't do nothing. Just stood there. Didn't act like he saw 'em or felt 'em. Then he clutched his chest and fell. Made a sound like he'd been stabbed, the swell did. Kind of gurgled, like he'd been stabbed. Then he just lay there."

"The lights?"

"The lights." Ollie's eyes shone white as they rolled. "Gawd, yer honor. Them lights. They was going round his chest still. Like a

St. Catherine's wheel. Then they went away."

"Did you go to him?"

Ollie nodded. "I told you. He was dead, dead as a rat under my boot. Had a hole in his chest where the lights were. A bloody hole. His clothes were gone there too. The bloody sparkler was gone. What the bloody hell does that mean?"

Chapter Twenty-five

She was up with the sun, dressed in the company of gritty fog, and came down the stairs just as the butler raced through the baize servant's door shrugging his coat on. Tendrils of mist floated across his nose, giving the impression of a dragon stoking his furnace for battle.

"You are too early, madam," he had the gall to say.

Margaret narrowed her eyes, in no mood to tolerate insolence. "You become predictable, Craig. Instead of a sneer, why don't you try fawning on me? A good solid fawn is as irritating as a sneer. Perhaps more effective; if you cringed and whined, there is a chance I would feel guilty at upsetting your routine by arising before the accustomed time. As it is, I want nothing more than to hit you over the head and scream this is *my* house and I will do as I please." She set her foot on the marble of the hall floor with queenly grace. "Fetch a pot of tea. The fog is caught in my throat."

The kitchen fire hadn't had time to heat, so she sipped tepid tea in the dining room with a dour butler breathing fire on her neck. He didn't take her advice. Oh, no, servility wasn't in his repertoire. Margaret attributed Craig's sullen mood to the same source as her own: the miasma in the air settled in bones, gave a chill. It couldn't be anything else.

The tea tasted gritty. Her skin felt gritty. Nightmares lapped at the edge of her thoughts, not quite forgotten. She imagined a twisted imp on her shoulder, digging claws in and breathing wispy curses, as it had done all night. Mist swirled. Broken men littered the ground; her father, grandfather—a line of her ancestors shed blood that dripped down the twin towers of her desk. It was the field of Waterloo and Napoleon's knights hacked at her knees. Emma screamed, clutching the rim of a bronze cauldron as it sank through a crack in the carved Chinese table.

Her husband had strolled the nightmares. Stirring Emma's bronze cauldron, James Treadway played cackling witch to her drooping Hamlet all night. No wonder she felt on edge.

Her fingernails tapped on the table, on the saucer, on the lip of the porcelain teacup. To distract from a vague presentiment of pain, she varied the tempo and beat. It didn't help. She steepled her fingers, wove them into pews and church, swung the doors of her thumbs closed and open, open and closed. In the dead silence of the dining room, the thuds of her thumbed doors sounded clearly.

There was one bit of good news. A note from Clarissa. Margaret opened it.

Meg,

Forgive the rush. I couldn't wait to tell you. Remember the mermaid we found in the shop? Sir Perth got down on bended knee and asked me to share it with him. Perth proposed! My Perth, if you please.

Don't look for me until our ball. We make a flying trip to tell his mother.

Ever your friend, Clary

With an impatient huff, she pushed the teacup away and rose. This was ridiculous. Her mood dulled even Clarissa's excellent news. They were only bad dreams. Everyone had them. If she went back to bed, she would sleep, dreamless.

Instead, ignoring the petrified maid peeking around the corner of the hall, she went to the solar, to the solace of Florence stitch, four shades of yellow wool, and a complex medieval needlepoint pattern.

* * *

"I must speak with Mrs. Treadway at once," Adrian Hughes said to the butler later that morning. "Where is she? I'll see myself in."

"Certainly, sir. Madam is in her solar."

It was a solemn moment, one of those times when a man paid homage. Finesse dictated. He practiced as his feet dragged him up the stairs. Each riser seemed higher than the one before; the stairs stretched as if he were climbing Jehovah's ladder to heaven or circling Dante's representation of hell. The upper hall smelled of exotic oils. For a moment he was at the feet of the shaman who trained him, but the word sounded and his mentor faded. There could be no assistance.

He must perform this task alone or be forever damned in his own eyes.

A maid shrieked and threw her dust cloth into the air when he passed her in the hall. Watching her run to the service stairs, he was momentarily distracted, but knocking on the fog damped panel of the solar door, the word echoed as it had not since Arthur passed into Avalon. Dire as Merlin's enchantment, final as Lancelot's banishment, the word resounded in his head, but he could not say it baldly. He must cushion the shock. So he practiced, as he had practiced the last several hours.

His knock went unheard. Shaking his head at the foolishness of further delay, he rapped smartly. A voice called, "Enter," and he swung the door open with due ceremony.

Margaret bent over a frame, gracefully setting a stitch in a piece of needlework. From the door, he could see the sun burst under her hands, corralled on canvas and bathing her fingers in a nimbus of light. The purity of the Lady's favor shone on her face and in her uplifted eyes. Bedazzling, she shimmered. He blinked and the illusion stripped away, leaving his beloved's fingers plying sunny yellow thread with a needle.

"Adrian," she mouthed.

"He is dead," he said baldly, closing the door behind him. No finesse, no practiced words these, but the agony of his soul hovered behind the word. Adrian crossed the room with a few long strides and knelt at her feet. "Margaret, I am sorry. Treadway is dead."

The breath caught in her throat worse than the fog. Unable to speak, she slipped off the chair and into his arms. He rocked, rubbing his stubbled chin over her silky hair when she buried her face in his neck. She rocked, smoothing the ridged and knotted muscles of his neck and back when he convulsively locked his arms around her.

Warmth seeped from one to the other. Comfort, caring, and love eased the moment, though Adrian's horror and Margaret's shock clung to them as tightly as they clung together. After a time, after an eon, when he managed to place her at a distance, so far from him that a single blade of grass might have slipped between them if it hadn't minded being crushed in the slipping, she found her voice.

"What happened?"

"He died." Margaret looked him in the eye and saw horror gripped Adrian. Lovingly, she caressed his cheek.

"Adrian, tell me." He shuttered his eyes as if blindness would cure his ills. Both still kneeling, he told her what he knew, his voice tight, the words clipped.

"Treadway was down by the docks. The magic killed him—it put a hole in his chest." Her eyes closed; lack of sight offered no more peace for her than for him. She crawled back into his arms.

"I waited too long," he continued. "If I had only acted sooner, this could have been prevented." He gave her a little shake, rocking both since his arms were once again locked around her waist. "Sweetheart, we cannot waste time. The duke is waiting for us."

"What duke?"

"Haverhorn."

Margaret raised her face from his cravat and blinked. "I can't see a duke. I have to...I have to... Hatchments. I have to send someone for mourning wreathes."

"That will have to wait. We have to see Haverhorn." He stood, pulling her up. "He is waiting for us." She looked at him vaguely and he shook her again. "Margaret," he said firmly, "mourning traps will have to wait. Go find Emma. We have to go see the duke."

The sternness of his voice penetrated the mist. Margaret swallowed hard, breaking free of the nightmares which had followed her to this moment. "We have to go see a duke? Now?" He didn't answer and the mingled tension and resolve in his face steadied her. "Yes, I see. We have to visit a duke. You say Emma should come also." She scrubbed at the wetness on her eyelashes. "Emma; I will go fetch Emma."

* * *

Adrian took them to a building shadowed by the castle of Camelot. Viewed through the veil of Margaret's tears, the unadorned red brick and plain black painted door of the building did not impress. The foyer and hall were equally unimpressive, but when they crossed the threshold of an upstairs room, luxury reached out and pinched Margaret's sodden senses. From the aroma of fine leather and well waxed wood to the muted tones of landscapes framed in flaming gilt, the room exuded wealth. Nevertheless, her attention was drawn to a young man sitting behind a desk. Sandy head bent over a stack of paper, he hummed a poor rendition of an aria from Vivaldi's *Griselda*.

He saw them and comically leaped to his feet, leaning over his chair to grasp a bell. The stack of papers sagged and started a shuffle to the floor.

"Morning, Mr. Moneypenny," Adrian said. His tone was such that Margaret did more than nod at the man behind the desk. She bent a careful assessing eye on him as, gathering papers, he slapped them into a cabinet built into the wall to his right. Rudely, the young man growled a greeting in answer to Adrian's pleasantry.

Good tailoring, efficiency and menace. Behind a cracked mask of manners, Mr. Moneypenny radiated enmity. Startled, Margaret realized it was aimed at her sister. She took an involuntary step forward, but Adrian's hand restrained her.

Emma, bless her oblivious heart, looked ready to dig out a sketchbook, not swat an enemy. Dark braids slapped her shoulders as her head swiveled.

"Look at the paintings," she said, awe drawling her words.

"Nothing good about this morning," Moneypenny said. "You are late, Hughes, in every way." Poised like a spear, the bell he had grabbed tinkled in his hand. Emotion, not announcement, shook it.

"You are not the arbiter." Adrian set a hand in Margaret's back and moved them to the center of the room. "Emma, join us." The command in his voice had Emma skipping from the wall.

"Mr. Hughes, the paintings are wonderful. I wish to admire them."

"You can enjoy them later," Moneypenny said dryly, ringing the bell again, this time raising a vigorous peal. Margaret had the impression he tightly reined his feelings. At her side, Adrian relaxed.

"He is waiting." Moneypenny turned to the door on the opposite wall from where they had entered and took a step. The desk chair was in his path. It wobbled and he tilted. "Damn."

He tripped over the chair, arms flailing. The bell sang an accompaniment to his dive until they hit the floor, whence it croaked once like a lead frog and was silenced. A painting fell off the wall, papers fluttered to the floor. Emma raced around the desk and grabbed his arm.

"Don't touch me," Moneypenny hollered. He pulled roughly away and rolled into the chair, a handsome walnut arm chair. It toppled atop him. "Get away, girl."

Adrian stalked around the desk. At that moment, the door opened. Margaret turned to see an older man, not too tall, not too handsome, gently raising a quizzing glass. His magnified eye, glacial gray, speared the rudesby under the chair.

"My, my, recent events have upset you, Moneypenny" the man drawled. "I had not realized the chair was in sympathy." Adrian snickered and the penetrating gray eyes turned toward him. Margaret was impressed that Adrian did not flinch. She wanted to crawl under the desk. Not the chair. That was occupied.

"I wish we had met before," Emma said, with eyes almost as large as his seemed behind the quizzing glass. "I need your advice, sir."

"You should have waited, young lady, until you did meet me. I don't appreciate having to pull you out of the soup."

"Yes, sir." Emma's braids dipped with her head.

"Well, let us get on with it. In my office, all of you."

The man's attention turned back to the floor while his visitors marched through the door as if ordered to Waterloo by Lord Wellington himself. "I heard, not an announcement, but a summons, Moneypenny." His tone was soft. "I know you dreaded facing her after suffering the effects in the paintings. Pull yourself together. It is not her fault and is nearly at an end. I promise, my lad, it will be a good end." He turned into the room, closing the door. His next whispered comment sent gooseflesh down Margaret's arms.

"If I can wrap my hands around the ether, it will be good."

The gray-eyed man walked past Margaret and Adrian as if they were lackeys and crooked a finger at Emma. She followed him the length of the room. Adrian took Margaret's arm and they drifted in their wake, past a lavish drawing room suite anchored by endless deep piled carpet and over a ballroom's worth of polished floor to the end of the room.

There sat the most astounding desk. Margaret almost drooled. She'd been writing letters on a dinky writing table jailed between two appalling faux castle towers; this man had a polished ebony expanse she could do the quadrille on. Two hefty stacks of paper drifted on the expanse like punts crossing the Atlantic. A single many branched candelabra threw silver shadows on black. She counted the arms. Seven. Good heavens, he disliked squinting.

The wood slab of the desk was supported by marble columns

more time worn and beautiful than the halls of Avalon with elaborate scrollwork at top and bottom. Peeking from the scrolls were faces. Not faces like the dreadful mirror at the Treadway townhouse, but the faces of ancient men, bearded, wise, and weary.

She jerked her attention from the desk.

Chairs sat in front of the desk, empty except for one. Mrs. Silvester sat on the last on the left. What a hackneyed description. Margaret's grief tinged smile dimmed to a bewildered scowl. Mrs. S did not sit. Back straight as a ship's mast with a furled sail bosom, she was more regal than the queen, less gracious than an archbishop, and madder than a rabid dog. Dressed as if for tea at Kay House, a fabulous string of pearls hanging from her neck to her lap, Mrs. Silvester glowered. Disapproval enveloped her as a cloud obscures the sun. The glare she directed at Emma could steam mussels.

Moving behind the desk, the imposing man introduced himself. "In the event you have not deduced it, I am Richard Shipley, Duke of Haverhorn. Maud Silvester you *should* know." His voice was as dry as the wind. "In the interest of coming to a conclusion as quickly as possible, I ask that you be seated, listen attentively, and," he focused on Mrs. Silvester, "keep your mouth buttoned."

Margaret plopped into the chair at the far right, next to Adrian, as far from Mrs. S as she could get. With efficiency of manner, the duke seated himself. "Emma, you have been creating magic. Describe the spells in detail."

"There is only one, sir."

"Describe it."

"I-I use black candles and—"

"In detail. How many candles?"

Emma looked directly at the duke. Folding her hands in her lap, she said, "I place two black candles, fresh ones each time—they are beeswax with ashes from the Christmas Yule log mixed in—they go in silver candlesticks my mother gifted me with. I always use a table; I understand that doing the spell on the floor weakens it. The candles on the table, I wrap a hemp rope around the candles in a circle." Margaret marveled that the duke's clipped interruption had settled Emma. She matter-of-factly and fluidly paid the greatest attention to detail, leaving nothing out, telling the Duke of Haverhorn every detail of the spell she had unwillingly conducted for the benefit of their stepmother, Eulalia, Lady Ridgemont.

The duke nodded, smoothed his index finger back and forth over ebony, and thankfully, kept his full attention on Emma. Sick at the thought of what the spell had wrought, Margaret drifted.

"To conclude the spell, I dismantle the table in opposite order from its construction. I sweep any leftover henbane up with a four inch tall straw broom I made from clipping the ends of a broom and a willow stick handle tied together with a bit of my sister's embroidery silk. The henbane goes on a bit of paper, which I burn once I am done, and back into the hat box."

Margaret turned her wavering attention to Mrs. Silvester, who did not appear as calm as the duke. Mrs. S's cheeks were puce. She shivered and Adrian caught her hand, giving it a comforting squeeze.

When her sister said, "The spell is done," the duke sat back in his chair and rubbed his chin. "What purpose does the spell serve?" Emma's eyes wavered for the first time. "Well?"

Her chin sagged toward her chest, Emma whispered, "It is to keep my stepmother alive." Mrs. Silvester shot out of the chair so fast, Margaret heard her knee snap.

"You dreadful girl," Mrs. S said, lips tight. "You were never to perform a spell for that purpose. I had it from your mother directly—she promised she told you it was forbidden."

"Enough," the duke thundered. "If you cannot keep quiet, Maud, you will leave." She turned on him.

"You can't condone her behavior, Richard. It is against all precepts—" The duke stood, seeming taller than before.

"I said enough." Margaret would not have been surprised if he growled or spat, but the smooth threat in the duke's voice made her cringe against the padded back of the chair. Adrian's fingers tightened about her own. To her surprise, Emma spoke up.

"Mama did tell me not to do such a spell, sir." The silence in the room took on the hushed quality one finds in a vast cathedral, as if sound was swallowed in shadows. This room lacked shadows in the corners; Margaret imagined sound running in panicked circles, looking for a place to hide.

The duke made a controlled movement. "If you cannot claim ignorance," the threat in his voice deepened and swirled, "what is your excuse?" Emma tugged at the skirt of her gown, but showed no other sign of distress.

"I have no excuse. I wanted to keep my stepmother alive because Papa likes her."

"Horrid girl. Unprincipled, undisciplined brat," Mrs. Silvester shouted. The duke sat and steepled his fingers against his lips while she ranted, "You break Merlin's law. Do you know the penalty? Never has a magician dared to go against the great Merlin." Mrs. Silvester leaned forward. "Mother Nature is not to be trifled with. Not even Morgan le Faye did what YOU have DONE."

"If you had done your duty, Maud," the duke said mildly, "we would not be in this pickle." The old woman whirled to face him, the string of pearls whipping her arm.

"You say it is my fault? I-I am to take the blame for this—this atrocious crime? How dare you, Haverhorn. Margery should have drowned these girls at birth. I had nothing to do with their upbringing. How dare you slander me?"

Clear gray eyes fixed on her. "It was for you to take charge when Margery died."

"I was in London, managing the Council for *you,* when Margery died. You were languishing in the country with the duchess, growing children. You were head of the Council, it was for you to handle."

The duke smiled, a slow, affable smile that made Margaret's toes curl. He lifted the crystal paperweight from the paper stack to his right, took up a sheet, and read aloud.

I, Maud Anne Mathilde Emerson Silvester, do hereby assume apprenticeship of any gifted offspring of the magician Margery Laycock Ridgemont in the event said magician is unable to educate aforesaid offspring. This apprenticeship shall be conducted in accordance with all principles of the Council of Mages, English Chapter, and expires upon successful completion of the rite of passage of all gifted offspring of said magician.

"This contract was executed October 31, 1793, the traditional date after marriage." The Duke of Haverhorn laid the paper on the desk.

Mrs. Silvester sank back in her chair, her face so white the lines around her eyes looked like scars. "Oh, my dear Lady," she said. "I forgot. I forgot until this moment. How could I forget?" Seeming to have forgotten the others as she had forgotten the responsibility she had promised, her dilated eyes lifted to the duke.

"Margery was as dear to me as my own daughters. Her pranks; I laughed all day when she made King George believe the Irish had voted to stick their tongues out at the pope and turn Anglican." A single tear dripped from her eye.

"If this crisis stems from my failure, I take blame. But I am ashamed of them," her arm swept to indicate the Ridgemont sisters, "and horrified they turned to dark arts. That any child of that dear girl's should follow the loathsome path of Mordred is revolting."

No one spoke for several minutes.

Margaret wrung her hands, wanting to comfort Emma, who must be stricken at Mrs. Silvester's charge, but was afraid to move. She piled the loss of Mrs. S's esteem, a surprising pain, on top of Emma's danger and James Treadway's death and froze in misery. *Adrian, save us.*

The duke was implacable; no sign of pity or forgiveness slid across the ebony desk. Finally, Emma, courageous Emma, spoke.

"It cannot be Mrs. Silvester's fault alone that she forgot. Why did you not remind her, sir?" The duke picked up the paper and waved it, a bitter twist to his mouth.

"She took responsibility when she signed the contract."

Adrian shifted to face Emma. "As the contract says, following the precepts of the Council of Mages mandates confidentiality."

"You mean secrecy."

Adrian nodded.

"No one talked about it? That's silly." Emma folded her arms across her chest. "You can't blame Mrs. Silvester for forgetting, sir."

In a morass of guilt over her husband's death, her fault for not stopping Emma's spelling, Margaret still marveled at her sister's daring. Emma wasn't afraid of the duke. She acted as if the spell she had set was no more than a child's peccadillo, not a disaster of epic proportions.

Mrs. Silvester spoke of a crisis, but no one had mentioned holes. They burned through Margaret's head as lethally as they had attacked Treadway. Not only was she to blame for his death, she would be faulted for any and all other damage the holes did. The Duke of Haverhorn probably had a second sheet of paper listing those felled by holes. It might comprise the remainder of the stack of papers at his right hand. The list could be as long as the accounting of knights killed at Waterloo.

And it was all Margaret's fault. She hadn't stopped Emma.

She hadn't done anything to counteract holes. Poor Emma. She had nothing to fear. Margaret was the one on trial, the person condemned.

A truth sneaked into her dulled mind. Emma felt no fear because she felt confident. In this room, discussing magic and the shadowy entity called the Council of Mages, Emma considered herself a peer of both older people. She couldn't know if her magic was as strong as theirs, but she was as important as the duke. Mrs. Silvester also. She rejected the charge of following Mordred into black magic.

No, Emma had naught to fear. Margaret's spirit gave a little cheer.

Sadness that Mrs. Silvester's friendship should splinter in this waterspout, awe at her sister's strength, yearning for Adrian's championship, and fear of the duke buffeted Margaret. She shrank in the chair and awaited events.

As if she had not been heard, Emma repeated herself. "You can't blame Mrs. Silvester."

The duke acted surprised at Emma's championing of the old lady. "Why should you defend her?" he asked. "She has done you no favor. Because of her negligence, you lack training. Your youth lacked the guidance that is your birthright." He rose, resting his knuckles on ebony. "As leader of the Council of Mages, it is my responsibility to pronounce judgment. Merlin knows there are more important matters to attend, but the Council dictated this brouhaha be dealt with first."

Mrs. Silvester stood, head proudly high. His words echoed, filled with unnatural power.

"Maud Anne Mathilde, I decree—"

"Emma is correct. Mrs. Silvester should come to no harm." Margaret's words, soft as they were, beat back the duke's pronouncement. His glare promised a Chinaman's torture, but surprisingly, it was Mrs. Silvester who spoke.

"You dare speak? In defense of my crime?" Mrs. Silvester lifted an arm and pointed at Margaret. "You have no gift, young lady. Your presence here is superfluous. You will keep silent before your betters."

Emma was out of her chair, her arm circling Margaret's shoulders. "She does too have a gift."

"What is it?"

The demand filled the room. Adrian was tense, worried for her. Margaret wanted to rise, but her legs were slammed by emotion, as weak as a shaft of hay pelted by rain. Emma knew Margaret's magic was minimal. She couldn't create spells; the best she could do was assist Emma with hers. How could Emma say Margaret was gifted? Gratitude for Emma's faithfulness mingled with love for her misguided opposition of the duke.

In every way the Duke of Haverhorn was powerful. He could and would swat her as a cook would take a towel to gnats, but Margaret's safety meant nothing. She had to protect Emma.

"Do not be disturbed by his words, Emma," she whispered. "They are not sticks and stones. I came to terms with my lack years ago." Emma shook her head and Margaret lifted a hand to grasp her sister's. "Emma, I know how you feel. You shouldn't. Not inheriting Mama's talent has not blighted my life. I am proud and glad for you, not sorry for myself." Emma's hand shook and Margaret squeezed it.

"If you are not to be charged with a lie, you will speak now. What is her gift?" Margaret glanced beyond Adrian's stalwart form and Emma's white-faced indecision to Mrs. Silvester. There was no hope for clemency, the old lady's face said.

"I have no gift," Margaret said. "By lashing out, Emma seeks to ensure my peace of mind." She took a deep breath. "You see, she always felt I was slighted because I cannot do magic. But that is not important. What matters is your concern over the holes my sister inadvertently caused. You should not blame—"

The crystal paperweight banged on the desk so hard it broke into four pieces. Margaret almost fainted. The duke, a magician as she now knew him to be, looked ready to blast her. Maud Silvester took a menacing step forward. What had she said?

She leaned into Adrian, who wrapped a protective arm around her shoulders. His warmth gave her a measure of—not courage, for facing enraged magicians was in no way emboldening—but steadiness. With him to support her, Margaret thought she might leave the room alive and with a modicum of sanity. Perhaps she would have wits enough left to find a deep hole, one made by a shovel, not magic, to hide from the duke.

A flicker went through the old lady's eyes, then astonishment filled them. She opened her mouth, closed it, and opened it again.

"A gift of empathy?"

Chapter Twenty-six

"Can't you keep to the subject, Maud?" The duke raised a fist and the floor shook. Margaret stumbled into Adrian's chest; he clung to her. Together they fought to stay upright as the room tossed like a boat on a stormy sea. Emma fell over a chair, six legs tangling on the floor, since two of the chair legs broke off with her fall. Behind them, several paintings fell off the wall, one frame cracking into pieces and skidding across the floor.

Mrs. Silvester remained upright, swaying but never losing her balance, her foot arched over a newly warped floorboard. "Really, Haverhorn. Weren't you taught to take your tantrums out of doors where they do less harm?"

"By Merlin and the grace of Jehovah, I am sick and tired of dealing with drivel. This is my office; I will destroy it if I please." The duke shimmered as if the heat of the sun poured from him, then he sat back in his chair, passing a hand over his forehead. Red faded from his cheeks, transmuting him from enraged magician to irritated man.

Using the contract as a shovel, he scraped the shattered pieces of crystal together, every move studied, and muttered. The duke set the crystal paperweight, in one piece, back atop the pile of papers.

"Sorry, Maud. My temper got away from me. We have gone off topic, and my patience is exhausted. Assigning blame will not solve the conundrum facing us. I don't care if the Council requires me to deal with your lapse, nor am I interested in exploring this young woman's abilities. I need to deal with the atmosphere. Now, before catastrophe strikes."

"That is the first sensible thing you have said for some time," Mrs. Silvester said dryly.

Adrian righted chairs and sat Margaret and Emma in them, standing behind as one chair was now out of commission. He had been silent for most of the interview, but now he said, "Emma's spell would not have the effect she sought, sir. It wouldn't keep a fly alive without arrowroot."

Emma's mouth dropped. "Arrowroot?" The duke waved her to silence. Margaret, dreading another movement of the wizard's arm, flinched and surprisingly, his cheeks darkened in a blush.

"Relax, my dear. I'm not going to do anything." The duke turned to Emma. "Arrowroot as a thickener. Without it, the spell runs off."

"Then what is making the holes?" Margaret, soothed by the duke's flush of embarrassment if not his matter-of-fact statement, groped blindly for Adrian's hand. His fingers wrapped around hers, firm and comforting.

The duke steepled his fingers and rested his elbows on the desk. "Mr. Hughes knows. Maud, you mentioned the source at the last Council meeting. Would you elaborate on the subject?" A bell tinkled. The duke held up his hand. "One moment."

He cocked his head. "Well, it is about time, Moneypenny. Send the boy in alone." A pause later, he growled, "Give her a chair, a cup of tea. Tie her up, I don't care. Just don't let her out of your sight."

The door to the reception room opened and a man strode in. Twisting in her chair, Margaret recognized Lord Brinston. *Now what.*

Long strides and a quick hop over a fallen painting brought Lord Brinston to the end of the room. "Sorry to be behind the time, your grace," he said in a deep voice as he bowed to Mrs. Silvester. "She was devilish hard to run down. I went by three drapers and four milliner's shops before I found her."

The duke nodded. "Bring another chair, will you, my boy." As Lord Brinston fetched a mismatched chair from along the wall, Mrs. Silvester regained her seat. Chair legs scraped, introductions flew around and the duke waved permission for the others to relax. Margaret's knees wavered as they bent; she was about at the end of her rope, what with all the shocks she had sustained.

With her again at the edge, an expanded arc faced the ducal desk. She was thankful that the duke's eyes were on Lord Brinston as he said, "We have not gotten far. Only to the point where it became clear a favorable outcome to your mission was imperative, Brin. Tell us, before I have Moneypenny bring her in, what did you find?" Mrs. Silvester opened her mouth, but the duke frowned and she closed it.

Lord Brinston crossed his long legs. "All the makings of a love spell were stuffed under her bed, sir, along with this." He reached a hand into a pocket in the tail of his coat and pulled out a tiny stone figure. Setting it on the duke's desk, he sat back in his chair. "It's a marble Cupid. Roman, blister her stupid soul. Looks like one Elgin had in his library."

"Probably stolen." Mrs. Silvester laid a fingertip on the statue. "It is warm at the core; I believe it has been used in the last day or so."

"Well, shall we bring this to a conclusion?" The duke whispered behind his hand and a door opened. Looking vastly pleased at the chance to raise his voice, the duke bellowed, "Mr. Moneypenny, escort her in."

She entered from the reception room, her chin high. A celery pelisse trimmed in olive and matching satin bonnet frothing with white feathers set off her dark hair, but a frown and glittering eyes, evident across the length of the office, radiated displeasure. Stalking over carpet and hardwood floor, she looked like a diamond, ready to cut something—or someone—to shreds. A white line of tension ringed her mouth. Moneypenny, a respectful three feet to her rear, could only be described as wrathful.

"May I introduce Mrs. Christine Whitmill-Ridgemont, your grace," Moneypenny said, his voice taut, once he was in hailing distance. He bowed and Margaret found herself relenting her dislike. It had been absorbed by her sister; Christine glared at him as she moved in front of the duke's desk.

The glare seemed to release a spring in the duke's minion; his stiff upper lip stretched. Moneypenny fisted his hands and blurted, "Your grace, I am compelled to voice a complaint. You said to serve the lady tea. I did so. "I used the new Wedgwood set her grace gave me for Christmas. I like it prodigiously. I like it so much I kept it at home for my private use until today. I only brought it to the office because her grace is expected this afternoon. I wanted to be able to offer her a cup of her favorite Bohea in one of the Wedgwood cups. It is ideally designed to sip tea from." He punched the air in agitation and the duke blinked.

"I didn't want her to think I lacked appreciation for her gift. Your grace," Moneypenny leaned forward, "I am grateful for her grace's thoughtfulness. I would never, ever wish her to think I don't like the tea set. It is a thing of wonder, each element is as perfectly wrought as the Round Table, as gracefully balanced as the Holy Grail . Wedgwood should be given the royal commission of King's potter." He gestured as expressively as an Italian soprano lamenting the death of an excellent tenor. The duke nodded encouragement as the secretary took a ragged breath.

"Your grace, I put the Sevres set in the closet. It is buried in three inches of reports," rigid fingers jabbed in front of his chest, measuring a good four inches of air, "delivered just before Mr. Hughes brought your guests in." At this, Moneypenny shot Adrian a resentful glance.

"*If* Mr. Hughes had waited *just* half an hour before he barged in, *without an appointment,* I may add, I would have had ample opportunity to file the reports." Moneypenny's forehead flamed dark red. "But no, he interrupted my routine and I put the reports in the closet until the office cleared. They are confidential, you know. No good secretary would leave them laying out for anyone to look over, and I," his chin jutted out, "I am as good a secretary as you shall ever find. Indeed, you may never find another secretary as adept as I at the nuances of your business. Thus, I am forced to lodge a complaint."

"What is the complaint?" Curiosity was writ on every line of the duke's face. Moneypenny drew himself up, switching from the dramatics of the Opera to the precision of the military.

"Your grace, tea is splashed over the wall behind my desk. Hot tea runs down the hill of the Constable landscape behind my desk. Hot sugared tea drips off the frame of the Constable painting, down the wall and onto the floor. One Wedgwood cup, one Wedgwood cup of a full set of twelve, mind you, is in pieces on the floor behind my desk. It sits, shattered beyond recall, in a puddle of hot sugared tea." He snapped to attention.

"Your grace, your guest threw her teacup at me."

The Duke of Haverhorn sat back in his chair with a sigh. Four fingers of his left hand slapped the wood of his desk, four fingers of his right hand followed suit. His thumbs marched into his palms and back out, swinging up and down as he gazed at Christine. His Grace of Haverhorn looked madder than he had when he made the room shake. Margaret held her breath and braced her feet against the floor, expecting a massive quake to rattle the room apart.

"Mr. Moneypenny, I share your outrage," the duke said, soft as a gosling. "All will be made good. I daresay her grace will insist on picking out another tea service so you may enjoy Wedgwood's excellent craftsmanship both here and at home." A smile of immense sweetness winged its way to the secretary. "Lady Coletta expressed a desire to visit the Wedgwood factory. You need not think you will be putting her grace out. My ladies will enjoy the outing." Moneypenny nodded, some of the red fading from his ears.

"Mr. Moneypenny," the duke added, "you are the most efficient secretary I have met in a long life. You are worth more than any Constable painting." The secretary tossed his head, looking immensely pleased.

"Mr. Hughes," the duke said in a normal tone, "I believe your presence is not required and you have ground to regain with the good Moneypenny. Would you be so kind as to wait without?"

The group sat—Christine stood—and watched Adrian trail the secretary the length of the room. Looking neither to the right nor the left, Moneypenny stepped over a bronze Buddha fallen from a table, opened the door to the reception room, and disappeared. Adrian paused to heft the statue upright, then went out, closing the door soundlessly.

Margaret sighed, missing his support. At least the duke no longer looked like a bolt of lightening. She eyed Christine, wondering why she had been brought here—and why she threw a teacup at poor Mr. Moneypenny. All would be made clear, she trusted.

The duke rested his chin on his thumb and curled his fingers over his upper lip, which lowered his head. His eyes looked through the stray hairs of eyebrows sprouted with age straight at Christine, but he spoke to Mrs. Silvester.

"Maud, remind me to speak to the duchess about Wedgwood, won't you? Moneypenny is an excellent secretary, it wouldn't do to neglect his grievance."

"I don't know how you stand his volatility," Mrs. S said dryly.

"I like the boy. Well, Mrs. Whitmill-Ridgemont," he drawled. The words bounced his head on his thumb. "What do you have to say for yourself?"

Chapter Twenty-seven

"I don't take your meaning." Christine looked around for a chair. The only one available was next to Lord Brinston, but his leg, folded over his knee, blocked the seat. She sniffed.

"I meant, dear lady, to ask in what endeavors you employed this statue." The duke's eyes wandered to the miniature Cupid at the edge of the desk, and then returned to Christine's face. His tone was mild. The duke presented the ideal of bored aristocrat idly watching a cotillion, but something told Margaret he was anything but disinterested.

It was as if her interview was a prelude to the storm now threatening to burst from the ducal brow. Margaret glanced at Lord Brinston, casually slouched in his chair. Like the duke, he watched Christine.

They looked much alike, these two lords. Father and son, Margaret belatedly recalled. Lord Brinston was heir to the Haverhorn strawberry leaves. He was already in possession of an inheritance of shrewdness from the duke. Neither would suffer a fool. What had Christine done that they were ready to tear her apart?

Her sister was oblivious to danger. She put out a finger and pushed at the cupid. It toppled. "This old thing? Why, I used it as a focus for some experiments a short time ago. They were not successful and I abandoned the effort."

"Let me guess," Mrs. Silvester said. "You dipped white silk thread in rose water, waited until it was barely damp, rolled it in thrice used tea leaves, and cut it into sections with your fingernail."

"Exactly." Christine threw the older woman an admiring glance. "And for strength, I rubbed the oil off feathers and smeared it on the thread."

"Falcon feathers?"

"No, I couldn't find any. I used Madame Celeste's finest ostrich feathers. Making the points was hard; the glue that held a single grain of salt on the end of the thread kept gumming."

"But you managed."

"Of course. I have always been artistic."

Mrs. Silvester turned the ring on her finger. "Who was the target?"

Christine tossed her head. "James Treadway."

"And what went wrong?" Mrs. Silvester's tone was interested.

"They wobbled when I threw them."

The duke's fist left dents in ebony. "Cupid darts. You were throwing cupid darts, you brainless chit." He rose, a straight pillar of outraged male. "Are you deranged? Not only were you performing a proscribed spell, every dart you threw punched holes in the atmosphere of our world." Thunder shook the walls; a jagged crack shot along the plaster behind him.

"The atmosphere, that wonderfully balanced, delicate web which gives our world life, is damaged. You—*you* are at fault. Do you know what that means?" The duke leaned forward over his desk. "The Council of Mages decreed long ago, in the time of William the Conqueror, the magician found to be at fault will bear the onus of repairing any damage created by his, *or her,* magic, up to and including sacrifice of life. There is no court of appeal, no higher power to crawl to for leniency."

Mrs. S frowned him down. "Tell me, Mrs. Whitmill-Ridgemont, when did you last throw a dart?"

"Oh, it was weeks ago. I hardly recall."

"Yet the effects were felt as late as last evening."

"Perhaps someone else is doing it also," Christine said. "I don't know why they bother; my power wasn't strong enough to do it. It is obvious the spell doesn't work."

Emma said, "Or you threw a bunch at one time, hoping the effect would increase, just as you did when you spelled Papa to make him allow you to marry Mr. Whitmill."

"So what if I did? One was not enough to affect Colonel Gooding."

"And cupid darts are floating around, looking for a specified target." Mrs. Silvester sighed. "Haverhorn, the burning rain in the park—was it a clump of cupid darts? Innocents were harmed. The darts are too dangerous to be left alone, unless they vaporize or quickly lose potency."

His Grace of Haverhorn wiped his forehead with his sleeve. "We can't count on anyone or anything rendering them harmless. We must do it. Maud, check the library. See if you can determine a way to leash those remaining darts." The duke snapped the order. "I have the joy of dealing with their effect on the atmosphere.

"But first, I want this woman out of the way." His finger pointed. "You, Christine Anne Whitmill-Ridgemont, are at fault. The Council will review your case and determine reparations to the atmosphere. Brinston, take her away." He turned his back.

Lord Brinston took Christine's arm and tugged. The duke, overcome by emotion, swung back around and shook a fist. "By Merlin and all the powers that be, Maud, you are right. Her sort should be drowned at birth."

Christine's chin elevated as she held her ground. "I deserve him. I put up with Martin Whitmill; I deserve a Corinthian for my second husband. James likes me, not Margaret, and I like him."

"You put paid to that," Brinston said, his voice chopped in ice. "Your asinine cupid dart found its mark at last. James Treadway died last night. Your magic bore a hole straight through his heart."

* * *

"Hughes, Brin, be ready to catch them." The duke handed fish nets over. "Maud, I want you to watch for holes; see what happens with them."

"Don't I get to do anything?" Emma, perched on the edge of the ebony desk, her foot wrapped around a beaked nose on a column, was eager to help. "I could catch darts."

"No," the duke said. "You are to hold the boat steady. The floor might churn, it might ebb and flow with waves. Do you remember how to snare the tide?"

"Of course. I need a silver spoon."

"Moneypenny, a spoon."

"Certainly, sir." The secretary hung the last of the landscape paintings, removed from the outer office and placed in a row on the long wall, and disappeared, returning in a moment with a teaspoon. "It is one of Paul Storr's. You don't mind the pierced handle, do you, Miss Emma?"

"It's pretty." Emma waved the spoon in the air. "And well balanced. It will do well." Moneypenny beamed.

The duke turned to Margaret, his voice gentled. "If you can hold the waistcoat still, Mrs. Treadway, the darts may travel less erratically. Do you feel up to it?"

At the moment, Margaret would have held Treadway's body up, not to mention his waistcoat, to make the magic stop. "I am ready, sir," she said, smoothing another wrinkle out of her husband's sage green, single breasted Marcella waistcoat, fetched by runner from the house on Mount Street. Aiding a group of master magicians as they repaired the damage Christine had wrought to the atmosphere would atone in a small way for Margaret's sense of culpability. She should have guessed Christine's determination to attach Mr. Treadway would lead to folly.

"Silence now," Mrs. Silvester intoned. Emma scooted to the center of the desk, folding her legs under her. Mrs. Silvester lit candles, Moneypenny cast herbs over the floor like a farmer sowing a field, and Adrian and Lord Brinston balanced on the balls of their feet.

Tossing a gold-tasseled rope to the floor and arranging it into a circle with his boot, the Duke of Haverhorn stepped into the middle, held his hands out, and with no further preparation, shouted "Sit vis vobiscum."

The power in his voice, the imperative of the words, shook the room. The crystal pyramid rolled off the stack of papers, coming to rest at Emma's knee. Margaret's chair rattled like a rocker missing a rung and a bit of plaster fell out of the crack behind the desk. A cool breeze blew over her shoulders.

Clouds gathered on the ceiling, rolling past crystal chandeliers, massing over the duke's head. They darkened and the acidic smell of struck lightening watered Margaret's eyes. Dimly, through the wet, she could see mailed figures marching to the duke's back, a ghostly army of knights answering the call of their liege, but when she blinked, they were gone.

In their place were fireflies gone mad. Darting points of light bounced off walls and changed course in mid air. One could not say they flew; rather they threw themselves back and forth. A series of lights formed a wedge, somersaulted Mrs. Silvester's shoulder, wheeled around Moneypenny's head and rammed Emma in the chest.

These were the cupid darts thrown by Christine in her quest to attract James Treadway, Colonel Gooding, or another gentleman into matrimony. There were so many that, had her aim been true, Christine could have had a man for every season, month, day and week of the year. They flew around the duke's office, summoned by Haverhorn's command.

Lord Brinston tossed his net in the air, snagging lights. Like Dodinel the Wild hunting game, he galloped his side of the room, jumping with dancer's grace to reach those skimming the ceiling. His net flashed past Mrs. Silvester's head to capture the twinkling cloud that flirted with her hair. Adrian was more whimsical. He flung his net in patterns, whipping the coarse hemp in figure eights and writhing arcs, playing tag with a fist-sized group of lights, then cutting swathes through masses of cupid darts. Coated with light, both nets soon swung with the brightness of pine torches, hurting the eyes.

Cupid darts. Amazed at the number, Margaret tried to count. Holding the waistcoat in the air as she had been instructed, her eyes flew, counting darts. They moved too fast to tag. Some pierced the Marcella fabric of the waistcoat and hung, quivering spears with fire at the tip. Others seemed to aim for the clothing but missed, traveling over and around her. Little 'hizsts' of sound buzzed by her ears.

Margaret held firm while Adrian and the marquess chased lights. Her arms straight up, she kept the waistcoat motionless in the air. A "huzzah' escaped her mouth when Adrian coaxed a shy dart from behind a desk column, but then she looked down and her cheer faded to a whimper.

The floor was disappearing. In its place was a rising tide of bronze, like the bronze invoked by Emma's spell, but larger. Much larger. She couldn't see the rug. She could no longer see Mr. Moneypenny's feet. And it was coming in her direction.

The waistcoat dipped toward her lap as her arms shook and Mrs. Silvester shouted, "Margaret Ridgemont, don't you dare drop that coat, or I'll blackball you from Almack's." Her heart a ball of yarn in her throat, Margaret found Mrs. Silvester with her eyes. The lady's feet were spattered with bronze drops. A wave lapped at her ankles.

Margaret opened her mouth. "Awk."

Adrian kissed her. "You said you were five, Meggie mine. No self respecting five-year-old is afraid of a dip in the pond." With a twinkle, he swooped and caught another dart. "Wait till you see the shore off Sunderland Point."

His words gave her strength and his kiss courage. She could

overcome trials as valiantly as Bedivere and earn a place of honor. Heartened, Margaret straightened her arms, spreading the waistcoat so it offered the largest target for cupid darts. Watching for darts, swaying her arms so they did not miss the cloth, she ignored the menace of a bronze sea. Sunderland Point; was that Adrian's home?

Soon, there were no more darts in the air. They stuck in nets and waistcoat, pulsing masses of light. Adrian and Lord Brinston carried their nets to the desk and heaped them in front of Emma. A glow lit the girl's face, giving her face a satanic cast. Adrian came to Margaret, lifted the waistcoat from her hands and spread it over the nets.

Mrs. Silvester waded through bronze to stand in front of Emma. She spread her fingers, as if warming her hands over a fire. Her face grew serene as she crooned a mish mash of sounds, no words discernable. Lights pulsed and Mrs. S crooned. Listening to her, Margaret's eyelids sagged. She was tired, so tired.

The darts grew tired also. The fire banked; darts winked out along the edges of the pile. Mrs. S still purred. More darts quenched their light, the pile dimmed. Mrs. S's voice soothed, whispered, coaxed. Margaret could no longer discern syllables; Mrs. S droned.

A touch on her cheek jerked Margaret awake. Adrian smiled; she blinked and took his hand. That smile was in her dream; she depended on seeing it, seeing him. Once this was done, she supposed she would go home. She wouldn't be in London, in any event. She would lose Adrian's smile, lose him. He could talk about taking her to wade in the ocean, but it would not happen. Pain unfurled its talons.

She clung to his hand.

Hughes, thinking her overset by events, hovered over Margaret. One more step, the most perilous step, remained. He shuffled his feet and glanced enviously from his shoes to Brinston's Hessians. If he had known Haverhorn's style, he would have been better prepared. Catalytis flooded the room, soaking everything except within the duke's circle.

Curious how the catalytis sea threaded copper, gold and silver in the bronze. Must be a reaction to the wealth of the Council. Or the duke.

He took a firmer grip of Margaret's hand. What came next might panic her. She had been through so much, she might lose that core of composure he gloried in. If necessary, he would buoy her up.

The duke lowered his arms. Roaring, *"Ad eundum quo nemo ante iit,"* he twisted at the waist and flung his arms like a farm hand throwing slops. Clouds and sea trembled, then surged in a tidal wave toward the desk.

Emma held up her teaspoon, an absurd defense against the primal savagery of wind and wave. The clouds, lighter than bronze, reached her first. Her spoon never wavered; it sucked clouds into the bowl, vaporized them, and cast pearls upon the hemp nets. Without pause, the bronze came next in an unending wall. Hitting the columns of the desk, it rose, splashed over the ebony of the desktop, flung itself atop the nets, and cascaded up to the spoon. There it eddied around the bowl. Like the clouds, it spewed forth as pearls, each one larger than the one before.

Then all was silence.

"Well, that was something to fill an afternoon," Mrs. Silvester said.

Chapter Twenty-eight

The sky over Hertfordshire was the clearest in the land and there were fewer distractions than in town. The shops in Puckeridge held little appeal for Emma, who had developed a passion for bonnets, but Margaret slept better with birds twittering outside her window than with the constant clatter of wheels. Visitors were discouraged.

The gazebo, its roof rebuilt, was their favorite site to hold class now the weather had stretched from the chilliness of spring to the warmth of June. The prospect of woods to the west, rose garden and house to the north, fields to the east and pond to the south meant their eyes were refreshed at a turn, but with little moving in the landscape, they could focus on matters at hand.

Firmly reminding herself she was content with her lot in life, Margaret pulled canvas from her workbag and threaded a needle. "I am glad Christine is happy," she said, introducing the topic that had filled her mind for the last week.

"I don't know how she can bear being stripped of her powers." Emma shivered.

"That is because they matter to you. For Christine, magic was only a tool to gain her end. All she wanted was another husband. Now she has married Mr. Gates, she won't have a care in the world."

Mrs. Silvester's tone was dark. "Until she wants something he will not provide."

Margaret shook her head. "I can't imagine anything he would not give her."

"No more of that. The two of you could argue about Christine till doomsday," Emma said, folding the paper of her latest lopsided drawing. "Margaret, you decided on your new embroidery; what is it to be?"

Margaret held up the canvas. Penciled on the weave was a shield, quartered like the fields of a crest. "When I am finished, a suit of armor. This is the breastplate."

Emma's eyes lit with interest. "Life size, in the Italian style?"

"Half size. I will try to duplicate the engravings from Papa's book."

"And it will all be needlepoint." Her sister sighed in ecstasy.

Their companion was not so easily impressed. "Singularly useless. I wish you heeded my advice and designed a shade for the south side of the gazebo. My nose was pink last night." Mrs. Silvester rapped a finger on the chair arm. "That sun is merciless after one o'clock. I may not be youthful, but I still have a measure of vanity."

"Your nose is peeling."

The society dragon stuck her tongue out at Emma. "Impertinent chit."

"I shall ask Papa to plant a tree." Margaret smiled at Mrs. S. "It will shade your nose better than a needlepoint screen, which would block the breeze as much as the sun."

"It'd take Denison three years to decide what to plant. I'll just act my age and start taking naps in the afternoon." Mrs. Silvester rubbed her abused nose, which to be truthful, showed no signs of reddening.

"Sassy," Margaret said to no in particular. Emma, who practiced impertinence deliberately, to Mrs. S's not so secret delight, set another fold in her drawing and sailed it into the air. The paper swooped past Margaret's head, did a flip and landed atop the tea tray.

The old lady snatched it up and threw it into a bush. "Listen to me, you two. Emma, I have an announcement to make. You should show proper deference."

"Yes, ma'am." The young woman fell to her knees at Mrs. S's feet, batting her lashes and pouting like a spoiled debutante. Instead of rapping her knuckles, something the grande dame had been known to do, Mrs. S laid a gnarled hand atop Emma's hair. Fondness threading her voice, she said, "Haverhorn is driving out today. It isn't a social visit; he is coming to conduct your final exam."

Emma gasped and Mrs. S nodded. "Yes, your training is complete. My dear, I have taught you all you need know about the practice of magic to be declared a journeyman. His grace will lead you through the exam, as required by the Council. Then, if you pay attention and pass it, next week we will travel to town to attend the Council of Mages. They will acknowledge your right to a seat at the table."

"I—I'm done?"

"No, you are never done. Magic is a life-long learning process. But you have taken the first step."

Emma's squeal could be heard in the house. Margaret dropped her canvas to hug her sister. "How marvelous."

"I have prepared your final lesson, Emma. You will spend the next hour soothing your stepmother," Mrs. S said sternly. "You recall she toadied to Haverhorn last month when he was here. He really doesn't like it. Do what you can to calm her down so she doesn't jump all over him this afternoon."

Emma made a face. "You give the hardest assignments."

"It is good practice and exercises your greatest failing, that of running riot. Try the Lucas Maneuver and pace it out. It's all a matter of timing."

"Yes, ma'am." Emma sped to the house, eager to race through the hours until His Grace of Haverhorn should arrive. Margaret gazed ruefully after her.

"I'll never match her for zest."

Mrs. Silvester grimaced. "You shouldn't try. You would go up in smoke."

"Or be riddled with holes." Margaret glanced up, fearful that holes would again form.

"No," Mrs. Silvester said with an unexpected lilt in her voice. "No more holes. Haverhorn included that news in his note."

"Then everything is finally repaired?"

"Yes. Evidently the atmosphere is more resilient than anyone imagined. It seems to have healed itself." Margaret sighed and Mrs S took Margaret's hand and patted it. "The unfortunate episode is at an end and we can relax our vigilance. I must say, I am thankful it was not Emma's magic that tore holes in the fabric of our lives. If she had been responsible, the Council would never admit her, no matter how powerful her magic."

Margaret's grin was smug. "She is exceptionally gifted. I told you so."

"I concede the point." Mrs. Silvester stood and set her hands in the small of her back. "I will turn her over to Haverhorn's supervision gladly. I'm too old to chase after the moonbeams she shot around the drawing room. Still, she is not my sole student, Margaret, though you reject my teaching."

"Because there is nothing special about my 'gift.' I care about people, that is all." Margaret made a dismissive gesture.

"And because I care about you, please, let me finish." Mrs. Silvester held a hand up when Margaret opened her mouth to object. "I wish to tell you what I have observed this past year. I have no experience of empathy, nor does any other I know. I do not presume to judge your abilities. Whether you have the skill or not, common sense and determination to do the right thing guide you. Both are rare, and I applaud you, though I can't say I have much faith in your ability to create needlepoint armor."

Mrs. Silvester fingered the lace at her cuff, reveling in the drama of the moment. "As a consequence, his grace has expressed satisfaction with my reports about you, and stands ready to put you to the test alongside Emma. I don't have a clue what he plans, but if you take the test and pass, the Council is prepared to scrutinize your credentials."

Margaret took a stitch in her needlework. "There will be no test."

"And so I told Haverhorn, but he wanted to be prepared. Remember, dear, I signed a contract. Dilatory as I am in my responsibility to Margery's children, I must discharge the contract with all due ceremony. When the duke arrives, I hope you will participate."

"Of course. Not wanting training does not mean I do not appreciate your efforts on my behalf."

Mrs. S laughed. "Thus speaks an empath. Now run along. I need to shut my eyes so I am sharp when Haverhorn digs at me." She retook her seat, stretching her legs like a man. "I'm not sleeping—don't you dare say I am sleeping."

With a laugh, Margaret packed up her needlework and went to walk in the gardens. Mrs. S needed a nap; Margaret needed the beauty of nature to prepare for the duke's appearance. Emma was going to be as jumpy as a puppy let loose among chickens, and as hard to control.

The herbaceous borders were reaching their early summer peak. Margaret wandered a gravel path, admiring the pink peonies stretched around a curve. She paused by a bed of iris and wiped a bug off a lolling purple tongue. The cordelyne bush, not a favorite, was doing well. It generally did not grow in Hertfordshire, liking the warmth of the southeast, but tucked in the lee of a brick wall the spiked leaves threw dramatic shadows.

Then she passed through the woodland behind the rose garden, head down, following wandering clumps of cushion moss. The head gardener had planted the moss where grass refused to grow for the shade. On a whim, she jumped from clump to clump, playing hopscotch.

She stopped when the clumps thinned and her breath came in gasps. Looking up, she spied a gravel path. The path to the swinging garden. Margaret's feet faltered. She would not take the Council's test, but a test was still necessary.

Could Margaret face her ghosts?

She hadn't been in the swinging garden for a lifetime, specifically, not since the day she played at being a child with Adrian Hughes. The time spanned James Treadway's lifetime and for that, she would always carry a measure of guilt and shame. She hadn't done well by James; she could have behaved better, as Mrs. S said. He was ghost number one.

And Adrian. She was not ashamed of her feelings for him. They were natural and need not be denied. But, powerful as they were, she did not know if they were returned. He had not written or visited; she had not heard from him for a year. His beaker reposed on the mantel in her bedchamber where she could see it before she slept and when she awoke. Could she face the remainder of her life with only that reminder of love? Without the love? Adrian was ghost number two.

Decision made, she moved into the sheltered roundel. Skirting the stone urn at the entrance to the garden, holding an orange tree heavy with fruit, she found she still hoped for the future. Kicking gravel, she moved to a swing, the same swing Adrian had sat upon. Margaret brushed a hand down a chain. His hand had clung here. His laughter had echoed off the yews.

She shook her head, impatient with sentimentality. She plopped onto the swing and pushed with her foot, setting the swing rocking gently. Swish, creak, swish, creak.

"I'm seven; how old are you?" The whisper was all too real. Margaret closed her eyes. Goose flesh ran down her arms, melding her fingers to the chain.

"I am six." She whispered it, an echo of the girl she had been before James Treadway strode into her life. The response was not an echo.

"That's not so old."

A smile tilted Margaret's cheek. "It's old enough. When I swing, I can touch the sun."

"Ah, but does it make you laugh?" She nodded so hard hairpins tumbled and her heart soared. Oh, yes, it made her laugh.

"Why?"

She whispered, "It tickles." Her eyes opened, sought and found the source of her joy. Flesh and blood, blue wool jacket and slightly askew cravat. A whimsical twinkle in hazel green eyes. Adrian cocked his head.

"I like to be tickled."

His smile warmed her heart. Then she was in his arms and she knew it was the glorious month of June.

~The End~

About the Author

Ann Tracy Marr gets so wrapped up in the Regency era that she forgets people want to know something about her. She admits to being fiftyish, which puts her firmly on the Dowager's bench at Almack's. There is an indulgent husband entailed to her estate and two unmarried daughters old enough to have made their curtseys to the queen but not so aged as to be considered on the shelf. To put syllabub on the table and keep her daughters in the highest kick of fashion, Marr tinkers with the devil's invention, computers. For non-Regency addicts, in plain English Marr is married with two daughters on the brink of adulthood. Her day job is computer consulting.

Be sure to read **Round Table Magician**, the sequel to **Thwarting Magic!** And watch for more Regencies by Ann Tracy Marr

~ Experience Historical and
~Regency Romance~

**Awe-Struck E-Books, Inc.
and Earthling Press**

In nearly all the electronic formats you could ever need, including Palmpilot, pdf, html, and of course, PRINT!

Surrey Secret by JoAnne McCraw
Round Table Magician by Ann Tracy Marr
The Lady and the Lawyer by Melissa McCann
His Majesty, Prince of Toads by Delle Jacobs
The Forgotten Bride by Maureen Mackey
The Unexpected Bride by Jennifer Lynn Hoffman

And *many* more!

E-books are increasing in popularity and can be ordered easily and received instantly!

Visit our site for easy ordering information of electronic and print titles! Find your favorite historical and Regency e-book
or **print** book at:

www.awe-struck.net
and Amazon.com

Made in the USA